The DRAGONS Keeper

The Keeper Series: Book 2

M. L. Burns

Copyright © [2024] by [M. L. Burns]

All rights reserved.

No part of this publication may be reproduced, distributed, or transmitted in any form or by any means, including photocopying, recording, or other electronic or mechanical methods, without the prior written permission of the publisher, except as permitted by U.S. copyright law. For permission requests, contact M. L. Burns. The only exception is a reviewer, who may quote short excerpts in a review.

This is a work of fiction. The story, all names, characters, and incidents portrayed in this production are fictitious. No identification with actual persons (living or deceased), places, buildings, and products is intended or should be inferred.

Book Cover: Katarina @nskvsky

Interior Design: M. L. Burns

Interior Art: Leonederic

Edited by: Vanessa Barbas

Formatting: M. L. Burns

Hardback ISBN: 979-8-9894808-2-1

Paperback ISBN: 979-8-9894808-3-8

First edition [2024]

Trigger Warnings

A note to readers.

This is an 18+ dark fantasy romance book, and dark themes are present throughout Book 2 of The Keeper Series. This book is significantly darker than the first.

Your mental health matters.

Stalking, Violence, Kidnapping, Abuse/Assault, Suicide, Self-harm, Rape, Sexual Assault, Manipulation, Gaslighting, Humiliation, Nightmares, Sexual Scenes, Racism (fantasy), and Mental Health Topics: PTSD, depression, anxiety, traumatic events.

Note: This book contains dark, triggering situations such as rape (These scenes are not written in full, graphic detail. However, please proceed with caution).

To those who made this possible:

My loving husband, Don Burns.
Sabrina Drummond, Cassie Hickin, and Tiffany Jarrell, for making this series happen.
Shannon Crittin, Taylor Brenchley, and Melissa Viccico, for giving me the confidence to not give up,

Thank you.
None of this would have been possible without you.

Dedicated To:

The ones who shed tears in the fury of their anger.
Because you would instead internalize it,
and choose to let it hurt you,
and not everyone else.
You are seen,
You are heard, and
You are not alone.

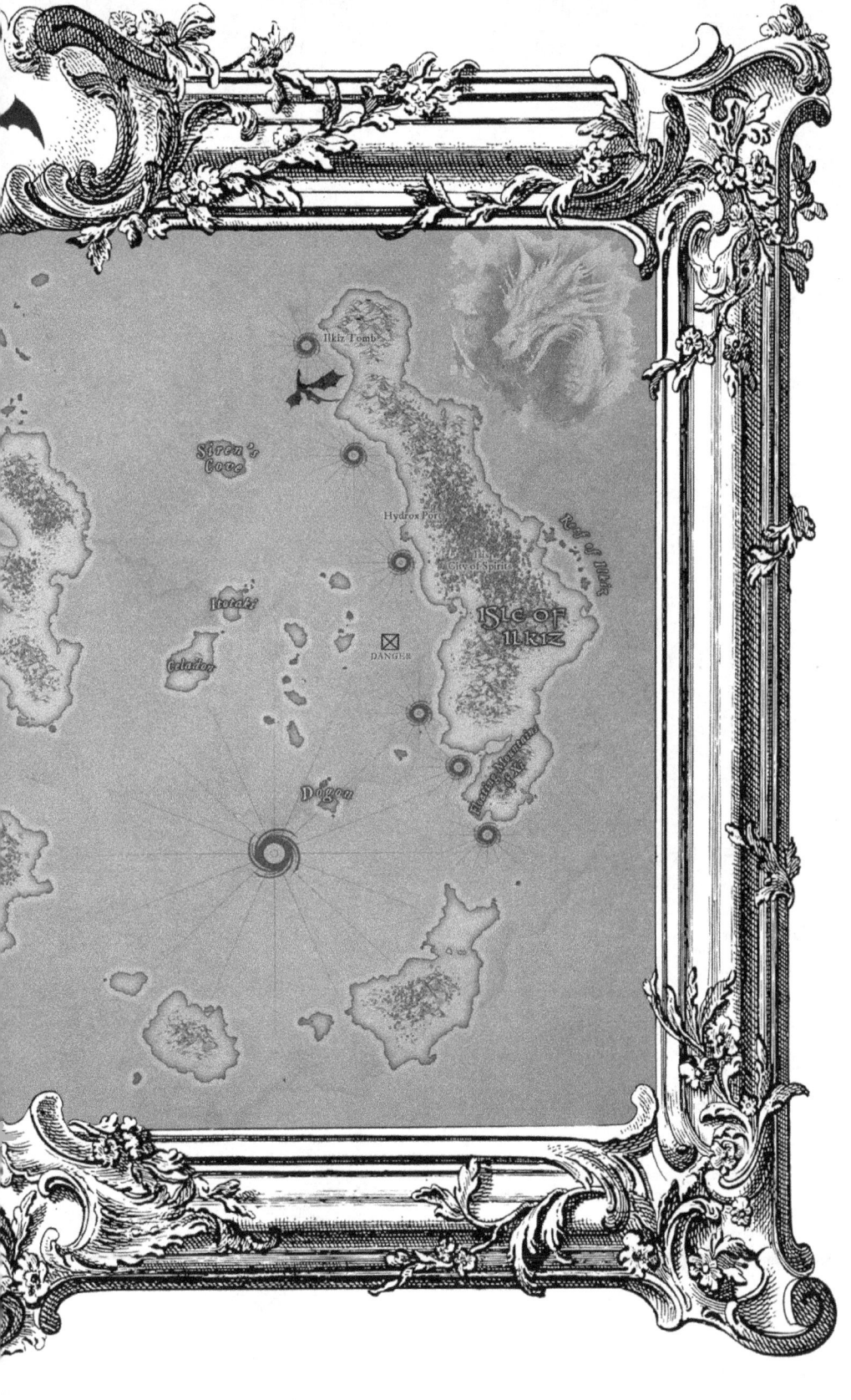

Playlist

Spotify

Amazon

Apple

Pronunciation Guide

PEOPLE

Azahara - Ah·Zuh·Har·Uh
Azahara (with accent) - Ah·Tha·Ha·Rr·Uh
Kaed - K·Ae·D
Ilkiz - Ill·Kai·Z
Alyse - Al·Iss
Xol - Sowl
Zayne - Z·A·En
Zephyra - Z·Ef·Er·Uh
Lucala - Luke·ALL·Uh
Tillin - Ti·Luhn
Goddrick - God·D·Rick
Akua - ah·KOO·ah
Kaen - K·Ay·N
Jaakobai - Jac·Uh·Bi
Zhal - Z·all
Illyan - Ill·E·In
Venruvemi - Vin·ruh·vem·e

PLACES

Naverra - Nuh·Ver·Uh
Höwl - How·El
Dogon - Doe·Gone
Celadon - Cell·Uh·Dawn
Itotaki - E·Toe·Ta·Key
Ilkiz - Ill·Kai·Z
Hydrox - Hi·Drox
Katsukazan - Cat·Sue·Kuh·Zan

They say, what beauty she had,
was a terrible beauty.
Like that of a goddess.

It was believed that
when you look at the face of a goddess,
or one that was quasi-divine,
dreadful things happened.
Desired by the Gods,
hated by man,
and in time,
they began to hate themselves.

What a terrible thing she is,
they say.

YEAR 6068 A.R.
PROLOGUE

The way they gazed at her was as if she were the embodiment of Death itself.

"Please stop looking at me like that," Azahara leaned back in the wooden chair, which squeaked in protest, "or at least say something. You are making me nervous."

A whole year had passed since the Temple of Ohrok incident and the appearance of Goddrick. It felt like it had swept by in the blink of an eye, leaving her in a constant state of unease. Every moment was filled with paranoid glances over her shoulder, seeking solace within the safety of her home, or tears soaking her pillow. She tried to convince herself it was just a nightmare, a terrifying creation of her imagination. But Mel and Skyy's relentless questions about her well-being kept dragging her back to that ominous day.

Her gaze shifted from Mel to Skyy.

Skyy broke the silence, her voice gentle and filled with concern. "We're just worried about you, Aza." Her hand reached out across the table, tenderly grasping Azahara's as if to provide comfort and reassurance. "Tomorrow marks the first anniversary of..." She let her words trail off, leaving the unspoken emotions to linger in the air, acknowledging the heaviness of the memories that day brought.

"I know, Skyy." she replied, her tone free of bitterness. She hoped the smile on her face would be enough to reassure her sister.

Mel closed the gap, pulling up the nearest chair and leaning in. Azahara mirrored the gesture, wrapping her arm around her sister and gently resting her head against Mel's.

Remembering Goddrick's words, *"Immortality is such a blessing, so there will have to be a catch, you understand."* She had expected acknowledgment of said catch throughout the year, but nothing ever came about. Everything had gone as smoothly as a year should go, except for the anxiety and depression that had come with the whole ordeal.

"You have no choice but to accept it. Only then will I remove this curse, and we will be together forever."

His voice echoed in her mind, as if he stood right beside her. It no longer seemed like Mel and Skyy were alone in her family's dining room; instead, it felt like the god who had nearly ended her life with a single strike was there, demanding her to become his Dikos Mou.

"Aza?" Mel called, bringing her back from her thoughts.

"Yes? Sorry—What did you say?" Azahara ran her fingers through her sister's long red hair.

"Are you scared?" Mel's body trembled under her hold.

"Why would I be scared? It's just another day."

"I think what she means," Skyy interjected, her voice tinged with a hint of embarrassment as she averted her gaze downward, clearly remorseful. It was her accidental activation of Goddrick's hourglass that set everything in motion. Although Azahara had been upset, she quickly forgave her sister, understanding her youth and curiosity. What mattered the most was that they all survived that day. "Is, are you scared of the curse that Goddrick put on you?" Skyy clarified.

Azahara sighed, straightening her posture as she summoned a forced smile. "You've all seen this year go by, and nothing has changed. He was probably trying to scare me into submission. The foolish god didn't realize that I, Azahara Rhay Rothwen, daughter of Alexandar Rothwen the Third and Jessalyn Rhay, am not someone to be trifled with." she proclaimed, her tone carrying a playful edge. Her words had the desired effect, causing her sisters to burst into laughter.

She masked well enough, but deep down, she was genuinely terrified.

"I love you both, don't worry so much about me. You have your year-end exams coming up," she was eyeing Skyy, "and you should be preparing to go into Upper Grade in the new year." She squeezed Mel's shoulder. "Trust me, if I think there is trouble, I will come running. I know that together, this family can do anything. We are the mighty Rothwen's, after all."

That seemed to sedate any concern that they had, and while she knew Skyy would be watching her like a hawk the next day, things would pass.

The hour had grown late, and they stayed up solely to welcome their father home from work. This year, he had been away more often than in the past, making every chance to see him a cherished moment for the sisters. After he arrived and they exchanged warm greetings, they bid each other goodnight and retired to their beds.

Azahara hadn't fully grasped just how exhausted she was. Despite her efforts to maintain a strong façade for her family, the past week had been nothing short of hell. The awareness that this day was approaching, and its rapid arrival, had sent her into a downward spiral.

It was the cause of her family's concern, and she knew it.

As her head hit the pillow, she gazed out the window for as long as possible. Not a single cloud adorned the sky, bringing her joy. Stars twinkled, momentarily vanishing and reappearing, while the encroaching darkness behind them gradually approached and eventually lulled her into slumber.

"*Such a misfortune to torture yourself.*"

No, please, don't do this. Her voice pained as his own ripped right through her.

"*You are mine, even if I must wait a millennium.*"

Why? Please, tell me why? She was begging for salvation through means of understanding.

"*Dikos Mou, the gods gave you to me. Who am I to deny such a gift?*"

His hand felt as cold as ice against her throat, and she watched as his eyes emerged from the darkest recesses of her mind. They bore down on her, rekindling the fear she had experienced on that fateful day.

"*Be mine, as you have already surpassed my patience.*"

Never. Not now. Not then. Not ever.

"*Then suffer as you have.*"

Her body was upright then, fingers combing through her hair, gripping it tightly. The rhythm of her heartbeat felt alarmingly rapid, as though it were struggling to break free from her chest. The world around her began to spin in a dizzying whirl, compelling her to pull her legs close to her chest and bury her face between her knees.

Please, make it stop! The agony in her head exceeded the pain in her chest, rendering it unbearable.

It was an endless torment that threatened to tear her to pieces. After rocking back and forth for several heartbeats, she finally managed to break free from the haunting dream and the previous day's events.

The scent of vanilla and peppermint wafted into her nose, and she instantly felt a sense of being home. She wasn't back at the Temple, and Goddrick wasn't there. Perhaps it had all been a dreadful dream, her mind just playing tricks on her.

There was no being ignorant to the fact that it wasn't a dream, even if she wished it to be. Carrying the sleeping figures of Skyy and Mel on her shoulders down the hill and through several villages to get them home would haunt her as much as the other event. The fear that they might have been dead the entire time, despite their hearts beating, drove her to push through her pain and dread.

A chill ran down her spine then. When she had dropped them off at the apothecary, they hadn't even asked to check on her. It only dawned on her when she took in her appearance in the mirror that she held no wounds. The hit to her face, the scrapes, and the bruises were all gone. Whatever Goddrick had done to her had healed all of her injuries.

Not that she would have thanked him. He had been the one to cause them in the first place.

Inhaling deeply, she cast her blanket aside and finally lifted her gaze. The headache had subsided and she suddenly felt the urgency to go and check on Skyy and Mel to ensure they were okay.

However, as her eyes finally focused on the room around her, she realized it wasn't hers. It bore some resemblances, with vines adorning the walls and doorframes, and meticulously placed candles in the corners and along the solitary windowsill. The bed was of a similar size, yet the sheets and blankets were different. And then there was the view outside the window; instead of a sprawling sky, towering mountains loomed in the distance.

She swung her legs over the edge of the bed and glanced down, noticing a rug of similar color to the grass, beneath her feet. However, it lacked the stain Mel had inadvertently caused while celebrating her birthday with wine one year. The red liquid had splattered the corner, and she had adamantly refused to replace it, deeming it a mark of character.

There was a sense of dread that was beginning to overcome her. "Where am I...?" She said aloud.

Standing, she moved to the closed door and was ready to run from it when a piece of paper caught her attention. It was pinned to the door, with **"READ ME"** written in big letters. She hesitated, uncertain whether to heed the message, as the handwriting didn't seem familiar.

It only took her a moment to decide to take the piece of paper and open it.

It was addressed to her:

Azahara,

I know this won't be easy to read, but I need you to stay strong. Wait to leave this room until you have finished this letter.

I am you, from yesterday. You won't have any memory of writing this, and that is because of the curse. The one that you believe to have been placed on you yesterday. When in fact, it has been nearly three hundred years.

There is no easy way to say this, as I, too, had to read a similar letter a year ago, but it must be told.

They are all gone. There is no one for you to go check up on. When you inevitably run out of this house searching for answers, a completely different world lies in your presence. Gone are the easy days of cooking, cleaning up after the twins, and looking after Skyy and Mel while they enter tweenhood. The mundane life, as you remember it yesterday, is no more.

The books that are downstairs, do not destroy them in a rage because they are yours and our future lifeline. We have written down our lives for the past two hundred-plus years once we realized what was happening. While it is a lot to understand, you will feel overwhelmed and will want to give up; please, at least try.

Every year seems to be different. I was able to embrace it entirely, but that isn't to say you will. Just know that whatever reaction you have, is valid.
You are strong.

There is someone downstairs who has just come into our lives. Allow them to help you. We have done this for so long that it will be nice to have a voice around.

Their name is Illyan, and they will love you as they have loved me.

We haven't found a way to break the curse, but there is one thing for sure, we will never give up.

I will never be his.
Be strong.

Azahara Starfall

Her hand was trembling so much that she could barely see the last lines on the page. "Three hundred..."

Just yesterday, she sat at the table discussing with her parents what had happened to Mel and Skyy. They couldn't be gone; they were filled with life. How could this have happened?

She couldn't even say goodbye to them...

"No..." She crumpled the paper into her fist as she swung the door open, the hinges nearly coming free as she charged into the hall and down the stairway. Every step felt like she was submerging herself in hell and would never come from its depths.

Standing in the kitchen was a beautiful, lanky, pale figure with long silver hair and pointed ears. They were staring at her, concern written in their lavender eyes. The urge to trust them was so strong that she feared it was a trick, Magic to keep her from finding the absolute truth of what was going on.

"Ladybug..."

"No—No, I don't know you. Where are they?" Her voice was broken, shattered under the weight of her despair. "Where are my **sisters**?"

The figure dropped its shoulders, "Did you see the letter?"

"It's a trick," she spat, her hands clenching into tight fists. "A trick from the gods, that's all." Her eyes darted towards the lone door, and she lunged for it.

Her legs propelled her forward swiftly, and she charged ahead as the figure stepped in her way. Using all her strength, she thrust them against the wooden door, which broke open with a resounding crack.

Though her forearms throbbed from the impact, Azahara wasted no time. She quickly descended a few steps and faced overcast skies and an endless expanse of nothingness.

There was no village.

There was no one.

Her legs only carried her a few more feet before they felt like sticks, and under the heavy weight of her sorrow, she crumbled to the ground. The flowers that surrounded her then, carnations, roses, spider lilies, forget-me-nots, hydrangeas, and lavenders, were all placed there with a purpose.

It suddenly dawned on her that this home wasn't coincidentally designed to create a sense of safety for her. It had been intentionally arranged this way. The flowers chosen were all favorites of her siblings, from the carnations Mel adored to the spider lilies which had been Skyy's preferred choice.

The scent of vanilla evoked memories of her mother's love for baking sweets, while the presence of peppermint reminded her of her father, who would always bring the treat home after being away.

The vines were meticulously placed throughout the room, a call to how relentless they were on her childhood home. Ultimately, she loved them and told her parents to stop taking them down, telling them she'd take care of the rodents.

Even the placement of the house. The forest at which she would hunt, the smell of the sea for her affinity for swimming, and the mountains, the ones she stared at in the distance through her window every night.

"It's true..." The embodiment of her sorrow poured in her tone, "They are gone." The hot tears that began to roll down her cheek were endless. How had she done this for three hundred years?

This was pain, and torture. Why me...

"Ladybug," It was, she had said their name was Illyan, that stood behind her. "It will be okay. I'm here for you."

She felt their hand on her shoulder then, and a sense of Magic ran through her core. She never dabbled in it, but she somehow knew what it was. Its warmth caressed her like a blanket.

They stood there as the sun crossed the overcast sky, and the night began to swallow the area around them. Time had felt meaningless, and she could have likely sat there for days without standing. Except, time was something that she didn't have on her side. It didn't afford her the comforts of forgetting its existence.

"How long do I have?" Azahara asked, defeat lining her tone.

"One year." Illyan said while putting their hand out to assist her. She looked up at them, their lavender eyes were gentle and held no judgment.

With a resounding sigh, she stood, "Let us get started then."

Day 4
CHAPTER 1

The darkness stretched endlessly around me, undeterred by the blazing fire. Its flames offered no illumination. "You are a monster." I don't know who you are.

There was so much blood on my hands. No, please, don't do this to me...

"You deserve to be locked in a cage." I know I did this to him. *His head rested in my lap, and that beautiful face I loved beyond my life lay lifeless.* Please come back to me. Please.

"It is you that should have died, not them." Fuck you. You don't know what I've gone through!

"They sacrificed everything; what did you ever sacrifice?"

I gave them everything. I gave my entire life for you ungrateful people. He died to save your useless existence. You will all burn. I will fucking destroy you all for what you did to him. What you have done to me!

Azahara bolted upright in bed.

The nightmares had jolted her awake, and the turbulent waters near the coast only intensified her distress. Everything around her seemed to spin, and her body trembled with fear. A dreadful sensation gripped her gut as she struggled to shake off the haunting image of Kaed laying lifeless in her arms.

The weight of having killed thousands on the battlefield in a matter of minutes bore down on her. The realization that the King wasn't seeking to bring her to trial, but to instead end her life intensified her despair. It meant she couldn't return home, but it wasn't as if she desired to, anyway. Despite the painful thoughts of never seeing Illyan and Zhal again, she couldn't bear to put them at risk because of her darkness.

Every part of her ached, yet she felt no pain. Her body was so numb that if the ship crashed into the bay and took her down, she would welcome dying to suffocation in peace.

In addition to everything else, regaining her memories from the past five hundred years felt like a journey through the underworld. Every sight triggered memories that would flash before her eyes, unleashing a whirlwind of emotions.

She lowered her head into her hands, curled her legs, and leaned between her knees. *Stop the incessant memories, by the Mother. Please help me.* Whether it was the random choice of black attire she wore onto the ship, a memory of wearing it to a Northern tavern flickered before her eyes, or something as simple as eating a peach, that transported her back to the moment when she had sliced her finger open while attempting to make a fruit medley pie.

The impact of her memories returning had nearly caused her to black out during the first few days. However, she'd gladly welcome those memories over the relentless flashbacks of that fateful day. Anything was better than reliving that.

"Come back to me!" "How fucking dare you!" "You swore!"

"How could I have done that to you? I am the monster..." Her voice trembled, barely audible, as she felt herself descending into the abyss of her thoughts. It was a place that would ensnare her in an endless loop, replaying that haunting moment on an eternal loop—the sight of Thall's sword piercing Kaed's chest, impaling her very heart.

If Thall had known her intentions, would he have stopped his tirade?

His soul lingered in purgatory until she joined him a few days later. The path she had discovered remained inexplicable, yet their conversation upon her arrival was brief but bittersweet, ending in her quest to vanquish him entirely.

"You took him from me," She remembered, staring at him with no remorse.

"You be—" Thall didn't get to finish his last words as she crushed his soul into oblivion. There was nothing beyond that. Once the soul was destroyed, it didn't move on or wander. He was no more, and that's exactly how she wanted it.

For Thall to be nothing, because he took her everything.

Tears streamed down her cheeks, and she felt no shame in letting them flow. It was all she could do to prevent the ship from crumbling in the breeze.

There had been a moment when she almost destroyed her home because she had been holding back her tears and emotions while trying to have a simple conversation about what jam she wanted on her toast.

"Ladybug? Grape or Strawberry?" The sun blazed relentlessly against my skin, making me uncomfortable. "Ladybug..." I wished the sun would set permanently. That seemed like the only solution. Could I destroy that, too?

"Azahara, do you want something else?"

"I don't want your jelly toast, Illyan. Can't you ever be quiet?" I could feel the power radiating between my fingers, pulsating through every pore. The chair I had been sitting on now lay in pieces.

The way they looked at me was pure fear. Good, they should be afraid of me.

A firm hand pressed against my shoulder, unafraid, preventing me from lashing out at what was left of my family. I would have destroyed them and the house that had become my only sanctuary.

"Eggs it is then," Illyan said, but my eyes were on Zhal. Her expression showed sympathy.

"Fuck your sympathy." The words were meant to hurt, but she didn't falter.

I cried then; the pent-up anger and pain I had held back finally burst forth in waves of salty tears. Zhal held me without judgment until I was sedated.

I hated myself. I genuinely hated myself.

The days following losing Kaed had been blocked out of her memory, and for once, she was content with that. There was nothing in this world she'd instead not feel, and those days were among them. If only she could erase the moment of his demise.

Why hadn't she lost her memory this time? Had it been Goddrick's doing, knowing precisely what was happening and being aware that she would suffer immensely if she remembered everything? It was as though the realms were conspiring to make her suffer more, as though she hadn't already suffered enough.

Now, curled into a ball in bed, she cried even harder. It wasn't a gentle release of emotions but a broken, unfiltered torrent of sorrow. Every inch of her trembled, and the tears that streamed from her eyes flowed like a relentless river, seeming as if they would never stop. The dam had broken, and there was no way to repair it. *No one can fix me. You were the only one who could. I am broken. I lied. Please—*

"Don't leave me. I can't do this—"

A rapid, urgent knocking on her door abruptly silenced her, and she fought back a whimper. Her body felt immobilized; she just wished to ignore the person on the other side. The issue was that she was a guest on this ship. If someone was seeking her out, it was for something urgent.

"Give me a moment," she whispered, which brought another wave of knocks. "Just one moment." She tried a bit louder, successfully quelling the next wave of knocks.

Tossing aside the blankets, she swung her legs over the bed and stood. Her bare body was drenched in sweat, even though the room was at a mild temperature.

She quickly grabbed the same black dress she'd worn for days, threw it on, and did her best to fix her hair before unlocking and opening the door.

Standing before her was an older man, his gray beard and hair showing the telltale signs of years spent at sea. Though not as captivating as hers, his blue eyes held a beauty of their own. She sensed a hint of flustered curiosity as he gazed at her and wondered if he had overheard her crying.

It was highly likely that the crew had indeed heard her. Whether it was her anguished screams during nightmares or her tearful outbursts of anger, there was no way they could have missed her emotional turmoil.

"Miss Rothwen, I apologize if I interrupted," he said, his tone trembling. She couldn't help but notice he was afraid of her, though she wasn't exactly sure why. For the past four days aboard the ship, her interactions with the crew had been minimal at best.

"It's okay. How can I help you?" She cleared her throat as she realized her voice was hoarse.

"The Captain would like to speak with you."

"He could have come to get me himself," she thought aloud, puzzled by the sudden request. The Captain hadn't hesitated to see her before. "I'll make my way to him now."

The man stepped aside, and she closed the door behind her.

The ship itself was as standard as one could get. Weathered wooden planks, burnished with layers of sea salt, stretched beneath her feet. Large white sails loomed overhead, bearing no crests or sigils. The crew was busy performing their duties, pulling the sails and moving cargo boxes around.

She ascended to the deckhouse, taking the single stairway up. Her eyes focused only on what lay ahead, never straying to the crew or the sea.

The ship was entirely adorned in wood, from the stairway to the doors, walls, and railings. Not a single trace of the color green caught her eye. She couldn't decide if it caused her more pain, or offered a fleeting respite. The absence of the color that reminded her of home was a stark reminder of those emerald eyes that once held her in their gaze and their love for her.

I miss you so much.

She knocked gently on the Captain's door, her eyes closing as she took a deep, meaningful breath. A rapid surge of pain had washed over her in just those few minutes since leaving her room, and she needed to center herself.

"Come in," the voice responded, and she entered.

"Captain," she addressed as she stepped into the deckhouse, a space that served as the Captain's quarters, galley, and meeting room for the crew. Maps sprawled across the massive round table, accompanied by various unfamiliar instruments that puzzled Azahara. "You requested my presence?" she inquired.

"Oh, yes, Miss Rothwen, thank you for arriving so promptly," he greeted. He appeared as a middle-aged human; nothing particularly remarkable about his appearance. His long, blond hair cascaded around his face, framing striking green eyes that proved difficult for her to meet while conversing. "Would you care to take a seat?" he offered.

"No, I can stand, thank you." Her hands were tucked behind her, fingers laced together.

"When you reached out to me, you were clear that your destination was just to be taken to the Port of Kortez. You know that is the Kingdom of Naverra's port, correct?"

"Yes, Sir." She felt her hand beginning to shake, so she shifted her posture. "Is that a problem? Can this ship not dock there?"

"No, no, that isn't it." His face softened, and he looked down at the table.

She narrowed her eyes at him, giving him time to find the words stuck in his throat.

"The King has informed all vessels that a woman is seeking passage off the continent to Ilkiz." He looked up at her through his thinning lashes. "Striking features, short curly scarlet hair, eyes as deep as the Casper Sea, and—" It seemed to pain him to say the last piece.

"A murderer?" Her voice was devoid of emotion, her face impassive. The permanent frown etched upon her lips revealed her indifference and lack of concern.

"And wanted for the massacre at Sunfall." Tension filled the room, though it didn't originate from her.

Staying neutral, she nodded. "Does this prevent you from taking me to the Port of Kortez?"

There was a look of bewilderment on his face. "My crew, they're also aware of this warrant for your arrest." It was as if he was attempting to make her grasp the gravity of the situation as though she didn't understand the implications of his words.

"They do not want to arrest me, Captain." She rolled her eyes and looked away from him. "How much?"

"Excuse me?"

"How much is the bounty for my capture, Captain?" Her tone was matter-of-fact. Not rude, but tinged with irritation. She was done with this conversation.

"A lot," he replied, and she noticed his throat bobbed with the words.

"What is your intention in sharing this information? Are you informing me that you've already reported me to the authorities, or are you looking for me to pay the bounty for your silence?"

The Captain, visibly fearful, stood. Perhaps he had hoped she would deny her involvement or claim it was all a misunderstanding. Unfortunately, neither of those scenarios would come to pass.

"We all heard what happened at Sunfall. It isn't my place to play bounty hunter, but I can't deny the danger you've put myself and my crew in," he said, and she only nodded in response. "Some of my men want to turn you over. However, this is my ship, and my word is law here." Their eyes met, and she could still see the fear he held so close to him. "Payment will suffice, but I also want to know, did you kill all those people?"

She felt her nostrils twitch and the heat of his gaze as he tried to stifle the sweat dripping from his forehead.

"You truly do fear me," she uttered aloud, though she hadn't intended to. It had been a mere thought, but its intensity compelled her to vocalize it. "Good. You should," she savored the power those words brought.

Visibly taken aback, the Captain gazed at her with an intensity that she imagined would become all too familiar.

A heavy sigh escaped her. "Yes, I did," she answered. Even if the Elf couldn't discern her truth, he would know she was not lying.

He nodded. "Thank you." For some reason, that surprised her. "At least you aren't a liar," he remarked, his posture straightening. He placed his hands behind his back and continued, "We will dock in the morning, and we won't alert the authorities. Your pay—"

"Here," she said, stepping forward, and she heard the distinct sound of his boots as he stepped back. Her head tilted inquisitively, and she halted her movement. "Captain, you know my truth. So when I assure you that I harbor no intention to harm you or your crew, find solace in that."

The familiar pain surged behind her eyes once more, and as she stretched out her hand toward the table, she noticed it trembling. "Not now," she muttered under her breath, frustration evident in her voice. Determined to regain control, she clasped her shaky hand with the other, gripping tightly.

Closing her eyes, she inhaled deeply through her nose, held her breath, and focused on the one thing that brought her peace. *You smell like black tea as it settles into the hot water. You will always be my sun... always.*

After a brief moment, she exhaled and grasped the pen. "Follow these instructions," she wrote, swiftly jotting down a few lines. She continued her message, "They will provide you with double the bounty's worth."

She turned away from the Captain and approached the door swiftly.

"Miss Rothwen," he called, and she lowered her head. "If it matters to you, whether I fear you or not, I don't consider you a bad person. We hear you suffering and calling for help. Whatever it is you seek, I genuinely hope you find it and that it grants you peace."

As her hand rested on the doorknob, she responded, "Death would be the only peace for me, Captain, and I don't believe I'll be granted that blessing for a very long time."

Day 5
CHAPTER 2

"It was always supposed to be him that survived. I wasn't meant to be the one to come out alive. He had his whole life ahead of him, and it was torn away because of something as foolish as love. How could I have been so selfish with his life? How could he have been so naïve to think he could survive being with me? I don't understand it, and it makes me so angry—so hurt. I am hurting so much."

Death's unwavering sunny gaze fixed upon her, devoid of judgment but filled with pure empathy and care. Not a single day had passed since Kaed was taken from her that she hadn't wanted to venture into Purgatory, seeking solace from Death.

They remained silent, attentively listening as Azahara rambled through her tears. "Now I have to unravel what the fuck is happening to me, all on my own. And don't dare say it was by choice. I would never willingly choose solitude; it was only for their safety that I had to."

Death only nodded, a gentle smile adorning their beautiful porcelain skin.

"I don't want this," she continued, her knees hitting the floor with a thud. "Take me with you, Death. Grant me passage into the afterlife. Let me be reunited with him, and yourself for all eternity." Bent forward, her body hunched and her face buried in her hands, she pleaded with Death for release.

A gentle sigh escaped Death's peach lips as they approached her. "My light, you know we have transcended such a choice," they spoke softly. Their skeletal hands came to rest against Azahara's head, and a radiant flood of light enveloped her. The pain dissipated almost instantly, replaced by a sensation of weightlessness. "As much as I long to bring you with me, I cannot do so. You are bound to this realm."

Azahara sat upright, feeling Death's fingers gently rest on her chin as they spoke further. "If I were to forcibly detach you from this realm, you would be forever lost, and I fear the realm itself would suffer the same fate."

Tears ran down her cheeks. "I don't want this. I never wanted this responsibility."

"I know, my light. All I desire is to free you from this pain," Death knelt, their eyes gleaming brighter than the sun as they locked gazes with her. "However, I am incapable of doing so."

Death gently pressed a kiss to Azahara's forehead. "You must not persist in visiting this place, for it will only lead you to oblivion," they cautioned. Their arms enveloped her, drawing them closer together. The long, black cloak enshrouded Azahara, and she closed her eyes. "I will forever be here for you. If he should manifest in my presence, I shall summon you. But for now, my sweet Azahara, this is farewell."

"Don't abandon me..." Azahara whimpered, fully aware of the pitiful sound of her plea. She recognized her weakness in begging the all-powerful Death to remain by her side.

"Never." Death reassured her before gently guiding her away, back to the harsh realities and the piercing brightness of the rising sun over the Kingdom of Naverra.

Azahara stood outside her quarters, resting on the railing as the ship came to dock. The city's port was already bustling with life, even at such an early hour. It would work to her advantage, making it easier to blend in when there were hundreds of civilians bustling about. She had to gather a few things before boarding her next ship, which she had already spotted arriving.

Her eyes locked onto it as it approached the port, and a rush of memories flooded back to her. It had been nearly two centuries since she last set foot on what was then known as The Neptune, sailing with Captain Hawthorn. She had been wandering the city aimlessly, unsure of her purpose when Captain Hawthorn had noticed her lost expression and offered his guidance. Trusting him had come easily because of his captivating aura.

From that moment, history had been made, and she had spent the next six months sailing aboard the breathtaking, all-black Neptune. Now, as she beheld the ship, it had transformed. The new Captain had adorned it with golden accents and pure white sails. While the change did not diminish its magnificence, it now stood out like a radiant gem in the vast sea.

Hearing footsteps approaching her, she straightened and pulled her black cloak tighter around her shoulders and chest.

"Miss Rothwen."

"Captain," she said, facing him as he leaned against the railing, his gaze fixed on the vast Kingdom. "Thank you once more for welcoming me aboard your ship." Despite their previous conversation, which hadn't been the most amicable, she still appreciated his willingness to assist a stranger, especially one burdened with a wanted status.

He let out a soft laugh. "It was no trouble."

They both fell silent, and Azahara wondered if he had approached purposefully. The feeling that he had something more to say gnawed at her. In her previous life, she would have given him the time and space to decide whether to speak, but she no longer had the patience.

"Is there anything else you wish to tell me before I depart?" Her tone remained composed, devoid of any trace of anguish.

"You have a knack for reading people," he allowed another laugh before continuing, "I just wanted to let you know we won't collect the coin. I thought about it overnight and felt like I was blackmailing you."

Azahara turned her gaze to the Captain, who fixed his eyes on the port. "I insist, please."

"I don't think you understand how much is at stake, little lady."

She took a deep breath, "I'm old enough to have fucked your great, great, great, great grandfather and bore his children, Captain; I am no little lady." The blush that immediately covered his complexion was gratifying. "With all due respect, please refrain from belittling me with silly nicknames.

"That being said, I appreciate that you care for my well-being enough to hold off on taking from me. However, I insist you at least take what you feel the trouble has been worth. It will not impact me, I can promise."

She fixed her eyes on him, and when a smile graced his lips, she looked back off the ship. The men nearest the dock began grabbing and tying the ropes for deboarding.

"You have a fire in you," his voice was gentle, "don't let anyone blow it out." He took his leave from her then, and she watched him from the corner of her eyes.

With a heavy sigh, she positioned her bag behind her, concealing it beneath her cloak. Flipping her hood over her head, she gracefully navigated her way to the slipway and disembarked from the ship. As she stepped onto the wooden surface, she felt the tremor caused by several other crew members leaving simultaneously, finally understanding the sensation of sea legs. Struggling to maintain her balance, she hurried toward the safety of solid ground. The last thing she desired was to slip and plunge into the water, drawing unwanted attention.

As soon as she stepped into the port, her senses were overwhelmed by the bustling activity around her. People were engaged in lively bartering, exchanging their early morning catches, and displaying pearls and other precious jewels from the sea for sale. This vibrant and crowded scene was exactly what she had hoped for, making it harder for anyone to single her out here than in an empty market.

She pulled the mask from her cloak and carefully positioned it over her nose, obscuring every visible part of her except for her eyes. She felt relieved knowing that the information about her appearance was outdated. The Captain had informed her that people would search for someone with two sapphire eyes. Ever since the Battle at Sunfall, one of her eyes had turned to sunset for solace, its gentle blue fading from its once-dominant hue.

Her first order of business would be to find the next captain. If the Neptune stayed in the family, they would likely have been a great-great-grandson at least, if not another generation down.

When she had sent the letter to the Neptune, addressing it to Captain Hawthorn, she hadn't expected a response, due in part to not providing any means for them to send a reply. The fact that the ship was currently docked on the day she had mentioned being in the port meant that it was either a remarkable coincidence or they had indeed received her letter.

The letter had requested safe passage through the Bathālisk Sea to the Isle of Ilkiz, and it included details about her identity and her previous sailing experience aboard the Neptune with Captain Hawthorn nearly two centuries ago. She hoped that would be enough incentive to get an audience with the newest Captain.

Making her way through the crowd, Azahara kept her eyes straight, never venturing to look at anyone or anything for long. Order scouts and White Cloaks were posted about. Still, they seemed more interested in the smell of food and the gypsy dancers than a cloaked figure moving about aimlessly.

The dock where the Neptune had ported was cleared of crew and boxes, making it easy to spot a figure standing against a post. They were distinctively female, with shoulder-length raven hair and stature similar to Azahara. It wasn't clear if they were admiring the ship before them or were part of the crew.

Azahara felt at least asking would be a good start. It might not have been the case, but the Neptune had been around for long enough that most, if not all, would know who the Captain was.

"Good morning," Azahara approached slowly, not wanting to startle the woman.

When the woman turned to see her, she was immediately taken aback by her beauty. She had light ebony skin and almond-shaped hazel eyes clear of flaws. Her jawline rivaled Azahara's, and her silky, wavy raven hair begged to be touched.

The woman stared straight at Azahara, blinking her eyes as if clearing a haze over them. "Oh, good morning." Her voice was rhythmic and melodic, strongly emphasizing the vowels. While it had a slight nasal quality, it still held a feminine incline. "She's a beauty, isn't she?" Her hand pointed out towards the Neptune.

"She is," Azahara agreed, "the Neptune, right?"

The woman hummed. "Yeah, what do you think of the new paint job?"

She wasn't sure if she had enough time for this conversation but held back any snarky remarks. "The all-black was mysterious, but the gold gives it a glow when the sun hits it. I imagine it would look like fire crossing the sea at the day's peak."

"See, you get it," the woman said, putting her hands on her hips with determination. "Men are so obsessively against change; it's irritable."

"Right," Azahara looked away from her then, "do you know the Captain?" She decided to get straight to the point.

"I do; who's asking?" The young woman was amiable and looked to be in her mid-twenties, if not younger, still getting her feet wet in the world.

"I am. I have business with them."

With a widening smile, her cheeks pushed up high, her eyes nearly disappearing. "You sent the letter."

Even with her face completely covered, the shock in her eyes must've been enough of a tell because the woman laughed. Maybe the Captain had shared the letter with the crew so they would all be on the lookout for her.

Azahara swiveled her head to ensure no one was coming up behind her. When the woman came back into view, her hand was extended toward Azahara.

"Captain Hawthorn, at your service."

"C-Captain—" Azahara stuttered, extending her hand to shake hers.

A sly smile crossed the Captain's lips, "Are you shocked because I am a woman, or that I am so young, because if it's for—"

"You are young; do not see me as daft. Women are just as capable, if not more capable, than men in all things." Azahara wouldn't entertain any conversation suggesting otherwise.

The Captain took her hand away then and nodded, "Good. My full name is Alyssandra Hawthorn, but I prefer Alyse. Formality is nice, but when it comes to my crew and friends, I'd prefer to be addressed as Alyse."

Azahara understood and gave her a nod of agreement.

"And you are Azahara Rhay Rothwen."

"Starfall, Rothwen was my family name. It's Azahara Starfall now. You can call me Aza, for short."

Once more, Alyse must have seen the confusion in Azahara's furrowed brows. The letter had only addressed her as Azahara.

"My great-grandfather talked about you. Not to me, but to his sons, and they onto theirs. You made a profound impact on him, enough that my father told me your story."

"Oh," Azahara felt her face heat up, but thankfully, the mask concealed her embarrassment.

"He didn't tell them everything, so don't worry, if you guys—you know—"

"No—no! We never."

Alyse giggled, "He spoke of your beauty and how no man was worthy of it. So, to hear you say that does bring me peace. I'd hate to find out that you were a great-grandmother."

Thoroughly blushing now, Azahara squeezed her eyes shut and laughed. Hot tears brimmed them at the feeling, opposite to how she had felt in the past several weeks.

With a shaky breath and another short laugh, Azahara responded, "I promise I'm not that. I can guarantee it."

Dramatically, she wiped her hand across her forehead as if she had been sweating. "Thank the goddess," a resounding laugh followed before Alyse continued, "I knew I'd like you."

Azahara smiled but kept her eyes as neutral as possible. Somehow, she knew that Alyse would be necessary to her journey, not only for being the Captain of her ride but a light needed in her darkness. *You are a monster; don't forget that. You could destroy that pretty smile in a matter of seconds.*

Swallowing the lump in her throat, Azahara shifted slightly away.

"Okay, so, you want to go to Ilkiz," Alyse said matter-of-factly. "We can discuss specifics on that later, and the crew is already aware of who you are, so—"

"Who am I?" Azahara cut in.

Alyse put her hands behind her back and tilted her head. It only took a moment for her to understand Azahara's question, proving she could fully capture a ship and its crew.

"They are aware that you are the one wanted for what is being called the 'Massacre at Sunfall.' A few days ago, well after receiving your letter, we also received notice from the King that a woman matching my grandfather's description of you, down to the freckles, would be trying to find passage to Ilkiz."

Azahara could feel her heartbeat quickening, yet she remained silent.

"None of us believe what happened there," Alyse continued, her voice steady and empathetic, "everyone, including myself, lacks your side of the story. Whether true or not, we choose to believe there's a reason behind it all."

Azahara's need for this ship to get to Ilkiz was pressing, and the idea of being abandoned here meant confronting a different kind of battle. She restrained her inclination for a sarcastic response and kept silent, allowing Alyse to continue.

The Captain's smile remained unwavering. "You've paid us more than generously, far beyond the bounty on your head. Furthermore, the crew and I share a strong disliking for the King and his rule, so... he can eat pig shit."

Hearing those words was precisely what Azahara had hoped for. Given the gravity of her situation, she was aware of the danger she was putting these people in, but needed their support more than she would have ever wanted to admit.

"Thank you." Azahara finally said.

Alyse winked and nodded.

Azahara felt an increasing unease deep in her stomach. The resemblance between Alyse's personality and Illyan's surprised her, adding to her pain in a way she hadn't anticipated.

"I noticed you don't have any bags," Alyse noted, catching Azahara off guard. "Do you need us to grab anything before we depart? We'll set sail as soon as you're aboard the Neptune."

Stealing her eyes away from Alyse, Azahara nodded. "I'm just going to get some essentials before boarding. It shouldn't take me long."

With that, Alyse instructed her to board the Neptune when she was ready and offered assistance if needed. They parted ways, and Azahara made her way to the center of the merchants market.

She had hastily left after regaining her memories, determined not to grant Zhal or Illyan the power to confine her and prevent her from going. She knew they would have tried, and the consequences would have been disastrous. Losing Kaed had already shattered her, and losing them and her home too, would have been unbearable.

It could have unleashed a devastating scene similar to that at Sunfall, leading her to destroy the realms and everything beyond. There would have been no world left once she was finished.

Clothes could be purchased, but her home and family could not. And so, that was where she found herself, browsing through the racks of a merchant's stall. The merchant sat quietly, diligently sewing in her chair. Azahara was drawn to the stall, sensing she wouldn't face bothersome haggling or negotiations here. Moreover, the hanging clothes all appeared exquisitely crafted, adorned with shells and colorful ribbons that evoked the enchantment of the open sea.

Azahara preferred the rugged, charming clothes over the elegant ones that Illyan would have criticized her for not choosing. After setting a few garments on the table with a pair of boots, she was ready to pay.

The older woman rose with expected haste. Not wanting to appear impatient, Azahara averted her gaze to take in her surroundings.

The air buzzed with energy as merchants proudly displayed their wares, vying for the attention of passersby. Colorful canopies stretched overhead, providing patches of shade and a vivid spectacle of goods. The aroma of freshly baked bread and exotic spices enticed visitors to sample the diverse culinary delights. Everywhere, animated conversations filled the air as locals and travelers exchanged laughter and stories, their voices blending harmoniously with the melodic tunes played by street musicians.

Children frolicked by one of the nearby merchants, two of them wielding play swords. At the same time, the other pretended to wield a bow without any arrows, pulling back invisible strings and "shooting" at their playful companions.

Azahara smiled, observing their innocence.

Trauma is dangerous; it strikes when least expected.

As one of the boys wielding a play sword turned against the boy with the bow, a sudden jolt robbed her of breath. With a swift and direct lunge, the sword pierced the boy, unleashing a searing wave of pain coursing through Azahara.

In the blink of an eye, the bustling merchants square dissolved, replaced by a haunting memory of Sunfall. The scent of blood and the stench of death filled her senses, casting a pall of darkness and foreboding. The ground was stained with crimson, and lifeless bodies lay strewn around her like macabre decorations.

Within arm's reach, Kaed knelt, his hand reaching out towards her while a blade protruded from his chest. His once radiant emerald eyes gradually dimmed, and their light faded into emptiness, leaving a profound sense of loss.

She could smell his blood above everyone and the salt in her tears falling down her cheeks.

"Are you okay?"

Azahara, still trembling from her vivid flashback, turned her gaze towards the voice that had called out to her. She blinked, struggling to refocus her vision and distance herself from the haunting memories that had gripped her moments ago.

Her hood and mask remained securely in place, shielding her face and the turmoil it hid from the world's prying eyes. With shaky hands, she steadied herself, determined to overcome the lingering effects of her traumatic recollection.

As she looked around, she noticed that the children she had seen moments before were now huddled behind protective adults, staring at her with wary eyes. The adults themselves regarded her with a mix of concern and unease.

Feeling the weight of their collective gaze upon her, Azahara forced herself to stand. However, the ground beneath her seemed unsteady, destabilized by her nervousness. She brushed aside the invisible threads of her past and focused on the present moment.

Following the voice that had reached out to her, she saw a man who appeared to be the source of the inquiry. His eyes held genuine concern, and she swallowed, her gaze settling upon him.

"I'm okay," Azahara assured the elderly man who had shown concern for her. He had a gray beard and long white hair cascading down his shoulders.

Azahara turned toward the merchant without meeting her gaze. She placed more coins on the table than the clothing was worth and added, "I'll take a trunk too, if you have one." In her peripheral vision, she watched the older woman walk away, hoping she wouldn't alert the guards out of misplaced concern.

The elderly man spoke again, "Do you need anything?" Azahara looked up at him.

"No, please, leave me be," she responded, shrugging off the approaching hand. "I don't need your help." She hoped her curt words would encourage him to walk away, but they had the opposite effect.

The man chuckled and asked, "Are you sure?"

Azahara locked her gaze onto his. Although he couldn't see it, her jaw clenched tightly, and she felt anger surging up her throat, ready to unleash a torrent of nasty words. However, his hand swiftly pressed against her shoulder before she could utter another word.

The red haze that clouded her vision dissipated, and her anger and sense of dread vanished. A soft exhale of relief escaped her lips, and she closed her eyes, savoring the kaleidoscope of colors dancing behind her eyelids.

The man's voice reached her, "There. Now, are you okay?" Azahara opened her eyes, and the man was smiling wider.

"Yes," she replied, her voice breathless. As he removed his hand from her shoulder, the calm feeling persisted. "Thank you."

"Miss, here is your trunk," the older woman called her attention, and she saw her packing away the clothes she had purchased.

The man chuckled and added, "Anything for you, Sunshine."

Azahara's head jerked back in his direction when she heard the term 'Sunshine'. However, he seemed to disappear before her eyes, as if he had never been there in the first place.

She spun around in nearly a full circle, scanning the sea of people for the familiar sight of the man in the blue shirt and brown trousers. But there was nothing, no trace of him in the crowd. She was utterly shocked; no man his age could have moved fast enough to seemingly vanish into thin air.

The soothing sensation of his touch was reminiscent of when Illyan used Magic to lull her to sleep. However, this feeling was different. Its warmth and raw power resonated within her, and she recognized it. That man had to be Sam.

But why did he leave? Why did he leave her?

Come back, please.

Day 6
CHAPTER 3

The events of the previous day had left her completely drained. Upon boarding the Neptune, she urgently requested to be escorted to her quarters. When the door closed behind her, she wasted no time, and her head met the pillow within a minute. She cared very little to explore the room or acquaint herself with the rest of the crew. The magnitude of the ordeal in port had drained her to the point where any feelings of guilt for not doing so were subdued.

As the ship set sail, she could feel the gentle movement beneath her, bringing her a sense of contentment. While she hadn't set a specific date for reaching Ilkiz, her primary goal was to spend as little time as possible in the Kingdom.

As she surveyed the space she had been given, the memory of Captain Hawthorn's kindness came flooding back. These quarters held the essentials and everything she could ever want and need.

The bed was comfortable, large enough to accommodate at least three people, with freshly laundered white sheets and an abundance of pillows as though it were prepared for company. The décor was rustic and functional for someone with the co-captain role, but not so much for her.

Towards the back of the room was a substantial wooden desk, adorned with various navigational tools and maps. Placed strategically next to a window overlooking the ship's rear, the views were breathtaking. She couldn't help but feel grateful to the Mother for this quiet escape, allowing her to enjoy fresh air without the need to step outside or engage in socialization.

Surprisingly, there was a place to sit and eat, which seemed odd, considering the ship supposedly had a dining hall on the lower deck.

Adorned in brown leather pants and a white tunic neatly tucked beneath a black corset, she slipped on her boots and hastily tied her hair into a messy bun atop her head. Though the disheveled appearance seemed unconventional, she lacked the energy to brush through the unruly ringlets and make her hair presentable.

Before she departed, she paused at the mirror. The eyes that stared back at her seemed foreign, but she knew it would work to her advantage, at least for now. It wasn't as if the bright scarlet hair atop her head was a giveaway, but that at least could be hidden.

Looking at herself now was nearly unbearable. Knowing that the person in the mirror had caused so much pain, not just to others but also to herself, almost made her want to shatter the mirror without even a second thought.

Tearing herself away, she bumped into the last thing of note in the room. An oddly placed porcelain tub, which she assumed was for everyone's use, given its size. If she had the choice, she would have it removed without hesitation. It haunted her, dredging up memories of the Idle Fox.

Shaking her head quickly, she tried to banish the vision of herself and Kaed in the tub, his fingers gently running through her hair. Tears welled in the corners of her eyes, and she bit her lip hard, willing the painful memory to fade away.

Fuck off, she cursed to herself, *leave me alone. Please.*

Making haste, she left her room and was immediately hit with the smell of the sea assaulting her senses.

Taking a large, nearly intoxicating breath, Azahara heaved a heavy sigh. This was the open water she was excited to smell and taste. While aboard the ship that brought her to the Port of Kortez, it had hugged close enough to the shoreline that they barely had enough wind to pull about her hair. Not on the Neptune. They were out at sea, making their way through open waters, and for the first time since the night at the Idle Fox, she felt a sense of freedom.

As if nothing could touch her.

"Oh, my goddess," she recognized the voice and immediately pulled her gaze to Alyse. "They did not lie when they said your beauty was not of this realm." The captain was wearing a traditional skipper's outfit; a loose-fitting, off-white shirt with billowing sleeves, allowing her unrestricted movement during the most turbulent of journeys. A sturdy leather belt cinched at her waist, showcasing a finely crafted brass buckle adorned with maritime symbols. Her lower half was clad in practical trousers tucked into knee-high boots.

Alyse stared at her with awe-inspired eyes. Her cheeks were darkened, and her mouth was slightly ajar.

Azahara sheepishly dropped her gaze, feeling heat gathering at her cheeks. "You flatter me, Captain."

"Please, I beg of you, call me Alyse," she closed the distance between them and immediately took Azahara's hand into her own, "We are friends here. I'm only Captain to the helm."

With a smile, Azahara conceded and nodded, "Alyse it is."

"Perfect, come; I need you to meet the rest of the crew." High on energy, Alyse pulled her then, nearly dragging her across the deck.

Several people were already out, but Alyse gave a high-pitched whistle that reverberated throughout the space, calling for full attention towards them. Azahara wanted to protest but dropped her gaze as a dozen eyeballs stared at her. This would be the first time she would have been in the spotlight like this since her show-stopping performance at the Outpost's training area, and it made her stomach queasy.

Pulling her up a few steps, Alyse turned her and presented her as though she were the next in the lineup of cows on sale. She knew Alyse meant well and didn't mean it that way, but it felt the same.

"Good morning, Neptune family," Alyse had way too much energy for Azahara, especially in her current state, "I'm super stoked to introduce—finally—Azahara!"

Okay, now I feel like I'm in a show, playing the part of the jester to dance for the King. Swallowing, she dared a glance at the near dozen crew members staring back at her.

She sighed roughly. *I hate this as much as I thought I would.*

"Are you good with names, Aza?" Alyse addressed her, and she was tempted to lie. However, looking out towards the faces of the crew, she spotted at least two Elves, which meant they'd know she was lying. With their loyalty, they'd tell Alyse.

It's a silly thing to lie about, and odds are Alyse wouldn't care, but she didn't need to give them more reason to dislike her. She could tell that a few in the crowd were less than excited about her presence there.

"Decent, yes," She felt tightness in her throat, accompanied by the sting of acid.

"Wonderful!" Her exuberant attitude was infectious, but didn't take away Azahara's nerves.

"Let me start with the co-captain, Rowlin!" The first of the crew stepped forward, a nearly identical complexion to Alyse with soft, deep blue eyes and a big smile. "This is my loyal second in command, Rowlin Jasper. Again, we don't do formalities here." He could not be older than twenty.

He said nothing to her, but she smiled in return, "It is nice to meet you. Thank you for allowing me aboard."

Rowlin then looked at Alyse expectantly. "Oh! How could I forget? Rowlin is mute and partially deaf."

"Ah—" Azahara nodded her head, brought her hand up, and began signing, "It is nice to meet you," spelling out his name to emphasize she was speaking to him, "Thank you for allowing me on board."

The utter shock on his face and Alyse's when she turned to her was amusing. "What?" It would appear that several years ago, she learned how to sign, and while it should have surprised her as well, it was just another thing that made her feel like a freak.

Turning back to Rowlin, he began signing, "No need to thank me. I am now happier than I was moments ago that you have decided to choose us for your journey across the sea." Reading it was a bit more complicated, but she got the gist.

The smile never left either of their faces as Alyse clapped her hands together once. "Off to a wonderful start; next are my First and Second Officers."

This was beginning to feel like a lineup that Skyy would talk about at school when they would do roll call.

A male with blondish gray hair, a matching beard, and green eyes stepped forward. He was a middle-aged human, very fit and with a squared jawline. His appearance was that of a laboring man, as though he was out in the fields working with crops. She imagined him to be a horse rider with his wider-than-average frame and sloping shoulders.

The other was a humanoid figure with white skin and piercing blue eyes that mirrored hers. Their lips were dark brown, and they had no hair. Stunning and different, Azahara couldn't help but stare longingly at the creature before her. She dared not assume they were human, but they had the distinct features of one. That, and their gender seemed fluid, like Illyan. Yet they held a feminine incline in their features, such as breasts—which she quickly stopped venturing to look at.

"This is First Officer Xol," Alyse gestured towards the white dove, "And this is my second officer, Théodore."

Azahara bit the corner of her lip as she moved her gaze to Théodore, "It's wonderful to meet you both," dragging her eyes back to Xol, she provided a weary smile.

With a gentle gesture, Théodore extended his hand and, after placing hers into his, graciously kissed it, "A pleasure, Miss Starfall." Her eyes barely left Xol long enough to see Théodore give her a bright, unfiltered smile. For a human male, he had aged beautifully.

"Now for the rest of the crew," Alyse picked them up one by one, quickly going right to the left. "Zayne, Carmen, Yelena, Tessa, Zephyra, Darian, Lucala, and Tillin." Each time she passed over them, they'd either give her a quick wave or nod. Most had a smile, all but Zephyra, the Elf she'd spotted earlier, and Tillin, whose bright blue eyes were nearly translucent.

Tillin was a Siren, without a doubt.

"It's nice to meet you all." Azahara didn't mean to lie; she had nothing against any of them, but personalizing herself to them felt wrong. Building a relationship with any one of them felt like a betrayal to Kaed, Illyan, and Zhal.

Zephyra rolled her eyes and turned from the group.

An unsteady breath escaped Azahara's lips as she dropped her gaze.

"Are you free to chat further about the journey, Aza?" It was Alyse, her hand coming to rest at Azahara's elbow. The touch sent a strange, painful feeling through her body.

She jerked away so quickly that Alyse was left stumbling back, slipping on the edge of the stairs. Azahara, with speed she had only seen on the battlefield with Thall, was behind her before she could slam her head against the railing.

The crew that had stayed stared at her, and she pushed Alyse quickly back to her feet. "I'm sorry, I—" She chewed on her lip, swallowing hard. She hated that she apologized instinctively. They had no idea what she had been through, and jerking away from Alyse was a reaction brought out of pain.

"It's fine; I'm very touchy-feely, but you wouldn't know that." There was a pained expression on Alyse's face, and immediately, Azahara felt a tinge of guilt rip through her stomach. "I'm sorry—I should know better."

Azahara didn't respond immediately. Instead, she gently placed her hand on the elbow that Alyse had grabbed. It was the very spot that Kaed used to touch first whenever he rushed to her, assuring her safety. It was such a simple yet meaningful action, something he always did.

After an awkward silence, she finally said, "I have time to talk."

Alyse didn't push the discussion further, and she led her towards the front of the ship. They passed what Azahara would assume was Alyse's quarters and made their way to the open area that looked out at sea. The ship was beautiful, but something about the open water took her attention from it.

In toe to them was Rowlin, who hovered close to her, but thankfully never touched her.

Alyse sat on a barrel, and Rowlin stood closest to her while Azahara was across from them. Her back was now against the railing, one leg crossed over the other.

"Are you familiar with the route to Ilkiz, Aza?" Alyse jumped into the conversation.

"No, just that it is tricky," Azahara crossed one leg over the other and watched as Alyse did the same, sitting now with her legs intertwined like a pretzel.

"Indeed, that's precisely why no soul has ventured to or from Ilkiz in thousands of years, not since the conclusion of the War of Ilkiz nearly three millennia ago," she spoke with a hint of awe, as if the prospect intrigued her. "We will try the Cyclops route first, which would only take us roughly ten days, and we would reach the peak of Ilkiz."

"Why is it called the Cyclops Route?" Azahara cut in, looking at Rowlin, who was intensely watching her. He appeared to be reading her lips, which was good because she had forgotten to sign for him.

"It is because it takes us straight through the roughest seas, and if you were to look at a map, it's a single point in the middle and appears like a cyclone or an eye." Without a map, Azahara had a hard time picturing it, but she wasn't the Captain, nor was she sea-trained. She'd take her word on the image.

"Anyways, we will attempt this route first; if we cannot complete it, we must take the longer route, which includes stopping in Celadon for supplies. Then we would take the safe route pass Itotaki, and after that it's a straight shot through the Crescent Crossing to the Hydrox Port, Ilkiz's only port.

"That journey will take nearly thirty days instead of roughly twelve. It is why we will try the Cyclops Route first."

Azahara nodded, not adding to the commentary.

Alyse turned to Rowlin, signing while saying, "Do you have anything to add?"

"Nothing to the route, but can I ask you a question, Aza?" Watching him, she gave him a nod. "Can you tell me the truth about what happened at Sunfall?" He signed back.

Azahara felt her hands begin to shake as the burning around her eyes instantly threatened tears.

Rowin continued, "I just want to know. I promise no judgment."

Azahara, unblinking, stared at him. It felt like her lips were sewn together and wouldn't pull apart even if she tore at them. *You aren't the monster; you wouldn't have done it intentionally.* Her mind was fighting a losing battle. *You are a liar. A killer and a fucking monster. You would have done it repeatedly if the outcome had stayed the same. If he died, they would die.*

Swallowing, she finally blinked, and the tears that had lined her eyes fell down her cheeks. "I don't know exactly what you want me to say; what you have heard is the truth," she moved her hands and watched as he shook his head.

"No need to sign. I can read your lips," That beam was still on his face, and with one glance at Alyse, she could see she was smiling too. "Tell us your story, Aza; we want your truth."

"I killed them. All of them. Whether it was for a reason or not, it doesn't change the fact that I—" Azahara's unsteady breathing took her back, not realizing that her entire body was vibrating. "I—" She began to hyperventilate, and the open sea felt more constrictive like she was being swallowed by it. The sun that kissed her was like fire and no longer comforting.

"Aza..." Alyse furrowed her eyebrows, stepping down from the barrel. "It's okay; I promise we aren't your enemy."

Azahara felt her teeth chattering. "You don't even know me."

"Let us know you then," Alyse sounded as though she were pleading. *"Let me in. Don't push me away."* The memory of Kaed begging for her to open up shot through her like an arrow to the heart.

"There is nothing to know," she turned away from them, not wanting to see what Rowlin would say. Nor did she want to see the sympathy Alyse had on her face. "See me as nothing more than a package being delivered. One that will eat infrequently and be seen no more than needed."

She felt exhausted, even if she had just woken not too long ago. Instinctively and without giving her body guidance, she began moving towards the stairs to head back to her quarters.

"Aza, please, he's sorry," Alyse called to her, and she could hear her footsteps against the wooden planks approaching her.

"He doesn't need to be sorry. This is your—" Before she could get to the steps, Alyse stood before her, and Azahara scowled. "This is your ship, and you do as you please. Question me, hate me, like me; I don't care. It doesn't mean I will answer all of your questions; it doesn't mean I'll hate or like you back. It is my—my fucking choice. I paid for passage from the Naverra to Ilkiz; I shouldn't be obligated to be anything for anyone here."

The entire world was red then, her body on fire like the flames within Ilkiz herself. Alyse was unwavering and stood with fervor.

Azahara could see her chest rising and falling quickly at the edge of her vision. She could only hear her heartbeat while she should have heard the waves crashing against the ship's belly.

"I—" Alyse emphasized the word so much that it nearly came out as a scream, "I am so sorry, Aza."

"Everyone says that, but do they even know what they are sorry for?" Azahara was overbearing, and she knew it. Alyse was nothing but kind. Her heart hurt for the Azahara before Kaed's death because she knew Alyse would have been a friend.

"I killed them, Alyse." Her words were matter-of-fact. "And I'd do it again if it meant a different outcome for him. Then you would ask me if I knew the outcome of what I did, would I have still done it—yes, I still would."

Her voice was full of anger, pain, remorse and pity, and she would not have been surprised if Alyse had thrown her off the ship.

Azahara could have sidestepped or thrown Alyse, but because she saw it coming, it didn't send her into a panic.

Alyse wrapped her sun-kissed arms around her neck and embraced her. She left her arms down, fearful of how they would react without guidance if given the means. The smell of honey reminded her of Zhal, and instead of triggering a painful memory, it only made her feel at home.

"Nothing that anyone will ever say to you will help," Alyse's voice was gentle, sending chills throughout her, all the way to her stomach where a pit had formed. "I can't pretend to understand, but you are obviously in so much pain. Take whatever time you need, and if you only want us as a means to an end, then so be it."

Azahara leaned her head up and closed her eyes. Alyse's grip on her never loosened. "Just know that I see you, and so do many others. You aren't as alone as you may think."

"They won the war for us." "War costs, sonny, whatever did that stopped the war." "They finally came to help after all our prayers." Memories of the tavern echoed in her mind. Did she truly stop the war then and there, or had she unwittingly played right into Jaakobai's hands? Some would praise her as the hero, while many would brand her as the true villain. The burden of perception weighed heavily on her heart.

Kaed had always been the hero. He deserved the songs sung about him. They should put him in the history books. If it weren't for him, the encroaching forces of Sunfall would have befallen them in secret. The Kingdom would have been no more.

Alyse thought her to be the victim, and while she was, it didn't overshadow what she had done.

Feeling a gentle hand atop hers, she didn't need to look to confirm it was Rowlin. Consciously staying as far from her elbow as possible, it would seem.

"Whether you believe me or not, I am a monster capable of destruction..." Her voice but a whisper, "Do what you must to protect your family, Alyse."

Azahara hadn't returned the gesture of comfort, and in time, Alyse released her. The smile on the Captain's face never faltered, and she was actively trying not to pull her eyebrows together in concern.

With a heavy nod, she navigated around Alyse, her steps unsteady as she descended to the main deck. She remained oblivious to any curious gazes that had lingered upon her. Her gaze fixated downward, not on the planks' gaps, but the shattered world beneath her.

With trembling hands, she clasped the door handle in a desperate rush, shutting it behind her with force. Within seconds, she collapsed to the floor; her body crumpled under the weight of her sorrow, the impact echoing the magnitude of her pain.

The bed was too much of a comfort for her. She felt unworthy, deserving only the unforgiving embrace of the solid, wooden floor beneath her.

Day 10
CHAPTER 4

There was so much blood on my hands, and I could swear it was mine. The way I was in so much pain. My body vibrated, and my vision shook like the world during a quake.

I would have lied down and accepted my fate if not for the lifeless body before me. I watched as the darkness took my vision and waited for Death's sweet embrace.

The face of a man I had only known for days, at best, was void of life. It had been the previous year, the life before this, that had mistakenly been careless with Goddrick's body.

She had forced my hand. The one gripping the blade was bloodied and marred with the heart muscle on its hilt.

It was penance for what he had done to me, not that it was deserved. When he lay with me that night, fucked me till we both were satisfied, he could not have seen this being the outcome. How could I have been so stupid as to think that a god would not see this as a betrayal? In his eyes, I was his property and had just given it away.

I could not be selfish with their lives, yet here I was, killing an innocent man because he fucked me and accidentally planted his seed.

The feeling of bile rising in my throat made me jerk away, tossing the blade so far from me that it disappeared into the darkened abyss.

His presence was so overpowering that I didn't need to look up to see him, but he forced me to anyway.

The grip on my chin was firm as he brought my attention to his. With me on my knees and him standing above me, I was the dog, and he was the owner.

"What have we learned?" His thumb brushed down my lips.

I was looking at him with such hate, and I wanted to hurt him, for him to suffer a mere inch of what I had. That only seemed to fuel him, and his hand tightened at my jaw, making me wince.

"How about you tell me, Goddrick, what did I learn?"

The grin that laced his face formed a lump in my throat. I hated him more than I hated myself at that moment. "You will come to me, if given enough pain and suffering."

Pain that was not physical destroyed me then.

When I had woken that morning to the painful sight, I had called to him, begged him to remove any means of it happening again.

"Just end this suffering, Little Mouse. Be mine." He knelt before me then, his piercing, fiery gaze nearly impossible to hold. "Let me have you because you want me." I could smell the wood and ash as he was inches from my lips.

"I'd rather die with this boy." I felt his hand twitch and anticipated the slap that came, or was it a punch? I'm not too sure.

My body crumbled onto the lifeless body, and all I wanted to do was run away. I needed to get away from the smell and taste of death that filled my mouth.

As if he would allow me the joy of choice to run.

He was on top of me before I could gather myself. His entire body enveloped me, and I felt both disgusted and mortified that he was lying on top of me, while I lay on the boy I had just murdered in cold blood.

"Get off! Get off of me!" I was begging then. I didn't want this, and I would rather have slit my own throat than be here. Why had I thrown the dagger so fucking far?

"I'm rewarding you, while also punishing you." His hand wiped blood across my face, and I screamed. The blood-curdling kind that would bring the hero running to save the damsel in distress. "You asked for this, Dikos Mou, my love. You called to me."

There was so much pain then; I knew it was my own. I wanted to look, but fear prevented me from doing so. "Keep screaming for me." He placed the opposite hand, the one that wasn't wrist deep into my stomach, behind my head and lifted it off the frozen body below me. "Scream."

I clenched my jaw tight.

Goddrick fulfilled his promise, ruthlessly stripping away any possibility of another man impregnating me, just as this poor boy did.

I didn't know pain like this existed, and while I did not want to scream, when his hands wrapped around the part of me that would have brought life into this world, I could no longer hold it in.

I had done this to myself. For my past life mistake, I was suffering immeasurable amounts of pain. He was physically pulling me apart without remorse for the feelings that accompanied it.

It was what I deserved for what I had done to the boy below me. I was a monster.

He ripped it from me then, and my body went into shock. As if it were a piece of trash, he tossed aside part of me and brought his bloodied hand to my cheek. The heat of my blood filled me with warmth like a blanket.

"You are such a bad girl." I was shaking so badly that my teeth chattered. "I really shouldn't do it, but seeing you like this, so weak and helpless, makes me feral."

I wanted to die. I hated myself for what I had done. I hated him for making me this person.

I wanted to wake up from this nightmare that was my past.

"Wake up, please."

After emptying the last remnants of her stomach's contents out of the wall-to-wall window, Azahara clutched the frame, inadvertently cracking the wood beneath her grip, drawing crimson blood from the splinters piercing her skin. Rage surged within her, and she cursed all the gods for allowing that creature to harm her for so long.

How could they have allowed Goddrick to do such things to a mortal that they swore to protect?

"Who needs them, anyway," she muttered as she ripped apart a piece of the window's ledge and hurled it so far that it disappeared from her vision before plummeting into the sea. She longed to scream, but knowing it would be ill-advised, she stifled the impulse.

Over the past few days, she had woken to the terrors of her past, and she knew they had not been quiet. Grateful that the crew's sleeping quarters were in the ship's lowest part, she refused to let embarrassment linger. There was a chance that Alyse, who was on the same level but across the ship from her, might have heard her, but Azahara was relieved that Alyse never came to check on her.

Azahara knew it was time to leave the room and eat. The only items she had were the fruits that someone, likely Rowlin or Alyse, would place outside her door, and even then, she didn't really eat them. Only the strawberries would she consume. She couldn't continue down this path; starvation was not how she wanted to go.

I need to apologize to them for what I said. I can't be that way... She lingered on her words before stepping out of the room. The hustle and bustle around her indicated that things were in full swing, which made the crew ignore her presence on deck.

Azahara carefully navigated her way towards the helm of The Neptune. To her relief, no one stopped her to engage in small talk. She just wanted to focus on apologizing, grabbing food, and avoiding the shutdown of her mental state, which would inevitably force her back into her room.

Ascending the stairs, she lifted her cotton-white dress, which was far too long. Alyse's conversation with someone caught her attention. "We need to exercise caution with the sails as we approach these danger areas," Alyse explained while pointing at a map spread across a few barrels. "If we can pass this point, we'll have a straight shot to Ilkiz."

Azahara soon realized that Alyse was talking to Xol, who wasn't looking at the map, but up at her. Alyse followed Xol's gaze and spotted Azahara, almost stumbling as she hastened in her direction. "Aza!" Alyse greeted her with the enthusiasm of long-lost friends who hadn't seen each other in years.

"You are outside," Alyse stated, her lips widening, "We were just talking about the route. Only a few more days until we reach the roughest part, so Xol will prepare the crew and coils of rope for everyone."

Xol was beside Alyse, staring at Azahara with unblinking eyes.

"Xol, you are being strange. Say something," Alyse nudged the ghostly creature beside her.

Azahara shook her head, "It's okay. You don't need to say anything."

As if dismissed, Xol bowed her head and departed the space. Azahara hadn't realized she was holding her breath, and when she released it, she felt relief. It wasn't like she feared Xol; something about her just made her feel strange. It felt as though she stood in the presence of a ghost from her past, unable to pinpoint the exact moment when their paths had crossed before.

Alyse rolled her eyes, "She's a great First Officer. Please excuse her."

"There is nothing to excuse," Azahara said before taking a deep breath and continuing. "I want to apologize to both you and Rowlin. I shouldn't have reacted the way that I did. You both have been nothing but welcoming and kind. I'm just—"

A warm hand was on her arm then, "It's okay. You don't need to explain yourself, not to me. Not to anyone."

Azahara swallowed, her heart bouncing between her chest and stomach, "Thank you for your kindness. I don't deserve it, but it is appreciated."

Their eyes held one another briefly, and while Alyse smiled, Azahara's lips stayed neutral. She wanted to smile, but it would have been forced. Being happy seemed like a betrayal of her true feelings, and she was tired enough as it was; the last thing she wanted was to act on top of everything else.

"I should apologize to Rowlin. Do you know where he is?"

"What timing, here he comes," Alyse waved behind Azahara, and she took a centering breath, steadying herself. "I also hadn't realized, but there was one more crew member I needed to introduce you to. He was downstairs, and I'm not sure how I forgot."

Azahara just shook her head, "It's fine."

"No, seriously. Like, look at him. How would I forget **he** exists on my ship?" Shrugging, she turned to look over her shoulder, seeing Rowlin first and beside him—

"Jayce..." Her eyes nearly popped from their sockets as she whipped her body completely around. "Fucking Latimer?"

No, no, don't do this. There is no way. Absolutely no way that I am seeing him right now. She raised her hands to her eyes and wiped vigorously. As though there was a filter over them, creating a figment of her imagination.

She dropped her hands, hoping to only see Rowlin when her vision returned, but to her dismay, there Jayce stood—a smile painted across his painstakingly gorgeous face.

He looked like an old soul in the body of a thirty-year-old; Perfect facial features, with remarkably high cheekbones and a masculine jawline and chin. A thick, dark head of jet-black hair came to just above his shoulders, and a soft layer of bristly hair covered his chin, jawline, and upper lip.

Jayce only stopped when he was a foot before Azahara, his head tilted downward. She had nearly forgotten how tall he was. He was well over a foot taller than her, and it wasn't just his height that overpowered her. His build was anything but compact, with broad shoulders, he was stocky and powerful, with hardened muscles in his arms and chest.

"Hello, Azahara. What a coincidence." His hazel eyes were gentle as he looked at her. The smell of mother nature and peppermint hung to him, causing her to fall into bliss. It reminded her of home, and while that should have brought her comfort, it only reminded her of what was still there. What she had left behind.

Rowlin was beside her then, waving his hand and sending her a wide smile. She could only see it through the corner of her eye, as she feared taking her eyes off Jayce would cause him to do something they'd both regret.

"Hi, Rowlin," Azahara murmured. To her surprise, Rowlin put his hand on Jayce's chest and pushed him back, giving himself space to step before her.

She watched him say, "I'm so happy to see you out of your room."

Azahara felt Jayce's eyes on her, and she was mortified. Pure fear ran through her. Rowlin must have seen it in her eyes because he signed, "What is it?"

Turning towards Alyse, she asked "Why is he here?" Her tone was shaky, and she was so surprised that she immediately cleared her throat.

"Ouch," Jayce forced a pained tone, "I'm right here, you know."

Completely ignoring him, Azahara eyed Alyse expectantly, begging for an answer.

"Uh, I didn't realize you knew each other. He is part of the crew, specifically for—" Alyse was cut off by Azahara putting her hands on her arms.

"Alyse, he is the First Commander of the White Cloaks to the King. The same King that wants my head. This is no coincidence." Azahara found her lips trembling, and she stared so profoundly at Alyse, pleading with her to understand the severity of the situation.

She nodded but didn't say anything.

Quickly releasing her, she turned to Jayce, Rowlin knowing to step aside immediately. She felt the now too-familiar bite of power rising to her skin. The sense that she needed to protect herself and the people on this ship drove her control.

"Why? You knew I'd be onboard this ship! Why are you here?"

"I didn't." He was lying through his teeth, and she knew it. "I left the White Cloaks."

"Bullshit!" Azahara spat, and he smiled.

God damn it, don't smile at me.

"After the battle and aiding with the cleanup, I resigned." His tone was so husky, and it frustrated her that he could be such a good liar, but he wasn't going to trick her. "Figured I'd try my luck at sea since land didn't serve me so well."

She shook her head, "No, absolutely no way. Where is Karver? Is he here, too?" She stepped towards him, and he lifted his hands in defense.

"Please, no need to be violent."

"Aza," it was Alyse, "we can always ask Zephyra if you want confirmation—"

"Wonderful idea." The thought of using someone for such a granular thing caused a buzz in her head, but she didn't care. They had to see him for the liar that he was. Alyse was too kind to throw him overboard, but when she saw his truth, hopefully, she would see reason and assist in feeding him to the fish.

Grabbing his wrist, she dragged him down the stairs and onto the main deck. Without needing to look very far, she saw Zephyra standing with Yelena, who was an Ossodian. Her green skin tinted as they approached, flustered at their quickened steps. Zephyra, who had shown no interest in being a friend to Azahara, scowled directly at her.

"Tell her now." Azahara said while grabbing at Jayce, moving him in front of the Elf.

"Demanding things before a date, huh?" he joked, slipping his wrist from her grasp and rubbing it gently. "You have quite the grip. Did you get stronger after the night we danced? I remember you being more delicate."

She despised that she was blushing. It only fueled her hatred and mistrust more.

Zephyra was staring at her but held a much softer expression when she looked at Jayce. "Tell me what?" Her voice was silky, and Azahara swore then that she was putting all her effort into seeming interested in whatever Jayce had to say.

"If I must," he inclined his hand towards Zephyra, and she, without hesitation, gave hers to him. "I was telling Azahara here that I am merely a crew member aboard this ship and serve only our Captain Hawthorn."

Azahara watched as Zephyra nearly melted into a puddle before him.

"Why are you telling me this?" Zephyra asked, biting her lip and fluttering her eyelashes.

Are you fucking kidding me? Azahara had her mouth wide open, unabashedly showing her surprise at the show that was happening before her.

"For you to confirm that I am telling the truth," Jayce kissed Zephyra's hand, and Azahara nearly punched him. She had no idea where she found the strength to restrain from it.

Zephyra's eyes bore into Azahara with a look of absolute disgust, a visceral reaction etched upon her face, "He speaks the truth."

"Are you sure, or is the leaking drain between your thighs hindering your senses?" Azahara gritted her teeth and turned from them, quickly moving back towards Alyse, standing as straight as she'd ever seen her.

Azahara barreled past her and rushed towards the opposite side of the ship. She could hear footsteps behind her, thankful that it was a light pair. That meant it would be anyone but Jayce following her.

Alyse, bless her, sprinted in front of Azahara, "Wait, where are you going?"

"I'm going to swim to Ilkiz from here," it was impossible, she knew that. Still, if no one was going to believe her, it was safer than being on this ship with someone directly connected to the King.

"That would be ill-advised," she was walking backward, Azahara stampeding towards her. "Please, Aza, talk with me."

"I told you who he is," she threw her hands up in frustration, "he is lying!"

"But Zephyra..."

Azahara felt her eye twitch, and it was evident that Alyse had seen it.

"Okay, okay—just slow down, please." Alyse collided with the ship's railing as they reached the farthest point at the back. "What do you want me to do?"

"Throw him overboard." She was so quick to respond that it surprised Alyse.

"I can't do that. I'm sorry."

"Then I'll go," Pushing Alyse forcefully out of her way, she stepped up on a box and onto the ledge. This had been the first time she looked straight down, seeing how far the plunge was from deck to the sea's surface.

It would likely knock her out if she didn't land properly. If she drowned, her body would float to land or be consumed by a sea creature. Would she come back from being dismembered by a shark?

"Get down from there," she was struck by the myriad of emotions conveyed through the voice that was now speaking to her, "or I'll drag you down myself." His tone, though stern, carried a sense of genuine concern in its unwavering firmness.

Azahara didn't look back, she only held tightly to the rope lines.

The last time they spoke, he told her to be careful on the battlefield. He had sent Karver there to protect her. She felt that every action he had taken before the battle had been out of nothing but care for her.

However, she couldn't ignore the fact that he had the closest connection to the King. Jayce was sworn to his duty, and no amount of words he could spew would convince her that he was there by coincidence. He was not there for her well-being.

"Before I get back to the sleepy King." He had all but protected that piece of shit while his people died on the battlefield.

"Jayce, I strongly suggest you just back off for now." It was Alyse with the voice of reason.

"With all due respect, Captain. No." There was no harshness to his tone. Purely straight to the point.

A mock gasp came from Alyse, "Captain? Pfft. Oh, now you've really done it." She was upset at the title, not the insubordination of her so-called crew member.

Azahara turned her gaze to Jayce. His arms were crossed over his broad chest, an eyebrow raised. "If you come down, we can talk."

"I don't want to talk to you. Anything I tell you will get straight back to the King. They are probably on our tail right now."

"They aren't," he answered quickly, "I promise."

"Your promise means nothing."

Alyse, from the corner of her eye, was slowly backing away. "I'm going to just leave you two to it. If you jump from this ship, Azahara Rhay Starfall, I swear I'll send Xol in after you." It was meant to be a funny jab, and while she would have normally laughed at it, Azahara stayed penciled into her fury.

Then, it was just the two of them.

Jayce took a deep breath and ran his fingers through his hair. "Do you want me to jump in and drag you back onto this ship?" His voice held a gentle tone reminiscent of their last encounter.

"No," she spun around and quickly stepped back onto the solid floor of the ship.

He visibly relaxed, "Thank you."

"Jayce, for the love of the Mother, what do you want?" She crossed her arms under her chest, her hands gripping the loose fabric of her flowing dress.

She watched him, his body language, and how he never took his eyes off of her. He leaned towards her as if wanting to approach and close the five or so feet between them.

"I'm here because—"

"I swear," she felt burning behind her eyes, "do not lie to me. I'm so fucking serious."

He stepped towards her, and she pressed against the ledge—the wood biting into the dimples of her back. He stopped then and didn't approach her further.

"I'm not here to hurt you."

She felt her lip tremble as pain flooded her, "You'd only give others the means to do so."

"Never," he shot out quickly.

"I don't believe you."

"Let me try to convince you then." He was pleading, and somehow, it made her hate herself more than she already did. While she knew he was lying, his genuine look made her disgusted with herself for being so hostile towards him.

"What makes you think I want you to convince me?" Her tone was anything but kind.

"Aza—"

"Don't say my name as if you care. You knew what your presence would do to me. It is no secret that the King is out for my head. So, what," she laughed without humor, her eyes narrowing, "you thought, why not take a job on the Neptune? No—it's not a coincidence. Alyse told me she discussed with the entire crew who was coming onboard. The King warned all passenger ships that a short, curly-haired redhead with bright blue eyes—"

"—and beautiful beyond comprehension." Jayce cut in, a brilliant smile lacing his lips.

Her nostrils flared, "No, would be looking for a passage to Ilkiz and was wanted for the Massacre at Sunfall." She stepped toward him, and his head gently tilted downward, "You knew I'd be on this ship."

A confirming nod, "I did know." He confessed, but it wasn't good enough for her.

"Your King sent you—"

"He did not. That is the truth. I volunteered to come." Jayce said with assurance.

"Why…" her voice cracked, and she hated that it did. All she wanted was to stay strong, not to cry and break down. "I don't want you here."

He stepped to her, and she shook her head, "Do *not* touch me." He immediately stopped, and she dropped her eyes downward. They were so close she could smell the worldly scents he brought. She was no longer on a ship but back in a grassy meadow surrounded by trees and an overcast sky.

"Why…" She repeated, and by the Mother, she hoped he would answer. "Please, just tell me why…" She wanted to hear that he had defied the King, only to ensure she was okay, that Karver was downstairs, hiding until he knew she wouldn't throw him overboard, too.

Instead, he said, "I'll get off on the next port; I will tell Alyse to detour to Dogon," she could hear the underlying defeat in his tone.

Her eyes closed, and she wanted to cry. *Gods be damned, Jayce, why did you come here?* As if there wasn't enough pain, why couldn't he have lived in her memory as someone who had once given her hope? He could have stayed in the bright light of her mind, giving her some semblance of peace of her broken past.

Now, he was her enemy.

"Goodbye, Jayce." Her words mirroring the broken pieces of her heart that would never be put back together. She was being tested at every turn and she couldn't understand why.

Haven't I suffered enough...

Day 15
CHAPTER 5

"Your move, beau," Théodore said after moving the knight across the board. His legs were crossed while he leaned back, confidence lining his face like he had already won the game.

Azahara scratched her cheek and looked at the board longingly.

While the past five days had gone by relatively quickly, there was something that Azahara couldn't seem to ignore. Her mood had somehow shifted, and although her night terrors continued to plague her, she came out of her room daily.

Some clarity had come over her as well. She took in the ship's beauty for the first time since arriving on the Neptune. She could admire the darkened wood that sprawled from front to back, and the gold trimming that she had observed from a distance before boarding. Alyse mentioned they put some extra work into it a few years back when her father passed, and it showed.

Nearly twelve massive masts pulled the Neptune along, four posts holding three pure white sheets each. All of which were maintained perfectly by the crew. Everything was like a well-fed and bred farm animal; nothing was left to question.

When it came to Jayce, she did her best to avoid him. Even if he actively did everything possible to do just the opposite. It was the most painful part of the day for her, seeing him watch her. He interacted with the crew as if they were his family, as though he and they had known each other his whole life.

Feeling a sting in her palm, she reached for her bishop and swatted away the knight that Théodore had just moved. The knight went flying off the board, clattering to the floor.

"Check." Azahara looked up then, a defeated expression riddling his handsome face.

She had developed a fondness for Théodore. He reminded her of her father in many ways. The subtle wrinkles on his face suggested that he has lived a long and experienced life, possessing the wisdom many of the younger crew members lack.

"—Mate! How?" He cried out with a joyful laugh.

Azahara smiled at him, and she could see him swoon. "It's about putting the pieces in places the opponent doesn't expect, and then backing them into a corner to be surrounded." The board looked crazy, but each piece, from her queen, rooks, and knights, had all been placed accordingly to put his King in the worst possible position.

"Beautiful and smart," to her dismay, it wasn't Théodore who spoke. "Can I get a turn?" Jayce's voice was raspy, deep, and low. Mainly when he spoke with her. The feeling of it made her entire body tremble under its caress.

Théodore slapped his knees as he stood, "I don't think anyone has been able to beat her, so as long as you aren't a sore loser, have at it." He stepped around the barrel where they played their game and nodded toward Azahara before disappearing behind her.

She glared up at Jayce, "I think I'm done playing," and began to stand.

"Wait," he interrupted, and she paused. "If you beat me, I'll leave you alone for good." After some consideration, she nodded and began reassembling the pieces on her side of the board.

Before taking his seat, Jayce leaned over to retrieve the knight she had knocked to the floor. He chuckled, and she rolled her eyes.

"Not everything revolves around you," she said, her tone tinged with sarcasm. "I just sometimes forget my own strength."

"Uh-huh, I'm sure," he replied with an unwavering smile. As he sat down, he seemed to relax even more, his shoulders dropping and his chest heaving as he sighed. Jayce was undeniably perfect in the looks department, and she couldn't help but wonder if this was how people felt when they looked at her. That thought was genuinely irritating.

He arranged the pieces on his side of the board precisely, showing that he, at the very least, knew how to play.

Azahara shifted her gaze towards the sea. The waters had grown choppier, and the previously cloudless sky had become overcast for the first time in nearly a week. It meant they were getting closer to the Cyclops Route.

"Winners go first?" he asked, calling her attention to the game.

"It's the winner's choice. You go first."

"Normally it's ladies first, but if you insist."

With a heavy sigh, she crossed her legs and turned her attention back to the game. The last thing she wanted was to miss him cheating.

"Can I ask you—"

"No, just play the game." She groaned.

He laughed, and her chest tightened, "E2 to E4. I told you what happens when you win, not what I get if I do."

She narrowed her eyes, watching as he moved one of his pawns. "What do you get if you win, Jayce." It was more of a frustrating statement than a question. "E7 to E5."

"To allow me to talk to you beyond hello." Jayce moved his knight, "F3."

Azahara took in a deep breath, "Fine. F6." She moved her knight as well, again mirroring Jayce's move.

He was beaming; surprisingly, she couldn't muster anger toward him. "Perfect. D4," he declared, moving his pawn. She bit the corner of her lip, frustrated at her stomach for fluttering with butterflies at the sight of his happiness about his possible winnings.

She moved her central pawn, claiming the pawn he had just placed. "E5 to D4."

"The Captain said your last name was Starfall?" He moved his bishop while asking his question, "C4."

Azahara paused, seeing that he was pressuring her knight, and quickly moved her pawn to defend. "C7 to C6. Yes, Starfall is my name."

He moved his King, "G1. That is a beautiful, unique last name."

Her eyes moved from the table to him. His hazel eyes were drinking her up. She leaned back and crossed her arms under her chest.

"Right, the game. I have to win, got it." He let out a chuckle, conceding.

Frustrated by how attracted she was to him, she shook her head and moved her next piece. After that, silence hung between them, save for their callouts. They continued for a full sixteen moves, capturing pieces, and safeguarding their kings from each other.

Their strategic moves had caught the attention of the crew. Most of them had fallen to Azahara in the past few days, with losses occurring in as few as five moves and in no more than ten. This had been the longest anyone had lasted.

Then came the moment when their final pieces were on the board, and they both knew who the victor would be. The crew hadn't realized it yet, but Azahara and Jayce seemed to grasp it simultaneously as their gazes met. It became evident that neither was willing to give up, much like the ongoing game of cat and mouse. They would continue, even when the end was nowhere in sight.

She leaned back, took a deep breath in and sighed.

"You're pretty good," she remarked flatly, "for a Knight. Who taught you to play?"

"I learned a long time ago, but Karver keeps me on my toes," he replied, pushing away from the barrel that had become the makeshift board table. "Stalemate."

A resounding groan emanated from the crowd as if they were disappointed by the lack of a clear winner.

She stood, stretching her arms above her head and releasing a sigh of equal parts frustration and relief. Technically, neither of them had won, and though she could have argued that neither would get what they wanted, something in the way he looked at her at that moment urged her to hold her tongue.

His eyebrow, as though waiting expectantly, coupled with that tender smile that called to her, was just too much. *Gods, I hate you!*

She brushed past him, and he interpreted her silence as an invitation to join her at the railing. The sea below had been sending water sprays cascading across the ship all day. The railing and flooring were damp, so she was mindful not to trust in it with how unforgiving the sea was.

His arm brushed against hers, and she looked up at him.

"What do you want to talk about, Jayce?"

He gazed down at her, keeping his head level. "Your last name."

"What about it?" She took a step away, putting some distance between them. "It's just a last name."

"Can I ask where it came from?"

"I saw a falling star one day and decided I liked it better than my family name," she replied, suggesting that he wouldn't receive more information than that. Trying to explain to him that she had seen the clouds part and a star falling toward her as she was dying was too complex to convey and contained too many details to bring back to the King.

"I see," she watched him as his expression became brighter, "I like it. Not that I'm sure that matters."

"It doesn't," she was such a liar.

Jayce laughed, "You can ask me something if that will help you trust me again."

"Who said I ever trusted you in the first place?"

"Fair point. How can I make you trust me?"

Azahara, deep down, wanted just that. To be able to trust him. Whether she was willing to admit it to herself or not, Jayce was the closest thing to her time with Kaed and her family that she had.

"By being honest, even if it hurts me," she leaned forward, her head resting in her hands. "I'm no stranger to pain." She couldn't see his reaction, and while she wished to, she knew it was for the best.

"Okay, then ask me, and I promise to be truthful." His voice carried a subdued tone, steeped with empathy and longing as if pain were concealed behind the words.

"Why are you here?" She kept her gaze on him, "Really."

"To protect you." Jayce was a matter of fact. "It's that simple."

"Why?" While her heart was ready to jump to the sea below for relief, her head stayed resolute. "Who am I to you?"

There was a pause this time, and she felt disappointed. Her head turned outward, looking at the vast sea and the clouds that threatened to pour into it.

"Ask me something else, please."

She crossed her arms on the railing and rested her forehead on them. Having Jayce here was a peculiar mix of relaxation and stress. She longed to trust him, yet she knew it was foolish. Jayce had always been elusive, even from the day he rescued her from the crowd at the Idle Fox. Everything seemed hazy whenever she reminisced about those moments with him, as if there was some sort of filter whenever he crossed her mind.

"Before you quit," she said with emphasis, "the White Cloaks, was there anything of value the King learned about me?"

"Yes," Jayce was quick with his response again, "he met with… interested parties that were seemingly somehow involved with you, plus his generals and myself."

"Interested parties?" She said, surprised.

There was a brief pause, but he answered, "The Fae's new Elder, Jaakobai, and the Goddess of War."

Azahara shot up so quickly that she slipped on the slick floor; Jayce's arm was behind her waist to grab her before she fell. His opposite hand took hers, steadying her.

"The goddess…?" Her voice broke in several places, and she felt her heart racing frantically.

Jayce nodded, removing the hand from around her back, only to bring it to her forearm to keep her steady. Was she wobbling? Or was that the ship?

Then that means Jaakobai told them everything about me. They knew about Death. About… Goddrick? Panic surged, and she pulled her hand away from his, cursing.

"Then you know," she said, looking down at his hand on her forearm. "You know what I am."

"I know who you are." Everything was spinning, and her stomach was tumbling. If they knew what she was and summoned the gods, this was not her running from the likes of mortals anymore.

"I cannot allow you, a mortal blessed with the power of the gods, to destroy using what we have mistakenly given you. I do not want to fight you, but I will."

Her body was beginning to fold, the trembling that would take over her body, and the need to run flooded her. The realm would collapse around her, trapping her under the rubble, for her only to survive and suffer eternally.

Before it got to that point, Jayce had his arms around her—his embrace parting the way for light to seep through. The rumbling in her chest began to slow, and as quickly as the panic attack started, it was demolished in his grip.

She swallowed, her head turning to rest against his chest. His heartbeat was steady, with no trace of worry in its rhythm.

"What do you know…"

"Not as much as you think," his fingers brushed through the coils of her hair while his opposite arm held steady across her shoulders, "you have the gods' and Deaths' power."

His touch caused her to straighten her back, and it felt far too intimate of a gesture. An emptiness gnawed at her chest, conflicting with the part of her brain that wanted to push him away.

There was another beat of silence. *But the goddess? How? Why was she there? Why in the world would she answer the call? They never dealt with mortal issues. Except… I'm not mortal anymore. I am their problem. Fuck…*

"I don't think them knowing that matters, what does, was the power you displayed. They could care less where it came from, especially the King. He is afraid of you."

"As he should be, I'm a monster…."

"Azahara—" She realized he was tightening his hold on her, his body radiating heat like an animal. She pushed herself away from him, and thankfully, he didn't fight for possession, allowing her to lean back and face him.

"Karver told me that Thall threatened Kaed's life, and instead of running to him, you stayed and saved his life. You are not the monster they, and you, portray yourself to be."

Azahara stared at him while staying muted.

"Everyone says they are sorry," he said, placing one of his hands on the side of her neck, "I'm sorry for so much, but above all else, your loss."

To her surprise, she didn't immediately start crying.

It was the first time someone had acknowledged that her pain was directly related to Kaed. His death was the single point of destruction that set her in motion, getting her to where she is now. Losing him was the pinnacle of her suffering.

Although she hadn't shed a single tear, her expression remained lifeless, marking her face with an unmistakable pain. Jayce didn't look away; instead, he stared down at her as she looked up.

"I should have died that day. Not him."

Jayce, surprisingly, did not say anything. He only lowered his gaze and shook his head in disagreement.

"Yes. Kaed was good. He—" Her shoulders dropped, and she deadpanned. "His life mattered, not mine." She paused, looking between his eyes, "Mine should have ended long ago."

"Don't—Please," he took a deep breath as if trying to calm himself before continuing, "don't say that."

She didn't want to ignore the way that made her heart feel safe, but she did and continued, "I am a monster. I can't even let Kaed go."

Physically, she couldn't release Kaed. His soul remained trapped between this plane and Purgatory because she lacked the strength to let him move on. That was what she meant, not emotionally or in her heart. He was gone, and she wasn't prepared to release him beyond this existence.

"No one would ask that of you," he said, trying to reach her. She wanted to understand why. Why did he care so damn much?

"I don't think I will ever be able to," she said flatly, "and forever is a long time for someone that lives for eternity."

Jayce didn't appear surprised by the comment. It was probably another detail he had learned from Jaakobai in his obsession with her. He was likely manipulating the King, just as he had done with his father and Thall.

"I am a monster, whether you choose to believe that or not," she continued, moving away from the conversation revolving around Kaed. "When they come for me, to try and kill me, I will lose control and destroy them and everyone around me. I am not afraid of death; I welcome it. I am not afraid of your King or Jaakobai or the gods." Maybe it was a realization as much for him as it was for her, "I am terrified of myself."

"I'm not." He said, a strength behind his words. "You don't scare me."

She gave an exasperated eye roll and shook her head, finding the strength to finally pull herself away from him, "You weren't there. I could destroy this ship in an instant. One slip of my emotions, one memory I can't overcome, everything and everyone—ash."

"I won't let you," he never once faltered. His strength did not come from Magic or the gods; he was merely human, yet he stood there as though he were immortal.

She groaned out, "Okay, Jayce." Pausing briefly, shaking her head in consternation. "If you say so."

He took a deep breath and sighed through closed lips.

A silence hung between them, thick with uncertainty. Azahara used to despise these moments, but now she longed for them.

Breaking the silence after a beat, she said, "Thank you," and placed one of her hands on her other arm, squeezing it and leaning to the side. She looked around Jayce, ready to slip back into her room, hopefully without Alyse finding a reason to engage with her.

Jayce gently directed her chin to face him, wearing a compassionate expression. "If I could—"

Her eyebrows furrowed as she cut him off, "Why do you keep doing that?"

Jayce hummed in question.

She remembered the first time he had lifted her chin to meet his eyes. It was back in the Idle Fox after he'd pulled her from the mob of people as if he had some claim on her gaze—a natural reaction to her looking away from him.

"Oh," he moved his hand after realization hit, "I'm not sure."

Azahara then stepped away from him, her eyes weary. "Try your best to refrain."

Unfazed, he chuckled, "I'll do my best—" It seemed he hadn't finished his sentence, the way he pressed his lips and shifted his gaze away.

She didn't care, "I think I'll retire."

"It's dinner time though, I was hoping we could—"

"You think that things have changed?" Her stare was cold. "I've thanked my enemies before, Commander. You're still getting off this ship in Dogon."

She was deliberately trying to hurt him. However, Jayce didn't seem affected by her words. He still had that smile plastered on his face while shaking his head.

"I'll see you in the morning, then." Jayce stepped aside, allowing her to walk past him.

Infuriating! Why can't you take the hint? She cursed under her breath as she passed him. Another huff of laughter escaped him, and she had no idea where she found the restraint not to turn and toss him overboard.

As she made her way towards her room, wide arms wrapped around her neck and hugged her. "Huh?" She looked, and it was Rowlin. He was slightly taller than her, but unlike every other male she had contact with, he didn't tower over her.

"Hi," she saw him sign when his arms released her, "do you want to have dinner?"

Azahara looked up at Jayce, leaning against the railing with his arms across his chest and smirking. *By the Mother, why am I so drawn to him?*

"You know," she signed, "yeah actually, I'm famished."

She dared a peek back at Jayce, who pissed her off by continuing to smile as if he were happy that she had decided to have dinner with Rowlin. Her nostrils flared, and he laughed instantly.

Mouthing 'fuck you' at him, she laced her arm around Rowlin's and headed down with him to the mess deck.

She enjoyed her time with Rowlin at dinner; Jayce had followed them down but sat at a completely different table. Alyse joined not too long afterward, but only after Azahara learned that Rowlin and her were complete opposites.

Azahara had asked Rowlin if he and Alyse had a thing, but he responded with a breathy laugh. He explained that while he found her beautiful, he had no physical attraction to her, or anyone, highlighting the stark differences between their preferences. They both shared a laugh at the contrasts between them. She couldn't help but express her wish to be the same way, hoping that Jayce was listening.

When Alyse joined them, she immediately jumped into the conversation. Azahara realized she hadn't stopped smiling throughout their time down in the mess. It was reminiscent of the time at the Idle Fox when she sat at the bar with her family, enjoying herself as if she had no other care in the world.

There was a big part of her that felt guilty.

It wasn't like she was happy. She was content, and as the night dragged on and more of the crew arrived, she felt the need to leave.

Especially when Zephyra and Tillin came down and seemingly intentionally put themselves all over Jayce.

Azahara wasn't jealous; that would be stupid, but it irritated her that they were doing it to get a rise out of her. Jayce, who was soaking in her burning gaze, played right into their little hands. At one point, Zephyra slipped into his lap and fixed her gaze on Azahara. A smile, slowly but surely, crept across the Elf's face.

They both stared at one another. Only did Zephyra fold when Xol joined the table, sat beside Azahara and pierced her deadly gaze at the Elf.

She couldn't shake the feeling that Xol was someone she had encountered before. However, as she sifted through her memories from a few days earlier, nothing came to her. She was confident she would have remembered the striking, pure white being with sharp features, a permanent stoic expression, and unyielding resolve. There was simply no way she could have forgotten her .

"I'll take my leave now," Azahara said, placing a hand on Xol, feeling the coldness of her skin seeping through her shirt. The familiarity of it was nearly shocking, and while it hadn't been the cause of her fall, it sure didn't help. The sudden, violent rock of the ship was so intense that she had no chance of remaining on her feet, propelling her straight to the floor.

The loud thud of her hitting the ground was followed by another, and a cry of pain that hadn't come from Azahara.

Jayce knelt beside her, "Are you okay?" His hand came to her, wrapping gently around the side of her neck.

"Yes..." her tone a mere breath of a response.

The ship began thrashing again, sending Alyse sliding down the elongated stool at their table. Jayce wasn't fazed and began putting his hands under her arms to stand her up.

"I'm fine!" Azahara pulled away, not wanting to be treated like a child.

She placed one hand down to the ground and the other into the hand of Xol, standing beside Jayce. "I just fell; gods, I'll survive." *Holy shit,* she thought as Xol threw her up into her arms. "You are strong."

Jayce was beside them both, looking at Xol. For the first time, she saw his expression shift. Xol looked at him, the stoic, angry expression never changing. There was so much tension between the two of them that she could have cut it with a knife.

It wasn't lost on her that Xol had her pinned against her like she was some teddy bear, and she was keeping someone from taking it away from her.

The ship was hit with another giant wave, but neither Xol nor Jayce stumbled. They both continued holding each other's gaze.

More than anything, Azahara wanted to be separated from the two of them. She feared for her safety. "What the hell is happening right now?" Verbally spilling what she was thinking, she quickly slapped her hand over her mouth. The two of them shifted their gaze to her nearly simultaneously.

"Okay, both of you are freaking me out. Please, Xol, I'm fine. You can let me go. Jayce, go check on Zephyra. You probably hurt her feelings more than her tailbone."

It hadn't occurred to her until that moment, seeing the Elf casting daggers right between her and Jayce, that he had likely thrown Zephyra off his lap to come to her aid.

He didn't move, he only watched as Xol followed Azahara's instructions to release her. The death glare he directed at Xol was piercing, and she momentarily stared in confusion, wondering what she had done to deserve such a look.

Consumed by their staring contest, Azahara took that moment to slip away, hurrying up the stairs and clutching the railing tightly. The night shrouded the sky in darkness, but the storm clouds were unmistakable, now casting a relentless rain down on the ship.

Just as she pivoted towards her quarters, a sensation of weightlessness enveloped her, and she was lifted off the ship's deck. It wasn't a great distance, but it was enough to unsettle her balance and make her tilt forward.

Then, accompanied by a resounding crack, she was forcefully thrown back down, plunging her into complete darkness.

Day 15
CHAPTER 6

"Azahara!" There were rough hands on her shoulders, shaking her and pulling her from the depths of the abyss.

Please leave me alone. I'm not dreaming for once...

For once, she wasn't plagued by nightmares. It was as if she had died and was sitting in Purgatory. The absence of Death was the only tell that she was not where she would rather be, but instead, alone in the confines of her mind.

"Get away from her; I'll take her." Jayce yelled, his voice tinged with possessiveness. It was a level of dominance she wouldn't dare argue with, given the force behind it.

Strong arms wrapped around her shoulders, and it was all she needed to begin to open her eyes slowly. Jayce was pulling her to his chest, his other hand pointing toward something she couldn't see.

"Rope up, now!" He screamed; the sound was so loud that it shook her heart's cage.

Jayce must have felt her shudder because he looked down at her, their eyes meeting.

There was chaos all around them, and she could feel the floor shuddering under them and the shadows that were cast by the few lanterns still lit.

She closed her eyes, ready to return to the darkness. "Stay awake for me," his voice was calm as if the ship wasn't under threat from the sea. When her eyes reopened, she noticed a flicker of fire in his hazel eyes, causing the corner of her lips to twitch with a huffed laugh.

"Five more minutes," she murmured.

"Was that a joke?" Jayce laughed, "You really must have hit your head."

The throbbing was nothing compared to what she had experienced over the past few months. If he hadn't mentioned it, she might not have noticed. "I'm fine," she said, beginning to sit up, and with his assistance, she managed to get to her feet.

Chaos was not a strong enough word for what was happening. The ship was tossed and heaved. Its hull creaked under her, the relentless assault of towering waves flooded over its sides.

The crew was scrambling to maintain control, desperately clinging to their stations and finding the ropes that Xol had securely placed on the masts. Everyone braced themselves for another hit when Jayce put his arm around her waist and hoisted her towards a spar.

As her back pressed against the solid wood, his body became a protective barrier, and his arms held her in place as the ship was rocked by a massive swell. Amidst the screams surrounding them, she clenched her jaw tightly and found the only place to put her hands for support: around Jayce.

She could hear Alyse shouting orders over the deafening roar of the wind and water, blending into a cacophony of urgency. Mayhem, there was so much of it that it felt like the Battle at Sunfall all over again.

Jayce cursed, followed by a loud, shrill scream that pierced through all other noise. She recognized the sound and immediately knew it was a Siren's call. She could barely see several of the crew members beginning to huddle over Tillin. The scent of copper filled the air, and she knew something terrible had happened.

When Alyse rushed to him and everyone moved, she caught sight of the pool of blood around him.

Azahara's eyes widened, and instead of seeing Tillin, she saw Zhal, helplessly lying there, dying. Flashes of them returning from Helgum and the image of the axe in her back caused a visceral wave of fear to surge through her. Blood was everywhere, and there was no way to stop it. "Zhal—" Her voice was soft, nearly inaudible.

The Siren had made it abundantly clear that he wanted nothing to do with her, but seeing him writhing in pain with his arm severed and hearing his cries for help made her feel sick. Her body trembled, and Jayce reacted immediately.

"What's wrong? Are you hurt?" Jayce leaned back to pull her into view, and he immediately noticed what had her unblinking stare. "Shit, we have to be careful."

"Jayce!" Alyse screamed, "Come help us move him!"

Azahara felt him move away from her, and her knee-jerk reaction caused her to grab his arm. She took an unsteady breath and looked up at him, fear ripping through her. Her lips parted slightly, "He's going to—"

"No, Azahara, it's okay." Jayce placed both hands at the sides of her neck, his thumbs pressing at the contours of her cheeks. "Hear my voice. He will be okay."

"I can't fight the sea," She had no idea what she was saying, but the urge to protect this crew was driving her to be irrational. "I can't do anything. I'm helpless, I can't—"

Jayce lifted her head and pressed his forehead against hers, "You are anything but helpless." His voice carried a tenderness reserved only for her, "Close your eyes, take a breath, and feel peace."

His hands moved behind her, pulling her to him. Once again, she was sandwiched between the spire and his massive frame as the ship was rocked.

She closed her eyes and took a deep breath. As she had that night in Höwl, she let go of her fear and focused on the light that burned in her chest. It was warm, and it felt like life and death simultaneously. Everything about it was welcoming, and she clung to it.

She focused on the moon and stars and how they brought light into the darkened night. How sad it was that the sun and the moon would never truly be together. They would forever be on opposite ends, but she knew that they both served the same purpose, to give light to the realm.

When she opened her eyes, Jayce was still there with her.

She didn't say anything, only nodded.

An affectionate smile lined his lips, "Stay here and tie up. I'll come right back to you," he moved away from her, rushing off to aid in moving Tillin.

Azahara grabbed hold of the rope that Xol had placed to secure them, and began wrapping it around her waist. She prayed to the Mother that the ship would endure the storm. Still, her hope dwindled with another wave crashing against the vessel and throwing everyone across the deck.

Another scream echoed through the hull, but this one surpassed Tillin's in sheer chilling intensity. It wasn't the pitch that made it dreadful, but the word that resonated from it.

"Rowlin!"

Azahara felt the world around her shift into slow motion, as if someone had taken her hourglass and tipped it on its side, causing time to nearly reach a standstill.

Her body had turned without invitation, and in her view, Rowlin was toppling backward off the ship. Even if he wasn't knocked out by the fall, the darkness of the sea would swallow him. He would be dragged under the relentless waves, and even if he managed to resurface for air, he couldn't call for help.

They were going to take him away right in front of her.

Not again...

"No!"

Azahara dropped the rope, and as she felt a rush of power coursing beneath her skin, she leaped over the edge just as he cleared the railing.

The look of shock on Rowlin's face was immediately hidden by her arms wrapping around his neck and pulling him close to her body. "Hold on, no matter what, do not let go of me!" There was no hesitation, and he clung to her tightly, his grip revealing both terror, and relief that he wouldn't be alone in the darkness that was about to envelop them both.

Time returned to its normal pace, and as it did, Azahara shifted Rowlin on top of her, feeling the solid surface below her slam the air out of her lungs. The impact sent a shockwave of coldness through her body, disorienting her senses. The tempestuous sea enveloped her as the unforgiving water swallowed them.

They plunged deep into the sea, and while she fought to suppress a panic attack, she tightened her grip on Rowlin. Her skin began to glow, and every instinct screamed for air. Still, the chaotic turbulence made orienting them and finding which way was up, challenging. Rowlin wouldn't survive without air, and although suffocating was not Azahara's preferred way to die, his life mattered most.

One of her hands extended, letting it go limp, and she watched as it began to float in the direction they needed to swim. Her body battled against the current, and with Rowlin's help, they kicked hard enough to find and break through the surface.

She gulped in the air, feeling the harsh winds against her face and the rain cutting into her cheeks. It was pitch black, with only the Neptune in sight, wobbling and drifting to their right.

As she attempted to breathe, she accidentally sucked in a gulp of seawater, sending a piercing pain through her throat, causing her to cough uncontrollably. Her hands slipped from Rowlin, but thankfully, he heeded her words and held her tightly. Her arms wrapped under his, keeping his head above water while her head dipped under.

Rowlin kicked hard, even though it felt useless. The waves were relentless, nearly drowning her every time she tried to take a breath. "Hel—" Water rushed down her throat, and she was pulled under; a current wrapped around her, and her grip on Rowlin slipped as he couldn't maintain his hold.

"No!" As the current pulled her downward, she screamed and outstretched her hand. He was still visible above her, but she lost the battle to get back to him as her legs and body weakened.

The darkness of the sea as she was dragged deeper blinded her, and the deeper she sank, the colder it became. She closed her eyes, and the sounds of the chaotic storm and thrashing waves slowly faded. Only the serene abyss below seemed to welcome her into its embrace.

When her eyes shot open, she saw a hand reaching for hers. Her body fought to straighten, her arm stretching out towards it. Their fingers intertwined and she was yanked upward with a force the relentless sea couldn't attest to. She was pulled into her savior's embrace as they rushed to breach the surface. Her lungs burned, and she cried out as they finally broke for air.

"I've got you, Azahara," Jayce said, his head resting against hers as he fought the current with his free arm. The other held her tightly at her waist, a grip that spoke of nothing ripping her away.

Her head pressed between the curve of his neck, and her legs continued to aid even if it wasn't needed. "Rowlin—"

She expected him to sound angry, but instead, there was only relief. "We got him."

Azahara blacked out momentarily as the time between him grabbing her and being carried up the ladder seemed to pass instantly. Relief washed over her as her legs found solid ground and the depths of the sea remained where they belonged, beneath the ship.

Every part of her felt heavy, likely due to the soaked dress that molded to her body.

"Jayce!" Alyse called to him, "Put her back in the sea, now!"

Huh... Azahara felt his arms tighten around her, nails biting into her skin.

"Look at her..." Alyse was beside him, and while Azahara had difficulty distinguishing what was going on, it looked like she was trying to pry her from him. "She—"

"Touch her," His voice threatening, making Alyse cower away, "and it won't be her you need to worry about being on this ship."

What are you seeing... She glanced down at her hands, which were resting in her lap. The dark shadow had erupted around her, and the bright light that had guided them to Rowlin was now gone.

Jayce put his arm under her legs and lifted her to him. Her head leaned against his chest, and she felt his heart racing. It was beating so hard that she feared it would break through him and attack her. The shouts behind them began to fade as though there was still chaos from the sea; she now posed a more significant threat to the crew than the storm around them.

"Throw me back," her voice was hoarse, the seawater disrupting her vocal cords, "please, I told them to—"

"Stop." He cut her off, his jaw clenching.

Heat poured through her eyes then, and she felt tears brim them. "It's okay," her hands stayed in her lap, even if she desperately wanted to grab onto him for support, "I don't want to hurt them. I never wanted to hurt anyone." As she spoke, her voice only broke and became nearly inaudible.

Feeling Jayce stop, she opened her eyes to see him staring at her.

"It's okay..." her voice a mere whisper.

"You're right. It is." He knelt, bringing her back to the floor.

"Jayce—" his grip was firm, and if she were to fight, there would be no escaping his hold, "If I—"

He sat her on his lap, his arms wrapped around her tightly. One of his hands rested at the back of her head, and the other around her back. His head nestled between the curve of her shoulder.

"Let me help you, please," his words were like silk in her ear, making her hold her breath. "I'm not afraid of you." Her head leaned against his, and she closed her eyes. "Think of something you love," he paused briefly, "for me, it's freshly baked bread and the sweet scent of honeydew."

"Your favorite color is green." She heard Kaed's voice, *"You choose the white flowers over the reds and yellows because the green pops out more in their stems. You prefer the moon over the sun. Your favorite drink is lemon water with peppermint leaves. Your favorite fruit is strawberries."* With those memories, she was a goner. Her arms were wrapped around his head, fingers through his hair as she sobbed.

"Your greatest fear is living."

I never wanted to live without you, Kaed.

"I love you, Red."

I love you so much... why did you leave me...

There was nothing this world could throw at her that would hurt her like losing Kaed.

If that was the pinnacle of her pain, maybe she could come to not fear losing control. Perhaps all she needed was to be reminded that it could always be worse.

Nothing could be worse than this... losing him... absolutely nothing...

"There you go," he said softly, his hand releasing her hair and resting at the small of her back. "I've got you."

Tears rolled down her cheeks, and she felt the darkness around her fade. She didn't need to see it to know that Jayce had pulled her from it. She clung to him, and he didn't push her away.

The pain of hoping he truly cared shot through her, adding tremors to her unrelenting sobs. She wanted to believe that this wasn't all about orders to Jayce. That it wasn't all a façade to get close to her. Yet, fear was stronger than the flimsy thing called hope, and it won the battle, tearing her apart.

"Please," her voice was shaky, "don't be lying to me. Don't hurt me. I—" She couldn't have imagined that he could hold her tighter, but he did. "I can't—"

He stayed silent.

"I am so scared... I can't take it."

If Death wouldn't take her, *he* would. The pain she would endure would be expected. There would be no tricks, no surprises, just unending agony.

At least then, hope wouldn't be ripped away from her; it would all be gone.

Day 16
CHAPTER 7

The ship and its entire crew made it through the night.

Tillin had suffered the loss of his arm while attempting to secure the rigging; a wire had become ensnared between his arm and the mast. Carmen, a half-elf skilled with Magic in its healing art form, provided medical assistance. Although they couldn't re-attach his arm, Carmen managed to stop the bleeding, ensuring Tillin's survival for another day.

Everyone else was battered and bruised, but alive. That was what mattered, at least to Azahara. When she came out of her room, Xol was the only one walking the hull.

When Xol saw Azahara approaching, nothing changed, but instead of continuing to walk, she stopped and turned to meet her. Xol hadn't spoken to Azahara yet, so she wasn't sure what she sounded like. Honestly, she didn't even know if Xol was a she.

Azahara had tried to converse with Xol, simply asking if she was okay or if they needed anything. As always, Xol stayed silent, only shaking or nodding in response to everything. It looked as though she was holding her breath too, which Azahara hadn't noticed before.

There wasn't enough energy in her to try and force a conversation, so she conceded and left the first officer to do her duty.

The night was tumultuous, only gradually settling as daybreak neared. Alyse had managed to gain control of the ship's course, redirecting it northbound. Which meant they would now be taking the long route to Ilkiz. Once they safely navigated the perilous path, the transformation in the weather was astounding. The skies cleared, and nothing but blue skies lay ahead.

From her understanding, their next challenge would be crossing the Cascade Passing between the cluster of islands and Ilkiz. While it presented its own difficulties, Alyse was confident that it paled compared to the treacherous Cyclops route.

The sun had nearly risen and everyone retreated to their quarters. Jayce ensured Azahara was fine and didn't overstay his welcome. He then receded down to the lower deck with the crew.

Now, Azahara found herself searching for him, a sentiment she loathed. With Dogon no longer an option, he would remain on the ship for an extended duration. The problem wasn't that he wouldn't be getting off sooner, it was that she was happy about the prospect of it.

What am I doing... Her head was in her hand, the pain in her temples rising, threatening to send her back to bed.

"Hey," the gentle voice of Alyse caught her as she was about to head to the berth, "how are you doing?" She slowly walked down the stairs from the helm, her head tilted downward. There was defeat in her expression, and it made Azahara pause.

"I'm fine, how are you? How is Rowlin? I imagine he is still sleeping." Azahara stepped away from the stairway leading below the deck.

"He is, thank you, Aza—" Her voice caught, and Azahara realized then that she was beginning to cry. "I'm so sorry." Her chest constricted, nearly audibly gasping. "I was scared, not of you, but for my crew. Your words echoed in my head about what could happen. I—I'm a coward for it."

Azahara closed the distance between them, and to her own surprise, she embraced Alyse tightly. "By the Mother, Alyse, do not apologize."

Alyse reciprocated the embrace, resting her forehead against Azahara's shoulder. They held each other for a while, and Alyse quietly sobbed, never letting go. Azahara couldn't help but feel the weight of putting Alyse in that situation and the difficult decisions she had forced her to make. Just days earlier, she had adamantly refused to throw Jayce off the ship, even scolding Azahara for suggesting it.

"I promise I wasn't afraid of you..." her words were choppy.

"Even if you were," Azahara ran her hand down her head, feeling the silky soft hair that seemed untouched by the sea, "I wouldn't fault you for it."

Alyse pulled slightly away to look at Azahara. Her cheeks were darkened, and her eyes puffy. Azahara brushed her thumb against Alyse's cheek, offering her a gentle smile. "It's okay, Alyse, I promise."

"Jayce—"

"Is overbearing," she rolled her eyes while shaking her head, "but I suppose we have that in common."

Alyse laughed, her hands resting on Azahara's hips. "Thank you, Aza," her tone sheepish as she leaned her head into her hand.

Azahara let out a soft sigh and stepped away, breaking their contact. She felt that being affectionate might lead Alyse on. At that point, it was apparent that Alyse was attracted to her. While the Captain was everything she would have ever found attractive, the last thing on her mind was building relationships beyond mere friendship.

"Speaking of, I am on my way to find that overbearing man. Have you seen him?" Azahara peered down the stairway; the darkened void spoke of a sleepy crew.

"I haven't," she said, brushing her shirt against her eyes to wipe away her tears. "This boat is only so big. I'm sure you'll find him in no time." Alyse did not comment on her pulling away, and was either oblivious, or actively keeping the rejection bottled up.

"I'll wander for a bit then. After I find him, I'll return to see if Rowlin is awake." Azahara bid her farewell and quickly made her way down the stairs.

After scouring all four ship floors, she couldn't locate Jayce. Even in the sleeping quarters, where most of the crew members were still fast asleep, he was nowhere to be found. She swore every inch of the ship was checked, but they might have missed one another if they walked different stairways.

She found Tillin in the medical bay, but only popped her head in to see how he was doing. Almost dying hadn't changed his opinion of her, and he only gave her a simple nod and waved her away with his good arm.

After what felt like days, instead of possibly an hour, she emerged onto the deck where Rowlin was standing beside Alyse.

Azahara rushed to him, and he must have felt the ground shaking because he turned to her. She wasn't sure if he was physically fine, so instead of slamming into him with a hug, she stopped a foot or so before him. He closed the gap and hugged her weakly, soft hums coming from his throat.

Her arms squeezed his torso, she was so happy that he was okay.

They discussed the events, and he apologized profusely to her, saying that he should have known better. All she cared about was that he was alive and okay. How the incident transpired didn't matter to her.

They ended up parting ways quicker than she anticipated. Alyse explained that she needed to get the crew up to work on the repairs. They were already heading toward Celadon and would likely be there in four or so days. Azahara had commented on the ship holding together, considering how rough the seas had been.

Alyse laughed and told her that the ship had seen its fair share of rough seas and the monsters in it. Somehow, that did not make her feel better about being in the open sea for longer.

Unsure of what to do, Azahara left them to their work and headed towards the front of the ship. The chaos of last night was evident in the broken barrels and shattered glass that riddled the floor. The cracking under her boot echoed in the silence; only the crashing waves against the boat were its competition.

Climbing up and straddling the bowsprit, she rested her back against one of the ropes of the sails. She sat there for a long while, alone, hoping that Jayce would come to find her.

"It's not nice to stare," Anytime she was alone, her mind always wandered back to Kaed. How she took his life away from him because of her selfishness in wanting to be loved. *"Five more minutes, or an hour..."* Her nose stung, *"Oh, you'll always finish, Red."*

There was a moment when her mind teetered on the sensation of jumping overboard. Her thoughts were nearly too overpowering to keep her from listening to the intrusive whispers that told her she was too much of a burden. Reminding her it was better for her to have died that day at the Monastery. To have left before the Battle of Sunfall. To have saved Kaed and everyone around her from her darkness.

"Hey," a gentle voice pulled her from nearly tossing herself into the sea.

Turning her head, Azahara found her gaze meeting the gentle face of Tessa. Her luridus-colored skin and elongated, dark brown exotic eyes were holding her.

"Oh, hi," Azahara looked around, surprised. No one had actively avoided her, save for Zephyra and Tillin, but they didn't go out of their way to engage her alone. To have Tessa here, approaching and sitting at the ledge of the ship an arm's reach away, was unexpected to say the least. "How are you? Last night was... something."

Tessa nodded, "I'm doing okay. Definitely the roughest seas I have ever encountered. Terrifying, really, but I'm thankful we made it out, save for a single arm."

Azahara pressed her lips together, trying not to laugh out of respect for Tillin's loss. "Yeah, I agree."

She watched Tessa aimlessly pick at the fabric of her pants, "Can I ask you something that is terribly rude?" She peered through her straight lashes, "You can feel free to tell me to fuck right off if it's too intrusive."

Azahara lowered her gaze, watching the waves crash against the belly of the ship, "Sure, no harm in asking." There weren't many answers she could give Tessa, and she didn't want to lie to her. If she couldn't give her one, she would say it.

"You have made it very clear you are just a passenger on this ship. Not family. Yet, you saved Rowlin. Why? Why would you risk your life for him?" She spoke softly, with a faint undercurrent of puzzlement.

Azahara knew that with Tillin being the only Siren onboard, and injured, he wouldn't have been able to jump in and save Rowlin. It wasn't even a question for her to try and save him, even if she was adamant about never being a hero.

Taking a deep breath and slowly releasing it through her nose, Azahara responded, "It was the right thing to do. I've hurt a lot of people, both intentionally and not. Maybe it's me trying to make up for that." Pausing briefly, she continued, "I also don't fear death. I welcome it."

There was a moment of silence between them, and Azahara peered up to her. She was likely assessing her truth and seeking the tendrils of her words for the lie. None would be found. While saying she cared for Rowlin wouldn't have been a lie, part of her wondered if it would be.

Tessa had a solemn expression about her, "Thank you," she offered a smile, "and I'm sorry."

Azahara pulled her eyebrows together, "For what?"

"For whatever has happened to you."

She felt her chest tighten and that all too familiar sting behind her eyes and down her nose, threatening to expose how emotional she was.

Tessa continued, "I'm here if you ever want to talk about it, or even just about boys or shopping."

Azahara took an unsteady breath, trying to find the joy behind the sentiment.

"We don't have to be family or even friends, and I won't push you, but just know there are people onboard that see you." She was standing then, likely seeing Azahara's eyelids turning a bright red as she was sucking back tears. Tessa could never understand how powerful her words were.

Even still, they felt undeserved.

"Thank you, Tessa."

"Don't mention it, Aza. See you around." She gave a gentle wave of her hand and turned from her.

Azahara looked down at her trembling hands. The warmth of her tears lit her cheeks ablaze. She wanted so badly to be happy, to accept their care. Part of her didn't agree that she didn't deserve it, but the other, more dominant side won the battle over her body. It pulled her away from what should have filled her with joy and turned it into self-loathing.

The other side of her torment, and she hated that it even played a factor in her ache, was that Jayce never showed up on deck.

After no less than minutes passed, she retired to her room, skipping dinner and opting for sleep instead.

Day 17
CHAPTER 8

"*Oh.... Little Mouse,*" The water at my knees was ice cold, and I knew that if I didn't get out of it soon, my legs would be no more. "*I do like a chase.*"

My clothes were drenched entirely, not just my pants. The water seeped through, leaving my skin numb, the sensation akin to tiny bites. With every step, the water became a relentless adversary, tugging at me, threatening to drag me back under its surface.

I could feel my muscles contract in an attempt to warm themselves, fighting against the numbing that was ready to make my legs completely useless. My breathing was becoming shallower, quicker as my body attempted to adapt to the freezing environment.

The river along the edge of my land was always a little frozen, but when it snowed, a thin layer of sleek ice formed atop it, making it even colder. My teeth were chattering, but I had to push through. I had to make it beyond the wards. There, I could be warm, and then I could run and call Illyan.

"*I find your lack of faith in my ability to catch you quite painful.*"

The slight incline in the river made me feel hope. I was making it across.

"*Gods, you are incredible when wet.*" When I felt relief from the stinging pain, a rough hand gripped my shirt collar and forcefully pulled me back.

There was no stopping me from tumbling backward, which sent me straight into the frozen river. A surge of adrenaline, coupled with a sharp intake of breath was all I could muster before I was under. The moment sent a shockwave of pain through me; any warmth my body had left was stolen, leaving me disoriented.

I tried to get up, but a hand pushed me to the bottom. My eyes burned as they opened, and above me, through the clear icy water, I could see Goddrick holding me under.

I let out a scream, bubbles marring my vision. The cold penetrated my skin, biting into my bones. My muscles tensed and sent every inch of me into a vibration.

Scratching at his hands was doing nothing but making his malignant smile grow even wider. The air in my lungs was depleting, and I felt my body turning to desperation, turning, and kicking. Fighting for the life I knew would be gone in mere seconds.

Finally, his hand moved to my neck and he lifted me straight out of the water. Once my lips felt the air, I sucked in a full breath, drinking it as though he would immediately submerge me again.

The freezing water and his overpowering presence stifled my desire to scream. Floating on the river's surface, his thumb traced the contour of my jaw. "When will you learn you can't ever escape me?" He asked, his voice filled with longing and frustration.

His hand moved from my throat, came under my neck, and he carried me back to land—Opposite my home, away from safety.

"Honestly, I may be sad when you finally decide to become mine and there is no longer a chase."

My body was failing me. 'Move your legs. Punch him. Run! Run!' It didn't matter. My mind was not connected to the rest of me. Everything was numb, and it was beyond just the cold. He had control over me at every turn.

"Dikos Mou."

"Goddrick—no... please..."

"That damn no..."

As I was thrown to the floor, a cry of pain escaped me, and I felt my entire body shatter as if it were glass.

"I'm so grateful you turned my hourglass." He was in my face then, my breathing erratic. "That you came to me."

I want to wake up.

"Azahara, please, wake up."

She sat in her window, her legs dangling from the ledge, with nothing but the sea below. The nightmare had torn her entirely from sleep, and after a fit of crying, she decided it wasn't worth going back to it. The sun was beginning to kiss the horizon, and soon, the crew would be up and about.

With the return of her memories, more and more about Goddrick was coming to light. None of these flashbacks were ones that she had ever written about, and she feared just how many more there were. She imagined the lack of journaling them was due to how traumatic they would be to read, let alone relive as she was doing now.

There wasn't a single part of her that didn't ache, and she could swear the chill of the water was translating to her now. Her bones hurt, and it was all thanks to that piece of shit god.

As her mind drifted back to the nightmare, knocks rocked her door. While she looked, she didn't move to open it. No one had come to her room since she boarded the Neptune, which made her curious enough to say, "Yes?"

"I've got strawberries." If there had been one voice she desperately wanted to hear, it was his. "Can I come in?"

"Yeah, there isn't a lock." It was as though he already had his hand on the knob with how quickly the door opened after her approval.

Jayce strolled through, ducking so he wouldn't knock his head, a basket of strawberries in hand. He wore black trousers and a loose-fit tunic with a few buttons undone at his chest.

She didn't make a move to leave the window ledge but gave him a slight smile upon entering. "Thanks. That is a lot of strawberries for one person. Are you sharing with me?"

He hesitated as he approached the center of the room, visibly tense. It was a stark contrast to his usual, carefree demeanor. "Only if you want." While his tone was always gentle towards her, now it seemed laced with worry on top of it.

Pulling her eyebrows together, she asked, "Everything okay?"

"I really should be asking you that question," he didn't approach further, and she slipped back inside, placing her feet firmly on the floor.

"Stop being cryptic," she demanded.

Jayce put the basket down on the table and crossed the room to her, "I'm sorry." She couldn't understand why he was apologizing, "I should have come to see you yesterday." Her head was shaking, and he must have seen that she was more confused than before. "Your hands."

Fear gripped her from looking down at them, and the sensation of her throat tightening silenced her from asking why. Her body seized, nearly overtaking her ability to stay standing.

Finding the strength she didn't realize she had available to her, she lifted her hands. Crimson liquid marred them both, and she stepped back in surprise. "What the..."

Turning around, she looked at the windowsill; broken pieces of wood splintered where her hands had been gripping. The poor window was done for if she kept going at her current rate.

She was met with Jayce's hard chest when she stepped backward. "Let me see." His voice was gentle, and she hated it. She wanted him to scold her for hurting herself and be angry at her for being so reckless the day before. Why was he so damn understanding?

She didn't make a fuss, and instead turned around and placed her hands, palms up, into his. There was no pain, which concerned her more than the cuts themselves.

"What did the poor windowsill do to you?" He joked, the gentle expression returning to his dark complexion. His thumbs brushed the back of her hands, "Let's clean these up before we touch the strawberries. I don't like blood with my berries."

She walked over to the sink, where he turned on the faucet. The water felt soothing, and she became aware of the warmth radiating from her palms. The cool, sweet sting of the water offered her much-needed relief.

"Thanks," she went to turn the faucet off, but Jayce did it for her.

"Anything—" He cleared his throat, "Don't mention it." He stepped away and moved towards the window, looking down at the damage she had caused.

Azahara held a towel between her hands, applying pressure to stop the bleeding. These minor cuts would be gone by midday, if not sooner.

She was at the strawberries, picking one up and popping it into her mouth, when Jayce took one and ate it. "What did you mean," she said between bites, covering her mouth so he wouldn't see the berry mushing around in her mouth, "you should have come to see me yesterday? There is no obligation for you to see me. I'm not your responsibility or keeper." She swallowed, grabbing another one, but finishing her sentence before placing it into her mouth.

He leaned his head to the side, watching her. *Why are you staring at me like that?* She wondered, feeling her face starting to warm.

"Alyse said you were looking for me."

"I was," she confirmed, "but that doesn't mean you have to see me. I was only going to thank you. For what you did for me."

He nodded, grabbed the seat nearest the rounded table, and sat in it. *Yes, please, make yourself comfortable.* She made sure to keep the comment to herself. "I wanted to see you. I just—"

"You don't need to give me a reason, Jayce."

He grumbled something inaudible and crossed his leg, his elbow on the chair's armrest while his chin rested in his palm.

Azahara turned away from him, and it wasn't because of her heart doing flips or the butterflies in her stomach. Deep in her chest, it was crying out for relief. She never felt her body dying for water as if it were dehydrated because of a *man*.

After a deep breath, she looked back. His fingers pressed against his forehead, but his eyes stared at her between them.

"What?" She asked, her lips slightly parted as she waited impatiently for him to speak.

"You had a nightmare last night," her heart dropped to her stomach. The color drained from her face immediately, and her hands looked for support.

"No," she stammered, her voice shaky. "I mean, yes." Before her hands could begin shaking, she placed them together. "I mean... it was a memory. Like the ones I mentioned before, the ones I fear not being able to overcome."

The devastation that came over his face hurt her. The kind of pain that should have sent her to her knees. It nearly made her start to cry.

"It's okay," she lied, "I'm fine."

She watched his chest rise as he inhaled deeply, "You are great at many things, Azahara, but lying is not one of them." When he sighed, there was frustration behind it. "Who is Goddrick?"

Gods be damned. "Did I—"

"You screamed a lot, but that was the name you said 'no' to. So, who is Goddrick?" His anger was palpable. He remained eerily still in his chair, devoid of visible signs of agitation. There was no need for shouting, wild gesticulations, or loud outbursts.

Her chest tightened, "It doesn't matter who he is."

Jayce narrowed his eyes, "It does." The pure rage radiating off of him would consume the space around them.

Steading herself, she straightened her shoulders and placed another strawberry into her mouth. She was buying herself some time, and he knew it.

"Azahara."

Every time he said her name, it wasn't just her ears that heard it. Every part of her felt it. *Why are you here, Jayce?*

When she swallowed, he moved his hand from his face, taking another berry and putting it into his mouth.

"He's a piece of shit." That wouldn't be enough for him, and she wanted to redirect the conversation elsewhere. "These are good strawberries; how do they keep—"

The sound of the chair sliding against the wooden floor caused her to pause well before Jayce stood before her, towering over her. Her heart was in her throat, and she couldn't swallow it. He didn't scare her, or did he?

"I will give you everything within my power and more if you tell me who he is. I will jump from this damned ship, Azahara, if that is what you wish."

I don't want that... A huff of air released from her lips as they parted.

Her life began to spiral when she told Kaed who had taken her life away from her. Was this the beginning of the downward spiral of Jayce's life?

Would she be damning him the same way as she did to Kaed?

Her jaw trembled as if she were cold, trying to find the strength to do what was right. *You have to lie to him, and this time, be better at it than ever. Save him from your darkness, no matter what it takes.* "Someone from my past. He enjoyed torturing me for fun." She took a deep breath and continued, "What I dreamt was him attempting to drown me. The other night's events must have triggered it."

He closed his eyes, his nostrils flaring as he breathed deeply through them.

She dropped her head, and he was so close that her forehead pressed against his chest. Her own breaths quickened the moment she felt his heart and its rapid beat. Never before had she heard a heart race as fast as his. It wasn't human—there was no possible way. He should be dead.

His hand was then gently pressing against the back of her head. His fingers laced between the strands of her hair as he held her to him.

"I'm sorry," she felt his chest rise.

"For being overbearing? Or..." She wanted to lighten the mood. What was he going to do, go out and find Goddrick? It made her want to laugh, but she knew it wasn't the right time.

"For not being there." He didn't falter from his current demeanor.

She leaned back and stared at him, "I don't—" pausing to search for the right words, "think that would have been possible if you didn't know me."

"Then I'm sorry for not knowing you sooner so I could have protected you."

"That is very knight-y of you," she stepped around him, "I appreciate the sentiment... I really need to get those nightmares under control; how embarrassing." Her hand was on another strawberry when she felt his arms coming around her. "Jayce—"

He pulled her to him with one arm across her chest at her collarbone, and the other snaking around her waist.

She dropped the strawberry that was in her hand. "What are you—"

"Can you tell me something to calm me down?" His tone was low and grumbly, and the heat radiating off him threatened to burn this ship to ash.

Azahara had no idea what to tell him, and with every second wasted, his grip on her was tightening, creating a fog in her brain.

"I'm from the North," she began talking about the only thing that she knew for certain. "My name; you said it was unique, and that is because it is. The way you say it, Azahara, with the 'z' pronounced, it's wrong."

He was beginning to loosen his grip but was far from letting her go. "You pronounce it with a 'th' instead of a 'z', and you roll the r at the end. Like A-tha-ha-rr-a." She swallowed, "My name is Azahara Starfall, and I prefer the Moon over the Sun because it's far calmer. My favorite color is green. I enjoy writing, especially when it is to tell a certain Commander they are bad at dancing." Her accent was soft and had an omission of certain consonant sounds. Her vowels were elongated, and she rolled the r's in her words, which was the prominent feature of her vibrant speech.

His grip began to slowly release, and it was then that she realized both of her hands were gripping his arm.

"Thank you," his words a mere whisper in her ear, "Azahara." He said her name correctly, and it made her smile.

"You can keep the z—" She leaned back against his chest, "I've come to prefer it that way."

A rumbling chuckle vibrated against her back, "As you wish."

After another second, he leaned back and let her go.

Not that there wasn't a single good thing to say about Jayce, but the one thing she could say for sure was he didn't make things awkward. Once he had released her, he returned to enjoying the strawberries at the table. He was much more relaxed, and they sat silently until the basket was empty.

It was strangely calming. It was probably the calmest and safest she'd felt in a long time.

She realized she couldn't leave him at the port in Celadon. Despite any ulterior motives he might have had for being with her, she felt deep down that she could convince him to stay on her side. Even without being an Elf, she could see the truth in his emotions. Some part of him, whether large or small, did care for her.

It just begged the question, why? It wasn't as though they had known one another long. They hadn't spent that much time together.

She was determined to understand why he cared about her so much that he would defy or leave the King. As well as figuring out how to stop the incessant nightmares of Goddrick. While getting to Ilkiz to try and control whatever powers she had inside her.

The most important one of all: heal from losing Kaed.

She had a long road ahead of her.

Day 18
Chapter 9

"I'm not going to break," Azahara's voice was firm, "I will get it out of you." Her eyes were piercing, never flinching, as she stared into the deep sea of Xol's blue gaze. There was no reaction from the pale lady; even more, she looked bored.

Azahara took a step closer, her head tilting, maintaining unyielding eye contact. "I'm begging you, please." All she wanted was for this mysterious creature to speak to her. Alyse hadn't indicated that she was also mute, and while she had never heard her talk to anyone, she knew that she could.

"I'll jump from this ship," at this point, it was her go-to threat. It was evident that Xol had this strange defensive nature towards her, the same as Jayce, which made no sense. She was right in her direction because Xol's eye twitched slightly.

They, Xol and Jayce, had such a strange energy between them, and she was dying to know why. It was where her question had come from.

After Jayce had shared the basket of strawberries with her, he left without a fuss to stay, and who stood immediately outside: Xol. He nearly ran into her at how close she was to the door, and at first, he was just going to move around her, but she didn't allow him to. As if through unspoken words, she scolded him. Her eyes were like a sharpened knife slicing through a peach. There was no effort needed to show her malice.

Azahara ended up stepping between the two of them before things got ugly. Even though Jayce hadn't indicated he'd be hitting the woman, she feared that if she did, he would retaliate.

"I'll do anything!" That was a lie, but Azahara was willing to push her limits to get what she wanted.

"She won't answer you," his voice nearly made her jump out of her skin.

Not that it was needed, but Xol put her hands on her arms to steady her. She was cold, as though no blood flowed through her veins. Never taking her eyes from Azahara, she stepped between her, and the sauntering Jayce.

His arms were crossed over his chest, and he was shaking his head, "You could have asked me."

Embarrassed, Azahara dropped her gaze, looking at nothing in particular to avoid making eye contact with both him and Xol.

Feeling Xol jerk, she peeked through her lashes to see that she was once again piercing Jayce with the stare of death. *Dear gods, why is that so terrifying?*

"Chill, she's just blushing," Jayce said, seemingly trying to calm the aggravated Xol gripping her arms. "You can let her go. I'm not going to harm her."

"I can't express to you both how awkward you two are, and how uncomfortable it makes me." Azahara laughed nervously and immediately stepped away as Xol released her arms. "You both act like an ex-married couple—" Jayce immediately bellowed out a laugh, and Xol's eyes widened enough to nearly send her eyeballs shooting out. "I feel like the child you guys are fighting for custody over."

Xol was visibly distraught, her back pressing against the stack of boxes she was bringing up from the lower deck just minutes before Azahara cornered her. She was shaking her head vigorously, swapping between looking at Jayce and her.

Jayce had his arms crossed over his chest, expressing a hearty laugh. His joy at her joke was infectious, making a bright smile line her lips.

"What is so funny?" It was Alyse, along with Théodore, who approached them.

"These two are my parents, fighting over who gets to keep me the longest." Azahara gestured between them, and while Xol didn't change colors, if she could, she'd have been blushing from the furtherment of the joke. She didn't need to confirm with Xol that she wouldn't touch Jayce with a yard-long stick, even if it were to have peace and quiet with Azahara.

Both Alyse and Théodore laughed alongside Jayce. Azahara stayed neutral, at least attempting to. She didn't want to make Xol feel bad. She wasn't there to attack her. They were both guilty of being weird around her, which built a mystery around the duo.

After their fits of laughter, Théodore took her hand and placed a kiss on her knuckles. "Afternoon, Miss Starfall."

She smiled, "Good afternoon, Théodore." He was old school, and she had already attempted to ask him to call her Azahara or at least Aza. When he insisted on being formal, she didn't argue.

Peeking at Xol, Azahara confirmed she was not upset at Théodore's attention towards her. Which just furthered her curiosity about what Jayce had done to deserve such fierce hate.

Jayce, who was eyeing her over Théodore's shoulder, seemed to be waiting his turn.

"Will you be joining us, Aza?" Alyse stepped up next, leaving Jayce in the background, "For the celebration tonight?"

"Celebration?" Confusion rocked her tone.

"Yes, a celebration for surviving the first rough seas of the Ilkiz territory!" There was no such thing, but Azahara wasn't here to argue with her. "We will have drinks and music on deck."

Azahara smiled warily, "I'll think about it." She didn't want to be antisocial, not at this point. They'd been together for twelve days straight and had already been through a life-and-death scenario. It was just that drinking and music felt like a bad idea.

"I'll take it," Alyse perked and turned away, "Théodore, Xol, we have work to do. Jayce—" He never looked at the Captain, only keeping his eyes on Azahara. Her cheeks burned at the intensity of it. "You promised to help with the—"

"The barrels of ale, I know. I'll get them when you call for me."

"Perf!" Alyse said eagerly.

With that, the three of them departed. Allowing Jayce to finally step to her and put his hand out towards her.

"Uh?" Unsure of what he wanted, she looked from his hand up to his face.

"Théodore can kiss your hand, but I can't?" His smirk was devastating, and she rolled her eyes and threw her head back.

He didn't budge, and she slapped her hand into his. "Afternoon, Ja—yce!" With a forceful tug, he pulled her to him, one of his arms wrapping around her back as the other brought her hand to his lips.

Her face was on fire, and a droplet of sweat immediately formed on her forehead and began rolling down her temple.

"Good afternoon, Aza," his voice was low, "how did you sleep?"

"F-Fine." She stuttered.

"No nightmares?"

That night, in fact, she didn't have any and felt truly grateful for that. Not only that, but no one had commented on her screams the night before. It was as if nothing had happened, and she wasn't some freak with reoccurring nightmares plaguing them. The memory of returning from Höwl and keeping everyone awake with her incessant screaming kept resurfacing whenever she'd get ready for bed.

The last thing she wanted was to be a burden, more so than she already was.

"No dreams," she confirmed.

"I'm glad." He placed another kiss on her knuckles before releasing her, allowing her to breathe. "Have a moment to chat before I get to work?"

With a gentle nod, she found a sturdy box and jumped up to take a seat. A desired breeze caught her hair. The cloudless sky gave no reprieve from the scorching sun. It was such a stark contrast to her typically chilly years, attributing to her pale tone, unlike Jayce, who was blessed with remarkably tanned skin that only accentuated his sharp appearance. She was a ghost, while he walked amongst the living.

Crossing one leg over the other, she adjusted her flowing blue dress and rested her hands beside herself.

Jayce made himself comfortable across from her, leaning against one of the masts. "Can I ask why you want to go to Ilkiz?"

Her lips pressed into a fine line as she stared at him. While they had become much closer, she still had reservations about giving up specific details about herself that may be conveyed to the King and Jaakobai.

Before she could respond, he continued, "I know promising not to tell the King won't do anything to soothe your worry, so how about I offer something equally as valuable."

Azahara narrowed her eyes, "Okay."

"The King believes that you are going to Ilkiz because of the Book of Aurora."

A quizzical expression marred her face, "The Book of Aurora?" She repeated, and he nodded, "Why the hell would I be looking for that? I didn't even realize it was located in Ilkiz. Honestly, I thought it was destroyed during the Conquering of Parádeisos."

He sighed, "It was suggested by Jaakobai that it was why you were going to Ilkiz. Nothing more than that."

"Of course," she put her hands together in her lap, her thumb rubbing against the top of her hand. "He is throwing your King off, which I'm not sure I should be thankful for, or worried about."

"Do me a favor?" He paused briefly, "Try not to call him my King. He is just the King."

"Sorry," she said sheepishly.

"It's fine," that irresistible smile returning to his lips, "so, why are you going to Ilkiz?"

Azahara wanted to say she honestly didn't know. It wasn't her intention to gather the Four Points of Rah's Star, but Power felt like the only thing that could help her contain the existing force inside her. The one that killed thousands in seconds and nearly started a war with the gods.

Jayce didn't pressure her. He just stood there waiting while she gathered how to answer his question.

"Have you heard of the Four Points of Rah's Star?"

"Vaguely," he murmured, "they also brought up Rah during the conversation. That you had half the power he did during the Reshaping."

That piece of shit, Jaakobai. What I wouldn't give to rip his wings right off his back. She moved her hand to her neck and rubbed at the knot forming. Maybe Jaakobai wasn't trying to throw them off. It's possible he honestly thought she was going after the book of Aurora. Was that how she would get Power?

"Rah, a shapeshifter according to historians, sought out the Mother for guidance on how to save the realm. There isn't any text on why he did, but it's assumed that it was on the brink of collapse. It is the only reasonable explanation that the Mother would call to gift him the four points that held it together: Life, Death, Power, and Magic.

"While the Mother only governs Magic, she called upon her friends, the God of Might, Death itself, and Ilkiz. With their combined power, Rah was given the means to reshape and create an entirely new reality. One of which would begin anew, wipe out history, and start a new future.

"It was said that Rah killed all living creatures besides Ilkiz and her dragons, but I don't necessarily believe that."

Jayce cut in before she could continue, "Why is that?"

"Someone doesn't willingly give up their life to destroy what they are trying to save." She could see the confusion in his expression. "The power gifted to Rah was too much for his body to maintain, and in the end, it killed him. So, I have a hard time believing that someone who knew they would die because of the Reshaping, would willingly kill... likely millions."

To her surprise, he seemed distraught, "I see." His tone was raw.

"Does that surprise you?" She was puzzled by his reaction, "He held four of the most powerful beings within him. A mere shapeshifter, equivalent to that of a human, can barely manage Magic, let alone the other three. I'm surprised I haven't been obliterated yet."

She shouldn't have made that comment. Regret immediately pulled at her as she stared at Jayce, who had bumps lining his arms, anger riddling his expression.

When her lips parted to speak, he cut her off, "If you could refrain from talking about your demise as though it is just another time of the day, I would appreciate it."

"Sorry—I didn't mean to," she lowered her gaze, "death is just something..." Her lips pressed together, and this time, she shut herself up. Death couldn't take her. She wasn't allowed to leave this realm, even though that was the only thing she desired.

"So what, then, you are going to Ilkiz to get another point of his star?" Jayce tried his hardest not to sound upset while moving the conversation along. "Then next, Magic? Is your goal to reshape this—"

"I don't want that," she was flustered, "I never asked for this shit!!" The anger wasn't directed toward Jayce. She knew he wasn't trying to upset her. "Five centuries ago, I only wanted a mundane, boring life. To live and then die like a normal human." The desire to scream nearly became unbearable to resist, so she quickly continued. "My life was nothing spectacular, and I was okay with that. I took care of my siblings and helped raise them. I put everyone's needs before my own. I should have been gone, married off, and bearing some nobleman's children. Instead, I stayed because they needed me." She was rambling, and he would not know what she was saying.

"I just wanted to be happy. Isn't that what everyone wants? Instead, do you know what I got? Misery. I never asked to be cursed by an obsessive—" Her hand clapped over her mouth so quickly it caused her to wince.

"Please... continue..." His words were delivered with a forceful and vehement tone.

She didn't want to look at him. Everything was spinning around her. *Great job, Azahara, what the fuck?!* She scolded herself, cursing internally every word she could fathom.

"Jayce, I'm sorry, I can't. That was so stupid of me." She buried her face in her hands. "No, I'm not going to Ilkiz—"

He moved towards her with a silent stride, and upon reaching her, he gently but firmly peeled her hands away from her face, prompting a sharp intake of breath.

He groaned in frustration. The grasp on her wrists carried a quiet but undeniable strength, his thumbs pressing into her palms with a potent force.

"Why are you afraid to tell me?" His tone still manifested anger, but she knew it wasn't towards her, or at least not directly. She kept her head down, her hands limp in his grasp.

"Because it is insignificant information that would only put you in danger."

His frustration faltered, "Look at me, please. I'm not angry with you."

A light laugh escaped that held no humor, "I know you aren't." She then tilted her head, seeing his warm eyes filled with remorse. "You don't deserve the trouble it could cause you if I told you my story."

"I won't ask again."

"Overbearing..." They both smiled at the same time, "...a god. A god cursed me." His hands squeezed hers, "To live for eternity, to forget my memories every year, until I accepted being his. Except... I now remember everything. So," she slipped her hands away from his grasp, "I'm going to Ilkiz because I have nowhere else to go.

"It is the only place that makes sense. I don't seek the power of Ilkiz to reshape this world, and to be honest, how am I supposed to obtain something that no longer exists? As for the Magic," she cleared her throat and leaned back on her hands, trying to put distance between them, even if he was standing between her spread legs, "I had the opportunity to take it after I destroyed Thall…

"I have no desire to do anything for this realm. I'm not its protector."

Jayce's eyes darkened, not moving from before her, "Is the gods name Goddrick?"

She only nodded her head and watched as his eye twitched. "I see," he deadpanned and stepped away from her. "I need to go help get ready for tonight."

"Jayce—"

"I'll see you tonight," His hand gently patted her leg before he stepped away and nearly ran to the stairs, disappearing into the ship. Pure shock and confusion marred her face. *What the fuck just happened?*

She was left sitting there, alone, staring down at the stairway. *Why are you here, Jayce?*

She felt horrible.

Absolutely horrible.

After waiting only a few minutes to see if Jayce would return, which he didn't, she tried to find Rowlin. He had been preparing for that night, and even Xol couldn't be bothered. Azahara wouldn't have objected to having Xol stare at her if it meant the feeling would shift from sickness to awkwardness.

Finding Alyse moving around barrels, Azahara nearly had to beg her to give her something to do. Finally conceding, she was tasked to cook something to snack on while everyone got drunk and likely passed out on the hull.

Without needing to be told where to go, she made her way downstairs to the kitchen. She hoped she would run into Jayce carrying up the barrels from the lower deck, but she didn't. He was elusive when he wanted to be, and she wondered if there were secret passageways throughout the ship that she was unaware of.

Deciding on potatoes, colorful peppers, and beef skewers, she got to work. Alyse only commented that Xol didn't eat meat, so she would pay mind to make a few without the beef attached.

She forgot how much being in the kitchen calmed her, especially when she was in it alone. Not that she ever hated having Kaed or Illyan with her while she cooked, but something about creating the magic herself brought her a sense of pride. It was her thing that she could do and do well. Nothing special was needed, just her hands and the time to do it.

Thankfully, she had plenty of time to make enough food for everyone. She got carried away and baked a few pies with the fruits, seemingly on their last day of life. The ship's kitchen had everything she needed. She cleaned up and put everything away before asking for help to bring everything upstairs.

Things were in full swing when she made her way up the stairs to the hull, a tray in hand with skewers stacked on top of one another.

"Zayne, Lucala—" They were the two cooks on the ship, both dark-skinned druids who looked no older than Mel and Skyy did in the year leading up to her curse. The two turned to her, "Do you mind grabbing the other trays downstairs? There are four pies, sliced, and another thing of these." She lifted her pan and moved towards the few barrels used as a table.

They gave her the thumbs up and rushed past her to grab the rest of the food.

"By the gods, those smell delicious." Yelena strolled towards her, leaning over and taking in a prolonged, heavy air intake through her nose. "May I?"

"Please, they are for everyone."

Everyone seemed to flood over just as Zayne and Lucala returned with the rest of them, and Azahara stepped away to allow them space.

The number of groans and moans that were received after they took their first bites made her blush. It was like feeding her family again, making her want to cry. Those tears, they would have been happy ones. The kind she hadn't shed in a long, long time.

Everyone, including Tillin and Zephyra, who surprised her over everything else, thanked her and told her how great both the skewers and the pies were. Xol had acknowledged with a tiny head nod in appreciation of Azahara thinking of her.

The absence of Jayce was gnawing at her. The barrels of ale were up on the hull, indicating that he had been there, but disappeared elsewhere before she could cross paths with him. He was, again, making her think that the ship had secret tunnels.

Once everyone was done devouring her food, they began drinking. At the same time, Darian pulled out a violin, and Carmen started singing in Elvish. Soon, with how they were all drinking, no one would know North from South.

Alyse, Rowlin, and Théodore tried to get her to drink and dance with them, but she opted to sit on the sidelines and enjoy their movements. She explained that it was like watching a show. Slowly but surely, the climax would come when everyone was too intoxicated to know their part of the story, and the comedy would ensue.

They all conceded and went back to their fun. Everyone enjoyed each other as one big family. Even Xol, who was only moving her shoulders was, she supposed, having a good time.

When Azahara blinked, she was brought back to the Idle Fox. She saw herself walking down the stairs, overthinking, and unable to keep herself upright because of her nerves.

"You are absolutely stunning." Kaed's familiar voice echoed in her head. She dropped her gaze to the floor. *"You're turning red."* She choked on a sob. *"It's my favorite color."* Tears brimmed in her eyes, and she stood and turned quickly from the crew.

While every memory of Kaed was beautiful, it always ended with the knowledge that he was laying lifeless in a void. His soul trapped because of her inability to let him go. She was weak, and in moments like this, she knew how much of a coward she really was.

Putting her head into her hands, she let the tears fall.

The memory of him taking her onto the balcony that night ripped her chest open. Her heart was bare and exposed, threatening to stop and end her suffering. The voice of Zhal, hoping that one day she could have her alone, broke her to pieces. Illyan, asking Kaed to dance, and him conceding.

That memory would live on in her mind as the best night to cause her absolute turmoil for eternity. She would never get that moment back, and pretending she could ever have it again was blasphemy. It made her feel guilty for standing near any semblance of happiness and joy.

As though she didn't deserve even the thought of moving on.

Her legs were in full motion before her brain realized what she was doing. The stairs were taken quickly. Nearly ten steps turned to three when she was down to the second floor.

"Jayce?!" She called for him, and she didn't know why.

When there was no answer, she ran down the next stairs, nearly tripping as she came to the third floor. "Jayce?!" Once again, silence. Only the sounds of the fading music above her as she rushed down the final flight, the darkest of them, which happened to be the storage facility.

"Jayce..."

Silence. The sounds from the hull were but a muffled buzz in her ears. It was still far too loud for her.

She wandered around, barely able to see two feet in front of her with how dark it was down there. None of the lanterns were lit, which made sense if they had no business there. It was another indication that Jayce wouldn't be there. Still, she found herself weaving through the boxes and barrels until the sounds of the hull were gone entirely.

Then, she found a space on the floor and sat.

She wasn't sure why she even ran to find Jayce. He couldn't bring Kaed back. He couldn't undo the past. Why was she searching for him then? He couldn't do anything for her.

Slipping from a seated position, she lay on the ship's floor. She was feeling the waves closely crashing against its belly. The swaying back and forth cradled her and soothed her into a quiet, dark sleep.

She didn't want to dream. Whether it was about Goddrick or Kaed, she wanted to stay in silent darkness and float in its embrace.

"I'm sorry, Sunshine." Sam's pained voice came through the winnox.

It's okay. I'm no stranger to pain. She knew her voice sounded just as pathetic as she felt.

"You don't deserve this," it felt as though he was caressing her through her window.

Who does?

"Not you. Anyone but you."

Day 20
CHAPTER 10

Someone had clearly found her downstairs, because she woke up in her own bed the following morning. There was no indication of that person staying, nor did they change her or put her into something more comfortable. That would have been awkward, to say the least, so she was thankful.

She ventured out only once to ask Alyse how long they had until they arrived in Celadon. When Alyse replied, "Tomorrow," she returned to her room. She didn't search very thoroughly, just around the hull, but Jayce was once again nowhere to be found. He must be a spy, to be able to disappear on a ship of this size.

When the next day arrived, it was the first time she felt no movement of the ship, indicating that they had docked or were preparing to disembark.

She knew that this island was tropical, so she strategically put a one-piece swimsuit, not particularly the best fit, under her gold and white dress for a quick plunge into the sea.

As she exited, the entire crew, including Jayce, leaned against the railing, gazing towards the island. She approached, maintaining some distance from the others, and fixed her gaze on the breathtaking sight before her. Celadon, an island resembling paradise, was revealed in all its glory. Her eyes widened in awe as she absorbed the vision of the small port nestled amidst the natural splendor. The surrounding beaches, with their glistening white sand, seemed to stretch endlessly, inviting her to step onto their pristine shores.

A gentle breeze caressed her face, carrying the scents of the exotic blooms and salty sea air. The temperature, perfect and balmy, enveloped her in a comforting embrace. For the first time in a few days, she felt a sense of tranquility wash over her as if the island itself exuded a healing aura. The brilliant hues of the lush greenery, and the vibrant blues of the surrounding waters painted a scene that resonated deeply in her soul.

With a smile playing at the corners of her lips, she felt a magnetic pull towards the island. She was captivated by its allure and was ready to dip her toes into the sand and swim in the water.

"Good morning," Tessa said at her approach, "will you be coming ashore with us?" She had a smile on her lips and seemed just as excited to get off the ship as she was.

"Yes, I'm dying for it, honestly," Azahara's giddiness translated in her tone. For once, that joy was not ripped away by guilt.

They were joined by Alyse and Lucala, who were all jumping for joy to hear that Azahara would be partaking in the day's fun.

According to Alyse, Rowlin would be requesting the supplies they needed in town and joining them shortly after that. The rest of the crew would be heading down to the beach together to take in the perfect weather granted by Celadon.

Azahara went to see if Jayce would be joining them, but not to her surprise; he was no longer where he had been moments ago.

"He has some business to attend to in the port," Carmen said, her hand brushing behind her pointed ear as she leaned towards Azahara. "He is in kind of a bad mood today. It's probably for the best."

"Jayce? In a bad mood? I'm more inclined to want to see that than not." She huffed and followed the crew down the ramp and onto solid ground. It was obvious that Azahara was not used to being on a ship for as long as she was, and her sea legs wobbled on the unmoving floor.

Darian, the other middle-aged human male, took her arm and steadied her. "Gotcha, little lady, it'll take sum' gettin' use to, but you'll get there." His accent threw her off as much as the stable ground did. How had she not spoken to him in the nearly fifteen days she'd been onboard?

"Thanks, Darian." He smiled at her, letting her go as soon as she could walk stably.

Azahara took in the breathless sight of the mountains that stood as sentinels, their peaks reaching toward Parádeisos. Verdant foliage adorned their slopes, painting a beautiful tapestry that blended seamlessly with the azure sky. Some waterfalls cascaded down the rocky cliffs, their crystalline streams creating a sympathy of soothing sounds she could hear even from here.

The mountains seemed to hold a rugged beauty, their imposing statures filling her with serenity and wonder. *This would be a beautiful place to live,* she thought, her chest rising as she took a deep, longing breath.

The walk down the dock went by in a blink, and soon, she had her toes dipped into the warm sand on the beach. Everyone parted then, and with some running straight for the water, while others—Zephyra and Tillin mainly—stripped to their bares and lay on the beach. The other missing soul was Xol, which she was a bit upset about.

Azahara was slightly curious about what she would look like in a swimsuit. Or, to answer the question, would she burn? Her pale skin did not seem like the kind that should stand the test of the sun.

Feeling embarrassed thinking about Xol that way, she shook free of the thought. Part of her wanted to take in the moment alone, walk along the beach, and seek comfort in herself. As she looked out at the crew bouncing a ball between them and splitting into two groups, she fought the prospect of companionship instead of solitude.

She had isolated herself a lot onboard.

"Come on, Aza!" If she joined, it would have made them uneven, but by the looks on their faces, they didn't seem to care.

Sucking in an intoxicating breath, she slipped her dress off and began rushing into the water. The swimsuit was white, with thick, stretchy material. It had black stitching, with a gold circle that pulled the front together. It was cut from her shoulders down to her belly button. The back was no higher, and she wondered exactly who in their right mind would buy this as an option.

Unfortunately, she had only been able to pick up two suits before the panic attack at the Port of Kortez. Neither of them was better than the other, and while this one screamed for attention, the other one was, well—she didn't even think it would cover her nipples.

"Oh my gods," Alyse's mouth nearly sank to the seabed. "Your body is illegal. Someone, call the authorities."

As her hips met the warm waters, Azahara rolled her eyes and felt her cheeks igniting. "Stop! You are one to talk, Alyse. Have you seen yourself?"

While the Captain had little in the chest department, her ass made up for it. That, and her beautifully curved hips, they begged to be gripped.

"I'm not interested in women, but jeez, I have to agree with Alyse," Carmen said sheepishly.

Tessa was giggling, and with one look at the men, she knew they were silently agreeing. The thought of running riddled her.

"I should have worn shorts and a shirt," Azahara confessed, turning back to walk towards the shore.

"No, no. It's fine. It's boys versus girls, and you'll give us an advantage." Alyse was hurrying and pulling her back, while she felt Tessa taking her other arm. They dragged her backward, not allowing her to leave.

"Okay, okay!" A giggle escaped her, "I'll stay, sheesh, just don't keep staring, or else I'm leaving!" That, thankfully, got a laugh out of them. "What are we playing?" She asked once she was released.

With Théodore, Zayne, Darian, and Lucala facing Carmen, Tessa, Alyse, Yelena, and Azahara, the Captain went into detail about the simple game with no name. They would need to keep the ball from hitting the water and only had three hits before it was returned to the other team.

They did a practice round, where Yelena served the red ball, which was about the size of someone's head, over to the boy's team. Zayne knocked it up with his forearms to Darian, who flicked it towards Lucala. Then, with a swat, the ball was hit right back towards the girl's team.

Not knowing exactly what to do, Azahara reached out and caught it as it made it to her.

Tessa laughed, "We don't catch it," gesturing for the ball, Azahara tossed it to her. "Once it's back to us, we will do the same and hit it back to them. If it drops into the water, the other team gets a point. Make sense?"

The real game began with a shrug of Azahara's shoulders and a gentle nod. She wouldn't say that the group was competitive; that would be too gentle of a term. The amount of name-calling and gestures of 'fuck you' and 'eat shit' would have made her think they were enemies instead of family.

Though, with the laughs and bouts of jokes, she knew it was all in good fun.

Azahara began to pick up the game quickly. By the third round, she was making plays as advanced as Alyse and Yelena. At one point, Lucala had jumped nearly straight out of the water and spiked the ball hard toward the edge of their invisible ring. With a thrust of her body, Azahara sprawled out, barely hitting the ball with her closed fist and sending it back towards the girls.

After reappearing from under the water, she heard the howls from the ladies, indicating she'd saved them from losing a point.

"That was some dive," It wasn't just his voice that caught her by surprise, but his proximity. Her head craned back when she stood to see Jayce standing mere inches from her. "Is there anything you aren't good at?"

Her body tingled as his bare chest graced her vision. He was sculpted to perfection, and she hated herself for feeling the tightening between her stomach and groin.

"Lying. Remember?" She found her voice, and when her gaze returned to his face, he gave her that handsome smile.

"Right." Without looking away from her, he continued, "Théodore, can I join?"

The girls groaned.

"Absolutely, we could use the help."

Jayce winked at her, and every part of her vibrated.

He walked around her and over to the guy's side. She looked at his back as he walked by; it was no less impressive than the front. There was no way he didn't exercise daily. If he were to ever lift her, he probably could do it just as easily as Kaed would, if not easier.

After finding the means to move, the ball was tossed to her. She hadn't served yet, and that prospect scared her. Everyone had their eyes on her, but the strength of Jayce's gaze made her tremble.

Centering herself, she tossed the ball up, and with a gentle smack, lobbed the ball over to them. The game began, and as before, it was just as competitive. Azahara found her mouth clamped shut, as was Jayce's. While she didn't mind bantering, the prospect of calling them names seemed too personal, and she didn't feel close enough to them yet.

The ball found its way to Jayce, and she knew he would immediately hit it right at her. Preparing herself, she angled her shoulders, and as he spiked the ball down at her, she put her hands together, allowing the speed of it to tap off her forearms with no additional force behind it. Alyse was moving to flick the ball upward, and Tessa came to spike it over just the same. It was hit with such force that she swore it was done to inflict harm.

Zayne, who was closest, only had enough time to put the back of his hand up to ward off the ball, hitting him right in the face. It ricocheted so quickly that Azahara had no time to react, as she had been in the front. The smack against her nose had her stumbling, a soft curse escaping while her hands clasped over her nose.

"Oh shit, Aza!" Zayne gasped. "I'm so sorry!"

The sound of rushing water towards her was drowned out by Jayce, "I've got her." While his voice was gentle, it held a resonance that spoke of it not being a request.

His hand rested against her wrist, "Let me see."

"I'm fine," she winced as she moved her hands. While it stung, she could tell nothing was broken. His hand was on her cheek, his thumb brushing gently against the crease of her nose.

The way he held her made her heart bounce around in her chest. The hand that wasn't against her face had the back of her head, cradling it to ensure she wouldn't go anywhere. *Fuck, I need him to back up.* Try as she might, she couldn't remove her eyes from his. It was as if she was bound to them, which was both terrifying, and calming.

"Nothing is broken," he gave her a nod. "Strong nose. At that proximity, it should have." She swore at that moment he was about to lean in and kiss her forehead, but instead, he shook his head and stepped back.

Releasing a breath, she visibly relaxed. She wasn't sure if she should thank him or not. The thick fog in her brain kept her from thinking coherently.

Alyse was the savior to their building tension. "Oh, Rowlin!" She yelled, and at that moment, everyone sensed the game was ending.

Thankful that Jayce was now a few feet away, she could breathe without tasting his worldly, peppermint scent that brought her a sense of calm and tranquility that she both loved and hated.

Unsure of what she should do, she turned away from him and looked up at the sky, a longing, desperate look about her. A breeze swept through, gently tousling her hair, which was beginning to dry. Some strands danced and swirled around her face.

She stepped further into the sea. The thought of going diving to round off their time here in Celadon crossed her mind. She smiled and was about to do it when Jayce intersected her thoughts.

"Lucky sky," he was walking up beside her.

"How so?" She brushed her hair behind her ear, crossing her arms under her chest and leaning away from him.

"To be looked at like that."

"Pfft," she scoffed, "the sky has never disappointed or hurt me. It can have any look it would like." That wasn't necessarily meant to be a jab, but she supposed it came out like one after saying it.

"Ouch," a verbal confirmation.

"Aw, where does it hurt?" A playful smile brimming at her lips. His eyes trailed to them, and she instinctively bit at the corner. "I can get Carmen to bring you some aid when we return to the ship."

"We?" It dawned on her that she hadn't talked to him about staying onboard. Maybe that was why he had avoided her yesterday and this morning.

Sheepishly, her eyes diverted away from him, moving to give them space, "If you want, that is."

His feathery chuckle would have been all she needed to confirm that he would be getting back on the Neptune, but he still said, "I'd love nothing more."

She splashed him, "Doesn't mean I'm still not a **little** suspicious of you."

As if he wouldn't have splashed her back, and by the Mother, did he. It felt like he pushed an entire wave over her, sending her underneath the surface. With an audible gasp, she came up, her red hair covering her face.

"Jayce!" She shrieked, her fingers fighting against the tangles, her forearm lifting and throwing her hair back. "I threw a fish; you sent the god of the Sea after me!" A laugh accompanied her outburst, and she fixed him with a glare.

His shoulders jumped as he laughed in mock victory, "Don't start the fire if you can't take the heat."

Reigning in how his laughter made her feel, she furrowed her eyebrows, "In all seriousness," she cleared her throat, "not that I was looking for you or anything, but where were you? The night of the party and yesterday."

He groaned softly, "I was around, not too far."

"Cryptic, but okay." She wouldn't push him, as he was nothing to her; and she was nothing to him. Neither of them had a claim to the other and needn't answer further than what they felt necessary.

That wasn't to say she wasn't curious though.

He was slowly closing the gap between them, and while she could say the current was doing it, she saw him walking in her direction. "If you'll allow me, I'll never be too far."

Her eyes widened, "Jayce..."

Quickly, he shook his head and put his hands up in defense, "I'm not asking for anything." Feeling her heart ready to run out of her throat, she quickly swallowed, watching as he closed the mere foot of distance between them. "Just don't shut me out."

"Then tell me why." Her voice was needy, and she hated that it came out that way.

It visibly took him back, and for the first time, she saw him needing to catch his own breath. "I told you, to protect you."

"No, that isn't good enough for me." She shook her head, "Who am I to you?" It was the question he gracefully continued to avoid.

There was a pain in his eyes, "What if I told you I didn't know? That I just feel I'm supposed to be by your side. In any way possible."

"I would say you are lying," she watched his eyebrow raise, "you aren't as good at lying as you think you are. I may be worse, but you are no expert." His hand came to her chin, but he paused and immediately dropped it. "Can I at least ask why you won't tell me?"

His stare was impenetrable, unblinking as he soaked her in, "Only if you don't ask a follow-up question, and we go for a dive together."

Thinking about it for a brief moment, she nodded. At least it was an answer; she already figured it would be cryptic.

"I don't think it is the right time, with everything going on. It wouldn't do either of us any good."

Time. It wasn't like I didn't have loads of it. Why did it matter what she was to him? Having him around was becoming the only reason she was looking forward to coming out of her room.

She still wanted to ask questions but promised to concede to his response, "Thank you. Even though I—" She wasn't going to banter him, but it may have come out that way to him.

His index finger pressed against her lips, "Ah—let's dive." She hadn't realized it until then, but his hands were soft, opposite from Kaed's, whose were rough from yielding a bow and fighting in battle. Jayce's were like silk and likely had women and men begging him to return to them.

They enjoyed hours of swimming before being forced out, or risk ruining their skin by pruning.

She found solace and contentment in this fleeting happiness, knowing that her life challenges could temporarily recede and be replaced by a profound sense of joy. Though she understood its impermanence, she cherished the genuine happiness that enveloped her in that moment.

Illyan? Before heading to the ship with the rest of the crew and Jayce, she held back for a bit. Opening the winnox, she reached out to her friend.

"*Ladybug. By the Mother, it is so good to hear your voice... or thoughts...*"

Illy, how are you—and Zhal? How is she?

She leaned against one of the deck's posts that led out to the Neptune. "*We are okay, just extremely worried about you. Word has spread that the King is looking for you, and the three of us.*"

Audibly, she gasped, *What... no...*

"*Don't worry, we have moved from your home. With my father now aiding the King, we had no choice. Thankfully, we had friends that helped us get moved.*"

Where are you now?

"*The last place they would think to look. I could tell you, but it is probably best that I don't.*"

Of course, and...

"*We have him. I wouldn't leave him, Ladybug.*"

Her hand covered her mouth as a soft sob involuntarily slipped out. *Is he...*

"*I don't want to hurt you Ladybug...*"

Just tell me the truth, please. Is he still... has there been any change?

"No, I'm sorry. He looks like he is sleeping. I'm unsure if it's because of the magic around him or something else. It's as though he is frozen in time."

I see...

"How are you? Have you found what it is you are searching for? When will you come home? When can we see you..."

Azahara wiped away her tears, staring out at the Neptune. Jayce was standing at the ramp, waiting for her to join him.

I'm broken, Illy. I've not found what I am looking for and probably never will, but I will come home to you and Zhal... One day, I'll find the strength to protect you both.

"Zhal and I both see how strong you are, Ladybug. It isn't always easy to make the best choice for yourself. You are courageous and hold everyone before yourself. While we are hurting that you aren't here, we understand."

She turned from Jayce and crouched down, her hands pressing against her face. *I love you both, forever and eternity. Please know I left you because I wanted to keep you both safe. I didn't want to leave you.*

"I know, we both know that... Zhal says she misses you and wishes she could hear your voice. But refuses to allow magic to penetrate her mind because she said she'd become scrambled eggs. Then she'd haunt me. And I can't have that. I just couldn't."

Azahara laughed and wiped away the tears from her eyes. *Tell her I don't blame her.*

"She wants you to know she's sorry and can't wait for you to come home."

What is she sorry for... There was silence, and she feared that the winnox had broken or it was closed. *Illy?*

"She is such an oppressor, gods. Such a bully! Always blaming me, she's so mean. I must go because now she's all over me to tell you, and I won't. Reach out more often...please..."

Sniffling, she rose to a standing position. *Okay, I love you.*

"Love you so much. Bye, Ladybug."

Taking a deep breath, she was ready to retreat to the Neptune when she collided into a body. It was Jayce, of course. "Sorry, I'm coming."

"Don't apologize," he tilted his head down, "you okay?"

With a weak smile, she nodded, "I will be."

Day 21
CHAPTER 11

I'm unsure how I know I am dreaming, but I can tell. It's like the space around me is fake, even if it holds an element of the truth. When I breathe, it tastes like perfume, which makes my tongue tingle.

"Lucid dreams. Fun, aren't they?"

"When I'm alone." I turned to see evil incarnate, Goddrick, standing there in my room. The sanctuary that was supposed to be mine on this ship. "What do you want?"

He was looking around then, taking in the sights. Remember, it's just a dream. He can't hurt me here.

"Are you warding me, Little Mouse?"

Narrowing my eyes and pulling my brows together, I scoffed, "Warding you? I don't wield Magic like that." My tone was harsh, nearly condescending. Goddrick knew that I held no incline in Magic, so why would he even insinuate it?

"Maybe you are doing it subconsciously," he took a step towards me, and instinctively, I took one back. "Do you know what you did to me? With that little trick of yours."

I laughed, "Trick?"

Goddrick's stare was fixed, intense, piercing me like daggers forged from malevolence. "Yes, dying intentionally and somehow pinning it on my little wrist slip."

"Slip —slip!!?? You broke my neck! All because you didn't get what you wanted!" My voice rose, and I feared I was screaming beyond the dream. The fear melted into terror as Goddrick was in front of me in an instant.

This is a dream; he can't hurt me here.

His gaze chilled me to the bone, and my body trembled under the pressure of it.

I could see the fury in his face, the eye twitch and flare of his nostrils. "What do you want, Goddrick?"

"Now that you have your memories back," *he turned from me and walked throughout the room, touching the furniture as he passed.* "I'm wondering if you are remembering everything."

Without hesitation, I responded, "I remember everything and am slowly seeing more of how much of a piece of shit you truly are. My decision to never give myself to you was the right choice."

He laughed, stretching his hand and pointing towards me, "You say that as if you weren't the one that sought me out, Little Mouse."

A laugh slipped past my lips, and I shook my head, "You're delusional."

"Am I?" *He sauntered back to me, his hand coming up and caressing my cheek. I could feel him as though he was there, which made an acidic taste creep up my throat.* "Or are you too traumatized to see? Shall I tell you the truth?"

His nails were sharp, pressing into my skin and threatening violence.

"You came to me that day. You turned my hourglass. You hated your life and begged me to take you from it." *My head was shaking, even though I didn't direct it.* "Oh, but it is true. You only want to remember your sister turning it because you want to be the hero deep down. You want to be the victim in your story."

My vision was blurring, and rage began to pour over it, "You are a fucking liar."

"Why wouldn't I have cursed your sister then?" *No, don't listen to him. He is lying.* "You hated your life. Your parents locked you away to help care for them and their needs, and you, poor Azahara, watched as everyone lived a life for themselves. You—" *Every part of my body tingled, and I was again on the precipice. I was going to go over the ledge.* "You were going to die unhappy, and you needed an escape."

"No. No." *I was shaking my head so hard that my eyes could not focus on Goddrick standing mere inches from me.*

"My power scared you, and you retreated, but it was too late. I couldn't let you go after seeing how miserable you were."

"No, no—no," I kept repeating it, kept saying the word, even as he spoke over me. "Stop it—"

"You play the victim so well." His hands came to both sides of my face, lifting me to his gaze. "I love it: my Dikos Mou, the manipulator. You have everyone wrapped around your finger." He bit his lip, making me want to vomit, "Oh, what we could do to this world if you would just give up this little charade. Hmm?"

I was so lost. I didn't know up from down. Good from evil.

"No—" I had no other words in my voice box. It was the only thing I could muster.

"Just know your little trick didn't work, and they believed me." He laughed, his hands squeezing at my face, "As if they would take the word of a mere human, deranged and seeking the power of Rah to annihilate this world." I panicked; every bit of my strength was gone, as fear took hold of my heart and tore it from my body. "Over their own kind."

"No—I don't—"

It's a dream...

I am dreaming; why am I afraid in my own head? Why did I care about what happened five hundred years ago? So what if they treated me like shit? So what if I wasn't happy then? I'm not happy now. Why did I care so much that I was used? It wasn't like I wasn't being used right now.

Who cared that Goddrick was back? It wasn't like I was ignorant enough to think he was truly dead and gone. Deep down, I knew they wouldn't reprimand him for what he did to me for five centuries.

He was going to hurt me regardless of whether I was afraid or not.

"Okay." I felt my voice strengthen, "Continue making me the victim," His façade broke ever so slightly, and I smiled without happiness, "Hurt me. I don't care. So-what if I was mistreated, so-what if I turned your hourglass, so-what if you weren't punished?"

Goddrick tilted his head, watching me, "Interesting."

"This isn't a memory where I have no control of the outcome. This is my head, present day, where even if you hurt me, I'll wake up safe." That wasn't necessarily true, and I knew it. Goddrick could be anywhere, anytime, but something kept him from physically coming for me. Was it possible I was putting wards around me without knowing it? Sure. How? I didn't have the answer to that question, not yet, at least.

He smiled, and it wasn't friendly, "When I come to punish you outside of your head, Little Mouse, please show me this resilience."

I knew my heart was beating rapidly against my chest. I felt my breathing pick up, but I had to stay strong.

"Because I want to break it, and Dikos Mou," His lips closed in on mine, and I felt his following words as they rolled from his tongue onto mine, "It's going to hurt."

She was upright in bed then, hyperventilating and gripping at the fabric of her frazzled black gown. Heart pounding and sweat dripping from her forehead, she fought to steady her breathing. The fear and anxiety still gripped her, even as strong as she had been in those last moments, making it difficult to distinguish whether she was awake or dreaming.

"Aza—"

Absolute terror ripped through her as she jerked her head to the side, eyes widened, and tears brimming them.

Only for her to see Jayce kneeling at the side of her bed, staring up at her. She felt her jaw trembling and swallowed the large lump that had gathered, keeping her from screaming in that moment.

"What..." She shook her head and wiped her eyes, clearing the fog and confirming that he genuinely was sitting there. "What are you doing here?"

Heat rose to her face as embarrassment flooded her entire being. "Was I—"

"No, you weren't screaming."

The surprise must have been lacing her expression because he immediately responded, "I felt your fear, and I came to check on you." She moved her hand down onto his, which was shaking, and he instantly held it. "I was going to try to wake you, but you just stopped fighting, and then you woke up."

She turned away, knowing the exact time he had found her. The flood of confidence she felt, the power to take her dream back, what if it had been because of him? Maybe she hadn't done it alone.

That thought didn't make her feel better; it only angered her deep down. Did she not have the power to fight for herself? Would she always be relying on the strength of others?

She would always be a failure to herself and to those around her. Illyan was wrong; she isn't strong.

"Azahara, what happened?" His voice was calming, filled with worry, and it felt like a lullaby trying to put her back to sleep, as if Magic was trying to put her back into the darkness.

"I don't want to talk about it," she responded flatly.

Jayce squeezed her hand, "Please..."

Speaking it would make it real, and she didn't want it to be. She wanted to play in the ignorance of her mind and forget it ever happened. Forget that she may have done this to herself.

Taking her hand from his, she slipped from the bed and walked towards the front door. Before her hand touched the knob, Jayce had her arm, pulling her backward. "Where are you going?" His tone was forceful, more so than she had ever heard before.

"To forget. Let me go."

"Aza, don't push me away." He was pleading, his lips forming a straight line and his eyes sinking, "Please."

"I'm not," His expression softened, but he didn't release her, "I don't want to push you away, Jayce, so please, don't make me." He took a deep breath and loosened his grip, allowing her to swing the door open and exit the room.

Alyse had mentioned that they would do another round of drinks with the newest supplies, and the music was still going. It meant that it was early in the night, and Azahara was thankful for it.

As she approached the hull where everyone was gathered, Xol stepped in front of her, halting her.

"Xol—excuse me." Azahara pulled her eyebrows together, "I'm... yes?"

At that moment, she thought she might have been still dreaming. "What are you doing?" Xol said, and Azahara nearly turned around and went back to bed. The voice was nothing like she had ever heard before. Clear of imperfection, as though not used and worn. It was beautiful and ultimately caught her off guard. Not just for the sound, but the fact that she finally spoke to her.

Her mouth slowly parted, and she finally said, "So you do speak."

"What are you doing?" Xol asked again, her eyes trailing down, taking in Azahara's appearance. "You are in your sleepwear."

Azahara narrowed her eyes, "Yes, good observation." The nightgown she had on was not the best for anything but sleeping in. It hugged her thighs and was held up only by thin straps, its fabric clinging to every curve of her body.

Xol, who was highly aggressive, stepped against her, "Go back and change at least."

Heat rose from her stomach straight to her face, "If you don't like it, don't look." That seemed to throw Xol off, and she took a step back.

"Azahara!" The joyful screech belonged to Alyse.

"How about I find out if anyone else has a problem with it?" Her anger was translating in her tone, and for the first time, she didn't care. "Alyse!" Calling to the Captain while still looking at Xol, she strolled around her, "Do you care if I'm in my jammies to drink with you?"

Azahara went down the few steps and saw nearly the entire crew, "Does anyone? —" Quickly, she raised her hand towards Zephyra, "Not you or Tillin; I don't care about your opinions."

There were bursts of laughter that came with her quip, and Alyse was there, her arms wrapping around her neck and squeezing her tightly. "No, who cares! Half of the crew gets naked in front of each other. Plus, you look amazing!" She had already been drinking, and Azahara was ready to be that drunk.

With fervor, she grabbed a tall green bottle, placed her lips at its opening, and threw her head back.

Immediately regretting the large gulp, she scowled, nearly spitting it right back out. "Oh my – what is this?!" The back of her hand was over her lips, trying to avoid vomiting immediately.

Another round of laughter, and she turned to see Alyse sheepishly rubbing the back of her head. "We can't necessarily afford the **best** ale here, okay?"

"Next stop, I'm getting us some better stuff. This is—" Taking another swig, which wasn't any better than the first, she grimaced. "This is fucking disgusting."

That was the last round of laughter before she started chugging bottle after bottle. She didn't even care about Xol or Jayce; her eyes were glued to the liquor, downing it straight, feeling it go into her belly, and then rising to her head.

It became her sole escape from thoughts of him. The idea of resorting to a drug for relief was something she despised, and she had dreaded this moment, fearing that losing Kaed would be too agonizing to bear. Yet, here she was, drinking not to find sleep, but to erase Goddrick from her mind, or more accurately, to vent her frustrations about him.

"Then, you know what he said. He said," she hiccupped, "'You are mine. If I must wait a millennium, then so be it.' How desperate can a god be?!" It wasn't funny then, and truthfully, it shouldn't ever be funny, but the liquor and the way she deepened her tone to mock the god had everyone bent over in laughter.

Spotting Jayce from the corner of her eye, she noticed he was not.

Azahara fell into step, telling everyone what Goddrick had done to her. How she had told him to fuck off and denied his advancements over and over for five hundred years. She was animated, drinking more as she spilled every detail of her life around that despicable god. Not **every** single detail, but close enough. She left things out like him taking her uterus like a toy she had outgrown, and other sensitive memories she never wanted to know herself.

"What a fucking prick. How can anyone worship those fucks—" Alyse slurred, leaning on Azahara, as if she wasn't also seeing three of everyone. "I hope he burns in Oblivion!"

Everyone cheered, and while Azahara did, she also tossed her middle finger straight into the air.

"Oblivion would be too good for you," she whispered, returning her fifth bottle before tossing it where the pile was stacked high.

She stumbled back as Alyse yelled at Darian to play music for them again. He had stopped to listen to Azahara ramble. Zayne also had a violin and joined in on creating lively, upbeat music for all of them to dance to.

Jayce was there, his hands on her arms, keeping her stable.

She leaned her head back, pressing it against his chest and staring at him. His expression was flat, and she wondered what he was thinking. "Hi." She spun, pulling her arms from his grip but not stepping away. "You going to drink with us, or scold me all night?"

Watching his throat bob, she raised an eyebrow, "Do I make you nervous, Jayce?"

"No," He sighed, "You don't."

"Good." Just as she was about to reach for another bottle, his hand swiftly moved down her arm, intertwining their fingers.

Every inch of her skin rose with bumps, and she gasped. "Do I?" His voice was captivating, completely enrapturing her. His other hand came around her back, resting it behind her neck and pulling her to him.

"Yes," she said breathlessly, and it made him let out a soft, feathery laugh. The heat in her face that the liquor had caused now tripled with his proximity to her.

He leaned down, his lips against her ear, "Good." As quickly as her body had filled with the sensation of him, it was ripped away. Jayce released her and stepped back. Her mouth was left open, and she cursed under her breath, feeling her stomach tightening.

She watched him through veiled eyes, a hint of mystery dancing in her gaze, and the corners of her lips uplifted ever so slightly. Whatever he saw turned his confidence in leaving her alone, to ash in the wind. It seemed like regret filled him, and she was determined to make him wallow in it.

Before he could gather his thoughts and return to her, she redirected her attention to Théodore, her voice laced with a playful tone, "Care for a dance?" He did not hesitate as he eagerly took her extended hand into his.

All things considered, Théodore was a great dance partner. While drunk, she would have had difficulty guiding them in rhythm, but thankfully, he could keep up. The music was upbeat, which made things a bit easier.

Poor Théodore, though. Alyse barely let him get through a single song before she was butting in and taking over. Tessa even joined them, welcoming the warmth between the two women. It would have been apparent then that she was comfortable with all bodies, the way her hands met every inch of Alyse and Tessa as they rolled their hips together.

When the songs would pause and move to a different beat, the three of them took a second to drink more, even if they genuinely didn't need it. Well, maybe the two of them didn't, but Azahara did. Flashes of the Idle Fox plagued her occasionally, and she'd find herself shaking away the memory and throwing back another drink to dismiss the pain.

She was proud of herself that she never shed a tear nor felt the burning sensation behind her eyes. It was likely due to the liquor, but still, she was grateful.

Xol, who she hadn't seen since trying to stop her from coming out in her jammies, stepped in between them.

Azahara raised an eyebrow, "Yes?"

"You are a fascinating creature."

"Did you just compliment me?" Azahara put an arm around her neck and grinned ear to ear, "Because it sounds like you did!"

A fit of laughter escaped Azahara, and Xol placed her hands against her hips. "I guess I did." There was little emotion, which heavily reminded her of Zhal. She couldn't shake the feeling that the strange affection that Xol was giving her was not out of lust. It felt like she was trying to protect her from an unknown threat.

Jayce had some issues with Xol, which she couldn't place. Even now, as Azahara tried to dance with the colorless woman, he burned his eyes at her.

Leaning closer to Xol, she slurred, "Why does my grumpy Jayce not like you, hmm?"

"He thinks I can't be trusted around you." She leaned closer to her, and she could see Jayce step toward them. "When it is he that I do not trust around you."

Azahara leaned her head back and grinned. "You both are so weird."

Somehow, that made Xol smile, "You have no idea, Little One."

Her drunken state prevented her from fully grasping the words, so she just nodded as if she understood every bit coming out of her mouth.

"May I?" Jayce was there, slipping his arm between them and forcefully dragging her to his chest.

Azahara let out a grumbly sound, "Guys, there is enough of me to go around. Please don't fight."

Xol pressed herself against the back of Azahara, "Don't test my resolve—"

"Xol." Jayce was quick to cut her off, "Don't."

"Mom and Dad are fighting again!" Azahara raised her voice and slipped her hand between Jayce's arm, snatching another bottle and bringing it to her lips. "I think they need to be the ones drinking."

Alyse and Théodore laughed and simultaneously agreed, "Here, here!"

Azahara looked up at Jayce; his hazel eyes were peering down at her. The lights of the lanterns flickered off his taupe skin, only accentuating his handsome features more.

After taking another drink, she handed the bottle to Jayce, and to her surprise, he downed the rest without even flinching. Her gaze traced a path of liquor down his chin, tempting her to lick it, but she mustered the strength to simply raise her hand and wipe it away with her thumb.

"I really dislike you," she told him as he placed the bottle down.

"I couldn't tell." He adjusted her to face him, one of his arms wrapping behind her back, the other resting against the side of her neck. "Can I ask what I did this time?"

Fighting a smile, Azahara placed her arms around his torso, "It isn't anything you can control, but," she groaned, "it's because you are so damn good-looking. It's frustrating."

That seemed to surprise him, and a chuckle slipped out. A throaty, deep one that made Azahara roll her eyes and put her forehead against his chest.

"You are one to talk," she bit down on her lip, feeling his hand pulling her closer to him, "the word perfection was created in **your** image, not the other way around." Her heart was in the sea then. Only moments now, and she would be dead.

Leaning back, she saw him looking down at her, "Dance with me?" Even if she didn't want to, how could she say no?

Giving a nod of approval, he stepped them into rhythm with the slower beat of the music. It flowed through them both, guiding them with an unspoken connection and allowing their bodies to do the talking.

For Azahara, everything but Jayce faded away in that moment. The violin notes wrapped around them, weaving a tapestry of emotions that enveloped her heart, and for a fleeting moment, she forgot where, and who she was. The outside world faded beyond the horizon, and she only wanted to escape with it. She knew well enough that the effects of the ale blanketed this moment. That the place beyond this, beyond Jayce, was out to cause her nothing but pain and suffering.

She felt his thumb pressing gently against her chin, lifting her gaze, "Stay here with me; don't fall into the darkness. Don't overthink. Just enjoy yourself." How could he sense her turmoil before it even settled?

The placid smile lingered on his lips, but hers curled downward, "How?"

Jayce shrugged, never looking away from her, "I can't answer that for you, but if you'll allow me, I'll help keep you here. Grounded." As if to make a joke, he lifted her off the ground and spun her, making her frown turn into a smile nearly instantly.

Her feet found the ship again, and she leaned her head into his hand, which shifted to hold her cheek. "Why?" She was now cursing the liquor that completely fogged her brain, making complete sentences nearly impossible to form.

It didn't matter; it seemed like Jayce was reading her mind, "Why do I care? Why am I here? It is so simple, but you want to make it complicated."

"Jayce—I, Kaed is—"

His thumb pressed against her lips, stopping her. "I'd never, ever, take what he gave you away. I don't think I could, even if I tried." Her body was no longer hers, and she felt elevated out of her skin, "I'm not asking you for anything. I want to keep you safe and happy. Whatever that makes me to you, I'm okay with."

Safe and happy...

Moving both arms around her, he embraced her. His fingers laced through her hair as he deepened his hold.

Her hands gripped his shirt, bringing herself closer, which seemed impossible. Every part of her brain told her that this was stupid. How could she ever be happy when she had hurt so many, including the one person she claimed to love beyond any other?

Yet, her heart wanted to embrace this unconditional care that Jayce was openly giving to her.

Closing her eyes and listening to the sound of his heart, she felt a calm wash over her. She hadn't needed to turn to the effects of liquor to bring her peace. It was right here, and she needed to allow him to help her.

"I can't guarantee that I will ever fully heal," she could feel his thumb brushing gently against her back, "but I don't want to be in pain forever, or, at least, not in it alone."

He took a deep breath, his head leaning in and burring into her shoulder, "If I could take all the pain away, I would." She tilted her forehead against him, "I would have died in his place for you."

Tears immediately filled her eyes, "Jayce..."

"I should have been down there, not Karver. If I had been, I could have protected you both. I have made too many mistakes..." His words in the Idle Fox echoed, *"I have so many regrets..."*

The liquor dragged her under so suddenly that it felt like an external force was trying to take her away. "No, don't say that." She was trying her hardest to fight it. "I wouldn't have wanted that."

The only person that should have died that day, was me. No one else should have to suffer for my life. Especially not you...

Feeling a solid surface behind her, she looked around for the first time since they started dancing. She was at the front door to her room, Jayce leaning over her, his face pained.

She sucked in a deep breath.

His hand cupped her cheek again, "I know you don't. Because you are kind. You only want what is best for everyone, but never yourself." That dragging feeling pulled her so hard that she needed the door to stay afloat.

"Go, sleep," his thumb brushed away, the tears still falling, "I'll be close if you have another nightmare."

"If I asked you to stay with me..." She was frustrated at herself for drinking so much, the neediness in her voice encompassing every drop.

His lips pressed together, "You would hate yourself in the morning."

One of her hands grabbed the door handle; the other, which had never released his shirt, gripped tighter.

"Ask me then..." His voice was husky, and it sent a buzz through her body. It wasn't just her heart that wanted him to stay, but an emptiness inside that begged him to fill it. Ever since she ran into him at the Idle Fox, that piece of her had been dying for him to fill its void.

The downward drag of her body and mind were too strong, and she was losing the battle, "Goodnight, Jayce."

He smiled and moved his hand from her cheek, "Goodnight, beautiful."

Day 21
Chapter 12
Jayce Latimer

"Jayce, wait!"

He took a deep breath, holding his position against the outer wall of her quarters, just around the corner. His heart thrashed around in his chest, threatening to give his position away.

He could hear her heart, too, even over her heavy breathing. Not only were her words calling to him, but her heart was yearning for him. He couldn't. It would only hurt her when she woke up and found them lying in bed together.

Even if every fiber of his being begged him to go to her.

"I hate myself either way." Her words were filled with remorse. By the Mother, he wanted to go to her. Wrap her back into his arms and protect her from everything that ailed her.

If she had gone running in search of him, he would have cracked and gone after her. Instead, with the resounding slam of her door, he was resolved in his decision.

It's for the best, but I promise I won't be far.

The following morning came quickly, and he was grateful that Azahara had slept soundlessly through the night.

When he felt the terror rip through her like a stampede, he couldn't stop himself from going to her. He had been firm about staying out of her room the times before when she had a nightmare, allowing her to pull herself from them, but last night, it broke him.

Thinking about it only put him into a sour mood, making his body tremble, and the veins in his arms surface.

Damn that god, he thought, gripping his hands into fists.

He was coming up the stairs, the sun carving out the horizon, when he noticed cascading hills on the port side. There had not been mention of docking anywhere, but he supposed he hadn't spoken with Alyse directly in days.

Noticing Rowlin standing at the helm, he approached with a friendly smile, "Morning, Rowlin," he signed, watching as the co-captain nodded in his direction. "Are we porting today?"

There was hesitation from Rowlin, but after a moment, he answered, "Yes, Itotaki is the small Island here. Since we can't stop until we get to Ilkiz, we wanted to stretch our legs and gather more goods. We should only be here for a few hours."

Nodding his gratitude, Jayce walked away.

Itotaki was a primarily port-based Island. Unlike Celadon, it was not tropical. Its high cliffs were lined with homes that spanned the entire length of the Island for as far as the eye could see. In the main docking area, there were several ships, unlike in Celadon, and shops and markets galore were stacked on top of each other. The beach was barely visible at the base of the cliffs; there would be no swimming there.

Hundreds of people were already out and about, which would suit his needs. In Celadon, he had to get a letter out to the King, but leaving Azahara alone nearly made him forget to close the letter and get it into the raven's claws.

It felt like the entire realm was after her, from that obsessive god to the King and the Fae Elder; he couldn't leave her alone. He wouldn't let any of them get their hands on her. Here, at least, with this many people, it would be near impossible for someone to grab her without making a fuss. Plus, all the way out here, they cared little for the politics on the mainland. Even if someone recognized her, they'd be more likely to try and swindle her into their bedroom before putting her in chains.

He would feel confident in allowing her to leave the ship while he took care of business and sent another letter to the King. Their separation would be minimal, and he'd get back to her within the hour.

After the events of last night, he needed to be careful. He came close to saying too much, and in the end, all that would have done was hurt her. Keeping her safe was his top priority; her knowing why and who he was did not make a difference to that objective.

Even if it pained him beyond belief.

Feeling the familiar tug, he stood and turned toward her door as it slowly opened. The wild, curly mop of hair covered her eyes, which, when he saw them, could tell they desired more sleep.

It made him smile, seeing her slightly dazed as though she didn't know where she was or how she had gotten there. She had at least changed from her black nightgown that nearly made him lose all restraint. Keeping his hands to himself was enough of a struggle. Watching her dance in said piece of clothing had him questioning his morals.

Adorned in a beautiful white silk dress that snaked against every perfect curve, she tiptoed around, peeking off to the side of her quarters' space. Was she looking for him?

She seemed frustrated, crossing her bare arms over her chest and throwing her head back. He didn't move, only observed her for a time. *How could anyone hurt you, my sweet girl?* With a deep breath, he turned his head just as she looked in his direction.

Hearing her huff and the pitter-patter of her bare feet against the wood made him need to fight back a smile.

"There you are," Her voice, while sleepy, made his body fight for ownership of itself, "Good morning."

He looked at her just as she made the few steps up to him, her lips pulled into a gentle smile.

"Good morning, how are you feeling?"

She brushed her fingers through her hair, trying to tame the beast atop her head. All Jayce could see was her breasts bouncing with the zero support she had under her dress. While he had been good not to stare at them, it was difficult not to see her nipples playing compass right at him.

"Good, no hangover again." She groaned, and it took him by surprise.

"You wanted a hangover?"

"Well, of course not, but I feel I deserve one for making an ass out of myself last night." Finally stopping her attempt at fixing her hair, she dropped her arms and sighed, "I'm sorry."

He narrowed his eyes, feeling oddly more confused by her apology than the prior comment. "For?"

She sunk her shoulders, and he fought his hands to remain at the ship's railing. "I tried to take you to bed last night, and I forced you to drink. Did I kiss you too, or was that in my dream?"

What I wouldn't have given... He thought before giving his answer. "That was in your dreams, but hey, you're dreaming of me now?" One of his hands moved to his hip, where he slouched, gave her a devilish smile and winked.

She was blushing from temple to temple, waking the dormant bees in his stomach.

"Now I'm thoroughly embarrassed." Her confession was not needed, he could tell by the way she was fidgeting with her fingers and pulling her gaze downward.

Again, his hands wanted a mind of their own; the urge to take her chin and lift her eyes to his was so strong he shoved his hands into his pants pockets. "Don't be. I had a great time. I'd say you did as well. I am sure Théodore will never forget last night."

She groaned louder and dropped her forehead to her crossed arms on the railing. As she mumbled, he moved closer to her. Not that he couldn't hear what she was saying, but for selfish reasons.

"Aza, I'm messing with you. Everyone had a wonderful time. They were happy that you joined, and while the circumstances of why you came out were not my favorite, I'm glad you did." He touched her back, gently brushing his thumb against her delicate skin.

She didn't pull away; he was thankful for it but knew to tread cautiously.

"Thanks," she turned her head to him, smiling, "for everything. Especially what you said last night. I remember, vaguely, most of it." He wasn't visibly tense, but his heart slowed a bit. "Kaed, he was—is—everything to me. I still can't accept that he is gone, and I've pushed everyone away because of it. Whether I think my reasoning is justified or not, I still do. I think..."

He waited, only watching as her face remained stoic. To have lost as much as she had, coupled with the torment that she had endured over the past five centuries, she embodied the term strength. The epitome of the word, and no one could take that away from her.

"I'm afraid someone will tell me it will all be okay. I'm not prepared to hear that because I won't be okay—not without him."

He only nodded, his hand never moving from her back.

"You don't expect me to be okay. You don't tell me it will be okay, because who knows if it will be." He watched her stand and step to him, her head had to crane to keep them looking at each other, and his willpower faltered. His hand rested at the side of her neck, and she sunk into it. "I do feel safe with you, and even if I don't think I deserve it, I find some happiness in the blank spaces of light you give me."

The pain he felt for not being honest about who he was to her tore at him. Here she was, pouring out her truth and expecting the same back. Knowing that it would only hurt her and would do her no good, he held his resolve.

A gentle smile crossed his lips, "That is all I want for you. To be safe and happy."

Her eyebrows pulled together ever so slightly. The gentle parting of her lips as though she were pondering what he said, beyond its most straightforward meaning.

From the first time he met her, all he had ever wanted was to keep her safe and happy. It was, and had always been, his sole purpose since meeting her.

After a moment of pause, she replied, "I know," her hand pressed against his at her neck, and the warmth filled him like drinking the sweet wine the Elves make, "Thank you. I hope I can give you a sliver of what you give me in time."

He wondered how long she thought he would wait. Would her eyes see a human with only fifty or so years to give her, or would she see that he would give a lifetime to her? He wanted to tell her he would be there for her forever. That time meant nothing to how deeply he cared, how he would eternally fight in this life and the next.

"Time is not a lot to ask for, so it is yours to have."

She was stretching up towards him, and he leaned forward for her to gently kiss his cheek. He loved to listen to those rosy lips spew profanity and watch them curl into a smile. They were everything, if not more, than what he imagined them to be.

He stood upright while gazing at her as she smiled ear to ear. "So, I didn't realize we were porting today. Will you be going to shore?"

"I need to take care of some business on board but will join you, maybe after you do your shopping."

There was mock pain across her face, and he couldn't help but laugh, "You think because I'm a woman, I'll go shopping?"

"Itotaki is a heavy shopping port of the group of Islands, where you could likely find anything. I imagine everyone on board will go shopping. Man and woman alike."

"I'm still going to take offense to that," she crossed her arms under her chest and pouted.

"I'll make it up to you," he said, brushing his arm against hers and leaning out over the railing, "or we can have a little fun."

A bright, eager smile crossed her lips, "I like the sound of that. Can I have both?"

A rumbling laugh rolled from his chest, "Greedy, hmm?" he watched her grin and nod, "Sure, I'll make it up to you. But for fun, let's have a little bet."

"Oh yes, what is the bet, and what are the winnings?"

"I bet you won't come back to this ship empty-handed," the way her mouth dropped immediately had him grinning just as wide as she had been moments ago, "and if I win, then you will *let* me win in chess while the entire crew watches."

The pain immediately ripped through his arm and surprised him, sending a resounding 'ouch' echoing down the ship.

"That's rude," she was squared up again, ready to punch him, when his hand came up and caught it. He pulled her to him, keeping her hand outstretched and watching for the other.

"So violent," watching her bite down on her lip, he had to take a deep breath to stifle his natural body's reactions to his attraction to her. *Holy fuck*, he cursed to himself. How could that simple action make him feel such a need that he would risk it all for this woman?

"Not that I think you'll win," he cleared his throat and spun her out, watching as she steadied herself and quickly turned back to him, "but what would you like if you win?"

"You underestimate me, Jayce Latimer."

"Never," he said confidently.

She must have seen his reaction to her biting her lip just moments before because she was about to do it again, but physically diverted to instead licking them, which was no better than the bite.

"I'd like a shoulder massage," He would give her that without having to win, and now he hoped that she did, "in front of Zephyra and Tillin. Who both seem to have a thing for you."

He narrowed his eyes and leaned towards her, "Do I sense... some jealousy?"

Anticipating the hand, he grabbed her wrist as she tried to slap him. "No!" Her voice was ill-confident, but he'd let it slide. "I don't do jealousy. But for whatever reason, both of them seem to hate my guts. So, just a little bit of a bite back without throwing them overboard."

"It's because you are beautiful," he confessed, and the shade of red she was turning made his heart skip a beat, "Sirens deal only in beauty, and Tillin finds yours to be given incorrectly to a human. While Zephyra, who has always felt she was the most beautiful on this ship, finds you a threat to that status."

"That crown goes to Alyse," she said sheepishly.

"I completely disagree," He released her hand and slid his thumb gently across her cheek.

"Okay, okay!" Making her flustered would become his favorite activity. "Do we have a deal?"

"You have yourself a deal, beautiful."

As if on cue, the crew emerged from below deck and swooped Azahara away from him. Not that he would have fought for possession. He needed to quickly finish his business and reorient himself before returning to her anyways.

Watching her stroll down the deck, he leaned against the railing, the corner of his lip tugged upward. She was turning her head to look back at him, and the notion that she was looking for **him** brought him pure, unfiltered joy.

Get yourself together, by the Mother, he scolded himself. He gave her a wave, and moved straight towards her room.

"First things first," he said, peering around before slipping inside. The smell of her hit him immediately, and he took a deep breath to soak it in. His eyes, the traitorous things they were, immediately soaked in her bed. He hated his restraint and the thought he could have been entangled in there with her all night.

It was for her; that was what he needed to continue reminding himself.

Karver, opening the winnox, he called out to his distant friend, *are you in a good place to speak?*

"Brother," he nearly instantly heard Karver come through his window, speaking directly to him. "*It is good to hear from you.*"

Same to you, how are you?

"*Oh, you know, taking care of this shit King of yours. How's your girl?*" Karver didn't even bother to ask how he was doing, which was rude. "*You better be caring for her, or so help me.*"

Overprotective as always of her, and here I am, the overbearing one. He groaned outwardly and shook his head. *Honestly, I don't know how to answer that. She's okay, at best. There is more going on than I could have imagined. However, I did figure out why she doesn't age... I nearly destroyed the fucking ship, Karver.*

While he went straight into the story of Goddrick and her curse, he was roaming around her room, picking up and looking at items that either belonged to her or didn't. From the photo, torn and mangled, of her at the Idle Fox five years before, to a scorched but intact patch. Everything had her scent, and it made concentrating difficult. Karver kept quiet for the most part, except when he got to the part about her dreams; that was when he lost it.

"*That piece of shit, and here I thought the King and the Elder were her biggest problem. Have you located him?*"

I've tried; any chance I can get. I'm moving through portal after portal to get a sense of his possible location. He isn't anywhere on this plane that I can find. I also don't want to leave her for too long. I'm really worried about her.

"*I know, brother, I am too. The battle was a mess. Thall was a means for Jaakobai to get closer to the King and gain his father's Magic.*"

Has he returned since my departure? Jayce moved to the bed and sat down, feeling the comfort below him and knowing this was where she struggled the most.

"Yes, only to look for updates from you. The King has been impatient."

He can lick my boot.

"As he should, but it's getting difficult to cover for you."

I know, a raven should be arriving today. It will inform him that we hit rough seas and had to redirect course. I indicated I was still determining our path but would update at the next port.

"Did you include any details about your girl?"

I did. Nothing of importance other than she hasn't been attempting to learn or use her powers. Which isn't necessarily false, but it holds no value.

"Do you know why she's going to Ilkiz?"

Not entirely, but it isn't to become the next Rah.

"We both knew that already." His voice was turning irritable, which Jayce understood.

It doesn't make it any easier. I should have killed them in that room and ended that part of her torment. He looked at his hand, a deep purple engulfing it.

"Jayce, relax. Don't be rash. You would have started a War with three of the four major powers."

For her, it would have been worth it. Jayce's tone was not to be challenged, even if Karver did attempt to.

"No, it wouldn't. Then you would be on the run, and they would still be after her. Think with your head, not with that damn soul of yours."

Karver—don't talk about my soul like you have any idea what it has been through.

"I can't imagine. However, if you want yours to survive and to find hers, be in the now."

He took a deep breath, settling himself. *I want you to send me Sunrise, please.*

"Coming your way," He had no hesitation. While Karver was annoying to his own fault, he truly cared about both him and Azahara.

To his left, a wëther portal opened, and flying through was a sword covered in a black matte sheath. *Got it, thank you.*

"Are you going to tell her?"

Soon. Holding the hilt, he pulled out the high-carbon steel blade he gifted her before the Battle of Sunfall. With an adored blue sapphire at its grip, it was a work of art, like she was.

There was silence, and in that time, he placed the sword near her bed, propped up at the base of the headboard. *I need to get going. I've got to get another raven out before catching up with my girl.*

"Keep me posted. We just got your first raven; the King is calling us to the war room. Talk later, brother. May the Mother protect you both."

For the Mother. Bye, Karver.

Closing the winnox tight, Jayce took one last look around the room to ensure everything was back in place and exited. He needed to hurry and get the raven out and find her. Talking about all the bad things that happened to her made his stomach turn, and the need to be with her that much stronger.

As he rushed down the dock, his eyes laser-focused towards the shops close to the port. There was no mistaking the curly red hair that stuck out like a sore thumb.

It only took him a moment to see that something was wrong. The crowd around her was parting, and she was backing away from something, or someone.

Every inch of him went into fight mode. Just as he was opening a portal to get to her, he heard her scream.

No... Not again...

And then came the explosion that rocked the port town, destroying everything within the vicinity of where she was standing. The sheer force of it sent a shockwave blast, sending him crashing into the side of the ship and straight into the water below.

Day 22
CHAPTER 13
PLEASE REFER TO THE TRIGGER WARNING NOTE

After watching Jayce disappear into the ship, Azahara redirected her attention to the crew that had forcibly separated her from him. Alyse, leading the charge, had practically threatened to have Xol physically hoist her onto her shoulder and carry her along if she resisted.

Azahara needed no further persuasion. Though she longed to linger and converse with Jayce, they had ample time for that. It was evident to both of them that he had no immediate plans to depart, and they still had at least twenty more days at sea before reaching Ilkiz. She didn't just want to know more about him; it was an insatiable need. Jayce remained a tantalizing enigma, and she was determined to unravel every facet during their time together.

Considering everything, she had a wonderful time with the crew, especially Tessa. They formed a close bond quite quickly, and Tessa reminded her a lot of Skyy, just with less attitude. Azahara had pleaded with Tessa not to let her purchase anything and to claim that Tessa had bought it for her if she found something. They both shared a laugh, knowing that, ultimately, it would ruin Jayce if he lost.

Théodore, Alyse, and Xol formed a group, searching for a better ale at Azahara's request. Meanwhile, Lucala, Carmen, and Zayne were stationed at the food stand, indulging in what appeared to be sweets. Zephyra, Darian, Tillin, and Yelena ventured further into town, spending their coins on more opulent clothing and goods.

Azahara and Tessa shared similar tastes, favoring secondhand items over newer, flashier ones.

"Do you think he'll like this one?" Tessa confided in Azahara, revealing her crush on Zayne and their past nights of enjoyment, which had never gone beyond that. Azahara assured her she wasn't an expert on love or relationships but offered her ears to listen.

"It's beautiful," Azahara remarked, gently tugging at the delicate lace shreds that left nothing to the imagination. "I'd like it."

Tessa smiled at her, "So, you like both men and women? Like Alyse?"

A small chuckle escaped her lips, "Not so linear; I enjoy everyone. If I'm attracted to them, then I pounce." She playfully jumped at Tessa, causing her to gasp and grab at her chest for support. They both let out a hearty laugh.

"What about you and Jayce? Is that a thing?" Tessa asked sheepishly.

"I'm not really in the market," Azahara said, picking up a piece of lingerie. She knew it was something she would typically purchase but instantly put it down to avoid temptation. "I recently lost the love of my life, and while Jayce is kind, caring, and beyond gorgeous—"

"Devastatingly. Dear lord, what does he eat?!"

"Right?" They groaned simultaneously.

"Though, I could say the same about you, Azahara. Whoever it was that blessed you must have favored you." Tessa placed the outfit back on the table and walked alongside her.

"I wouldn't say I'm blessed, but thank you," she sighed. Azahara wouldn't openly admit it, but whenever someone commented on her luck or being "blessed" in the looks department, she wondered if they realized it was equally a curse. She might never have become an obsession if she had been the ugly duckling. She'd just be an ordinary, run-of-the-mill human.

Sensing her compliment didn't have the effect she wanted, Tessa aimlessly picked up an item from the table. She continued, "The only reason I ask about Jayce," she cleared her throat, "is because... well, the way that he looks at you," her tone sheepish, peering over at Azahara, who was beginning to blush. "I wish someone would look at me like that."

Taking a breath of air through her nose, Azahara looked at the Neptune. The high cliffs of Itotaki granted a stunning view of the docks.

"I'd be lying if I say I didn't love the way he looks at me," she confessed.

"And the way he protects you, by the goddess, what I wouldn't give for someone to be possessive over me like that," Tessa cooed.

Safe and happy... She drew in a sharp breath.

"I cannot tell the future, but I do know that there is someone that lives for nothing more than to keep you safe and happy. Above all else." When she woke that morning, she remembered that Death had said those words.

Was Jayce that someone Death was speaking of?

"That is all I want for you. To be safe and happy." Those were his exact words.

Needing to extricate herself from her overthinking mind, she shook her head. "Yeah, doesn't make him any less overbearing at times though." Some would likely say the same about her. He remained extraordinarily patient, which continued to raise the question: Why? Was it truly because all he wanted to do was make her happy? To keep her safe? *How... why... I just... I just want to understand.*

Tessa chuckled. "Most men are, let's be honest."

That made her laugh; Tessa wasn't wrong.

"And," Tessa put her arm around her and drew out the word, "I'm sorry for your loss. I can't imagine." She placed her hand on Azahara's, smiling at her.

She was getting ready to tell her about Kaed, because while Jayce was incredible, so was he. That one day, a delusional part of herself hoped that he, too, could sail on the Neptune with everyone. She knew that Tessa would like him.

Amidst the bustling market, a voice reverberated around them, carrying a sense of dread. "I can't imagine either," it said.

It was an unimaginable feeling, the fear that immediately took over her. Rolling bumps began at the back of her neck and ran to her toes, as when she turned to see him physically standing before her, she nearly threw up.

"Holy smokes, speaking of painstakingly beautiful men—" Standing there, with a disgusting smirk across his face, was the being of her nightmares. As he took a step toward them, he utterly overwhelmed her senses. His sharp features were a stark reminder of how deadly he was to her, causing her body to tremble.

"Tessa, get behind me." Azahara placed a hand on Tessa, guiding her to stand behind her. "Goddrick..." The name on her tongue made her nauseous. He rolled his eyes back, visibly reveling in hearing it come from her tongue. His sharp jawline was set, and as he smiled at her, those slanted crimson eyes devoured any strength she had, rendering her utterly powerless.

"This feels like déjà vu, wouldn't you say? Or, at least, in your mind. We both have different memories of the day you came to me." Her breath was shallow, and she could feel Tessa trembling as she clutched her dress.

It was highly unusual for Goddrick to appear with an audience, which made her fear all the more palpable. He moved closer, and she extended her hand towards him while stepping herself and Tessa backward. Her skin began to glow, illuminating the space around them, the shoppers started to part. "Back off." Her shoulders angled towards him as if she were prepared to fight **a god.** "What do you want?"

A snarl contorted his face, devoid of any smile but filled with pure anger. "I'm collecting what is mine."

In a whirlwind of events, he surged towards her, seizing her wrist in a tight grip. Then came the explosion. Azahara barely had a moment to turn, witnessing Tessa's body disintegrate right before her horrified eyes.

The realization that the encroaching darkness had extended close enough to ensnare Tessa, and just as she had done to Thall, her body was obliterated. "No! Tessa!!" Her scream was so piercing that it caught in her throat. It caused the ground to shatter, and fragments of it to lift as though gravity had been removed.

Anger and pain, much like that fateful day, consumed her, setting off another explosion that unleashed a shockwave of raw power cascading across the entire port. The island quaked, causing the buildings to tremble and the cliffs to topple, sending them plummeting into the sea below.

Goddrick's laughter reverberated in her mind, and it was the last thing she heard before darkness completely enveloped her.

When Azahara awoke, there was no light, and she had to blink several times to confirm that her eyes were indeed open. It felt like she was blindfolded, though nothing obstructed her sight. It wasn't just her vision that had been stripped away, but all her other senses as well. There was no scent, no sensation of hot or cold, and she couldn't perceive anything beyond the hard metal encircling her wrists.

Her bare feet shuffled on the solid floor beneath her, and even though she couldn't feel the sensation, she knew she was standing. She jerked her shoulders, attempting to free her arms from above her head. Still, she couldn't discern whether she was pulling or just flailing around.

When she looked down at herself, it was as though she were a light in an abyss of darkness. The dress she had been wearing was gone, and her naked, bare body was exposed. Although there was no vibrating sensation, she could see her skin trembling.

Tessa... Seeing her beautiful face turn to ash in mere seconds sent pain straight through her body. The tightening around her lungs threatened to suffocate her, and she tried to kneel, but the chains that gripped her wrist had no give. *Did I do that to you? No, I would never have. I would have never hurt you like that.*

Tears streamed down her face, yet the numbness in her body offered no confirmation of their presence. As they fell and hit the floor, there was no sound of splashing or sobs in the void she stood in.

"Help..." No audible sound emerged from her throat despite her efforts to vocalize. Struggling to figure out how to speak, she tried again, and again, and again, but silence was all that met her attempts.

She couldn't even discern whether it was her voice that was gone, or her hearing. Inhaling a deep breath, she attempted a scream. Her chest strained as she unleashed a prolonged, intense cry. Still, there was no sound, but she felt the soreness in her throat, giving her hope that her hearing might have been the only thing lost due to the explosion.

Oh, Tessa...

Then, suddenly, she realized she wouldn't know if someone was present without her hearing and in the pitch-black surroundings. The space felt constricting, and she began to feel like she was suffocating, trapped as she had been in that crusher, teetering on the brink of becoming nothing but a lifeless heap.

Her perception of the world was akin to floating in a void without any sensory reference points. Her sense of self and connection to the external realm was becoming distorted and garmented.

All she had were her thoughts, which were the worst parts of her, and she would soon begin to drown in her sorrow.

Her eyes closed, though it didn't alter the world around her. She tried to manifest their faces, piecing together fragments of their features, needing them as an anchor to prevent her mind from spiraling into a whirlpool of thoughts. It was a way to avoid thinking how she might have just killed hundreds at the port, including Alyse and the crew she wanted to call family one day, or plunging into the depths of her past.

She fought against reliving Kaed's death and its ripple effect on her life. She pushed away thoughts about how it should have been her instead of Zhal, who had taken the axe.

And then, the most gut-wrenching one, the possibility that she might never see Jayce again.

"Not so strong now, are we?" His voice resonated in her mind, bypassing her ears. A shiver of terror coursed through her, and she screamed, though it was futile. "So confident behind your wards, but now that you're in my realm, you're just another Little Mouse."

Her eyes remained closed, refusing to open and confront the god standing before her. If death was imminent, she wanted her last image to be Tessa's face—those brown eyes brimming with love and innocence. She vowed to hold onto that memory and let it accompany her in her final moments.

"Don't worry that pretty little head of yours," his voice was low, full of desire and joy. "I'm not there for now. I just wanted to visit you and give you something to think about."

What do you want? She thought instead of speaking aloud.

"To punish you first."

Azahara put her head against her arm, baring her teeth and sobbing. *I didn't do that to you, and you know damn well I didn't!*

"But you did. You tested my resolve, and I broke, all because of that fucking Elf. Who, in the end, died anyways."

She couldn't feel her legs give out, but she didn't try to stand back up when she dropped and was hung entirely by the chains around her wrist.

"Did I hit a soft spot?" He was full of pride.

Another scream came from her, and while she still couldn't hear it, her body shook with trepidation and sheer force.

"I love it when you scream. I plan to have you do a lot more of that." His tone was unsettlingly joyful for the words he uttered. "I will be with you soon, but like I said, I wanted to give you something. Your full memory."

I don't want it. Take it all back.

"Oh no, my love, it is a little too late for that. Because I couldn't come back here after the year to wipe your memory, you now have to deal with the consequences you brought upon yourself." Though he wasn't physically there, she felt his presence as if he stood before her, reaching out and gripping her as if his burning fingers were made of fire, coiling around her mind, and squeezing.

It was painful, but not nearly close to what she would soon feel. "I pulled these memories, all seven hundred and forty-three of them, individually. I wanted you to come to me willingly, and if you remembered them, you would write them in your journals. Those damn journals you kept locked behind your wards would ruin any chance you would come to me."

The first memory came as clear as if it were happening right in front of her, his words becoming a commentary on what she was seeing. "I was not as patient as I had hoped. You were put on this world to tempt me, like the seductress you are."

His hands were on her, even as she fought. She had no strength to get him off of her, and she knew he wouldn't stop. This was not a dream she could pull herself from. No one was going to wake her before the breaking point.

Goddrick tore at her clothes, "I couldn't resist, you see."

He removed his clothes, and she watched herself run in the briefest moment of freedom she could get.

"The more you ran, the worse it was for you, but the better it was for me."

Even when she closed her eyes, the memory continued to play. It was no trick, because as Goddrick grabbed her and threw her to the ground, she could feel it. The dirt between her nails as she tried to pull away from him, the rocks digging into her skin. Then, she felt when he ripped open her legs, and without a single bit of remorse or hesitation, took her.

There was no stopping the vomit that crept up her throat and projected from her. Tears accompanied it, and she screamed over and over again. She was pulling at the restraints on her wrists as another memory flooded her mind.

It was as though she was living through hell again, watching as if it were on repeat. Him violating her until she was nothing more than trash for him to toss to the side.

"Enjoy your memories, Dikos Mou. I'll be with you soon."

Death, can you hear me, please...

Please... Illyan... Kaed... Sam... Jayce...

Jayce...

Anyone... Save me...

Day 23
Chapter 14

PLEASE REFER TO THE TRIGGER WARNING NOTE

When they speak of pain, they can't be talking about this. Her mind was shattering, unable to comprehend the words she wanted to say aloud. *There is no way a four-letter word can equate to this. This isn't pain.*

Slowly, her senses began to come back to her; first, it was her sense of smell, and she only knew it because the contents of her stomach were still splattered on the ground. Next, the sensation returned to her body, and she could feel the liquid dripping from her wrists as she desperately tried to escape her restraints. Then came her hearing, which she immediately wished she could take away.

Every memory had its own sounds attached to it. Then, she blacked out, unwilling to hear herself cry for help again. To listen with no salvation as he destroyed whatever peace she had.

When she regained consciousness, she was no longer standing, but lying on a bed. Her wrists were still bound, but now spread apart and taut against the headboard. As she struggled to pull on them, there was no give. Her feet were secured, but at least she was able to move them, allowing her to curl them nearly to her stomach and cross her ankles tightly.

The room remained silent, and though she couldn't explain how, she knew no one else was in there with her. The only sound she could hear was the thundering of her heart in her throat. Fear and anger caused it to race, both emotions vying to silence her.

That is all she wanted, for her to somehow die right then. She would beg Death to keep her, and release Kaed. Then, they could be together in the afterlife without pain and suffering. To forget all of this and leave this realm and its darkness behind.

"I cannot separate you from this realm," Death had said, and she knew there would be no convincing them. She would return to this hell even if she were to end her life.

"My love." His voice triggered a scream, and it wasn't a subdued one. She unleashed the full force of her rage and pain and had no intention of holding back.

"Yes, scream for me." Her arms strained, and she kicked, putting up a desperate fight against the inevitable. All her power, every last bit of it, was gone.

He came into view then, a filthy smile on his face. The blazing crimson sun in his eyes glowing in the darkened room sent terror through her.

"No one can hear you but me."

His words silenced her, and she felt her jaw trembling, tears streaming from her eyes again. The knowledge of what was about to happen sent shivers inching across her skin.

"It's been over a year since I've had you," he said through a sigh.

The way he spoke made her feel nauseous, and while she only managed to gag, she whimpered and pleaded for mercy. "Goddrick, please, don't do this…"

"Don't do what?" He took a single step toward her, and she shook uncontrollably, crying out in sobs.

"Don't touch me. I'll forgive you for everything you have ever done to me. I'll never speak of it. Just please don't—don't—" Every word was fractured, requiring fixing before she could form complete sentences. The bed trembled beneath her due to her overwhelming terror. As he continued his approach, she clenched her legs tightly together.

"I don't want your forgiveness," he came around to the side of the bed, and she immediately turned her body as far away from his as possible. "I haven't done anything wrong."

He sat beside her, his hand brushing against her cheek and down her neck. He dragged his nails down her naked body as he spoke, "You are mine. Mine to do whatever I want with. You agreed to that when you turned my hourglass over. You will remember in time. We have plenty of it." When his fingers traced over her breast, she clenched her teeth together so hard she swore they would break.

The opposite hand that wasn't creating invisible scars across her body, came to her neck and turned her to face him, "My immortal. My love."

She gritted her teeth, her voice trembling, "You don't love me. If you did, you wouldn't hurt me like this." Tears cascaded incessantly from her eyes, blurring her vision with each passing moment.

His facial features hardened, the lines of his face becoming pronounced, "And you claim to understand love? An Elf who prioritized duty above all else. A Fae who manipulates and lies. Is that your interpretation of love?"

Kaed loves me. Illyan loves me. That is true love. Not this. Not him.

"For a little sacrifice of your body, you could have been everything. Now, you are nothing." Leaning into her, he licked her lips, and she spat, which didn't deter him—he just continued smiling while releasing her face with a shove. "You will go down as someone who not only murdered thousands during the Battle of Sunfall," he was slipping his shirt off. She looked away, biting her lip to stifle another scream. "But also, for the deaths of hundreds at Itotaki. No one will come looking for you, Little Mouse."

If she hadn't already been consumed by hopelessness, now it overwhelmed her entirely.

"You won't be able to do any of that here. Those shackles were made specifically for our kind, including Death. You're nothing here, as you were nothing out there."

Fighting him would be useless, but there would be no way she would give in to him, even in the end; she was not his, no matter what he spewed. She shut her eyes tightly, yearning to be devoid of all sensation again. She longed for the comforting embrace of numbness, praying for it to envelop every fiber of her being, shielding her from the impending torment he was about to unleash.

"This time, I won't take the memory of me away from you," his hands gripped her knees, and with zero effort, he spread her legs. Immediately, she kicked him, her hips lifting to propel her feet straight into his jaw.

"Ow, you always have been a fighter." As suspected, he wasn't even fazed, and she uttered a weak scream of defeat.

His hands squeezed her thighs and spread her, while she screamed, "No, please!" Pulling at the restraints on her wrists, feeling them cut into her skin. The smell of copper filled her nose as blood ran down her arms.

She wanted to feel anything other than his fingers slipping between her, "Mm, you're not wet for me, don't worry—I can fix that."

"No! Goddrick, please! I'm begging you, don't!" There was nothing she could do but continue to pull and feel the slicing of the metal into her wrists.

Abruptly, a searing pain shot through her leg, causing her to halt her pulling and direct her gaze downward. The knife in his hand glided a perfectly straight line straight down her thigh, the blood pouring down and pooling between her and the sheets.

"No…" Her voice was weak and sounded like a mouse squeaking to be released from its trap.

"That bloody no is going to keep getting you in trouble," He pushed up against her, one of his hands gripping her neck and the other propping himself above her. "Tell me you want me, and I may be gentle."

A high-pitched noise rang in her ear as her vision blurred. She was nothing anymore—a doll to the puppeteer.

"You do want it rough then," he groaned.

"I hate you," she said, and it only fueled the smile on his lips. "I'm going to send you to Oblivion one day." Her voice was emotionless; her jaw trembled as she clenched her teeth.

"I love that you think you are ever getting out of here. I love that you have hope. I love that I will take it away from you." He broke through her then, and she disintegrated into the pain and sorrow each thrust brought.

He would never let her go.

"I love you," his voice was breathless. He tightened his grip on her neck, taking away the breath that would never belong to her again.

Nothing would ever belong to her again.

Azahara was gone.

Day 44
Chapter 15

PLEASE REFER TO THE TRIGGER WARNING NOTE

"I've come to terms with my sentencing," her voice was hollow, "he has been right all along." Azahara lay in a few inches of water in the middle of the darkened room that she had come to miss.

Death was crying for the first time, and she wondered if the water was from their tears. This beautiful creature shouldn't be sobbing, not because of her.

Death approached her, knelt, and placed their warm and inviting skeletal fingers against her face. "You have to fight," the sun in their eyes, fading as though it were setting over the horizon. "Please."

"I tried." Her tone was as lifeless as she was.

"You must try harder," Death leaned down and kissed her forehead. "Take all of my power, break through his hold on you. Do it, you must."

Azahara's own eyes were hazed over, the blues and reds muted. No vibrancy radiated from them now. "Do you know what he did to me when I fought back?"

Death leaned back; the pain on their face should have hurt her, but she felt nothing. "I tried to run. I tried to escape, but I couldn't see. I saw nothing. Then—" They grabbed her and tore her from the ground, placing her between them and the cloak that took hold. "He showed me."

The scream that erupted from Death was both powerful and enraged. It shook the void around them, and she knew that the underworld cried out in harmony with Death's pain.

"He showed me what he had done to me. The bruises, the cuts, the markings; he showed me just how weak I am. Then, he made me feel how powerless I was."

Around Death, she could see the sun's soft glow, and she reached out for it. The beautiful aura of its radiance was something she desired beyond life itself. She gently brushed the contours of her dearest friend's face with shaky fingers. "Light... It was your power that I thought was from the gods."

Death looked down at her, a face filled with sorrow and pain. "Death is never the end, which is why we provide the light. The light at the beginning of a new life. You are their light, and now I wish I had never given you a choice." Tears of gold streamed down their face. "I should have taken you when I had the chance. My love, my light."

"You gave me what no one ever did," feeling a soft tug on her heart, she knew she was being dragged back to her version of hell. "I thank you for it."

Another cry bellowed from Death as Azahara was torn away from the warmth of Purgatory and brought back to her reality.

"Fight, please. He is looking for you. The Fae. Fight for me, fight for him, if not for yourself." Death's final goodbye lingered in her ears as her eyes opened to darkness. Instead of the warm and inviting Purgatory welcoming her, it was her cold and desolate prison.

"Did you sleep well?" The bed shifted beneath her, and she attempted to swallow, but her mouth was too dry to complete such a simple action.

She lay there, motionless, feeling the sheets wrapped around one of her legs while the other hung limply off the edge. Lying on her stomach, she could smell the salt in the pillow, and she was surprised that she had enough liquid left in her body to even cry.

The bed moved again, and she heard footsteps. He circled around to the other side of her and knelt at the bed's edge. A sinister smile adorned his face as he spoke, "I'm talking to you."

Finding the strength, she shifted her gaze to his, "Yes."

Feeling a sting in her leg, she hissed through her teeth, "Yes, Deus Meus."

He visibly quivered joyfully as the knife he pressed into her leg slowly withdrew. Her disgust grew as he leaned over and licked the blood, leaving a trail down her leg that made her feel nauseated. The problem was she had nothing left to project. He hadn't fed or given her anything to drink since she arrived.

Death's words lingered in her mind, "Deus Meus..."

Goddrick moaned, "Yes?"

"I need to eat, please." Begging had never been in her plans. She had accepted that even if he fed her or gave her water, no power in the world could free her. But she knew Death would never give her false hope.

He ran his hand across her cheek, brushing her hair over her ear. "What do I get in return?"

Piece of shit— She stifled her comment to a thought before answering, "Anything." Her stomach turned, but there was nothing worse he could do to her that he hadn't already done.

The speed at which he turned her made her dizzy, and she had to close her eyes to avoid dry heaving. He was straddling her, his hand lifting her head up off the bed. Even before she began to wither, his body overpowered hers. Nearly twice her size, she felt like an ant under a boot.

"Anything?" She could only nod weakly, and he began with a small laugh that grew louder.

Her jaw trembled.

"How humiliating for you." His lips were on hers then, roughly breaking through the layers of her.

She hated the way he was beginning to taste *normal*.

How she could smell and taste herself on him.

She didn't fight, allowing him to have his moment before he pulled away and dropped her head. "Let's see if that holds true."

She released a shattered breath and sobbed a tearless cry.

Day 45

He still hadn't fed her, and after getting nothing in return for her sacrifice, she shut down. It had pleased him enough to leave her alone to suffer in silence.

She wasn't healing, which was all she had ever asked for. Her exterior mirrored the broken, battered, and beaten state she had struggled with for the past five centuries.

Looking up into the endless darkness, she searched for the hope Death had given her. She yearned to hear Sam reach out in her mind, or Illyan, whichever Fae Death had spoken of. She needed to hear them, for them to remind her she wasn't utterly alone in this world.

She thought of Jayce on numerous occasions. How she remembered every single detail from the night before she was taken, only playing dumb to see if he would lie to her. She thought about how much he cared for her and how, in time, she might have been able to let him in. Allow the missing piece of her to have him because it called out for it. Even if her heart still called to Kaed, he would have been okay with that.

Reaching weakly out towards the darkness, she begged for anyone to grab hold and pull her to safety. The sight of the wounds, bruises, and scars he had inflicted upon her shattered every fragment of her that had managed to hold on.

She should never have gotten off the ship.

She should have never accepted coming back when Death offered her the choice.

She should have never fallen in love with Kaed.

She should never have taken her sisters to that temple.

She should never have been brought into this world in the first place.

Sam...

Please...

I beg of you, save me...

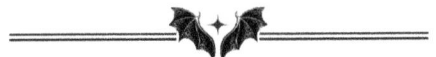

Day 47

"Dikos Mou," the scent of bread made her open her eyes, and the confirmation that it wasn't a trick of her senses filled her with unfiltered joy. Although she was physically too weak to show it, her eyes widened, and a broken laugh escaped her lips.

A tray of bread, fruits, cheese, and meats sat before her. Next to it, a glass of water.

Pathetic was the only word that she could think of to describe herself in that moment. It repeated in her head as she stared at the food, too afraid to reach for it, fearing that he would immediately toss it to the floor when she extended her hand to grab any part of it.

"What do you say?" Hate was not a strong enough word for how she felt toward him.

"Thank you, Deus Meus." He forced her to call him 'her god' and dragged her through hell to pull out the accent she had disregarded hundreds of years ago.

He stood, and she looked at him as if seeking confirmation.

"Eat." Pathetic.

Summoning the strength to sit up, she steadied her breathing and ate slowly. Everything tasted better than anything she had ever experienced before. The grapes were juicier, the bread was softer, and the cheese was fresh, nearly straight from the source.

When she took the water, it was challenging not to down the entire glass in a single gulp. She found the restraint and took sip after sip, putting it down to savor what would likely be her last meal and drink for another, however many days.

Time had no concept here, with no light source to determine day and night. Everything was one long, drawn-out day. She knew it had been weeks, with how she began to deteriorate.

Unable to heal, it had even caused her body to change. Her stomach was sunken, and her ordinarily full face felt like a skeleton. The bones in her wrists and collarbone were nearly protruding, and she wondered how Goddrick even found her attractive. She could think the only reason behind it was that he could heal her back anytime he wanted.

That was the next part of her plan, if she could even call it that. At this point, food was all she thought about. Even as he violated her, the thought of eating something filtered out his moans and her cries.

Halfway through the platter, she began to feel slightly better and was able to look at him. He watched her the entire time, and she had to swallow the lump in her throat.

"Yes?" He asked, and her back straightened.

Resolved in the knowledge that she had no other choice and that if she ever wanted to be free, she would need to endure further suffering, she uttered, "I'm sorry." Given how feeble and painful her voice sounded, she would have believed herself if she didn't know that she was lying.

He also seemed to feel the same, "Oh, and what for? Please, do tell."

"Everything," she took a quick drink of water, feeling the nausea rearing its head, "for not seeing that I was truly yours from the beginning."

"If you think I'm removing your restraints, you are wrong, Little Mouse." The shackles had never come off, but he had unclasped them from the bed. He complained that fucking her in the same place wouldn't do him justice.

Shaking her head, she dropped her gaze, "I don't want to leave."

Goddrick shifted back onto the bed, grabbed her ankle, and, with fervor, pulled her to him. Her legs dangled from the bed, her arms raised above her head. His crimson eyes bore down at her, an expression she couldn't place. She couldn't tell if he was angry or trying to read her.

"If you think—"

"I want you to bleed for me," his eyebrows pulled together as she cut him off, "like I've bled for you." His gaze was hardening, but the corner of his lips pulled into a grin.

"I'm listening," he brushed his hand against her cheek, feeling her tremble.

The manipulator.

Swallowing, she continued through shaky breaths, "I want to take you, and for you to bleed for me while I do." His hand rested on her neck, drawing his thumb across the contours of her jaw. "Deus Meus, please…"

"All it took was for me to feed you?" his tone echoed his doubt.

"All it took was for all of my hope to be taken away," tears filled her eyes. "No one will come for me, not because they can't, but because I'm a monster. I know that now. I'm alone, but at least I have you here." Nearly choking, she sobbed, feeling her words fill her with regret. They felt like truth, even to her, and she was hurt beyond belief. "I have only been lying to myself, and there has only ever been you."

He was kissing her then, just as rough as before. There would never be any gentleness with him, and that was okay. She wanted to hurt and never wanted to feel good because of him.

Her arms moved shakily over his neck, running one hand down his back and the other through his short hair. She felt him groan, and her mind went to a distant place. Instead of Goddrick wrapped around her, it was Kaed. His warmth embodied her, ready to please her before even thinking of his own pleasure.

When Goddrick flipped her on top of him, she wanted to keep her eyes closed, not to see the face that caused her so much misery. Except she knew that she needed to. She had to face this pain head-on to get through it.

His hand gripped her hair and pulled her back, and she used the moment to look at him. There was hunger in his eyes.

Blinking, she replaced the monster that tormented and destroyed her with Jayce. She envisioned the handsome smile that seemed to call to her, filling the emptiness inside her. She imagined how he would put his hand on her neck, protecting her forever from anyone trying to take her breath away, as if it were his to claim and no one else's to have.

"Sit," his voice demanded, and while her heart was ready to escape, she did as commanded. Her body shook in protest of the simplest actions, barely managing to stay upright. "See how much easier it is."

She nodded and adjusted her legs to sustain her posture. He hadn't moved her to take her, he only stared up at her. Equally, she looked back through veiled, heavy eyes. She was so tired, and her entire body ached. He knew how badly she hurt, and it only fueled him.

Moments passed until he presented the dagger he had been violating and cutting her with. Looking from the dagger to his eyes for confirmation for her to take it, she took it with a shaky hand. She gripped the hilt so tightly that her knuckles turned stark white.

She stared into the blade; the reflection that stared back was someone she barely recognized. The sunken eyes, bruised temples, swollen lips, and cut nose.

Then her eyes slid to Goddrick. His hands were gripping her hips, with a wide, wanting smile. "Tell me you love me," he was moving her back, and she knew what was about to happen. She took a deep breath and held it. "Then do with that as you please," he gestured to the blade, "after that, it is my turn to make you bleed."

She leaned forward, using her hand to prop herself against his chest. His skin under hers felt like fire, and she began to hate the sun. The warmth was not her friend, and she longed for the embrace of the icy river beside her home.

Biting her lip, she lifted the dagger, just as he simultaneously did to her. There was only pure sinister happiness on his face. He was getting what he wanted; why wouldn't he be happy?

"I love you, Goddrick," with strength she hadn't realized she'd been granted, she plunged the dagger deep into his chest, right where any heart would have been. He took her with equal force while letting out a pleased sound. Her body, with zero energy, fell onto him.

If he was nothing else, he was predictable.

His hand gripped her hair as the other ripped out the blade that protruded from him. Her face was shoved into the pooled blood, and without hesitation, she ran her tongue along the gash. That only sent him further into desire as his movements became more rapid, and she mentally checked out.

There was no guarantee that this would work; maybe she just signed her permanent contract with the god.

Anything was better than giving up.

Even if there was a sliver of a chance that she could see the light.

She would continue to suffer.

She needed to escape.

She needed to get back to them.

Day 48
Chapter 16
Jayce Latimer

"*Please tell me you have good news,*" Karver's voice was broken and angered.

I don't... I've scoured this entire planet, Karver. She's nowhere, and it makes no fucking sense. Jayce's tone was no better.

He was standing atop a snow-capped mountain. The wind was so strong at that height that most would have flown from its peak or died from the lack of oxygen. He was neither fazed, nor did it seem like he was concerned.

"*Brother, call me to come. Summon me, and I will join you in finding her.*" Karver was nearly on the verge of tears; he didn't need to see him to know that he was breaking down for his girl, "*It has been nearly—*"

I know how long it has been. Do you think I could forget? He hated that his tone was unforgiving. Karver didn't deserve it. He was just as concerned for Azahara as he was.

After the explosion that sent him into the sea, he recovered immediately, finding his place right where she had been in mere seconds. He had taken her right from under his nose. "*I do feel safe with you.*" were close to her last words to him, and he had failed to do the simplest thing: keep her away from that god, the King, and Jaakobai. That was all she wanted from him.

Xol confirmed that she— Jayce swallowed, incapable of even the thought of her being dead. Not again.

"*At least she's good for something. Fucking monster.*"

Stop! The mountains below him trembled, and he hadn't even uttered a word. *At this point, she's been the most significant help we have had.* It was true. While Xol held no Magic to traverse the world in a matter of seconds, she held the ability to speak with Death itself.

Death confirmed that they did meet with Azahara, but refused to tell her anything else. Xol... she looked into Death's eyes and saw a glimpse of her. If I couldn't pull the image from her myself, she wouldn't have told me.

He paused and heard Karver speak, but the words were indiscernible.

I nearly destroyed the ship.

"We will find her, Brother. I swear on my wings."

I know. I will never give up on her and I will kill that fucking god for what he has done to her. To my girl...

"Fuck—"

What, what's wrong?!

"I need to go. Your King is a piss rat. I'll check in later."

With that, Karver closed his end of the winnox, leaving Jayce in an unsettling silence. He couldn't find the peace he needed to stay calm, and the burning desire to bring Parádeisos down from the clouds to find her consumed him. The challenge lay in the fact that he knew she wasn't there.

He had no connections to the gods above, but their realm lay linear to Höwl, and he was old enough to know how to connect with it. It had been the first place he checked, and they were fortunate that he hadn't attempted a physical visit.

Taking a deep, resigned breath, he summoned a portal and stepped through it. The sun's warmth caressed his skin as the ship came into view. They hadn't departed from the port, not due to his request, but because of Alyse's unwavering orders. She refused to leave without Azahara despite the passage of nearly a month since she was taken from them.

A sickening feeling gnawed at his gut, forcing him down to his knees. He closed his eyes and buried his head in his hands. He had been trying to open the winnox to find her every day, nearly every hour. However, each time, he was met with an impenetrable wall. Whatever the god had done, it had entirely severed Azahara from him.

It didn't deter him from trying. He would never stop searching for her.

He took a deep breath and extended his mind, searching for her unique window—the one that unfailingly pulled his soul towards it. It was always there, no matter where she was, waiting, wrapped in vines and illuminated by a candle that could never be put out. Beyond the window, which always opened, he would find her bright smile, welcoming him home. Even if it was under the pseudonym—

"*Sam...*"

He stumbled through his mind, almost losing the connection to his winnox as she appeared at his window.

"*I can't see... am I here?*"

Sunshine... Hearing her voice flooded him with renewed hope, even in its broken state. She had found him.

"*Sam...*" A sob cracked in her voice, and he longed to reach out. He was going to get to her and protect her for all eternity. "*I need help...*"

I know, by the Mother, where are you?

"*I-I don't know. I can't see, even after healing enough to push through to your window, I can't see.*" The shudder in her voice broke his heart; she was absolutely terrified.

His teeth clenched, and his shoulders tensed. *I need you to see. I need you to break through whatever he has around you, even if it's only an inch.*

"*I'm... I'm trying...*"

I know you are baby girl. Take your time.

"*He...*" He was trying to reach through her mind. To take hold of her eyes and see for her. He only needed to see a glimpse of her surroundings. "*...Sam...*"

I'm here, and I'm not going anywhere. You stay with me, okay?

"*If this doesn't work—*"

It IS going to work.

"*—Can you tell Jayce and Illyan something for me?*"

This is going to work, damn it. Concentrate on seeing. Please—

"*Tell Illyan to release Kaed, so at least in death, I can see him.*"

Azahara, I'm going to get you out! His eyelids burned, feeling the onslaught of tears spilling from them. *I will come for you. Please don't give up.*

"*Tell Jayce I am thankful for him, if you can find him.*"

It was no use; she couldn't see, and neither could he. The god's ward was far too powerful. It blocked out absolutely everything. Not even his Magic could penetrate from the outside. It would have to be her. She would have to be the one to break through it.

"I don't blame you. It's okay," the defeat in her voice made the hold on his reality fracture and the gravity around him shift.

This isn't goodbye. I will never say goodbye to you. I would search for eternity for you, Azahara, but I won't need it. I'm getting you out now.

"He's coming back. I have to go—"

Do not break this connection! He nearly shouted through her window.

"...I do not want you to feel what he will do to me. I don't want you to feel my shame. I cannot let you see me like this..."

You are strong. You got to me now, don't –

"You don't know what I had to do to get this far! He is here, Sam. I never wanted to give up. I want to see him again..." She was breaking down; he could physically feel her body trembling and fear rapturing through her.

You will see Kaed again. I will make sure you do.

"...I want to see Jayce." A full-body chill ran through him, *"I want to tell him he isn't a bad—!"* The terror in her scream echoed through the winnox, cutting her short and ripping her away from his window.

The god knew, *Azahara?!*

He had no other choice. If they lost the connection, he feared what might happen. *Leave it open and look into his eyes, Sunshine. Let me see his face, and then I will come for you.*

There was only silence that followed, but he knew she was there; she was trying to save him from her pain.

Please, trust me. Let me see. Open your eyes. He gently caressed through her mind.

A moment passed. His heart was in his throat, silently begging her to trust in him, that he would come for her.

His girl did it, and as those crimson eyes came into view, he saw everything he needed to. When the perspective shifted, and her beautiful face was now captured in his view, that sense of calm he had from her turned to rage. That would be the last time she ever looked into his eyes, the last time she would ever feel fear and loneliness like that.

Jayce saw the space around them and knew exactly where he needed to be. Ripping open a wëther, he shot through the darkness, and without hesitation, went straight for the damned god.

His fist met Goddrick's jaw, sending him flying across the room with a rocketing sound wave. The boom from the impact, accompanied by the crash from his body, was music to Jayce's ears. Any mortal would have died from that alone, but as a god, Goddrick got to his feet and stood to his full height.

This was the first time Jayce had seen this piece of filth in person, and it filled him with even more anger and hatred. Standing nearly as tall as him, Goddrick was twice the size of Azahara. He took advantage of her as though she were cattle.

Massive wings expanded across the space, stretching outward and curling between the room. Goddrick's expression shifted, understanding what he was up against. While he may have known that a Fae was warding her, as Azahara had mentioned that night during her drunken slurs, he obviously had no idea just how strong Jayce was.

"You…" Goddrick covered himself in a black shadow and shifted his gaze away.

Jayce briefly looked to where Goddrick's eyes were to see them on Azahara, who was barely holding herself upright, leaning against the wall where he had her pinned just moments before. He shifted his black and midnight blue wing, reminiscent of a raven, in front of her, completely blocking her from his view.

"You will never lay as little as your filthy eyes on her again," his tone dripping with unmistakable venom.

Goddrick looked back at him, "If you leave this room, Little Mouse, I will destroy your world when they come for you."

Her soft weeping was enough to force his attack. Jayce reached out and gripped the very fabric of gravity around him. He watched as Goddrick's eyes widened in fear as Jayce obliterated the space nearest him into absolutely nothing, sending pure elation through Jayce's veins. It completely disintegrated the area, imploding the wall that brought in light from the area beyond it, leaving crystallized elements that represented the air and gravity that once housed that space in time.

Goddrick was gone, but Jayce knew his dyspoxii had saved him from turning into nothing but matter. He was ready to chase and fight until one of them was dead, when he felt a gentle tug on his wing. He glanced over and saw Azahara leaning into it, taking it, and wrapping it around her like a blanket. While Fae wings weren't ordinarily sensitive, having her touch them sent a sense of calm through him. She was his priority, not the god.

Plus, he couldn't take away the opportunity for her to destroy him herself. He would never leave her side, and Goddrick would never get to her again.

There was a choice: would he expose his identity to her or keep it a secret to protect her. Everything told him to show his face out of the darkness, but as she began to cry, he knew what she needed.

"...thank you..." her voice barely audible.

Gently, he lifted her frail body, which felt far too light, with his wing and slowly placed her outside the wëther. He knew the sun would be too much for her to bear and would give him a moment.

"Goddrick," Jayce said, tucking his wings back and stepping towards the portal. "Come for her, and I will destroy you. If I sense you lingering near her mind, I will rip Parádeisos right back down to this world in your name, just as it was thousands of years ago."

There was no response.

"I will only say this once." Jayce's voice dripped with seething rage and loathing. His hand shrouded in the element of Space as he took control of gravity, and with one step back, he collapsed the entire area around him into nothing but ash. The sound of cracking glass and pouring sand filtered through his senses.

"She is **mine**." And with that, the place that had been her prison was no more. A strange rush passed through him, a tingle of warmth caressing his soul.

His wings vanished instantly, his head swiveling frantically in search of her. She wasn't waiting at the wëther's entrance, and a shiver of fear coursed through him. The fear subsided when he spotted her standing with her back turned to him, gazing at the sea.

Reluctantly, he allowed his eyes to assess the damage Goddrick had inflicted upon her. He could discern each bone in her spine, visible from the nape of her neck down to her tailbone. Her skin bore the evidence of bruises, cuts so deep he could see her muscle, bite marks, and lashings, but it didn't stop there.

"Aza..." He didn't want to startle her, so he spoke softly, yet loud enough for her to hear from a distance. To his astonishment, she didn't even flinch. Instead, she turned slowly in his direction.

His shoulders slumped as he saw her sorrow, and he almost wept with her. The depth of her pain was something he never wished to witness again.

He stepped towards her, but she was already running to him. He couldn't fathom where she found the strength.

She never ceased to amaze him.

"Jayce!" Hearing her call for him felt like a comforting melody from the Mother herself. When his girl called for him, nothing would keep him from going to her.

He closed the gap between them and sank to his knees, enfolding her in his embrace. His arm gently enveloped her, careful not to squeeze too tightly. She clung to him, her grip solid and desperate, as if she feared he might vanish.

His other hand threaded through her tangled hair, his face nestled against the curve of her neck. Her arms encircled his neck, holding on for dear life, while her legs clung to him as if they were her lifeline.

Amidst her torrential tears, a gut-wrenching scream erupted from the depths of her soul, echoing through the air and carrying every ounce of her pain.

"I know," he whispered softly into her ear, "I know, I know..." Each cry out for him, he'd soothe her. "I know, baby, I have you."

His tears flowed silently down his cheeks, his hold on her unwavering. "I'm here," he assured her. He would let her scream and cry; she did not need to hold it back, not with him. "You are safe. I swear it."

She trembled so violently that he feared her bones might shatter under the weight of her anguish.

"I promise I'll never leave you again," he continued to comfort her.

When she drew in a shaky breath, her screams subsided, turning into steady sobs, until she fell into silence.

"I'm so sorry," he whispered against her tangled hair.

Azahara clung to him, the sun arching overhead as time passed. He knew it was time for them to return to the ship, where his wards would once again offer protection.

After a struggle to get his shirt off of himself and onto her, he gently lifted her into his arms. She curled her body toward him, her face nestled in the crook of his arm, never opening her eyes. He wished he could simply wëther them into her room to avoid dealing with the crew.

Before too short of a time had passed, he was crossing the dock and stepping onto the ramp towards the Neptune.

"Oh my god, Alyse!" Carmen's voice pierced the air as he began to ascend the ramp.

Everyone, except Tessa, had survived the explosion caused by Goddrick, and the aftermath was nothing short of chaos. He hadn't stayed to assist in the cleanup, but every time he returned, someone was discussing it. Predictably, Zephyra, who had the sharpest tongue, and was now standing between him and the Neptune.

"Get out of my way," he said, devoid of kindness.

"You cannot bring her onto this ship," while her words were strong, her fear poured through her shaking hands, "she is a threat to us."

Jayce narrowed his eyes, his nostrils flaring, "I will not repeat myself."

"Alyse said we would stay till she returned. She's back, and both of you can stay on this damn island for all I care." Zephyra didn't move, and Jayce felt his resolve failing.

He pulled Azahara closer to his body and was ready to mow her down when Théodore grabbed Zephyra by the arm and threw her aside. "Your little jealousy act is getting old, Zeph. Now, back off!"

With that, Jayce stepped on board, "Where is Alyse?"

"I'm here..." Alyse rushed to him, and she was evidently falling apart before laying eyes on Azahara. As she neared, tears streamed down her face, her hand resting on Azahara's bare leg, seeing only a fraction of the bruising marring her body.

Azahara's entire body quivered under her touch. She whispered in agony, "Stop, please—it burns—please—" Her voice was barely audible, even to him, as she shifted and turned deeper into his hold.

Jayce took a step back, breaking the contact. Alyse quickly retreated, her eyes widening into circles in response to Azahara's reaction.

"No..." it must have dawned on the Captain then what had happened.

Jayce dropped his gaze to Azahara, whose eyes were closed and who was feebly attempting to hide her face with her hand.

"Alyse!" It was Zephyra's sour mouth, "She killed Tessa and hundreds more! We have been lucky up to this point; don't risk everything your family built for someone you barely know!"

He just stepped around Alyse, who was now snarling at the Elf. "This is my ship, and my crew. I decide what is best!" she seethed through her clenched teeth.

"You will get us killed, and for what, because you find her attractive? Look at her now..."

It wasn't just Jayce that went cold. The entire ship dipped in ice, and Zephyra knew she had made a mistake. Everyone agreed with Alyse when she asked them to wait for Azahara. In some fashion, they all cared for the redhead who had just fought like hell to get back to them.

Azahara was awake and, to his surprise, had curled into an even smaller form. He locked eyes with Zephyra, who was now taking a step back, recognizing the gravity of her error.

"Get off my ship," Alyse spat, "and you too, Tillin."

The Siren hadn't spoken, but that didn't mean Alyse didn't have enough of a reason to throw him off, too.

"A-Alyse..." Zephyra was in disbelief, and that was enough for him to be happy about the decision. "I sailed with your grandfather—"

"Xol," Alyse called for her First Officer, who did not hesitate to grab the girl by the collar of her shirt and forcefully throw her off the ship.

Jayce was gently pulled away by Carmen, their onboard medic, who placed a reassuring hand on his arm. "Let me look at her, please." He didn't want to move Azahara, and she seemed reluctant to be separated from him. Still, he knew that allowing Carmen to assist her was the soundest action, aside from using his own Magic.

With a soft nod, he adjusted Azahara slightly, making it easier for the Elf to examine her. Carmen lifted the bottom of his shirt to assess her leg and ran her fingers across Azahara's body without making physical contact. Jayce felt a deep appreciation for Carmen in that moment; she understood the extent of what had been done to Azahara without needing to be told.

She leaned away and looked again at him, "It's bad. She needs to eat, and we need to get liquid into her right away. I can try to heal her wounds, but it will take time, and I will have to... you know."

Azahara swiftly hid back into him. Her cold hands against his skin felt like death itself. He wanted to take her away, heal her himself, and take away the memories of the past month.

With a nod, he turned away from everyone and, with Carmen in tow, walked to Azahara's room. It hadn't been touched since she was taken, and her scent of sweet honeydew still lingered.

He sat on the bed, her trembling body sinking into his lap, and he didn't have the heart to lay her down. She hadn't looked up at him yet, but by pressing her nails into his skin, he knew she was just as afraid to be let go.

"Jayce," Carmen closed the door and crossed the room to them, "you'll need to put her down. I know you don't want to, but…"

He didn't move or respond.

Carmen sucked air through her teeth and sighed heavily. "The shirt, too. I need to see the full extent of her injuries. If I go in blindly, I could do more harm than good."

He felt Azahara move and tilt her head back. Her darkened eyes and glazed-over expression made his breath shaky. She didn't need to say anything. He knew what she was telling him through her silence.

With a gentle nod, he shifted and put her down into the bed, laying her flat on her back and quickly moving to the other side. His hand captured hers as soon as he was situated beside her. The squeeze was that of a child, even if she tried to hold him tight.

Carmen stepped over and slipped the shirt over her first arm and then her head, and when it came to his side, he did the rest.

Nearly immediately, Carmen looked away and took a trembling breath. Jayce held her mismatched eyes as they stared blankly up at the ceiling. "You're safe," he ran his hand across her temple, wiping away the single fallen tear.

After a moment of gathering herself, Carmen came back.

The door opened, and Jayce glanced at Xol, who was stepping through. "What do you need?"

Carmen, leaning over Azahara, said, "I'm going to move you a bit, okay?"

Azahara didn't object, which was all Carmen would get for confirmation. Moving her leg over, Jayce peered down, seeing new and old cuts marring her thigh. It astounded him how she even managed to walk with how bad they were.

"Water and crackers. Just to start." Carmen said to Xol.

He moved his eyes to see Xol staring down at Azahara. The forever neutral creature faltered and pain pulled between the space between her eyebrows. "Is he dead?" She said, an echo in her voice reverberating in the small space. His eyes trailed to Carmen, who was heavily focused on pushing her Magic through to Azahara.

Jayce shook his head, his jaw setting as anger ripped through him.

Xol exited swiftly then, hastily making her way.

He returned his gaze down to her and rested his opposite hand against her cheek, turning her to look at him.

Caressing her sharp jawline, he watched her eyes slowly return from the haze. He could never understand how someone could hurt her, never like this. A breakup, accidentally knocking her over, or the death of a friend or family member was the only pain she should ever have to endure. Not this, absolutely anything but this.

As she looked at him, the tears stopped falling from her eyes. Her pupils focused on him as though she was coming from a darkened room to one filled with light. His thumb was gentle as it brushed against her cheek.

"I've got you," he whispered, and while she made no move to acknowledge, she hadn't needed to; her soul confirmed she knew. It had returned to her and was finally back where it belonged.

"Jayce..." Carmen called to him, and he shifted his gaze to her. She slowly closed Azahara's legs, pushing them together and shutting her eyes. "Can I speak with you outside?"

Feeling Azahara's hand squeeze, he was going to say no, but when the door re-opened with Xol and Alyse walking through, he conceded. "I'll be right back; you won't be alone." He slipped the sheet over her, covering everything but her face.

She didn't fight for him to stay, and when Xol sped to her, he passed her hand over, moved quickly around the bed, and headed out the door with Carmen.

"Make it quick, please," he said with haste as he closed the door.

"He—"

"I know," he cut her off.

"No, Jayce, you don't know." She lifted her hands, and they were shaking, "I tried to repair what he did to her, and it took every bit of my Magic nearly instantly. I didn't even get one of the cuts completely healed."

Somehow, that did not surprise him. The extent of the damage that he did to her, and that it was inflicted by a divine being, to that of a mere human. He was going to make sure that piece of shit suffered.

"That's not all," she hesitated, "I can't tell if it's new, but..." She explained then that the first thing she looks for in these situations is if she could be pregnant. With as long as she was gone for, it would not have surprised her. While no one has ever been known to birth a gods child, it didn't deter Carmen from checking.

She then went into detail that she detected no means for her to carry. "There is major scarring inside, and I don't think it's new, nor do I think it was done by... someone trained for that."

Jayce straightened his back, needing to find peace, or else he'd destroy the ship. "Okay..." *She loves the color green because it reminds her of home. Her favorite flowers are Oenothera because they only bloom at night. She bakes the best bread this realm will ever be graced with...*

Carmen continued, "I've healed victims of rape, but this is something else entirely. I'm unsure if it's because he is a god or the constant repeat abuse, but... I truly don't know if she will completely heal. There may be permanent damage." Everyone on board knew her affinity to self-heal through her drunken tirade. However, even with this knowledge, she still tried to bring what fraction of Azahara she could back to him.

Carmen's pain came through in her sigh, "Stay with her; just be by her side. She needs to eat and drink. I'm not sure how strong her healing is." He would give her the strength to heal. Secret be damned, he wouldn't allow her to suffer longer than she already had. "Even with all the Magic in the world, I don't know if she'll ever—"

Her voice cracked, and she let out a cough. She was trying to keep herself together.

"Thank you." He touched her arm for support and gave her a gentle nod.

"How could a god, someone that is supposed to protect its people, do something like this?" Her voice was shaky, and he understood her trepidation.

"I don't know, Carmen, but I need to get back to her. We can talk later. Go get some rest. Restore your Magic." He left her then and returned back to the room. Alyse had her face into the bed, sobbing, while Xol stood beside Azahara, still holding her hand.

Jayce didn't want to push anyone away from her, but he needed to try and get to her. For her to speak to him and find out where to help.

"Did she drink?" He asked, closing the door behind him.

"With help," Xol stated, "I'm going to fucking rip him apart."

He crossed the room, sitting beside her and resting his hand over the sheet on her leg. He slowly poured tiny bits of Magic through her. It would be nearly indiscernible, which would take a lot longer for her to heal, but at least it would speed up the process.

Alyse lifted her swollen eyes to Jayce, "Where did you find her?" She was barely able to form her question.

"She was on the beach, walking..." He watched for any reaction by Azahara, but she just lay there with her head tilted towards Xol. She had her eyes closed as if she were sleeping. He knew she was awake, embracing the peace she had fought so hard for. "A portal of some kind—" Xol tensed beside him, "opened, and I ran to it. Then, she was just...there."

Alyse choked and wiped her tears away, "Did she make it..."

"I don't know." He said quickly, not wanting to prolong his own lie.

Xol knew his truth, and she eyed him with both anger and understanding, translated through a soft nod. Her mouth moved, 'thank you.' Her blue eyes glossed over before they looked back at his redhead.

"Can I ask for you both to leave?" He understood why both of them were so close to Azahara. Alyse, who had bonded with the redhead nearly immediately on the dock, and Xol, who was only who she was because of her. The last thing he wanted was to push them away, but he needed her. Just her.

There was a moment of hesitation, but in the end, they both conceded. Xol told Alyse they needed to get moving, and that would be what they would focus on before coming back to check on her.

When they were alone, Jayce went to his knees beside the bed, her hand cupped between his, "Hear my voice," he watched as her eyes slowly opened, "I'm here. He will never get you again. I swear it."

She turned her head towards him, her hand shifting to try and hold his. The bruises on her face were so deep, so prominent, that he knew she could still feel the pain as if what caused them was still being inflicted on her.

"Where..." her voice cracked, struggling to speak, "is Sam?"

Jayce ran his thumb across her palm, "Who?"

Her eyes closed then, and a stream of tears rushed from them. He hated himself for not being honest with her.

"Thank you," she opened her eyes again and looked at him, "for finding me." The cut on her lip would sever if she smiled, but she attempted anyway.

"Always—" he was cut off by her broken sobs. Her body tried to turn towards him but failed. The frustration in her expression was evident, and as she tried to turn again, he didn't let her fall. He placed his hand on her hip and helped her to face him.

Her tears continued to cascade from her eyes. "Tell me what you need." His entire being called to take the pain for himself. Seeing her suffer tore him to pieces.

Feeling a chill against his cheek, he focused, now seeing her hand wiping away his tears. "You." Her hand moved down his face to behind his neck and tugged him. "Please…"

There was no hesitation. He shifted her gently and slipped under the sheets beside her. His arms took hold of her and brought her to his chest. The trembling that was a steady vibration of her body began to slowly reduce until it was just a mere twitch that would come from time to time.

Her head rested against his chest, arms tucked between them, seeking warmth and protection. She cried until silence flooded her and she fell into a deep, unhindered sleep. She was so still that he'd fear her dead if it weren't for her heartbeat.

His arm moved to the small of her back, pulling her closer to him, curving her body to his so he could warm her.

She needed to eat and drink. But Jayce knew that she would do what was best for her. If this was what she needed, then so be it. He could protect her like this, keep the memories at bay. Hold off the darkness that would try to take her from him.

Placing a gentle kiss on her forehead, he rested his head on the pillow, slowly moving Magic in fragments into her.

Oh Sunshine… I am so sorry.

Day 52
CHAPTER 17
Jayce Latimer

The mood on the ship had shifted with Azahara's return, but it would never be the same as before she was taken. Her affinity to bring others to her, both good and bad, astonished Jayce. Everyone onboard felt the weight of her pain, even if they had only known her for a few weeks. It was just a testament to how incredible of a person she was.

She was not pressured to come out of her room, even though he wished she would.

Since departing Itotaki, she hadn't stepped more than five feet from her bed, let alone outside, onto the deck. No one ever made her feel guilty, but it still brought a sense of dread to the already silent ship.

Anytime someone would go in and come out, there was a hope that she would be with them. It would take time; they all knew that. He ensured no one pressured her and they hadn't fought him on it.

Her healing, at least physically, began to slowly make progress. With his constant outpour of Magic and her self-healing, she was physically returning to the person she was before Goddrick took her. Mentally, that was a completely separate challenge.

Oddly enough, she would only speak when Jayce or Xol were in the room. Not even Alyse could get a word out of her, and he partially wondered if it was because Alyse was always crying when she was in the room. The rest of the crew minded little; they had made it clear they were just happy she was back home.

When Alyse had uttered those words to her, 'back home,' Azahara broke down and cried for nearly the rest of the evening. Alyse felt so bad that she about tossed herself overboard. Thankfully, Rowlin was quick to keep her from causing a scene.

There had been no judgment by Jayce for Alyse and even Rowlin when they would break down after coming from seeing her. They loved her unconditionally, and it was everything she deserved.

Hearing the gentle footsteps approaching him, he rolled his shoulders back and stood from the railing. "Hey, Jayce."

"Carmen," she had just come from seeing Azahara, sending Rowlin and Xol in next.

Giving him a nod, she leaned against the ship's railing, her forehead pressing against her arms, "She was whispering," his back went taut, "when she was sleeping."

He had made it a point to always be in the room now when she slept. The nightmares, Goddrick, they wouldn't get to her. He was moving around her, about to go into a full sprint, when she grabbed him, "Stop, let me talk to you first." Her grip was tight, and although he could have easily slipped through it and gone to her, he gave her a moment. "I can't—" she sighed, "I don't want her to hear, and this is the only time I can get you without you being with her."

"Go on," he said, stepping back to stand beside her.

"She's counting." Carmen turned to look at him, her face pained. "I can't say for certain what it means, but I fear I might have an idea. If that is the case, Jayce..." the pain in her voice was palpable.

Jayce pulled his brows together, allowing her the silence to gather her thoughts to form into words.

"It's... She's..." She took a deep breath, and he stepped closer.

"Carmen, just say it, it's fine."

She swallowed, and his stomach dropped as her heart began to speed nearly immediately, "She started counting at seven hundred and forty-three." He could hear her heart in his throat as if he were devouring it. "Given the time she was with him, even if it were every hour of the day—" she dropped her gaze, "she said she was five hundred years old? I suspect this was not the first time this happened."

He was shaking, "I left just after she broke eight hundred—" his abrupt departure cut her off.

Jayce was gone, crossing the hull and opening the door to see Xol and Rowlin sitting next to Azahara, who appeared to be sleeping.

Xol stood, "What is it?"

"Speak with Carmen, only you, Xol." She didn't take orders from him. They did not have that kind of relationship. However, the seriousness of his expression, coupled with the understanding he would never demand anything of her unless it had to do with Azahara, made her move towards the door.

Jayce grabbed her arm before she could walk out, "Keep calm, but I need you to know. I hate to say it, but I need you angrier."

"I don't think that is possible."

Jayce gazed down at her, "It is."

With a twitch of her eye, she exited. His attention turned to Rowlin, who quickly stood with the piercing gaze that Jayce gave him. "Can I have the room?" Rowlin watched him speak.

Signing, Rowlin responded, "What happened?"

Jayce shook his head, "For her sake, I'd rather keep it between as few people as possible."

Rowlin cared deeply for her, and it was apparent by how his hands trembled when he signed. "Is she okay?"

Jayce didn't know how to answer that question, truthfully. Looking at her, seemingly sleeping peacefully, he hoped she was. Only time would tell if she would be, and while he would give her everything to heal, there was no pressure for her to be okay.

Rowlin moved around the bed, and stood in front of him, "I saw you," there was confusion that hit his expression, "in Celadon. You sent a raven." Jayce didn't react but cursed himself for not being more careful. That explained why Rowlin had been so strange towards him when they arrived in Itotaki and throughout the past several weeks. "I want to believe that you are here to protect her. Please be honest with me. Are you really working for the King to bring her to him?"

"No," he placed his hand into Rowlin's and shared with him, in a series of images, who he was to Azahara. Seeing them for himself reminded him exactly why he was there and how strong he had to be so she would stay safe. "Please don't tell them. Not yet."

Rowlin pulled his hand away and looked up.

Jayce peered over to her, still asleep, and said aloud, "She is my everything. Always has been, and always will be."

It didn't take more than that for Rowlin to exit the room, and when the door closed, he crossed the room to her. He sat down at the side of the bed, his fingers brushing the head of red curls away from her face. Someone, likely Alyse, had taken a brush to it.

Touching her seemed to rouse her, watching as her eyes slowly opened to greet his.

The edge of her lip curled up ever so slightly, and she said, "Hi."

How do you have it in you to smile? He thought, placing his hand at the side of her neck, and smiling back at her. "Hi, I didn't mean to wake you. You can go back to sleep. I'll be right here."

"I know you will…"

Running his thumb across her jaw, he could see her coming back to life. The color in her skin was returning, those unique red freckles finding their rightful place across her face, and sea-colored eyes that the sun was invited to set upon were back to their original beauty. However, it could not mask the torment and pain she felt inside.

"How long was I gone?" She went to lean up, and he instinctively placed his hand behind her, assisting her to rest against the headboard.

"Twenty-six days," he went to move his hand away, only for her to take it into both of hers, gripping it tightly.

Her strength had returned, which he was thankful for. She had been a champ, eating and drinking when it was brought to her. Carmen would comment every moment she could about her strength, which would fall on deaf ears. Azahara would shut down anytime someone would talk of her strength.

While Jayce could argue to the contrary because she was the strongest person he knew, he never brought it up. Goddrick had stripped her of everything, making her feel weak, and she had begun to think that it was true after so long. Not only with Carmen's observations about her body but with him physically watching the damage heal itself, Goddrick was brutal towards her. It made him sick and only fueled his need to destroy him further.

"Seemed longer," she took a deep breath, sighing through her nose and looking down at their hands. "I had no sense of time. You could have said years, and I would have agreed without a second thought."

"We never stopped looking for you," she looked up at him but quickly returned to their hands.

"I... I thought..." her voice shook.

"I would have never stopped," he could feel her heart rate picking up, and he only wanted to shield her from the onslaught of pain.

"I thought I was never going to escape. There was one point I didn't want to. Not after he—" She squeezed her eyes tightly, and he could see the physical chill run down her body. He fought his arms to stay at his side. All he wanted to do was hold her, to protect her from the suffering.

She continued, "I had to do things I'll never forgive myself for," he closed his eyes, sensing the turmoil in her words, "but I'd do them again in a heartbeat, knowing the outcome."

Her head was against his chest then, and he didn't hesitate to wrap his arms around her, closing the gap that had been there. She mirrored him, lacing her fingers behind his back as best she could. His chin rested on her head, taking her in.

"Can you do me a favor?" he kissed her forehead instinctively, not thinking about it. When she gave him a gentle nod, he continued, "Talk with Carmen or Xol. Only when you are ready, though. No sooner." There was no rush where her healing was concerned.

"I can't talk with you?" His heart picked up, and he knew she could feel it under her temple. "It's a lot...but—"

"No, nothing is too much for me when it comes to you. I'll listen. I just don't want to be overbearing." It had been the term she used to describe him, and while Karver would agree, he still didn't see it.

The unthinkable happened then, and she let out a minuscule laugh.

"I'd rather talk to you," she lifted her head, peering through her long lashes up at him, "but I don't want it to be too much for you, and you leave because of it." His hand was gentle when it came to rest at the back of her head, his other arm pulling her up and closer to him. "I'm afraid that the only reason I feel even the slightest bit okay is because of you."

Tell her, by the Mother, she's strong enough. He fought with himself.

"I just want you to know that if it's ever too much, it's okay to tell me. It's okay to walk away. I'm okay—"

"Azahara, you are not okay." Her strong façade broke, and she looked up, her lip trembling, "And by the Mother, it is okay that you are not okay." He paused, looking between her eyes, "Tell me when you are ready, call to me when you need me. I will always come. Always. I am not going anywhere. I will be strong for you, so you don't have to be. I will be whatever you need me to be."

All he ever wanted was to be something for her. When he saw her again in the Idle Fox with Kaed, he found himself jealous. Even the Væragi made him feel that way, but the more he observed and felt her happiness, the more he wanted to just be a part of it, however small. Even if he were to have a sliver of what she gave to them, he would be okay with that.

Tears rolled down her cheeks, and he went to brush them, but she stopped him, "Don't." He reassured her with a smile before putting his hand back behind her. "You saw what he did to me." Once again, he nodded, allowing her to say what she needed, "He did the unthinkable to me, even before he took me away from you."

His vision was beginning to distort with red, and he knew that he needed to stay some semblance of calm, or else he would expose himself right then and there.

"Seven hundred and forty-three times." He was thankful Carmen had told him before, and while it did not make it any easier, at least he had already come to feel the anger that the number brought to him. "How…"

His fingers were gripping tightly at her gown.

Her strength for even being able to speak of it this soon knew no bounds.

"How do I move on…" Her voice broke as she sobbed inwardly, "How do I not see him on top of me?" Closing his eyes, he took a deep breath, wishing he had run after Goddrick and taken his head. "How do I not feel his hands on me?"

He ran his hand down her back, feeling her tremble, concluding that he would risk everything for his girl.

No answer would be the right one. The only one he had was that of time, and he knew that time had never been her friend. It hadn't been to either of them, but no more so than her. Her eyes were soft, but the expression lacing her lips was made of pain and sorrow.

With a deep breath, he pulled her back and placed his forehead to hers, "If you could take it all away, would you? Forget it all? It can never be undone, but would you want to forget?"

He wasn't sure he could pull that many memories from her; he didn't know if he could even erase the most recent ones, but he would try. He would try and do it if she wanted to forget, even if it took all of him. Every ounce of Magic he had would be hers. He would give her his wings to heal her inside and out if she only were to ask. Everything of his was hers, whether she knew that or not.

She shook her head, and the response surprised him so much that he leaned away and gazed down at her. "... I'm tired of people taking my life away."

He brushed a lock of hair behind her ear, "Tell me what you need, and it is yours."

With that same fiery resilience he had seen so many times before, she said, "Help me become powerful enough to kill that son of a bitch."

Day 60
CHAPTER 18

Despite her fear of stepping outside the sanctuary of her small room, Azahara knew she needed to get out of that space for the sake of her sanity. It had been twelve days since she had seen the sky, and the thought of leaving terrified her, but deep down, she understood that it was necessary for her well-being. She was safe onboard and Goddrick wouldn't be able to get to her, not here, not when *he* was watching over her.

It wasn't just she who wanted to see herself beyond the four walls. Every one of them had been trying to edge her out slowly. The one thing she was thankful for, was the people around her. How had she been so lucky to meet Alyse and her crew? Crazy to think that if she hadn't met her greater grandfather, where would she have been today?

Then there was Jayce, who, even then, was sitting at the end of her bed, flipping through a map and looking at where they were, and where they were heading. He hadn't left her side since she was brought back, save for the few instances where he stepped out for everyone else to have a moment with her. He hovered, but never more than she wanted.

Only once since escaping Goddrick had she dreamed, or thought of what had happened, and it was all because of him. He was keeping the memories at bay. He made everything better, and he expected absolutely nothing in return from her.

He and Kaed were so much alike in so many ways, but also different in others. It made her miss him beyond words, but was thankful that he hadn't been there. The knowledge that he would have been walking with her when Goddrick came for her tore her heart in two. Instead of Tessa, it would have been Kaed disappearing into Oblivion.

Her thoughts went to Tessa being ripped from this realm, and any beyond it. That thought made her hunch over and feel nauseous.

Not to her surprise, the map was on the floor, and Jayce was sitting beside her, "Hey, hey," his hand was on her arm, and she looked at it before meeting his gaze. "I'm here; what's wrong?"

Shaking her head softly, she leaned towards him, and he put his arms around her. He never advanced on her, only making a move when she would approach him. She never needed to ask; he just somehow knew. Everyone else struggled to see her cues and would reach for her when she didn't want it. Not him, never him.

"I was just thinking about Tessa." Her voice sounded pathetic, and she hated it. "How she..." When she closed her eyes, she saw her face disappear into ash, "I should blame him, but I know if it weren't for me, she would be here." She took an unsteady breath, "Instead of being..."

She slid closer, allowing him to completely pull her into his lap, his arms encircling around her shoulders, "Maybe Death can find her soul and bring it back." He comforted her, his forehead pressing against her head.

"From my understanding, once your soul has been obliterated, there is no coming back."

"Didn't you obliterate Thall? I thought his soul was waiting in Purgatory."

She nodded, "I did, but I told Death to allow me to destroy his soul separately. Tessa had no guidance to Purgatory. Obliteration comes instantaneously and doesn't give Death time to collect. She..." Feeling her hands tremble, she clasped them together, and Jayce held her tighter. "She was alone that moment in death, and without her carrier, her soul too, was obliterated."

The urge to begin breaking down was ready to wash over her like a tidal wave, but an overwhelming light filled her heart. As though her own soul was being comforted and it was healing before it had the opportunity to hurt.

Pulling away slightly to find him looking down at her, she found a frown etched onto his face. "I'm so—"

His eyes widened, and she pressed her lips into a tight line. Jayce never wanted her to apologize for anything that was out of her control. That was probably his most overbearing feature these days.

She only wanted to keep apologizing because she feared that her mental health would become too hard for him, and even though he was adamant about not leaving her, the thought still lingered. It was why going to sleep without him in the room was nearly impossible. Anytime he would leave, she would feel fear and wake. He somehow figured this out and stopped leaving when she would fall asleep.

With a resounding sigh, she leaned away, and he released her, "Can we go for a walk around the ship?"

Jayce didn't look surprised, just gave her that warm, handsome smile she was so afraid she'd never see again, "I think that is a great idea."

This was not a great idea, she immediately regretted the decision to leave her room the moment she stepped outside. It had nothing to do with the sun that bore down on her, or the heavy winds that came with venturing further East, it was the rushing of the crew towards her that sent a wave of anxiety throughout her.

Thankfully Xol, along with Jayce, was there to save her. They both stopped a rushing Zayne, Lucala, and Yelena. As they rarely went into her room, not because they didn't care, but more for their well-being, they were elated to see her outside. Théodore and Darian came up behind them, both equally exuberant and happy to see her. It was too much joy for her to take in. It didn't feel right, and it formed a pit in her stomach.

"Give the girl some room," Carmen said, with Alyse following right behind. They both had smiles but made sure to leave space for her to breathe. Rowlin came between them, looking between her and Jayce, before settling his gaze on her.

Rowlin had come to see her the most often, next to Alyse, Carmen, and obviously Jayce. He had been a bit weird, but she chalked it up to everything happening. Frankly, those that were acting normal to her felt worse.

As she waved at them, she moved to position herself behind Xol, her voice carrying a stern edge. "She just wants to take a peaceful walk. Can she have that?" Azahara was relieved her sharp tone wasn't directed at her.

With that, they dispersed. Jayce gently guided her to the ship's edge, ensuring she had the best view. Xol, true to her nature, followed behind them silently.

As far as the eye could see, there was nothing but the vast expanse of the sea. The scent of salt and the lingering sea life filled her senses. She had longed for this moment, yet it didn't have the effect she had hoped for.

Feeling the grooves under her nails as she dragged her finger along the ledge, she let out a frustrated sigh.

"It's okay to not be okay, remember that," Jayce said, placing his hand on the small of her back. "It will take time; don't rush your healing."

She desperately wanted to rush it. If she could snap her fingers and be back to who she was before, she would. She hated being this empty shell. Fear had become such a constant companion in her daily life. Even just thinking about it made her want to curl up into a ball in the dark and let the pain in.

When she would wake, she immediately looked for Jayce, who was always there. They had to cover the mirrors so she couldn't see herself because she feared what she would see, even if she was physically completely healed. Whenever she ate, she looked for approval or direction to do so. When anyone tried to touch her, that wasn't Jayce or Xol, she would recoil. When someone talked too loudly, she covered her ears, immediately taken back to Goddrick, demanding her to scream for him.

But the most dreadful of all was the word "no." The very idea of uttering it sent searing sensations across her skin, like blue embers of a flame.

"That no is going to keep getting you in trouble, Little Mouse. Say it again and I will carve it into your skin."

Her days were meticulous, making sure nothing triggered a response. It hurt to be so careful. Yet, the outcome of that caution had her here, walking outside and at least attempting to have a peaceful stroll.

Jayce knew at that moment what she needed and moved his hand from her back and found hers. Their fingers laced together, and he held on tight. She didn't realize his support would be so powerful, and the thought of him not showing up on this ship on whosoever's orders haunted her. The 'what if' of him not being here was another spiral she would find herself ready to fall into, but thankfully, he never let her.

"Already halfway around," Jayce remarked. She hadn't even noticed they had reached the helm, with the expansive view of the ship's front before them. "Would you like to keep going or head back?"

"Let's keep going," she said. As they resumed their walk, Jayce fell into step beside her. "Can I ask you something?"

"Of course," he replied without hesitation.

"When you... found me on the beach," she swallowed hard, not eager to revisit those memories but recognizing it was a part of healing, "what were you thinking?"

She had spoken a lot about her feelings, and Jayce graciously listened to her without ever bringing up how he was. While she asked, he would always direct his emotions and feelings to however she was doing. It was never about him and was instead, always about her.

A soft hum escaped his lips before he responded, "When I got to you, I knew I would never let you go again."

Her heart raced. "And you have kept to that." Her hand squeezed his.

"What about you—I couldn't believe you had it in you to run, but you did, right to me."

Returning to that moment, after being thrust out of the portal, she was assaulted by the sun. It blinded her, but that wasn't enough to keep her from running. Feeling the sand between her toes, and the feeling of fresh air hitting her skin, it made her open her eyes. While she couldn't see anything, it was not Goddrick; that was all that mattered.

Then she heard him call to her *Aza...*

"That I had to be the luckiest person," she looked down at the ground, but almost immediately, Jayce lifted her head and turned her gaze out to sea. Sealife leaped from the waves, splashing and sending sparkles through the air. "That you were there, and you hadn't forgotten about me. That I hadn't lost you too..."

Jayce let out a soft laugh, not out of humor that she had said something funny, "How could anyone forget you?"

"That is your takeaway?" She, too, laughed softly. It felt good; her chest seemed to loosen, and her heart fell back into a steady rhythm.

As he came to a halt, she mirrored his action. Gently, he placed his hands on her shoulders and guided her to face the sea that stretched out as far as the eye could see, its vibrant life dancing in perfect harmony with the ship. Standing behind her, he enveloped her with his arms, aligning his gaze with hers. He maintained a respectful distance, leaving a few inches between them, granting her a sense of freedom, unencumbered by any restraint.

"You won't lose me," he said, placing his chin against the top of her head.

"Kaed once said that to me," she felt that familiar sting in her eyes, "he actually said that to me so many times, and yet, here we are."

She felt Jayce nod and began to move when her hand rested on his. "Don't go, I didn't mean it that way..."

"I'm not going anywhere, your hair is in my mouth." She wasn't sure why, but that made her let out a full laugh. His hand slipped from hers, grazing down her head and moving it back quickly, but this time over hers. "That's better, it's not as delicious as it looks."

They shared a chuckle, and she leaned back slightly, signaling her invitation. He gladly accepted, moving closer to her. Together, they leaned forward, aligning their heads side by side, each supported by one of their arms.

"Kaed meant what he said because I can't imagine someone loving you as hard as he did and not meaning it." He watched her, ensuring she was okay with talking about him. She turned to him and nodded, wanting to hear it. "Karver told me how much love you both had for each other. That you both would have sacrificed the world for one another, he would not have left you willingly. No one would."

She felt a pain in her chest, and Jayce wrapped both arms around her, "If I were Kaed, I would not want you thinking I left you on purpose. I would want you to know I fought like hell to come home to you because you were the priority, above all else."

Looking at him then, he had a genuine smile, and while she felt the sorrow of losing Kaed all over again hit her like the waves against the ship, she returned one to him. "Thank you."

He nodded and placed a gentle, quick kiss on her temple. "Anything for you."

They stood there for some time, his arms keeping her cocooned and safe. There would be no stronger force to take her when he was around, and she truly felt that now. This was the safety she felt behind her wards before Jaakobai ruined that for her. She wasn't sure what Jayce would be to her at the end of all of this. She just knew that she wanted him to be there until the end.

She didn't know if she could give him what she gave Kaed, especially after everything that transpired with Goddrick. If there was enough love for her to give to him and Kaed because even in the end, her heart still had a place with him. For now though, she would do her best not to overthink it.

Jayce was here, and they were closing in on Ilkiz. That would be another chapter she would struggle to overcome because what was she even looking for? She had no idea what to do once they ported into the abandoned Ilkiz.

At that point, she would be drawing a line blindly, and without thinking, she sighed out loud in frustration.

"Do you want to go back inside?" Jayce leaned back from her, and she shrugged her shoulders. "This was an amazing first step, Aza."

"I know," she turned from the sea and looked up at him, worry in her expression, "I'm just not sure what to expect in Ilkiz, and I'm, of course, overthinking it." She watched his shoulders rise and fall with his soft laughter. **He** made her smile.

"The overthinker, and the overbearing one; I couldn't write it better myself." His arm snaked over her shoulders and pulled her back into step. "Let's start off with the easiest question, what do you want from going to Ilkiz."

Placing her head into the crook of his arm, she walked in stride with him, "Power." She felt his thumb rub gently against her arm.

"Good, so now, how do you get it?"

"That is the thing, I don't know—" While she had been so confident in her decision to go to Ilkiz, she never thought about what to do when she stepped foot onto it. In the darkest part of her mind, she wondered if she felt that she would never make it there.

"I think you'll find answers to what you're seeking at Ilkiz's Tomb." He said it so matter of fact that she didn't even react at first. When it registered, she leaned her head up and stared at him. "What, you think I wouldn't have done my research?"

She narrowed her eyes, "And you are just now sharing it with me?"

"Uh oh," he was beginning to slip away from her, but she pulled him back with force, "Don't hurt me. I'm fragile." He let out a gentle yelp when she pinched his side, his weak excuse of a plea not working on her.

"Tell me, Commander, or else."

Only when she heard Xol laugh did she remember that she had been following them this entire time. It seemed as though Jayce had also forgotten and turned to give the 'don't test me' look.

"Be nice." She whispered, placing her fingers again at his side.

"I know, I'm sorry." He pulled her closer and grabbed her hand for safe measure. "Many texts regarding Ilkiz have either been destroyed or locked away. They truly feared Dragons and felt that keeping their history would somehow bring them back."

"Could they?" She cut in, "Come back?"

Jayce took a deep breath, his fingers playing with hers before interlocking them, "I'm not sure. When a rogue Spirit Rider killed the King that ruled, which set off the War, there were thousands of them. They were gentle, unless provoked. They were a symbol of Power but utilized for keeping the Realm safe. It was Ilkiz's call, and they had been peaceful for nearly four thousand years.

"When Kuraiō, the Spirit Rider, was captured, he claimed his innocence. The problem was, thousands saw him riding Zuru, and destroying the Kings Keep. Or so says the written text. Ilkiz didn't want War, but she didn't want to see her kin and their Spirit Riders perish. So, she made the ultimate choice to wage War with the mortal realms." Not only did Jayce sigh, so did Xol, "We all know what happened in the end."

She felt Ilkiz's pain, she never wanted to fight either. All she ever wanted was to live in peace, to have her own life that belonged to her. "I can't believe that mere mortals could even win in a battle against Dragons."

Jayce let out a huff, "It's because the gods got involved, again, says the texts. These are all accounts likely rewritten over, and over, so take from them what you will."

Her lips pressed together, "Did the Fae fight with them?"

"They tried to stay neutral, at least in the beginning they did. They ultimately sided with the mortal realm."

"I see." She wondered if Helio had been a part of that, and—

"Getting back to what you need," Jayce cut in before she could get the thought out, "Ilkiz's Tomb, it maybe the best place to start. Maybe there are books written by Rah himself, or even her Spirit Riders, that could help."

She nodded, "We will start there then, and Jayce?"

He looked down just as she looked up, "I need you to promise me something, and I'm so fucking serious." She wasn't sure why, but whenever she used profanity, he fought the biggest smile. Like it was funny to him.

"I already know what you are going to say, so I promise." They came to a stop, right at her room.

"I'm still going to say it, so there are no misunderstandings," Turning to him she felt his hand coming up to rest at the side of her neck. "Do not, and I repeat, do anything stupid to get hurt. Don't be a hero. Don't die—" Tears had fallen so quickly, she hadn't even felt the heat in her eyes, nor the all too familiar stinging sensation that crossed over both cheeks.

Jayce was leaning in, his forehead pressing against hers, "I will **never** leave you. Ever. You are stuck with me. Until you no longer want me here."

"Ugh—"

"Xol, I swear to the Mother." Jayce straightened his back and glared at Xol.

They were about to start bantering, and honestly, she didn't want to stop them. This was the normal she wanted, not the inevitable depression that would come with her lying back in bed. Even if she felt exhausted, seeing the two of them about to go at each other's throat, brought her back to life.

Her eyes slipped from Xol to Jayce, *I'll never be able to thank you enough, and I trust you. I trust that when the time comes, we will be ready.*

Day 62
Chapter 19
Jayce Latimer

"Thank you for updating me, Brother," Karver was nothing but patient after Jayce had communicated that he had located her and brought her home. Finally able to provide him with some updates, Jayce spilled the last twelve days and his girl's progress.

"The King has been made aware of the incident in Itotaki and wants an update. I forged a letter that said that after deliberation, you guys decided to get back on track from Itotaki to Ilkiz. The only update in the letter about Azahara was that she was provoked and was claiming her innocence. Anything else would have held too much suspicion on you. I'll keep creating mock updates, at least for now. He makes me read them anyways, not that he'll catch on to the writing."

Do you think he is suspicious?

"I wouldn't say he is, but Jaakobai, that is another story. He nearly made the decision himself to send out his forces to find her when the news came of her destroying—"

It was Goddrick, not her, that destroyed Itotaki's port.

"Apologies, those were the reports, I know it wasn't her."

It's fine, Jayce had his arms wrapped around her then, she was sleeping soundlessly against his chest. *Please, continue.*

"He was only sedated by the King, surprisingly. I honestly don't know why Jaakobai would go through the trouble of an alliance with the King when he will likely betray him anyways."

The King is either too stupid to notice, or does, and is riding out the wave. Either way, they are both a threat to her.

"*Agreed.*" Karver paused momentarily, and Jayce knew he wanted to say more. Giving him a moment, he twirled a strand of Azahara's curly red hair between his fingers. The bounce when he released caused a smile to line his lips. "*I can sense her soul now.*" He finally continued.

I know. It's home.

"*Did that mean he had it this entire time?*"

I'm not sure, but the thought of that being the possibility hurts beyond belief. To think that was why I could never feel it this entire time... And why hers never... Even just the prospect of saying those words were painful. Though, it made sense, all of it.

"*Jayce,*" Karver's voice was pained, "*has she said anything about it?*"

No, I'm not sure if she has noticed. Humans don't normally have a physical connection with their souls like we do. He took a deep breath and released it softly. *It's strong, just like she is.*

"*I know, it's why I can feel it, even without the bond. Being locked up for five hundred years, I imagine it's just as pissed off as you and yours.*"

Jayce would help her understand just how truly strong she is. Even if it took years, hundreds, even thousands of them, she would come to realize how powerful both physically and mentally she is.

Karver must have taken his silence as ending the conversation regarding her soul, and reassured him, "*It's here now; that is what matters. We can protect it now.*"

His fingers brushed against her cheek, looking down at her perfect complexion and the freckles that lined from ear to ear across her face. Those plump lips were lightly parted, ready to spew words of both affirmation and profanity at any given second. A perfectly bridged nose that, when she scrunched it in frustration, only made him fall harder.

Even with her insides being scarred and battered, his girl was still a beautiful person. She fought so hard and would never stop fighting.

We will keep her protected while fighting beside her. After what he did to her, she won't allow herself to be the damsel in distress. As she did then, she will fight like hell, and we will not stand in her way.

"*Exactly, Brother, and—*"

"Sam?" Feeling a rippling sensation tug at the side of his mind, he immediately threw out Karver and closed his eyes.

"*Are you there?*" She was at his window, and a tinge of fear rippled through him, shooting bumps down his arms and legs. "*Don't hide from me, please.*"

Stifling an audible noise, he opened up and let her in. *Sunshine, I would never.*

It felt like she was trying to reach for him through his mind, to find him and see him, but she wouldn't be able to. He wouldn't allow her to, not yet. *I'm proud of you.* He said, knowing that she hadn't spoken with him since bringing her home.

"*You saved me, thank you...*" Her voice was broken, and he understood why. She wanted to know who Sam was. To thank him properly, not through the darkness she was seeing.

You did it and went through unimaginable things for me to get to you. I just showed up.

"*That is the thing, you showed up for me. I still don't understand why.*" When she confessed who Sam was to her, she observed him for his reaction. It was a similar look to the one that he had given her when he brought up Zephyra, watching for some sign of jealousy from her. Little did she know that it was impossible to be jealous of himself.

So many people want to keep you safe; you have no idea. I am merely one of them. He felt her shift in his arms. *I can protect you, so I will. I failed you in the moments that Goddrick took you, but never again. Never, ever, again.*

He wondered if she was awake then or at least coming to. Her hands were gripping tightly at his shirt, and her face was nuzzling against his chest as though she was hiding away from him.

"*Sam...*"

Yes, Sunshine?

"*I may not know why everything is happening the way it is, and sometimes that frustrates me. I want to know what I'm getting into. My life, I want to be in control of it for once.*" Her tone was mirroring pain, but he felt the strength that it held. "*I hope one day you'll come to me as you are. To be fully in my life, because, truthfully,*"

He hadn't expected to feel her soul reach out and touch his. The feeling was impossible to explain, but it was identical to being at the highest point in the realm, where the air was thin and crisp, and breathing it brought forth a sensation of exhilaration and awe. It was a profound warmth that ignited him, transcending all boundaries, and encompassing the intertwining of passion, compassion, and a connection that could never be broken.

It felt like **love.**

"I don't know all of you, but I know what love feels like, and I hope to be able to give it to you one day."

He needed his heart to slow. It was pulsing at a rate even he couldn't bring down. Everything felt hotter then, and he was both happy, and angered. Happy that the soul he was meant to have was finally back where it belonged. And angry at himself that he couldn't just tell her.

Swallowing, he looked down at her and took a deep breath. *One day, I promise you, I will give you everything that I am.*

Feeling her shift her leg across him, as if she was trying her hardest to get closer, she said, *"I have nothing but time, Sam. I trust you."*

She left then, and he adjusted her a bit. Her leg was wrapped around his hip, one arm draped across his chest and the other tucked between them. Her face was hidden, and he watched intently to see if she would wake.

She was still asleep, thankfully. He could tell by the rate of her heart and the subtle twitches of her hands when she would slip between the darkness of her mind to a mild dream.

It surprised him how in-tuned to Magic she was. Being able to open the winnox while she was sleeping was not an easy feat.

He turned to his side, wrapping his arm around her neck and with the other, brought her leg up and over his hip. With her arms tucked between them, he wrapped her in his embrace and tucked his head into the curve of her shoulder.

He felt her falling into a dream and drug out the onslaught of memories heading her direction. They were relentless, and he wondered if Goddrick had any hand in their frequency.

Having to see what he did when he pulled them from getting to her, was a test of his patience. She was going to destroy Goddrick one day, and he was going to help her. That was what she deserved; to have her revenge.

She deserved the world.

But nothing more than that god's head spiked upon the realm as a warning to the gods. No one would touch her, and if they dared, he would wage war upon them.

Day 65
CHAPTER 20

The feeling of hands on her shoulders, gently shaking, pulled her from the depths of her sleep. "Hmm?" Peeling her eyes open, she saw that it was Xol, instead of Jayce.

Not that she minded, Xol had been fine to have by her side, and she quite enjoyed her slightly more depressing presence at times.

"We are coming up on Ilkiz, Jayce asked me to grab you, so you don't miss it."

"He... asked you?" There was no hiding the shock in her tone.

Xol sighed and rolled her eyes, "Overbearing hunk of meat." Her hand was extended to Azahara then, giving assistance to her out of bed.

Swiftly donning an outfit more fitting than her nightgown, she gracefully exited the room accompanied by Xol. Without hesitation, she instinctively embraced herself, warding off the chill in the air.

A dense shroud of mist enveloped the deck, casting an icy ambiance. It cocooned her in a gentle, damp embrace, creating an ethereal blur and muting the rhythmic sounds of waves colliding with the ship. The moist air clung to her skin, eliciting a shiver as she felt the peculiar presence surrounding her. It wasn't ordinary fog; there was a mythical quality to it, an enigma that hung in the air.

This atmospheric shift was a stark contrast from the tropical weather of just days prior, leaving her contemplating the inexplicable transformation. As they strolled, Xol, with a thoughtful pause, retreated to her room and emerged with a blanket in tow, its soft drag echoing their footsteps.

"Thank you, Xol."

Azahara skillfully maneuvered through the dense fog veiling the ship's hull. Fortunately, her familiarity with the Neptune allowed her to navigate each step with confidence. Yet, the thick mist posed a challenge—how were they able to discern anything beyond it?

A subtle undercurrent of fear pricked at her stomach. How could they be certain they wouldn't encounter obstacles like abandoned ships or the port itself? Clutching the blanket tightly, she briskly moved across the ship's deck.

Soon, Jayce came into view, leaning over the edge and peering downward. Following suit were Alyse, Rowlin, and Théodore, each absorbed in their contemplation of the obscured depths.

Perhaps he had heard the pitter patter of her feet against the hull, because as she approached, Jayce leaned back with a smile on his face, extending his hand toward her. "Come see," he invited.

She took his hand, and he pulled her to the ledge while coming to stand behind her. He wrapped his arms around her, offering another comforting layer from the chilly air that surrounded them. "What are you guys—wow—"

When she looked down into the water below, she was immediately mesmerized by the ethereal spectacle before her. Bioluminescent lights danced across the surface and within its depth, casting an enchanting glow upon the waves. There was every color imaginable, from beautiful hues of gold and orange to vibrant blues and purples.

In the depths, she could see sea life shimmering and gliding through the illuminated currents, leaving trails of radiant magic in their wake. She could only imagine what it would look like at night. The breathtaking display of nature in this part of the world was a form of celestial artistry, which completely captivated her. There were creatures she had never seen before, and she wanted to swim with them. The urge to do so was so strong, and she couldn't quite place why. It was like the sea was calling her to jump in and embrace its magic.

Thankfully, Jayce had a very sturdy hold on her, so she wouldn't be going anywhere.

"This is—"

"Beautiful." Jayce finished, and she knew he wasn't talking about the water. When she gazed up at him, he was peering at her, not at the sea.

Hating that she couldn't stop smiling, she shook her head and looked back. The fog was too thick to see anything ahead, and she wondered if the water was what Jayce wanted her to see.

Feeling him lean down, his cheek brushing against hers, "The fog will break, at least that is what the map projects. Everything so far has followed it, so if it holds, then..." He turned his head, which caused her head to turn slightly from the pressure of his cheek against hers, "We should be breaking through right...now."

The fog parted as if it were a curtain, and the show was to begin. The ship cut through, exposing the beauty of the Isle of Ilkiz, home of what was once both the Spirit Riders and their great Dragons.

The Hydrox Port was a captivating sight. The harbor itself was a spectacle, adorned with magnificent dragon statues standing sentinel at the water's edge. The colossal creatures, crafted with meticulous detail, had their mouths open, which spewed forth cascades of water, transforming into majestic waterfalls that gracefully fell to the harbor's depths. The roaring sound of the rushing water added an enchanting ambiance, echoing through the air and casting a feeling as if they would come alive at any moment.

As the Neptune broke through the harbor, she could see more towering statues depicting the legendary Spirit Riders. Frozen in time, these larger-than-life figures captured the essence of a bygone era. With their stoic expressions and ethereal aura, they evoked a sense of mysticism and stories untold. Even the test of time stood no chance of taking the intricately carved statues down.

Amidst the grandeur, she couldn't help but feel the eerie undertone that permeated around her. As she expected, this once thriving city now lay abandoned, with dilapidated buildings standing as ghostly remnants of the forgotten times. The structures, now weathered and worn, bore witness to the passage of age of time and lack of mortal interference. Vines and ivy crawled up the walls, nature reclaiming its territory after thousands of years. She imagined it was the only reason these buildings still stood and hadn't fallen victim to time.

Azahara stepped away from Jayce, dropping the blanket and with a quickened pace, made her way to the ship's helm. Her arms pumping at her sides as she nearly sprinted. When she reached the furthest point of the deck she could, she stepped up, holding tightly to the rope, and watched in awe as the place where they would port, came into view.

At the end of the harbor, where the Neptune would soon find its place, towering gates commanded her attention. The colossal structure, reaching hundreds of feet into the sky, was a testament to the magnitude that was Ilkiz herself. Crafted with jade and black iron, these gates stood as guardians, both welcoming and daunting.

She couldn't help but feel a sense of anticipation and wonder as they began to slow. This place was calling to her as if Ilkiz herself were beyond that gate. It felt like when Helio's Magic called to her, but this was different, less abrasive. She didn't feel out of control; instead, the power felt more complimentary to her, enhancing her rather than being a mere desire to possess.

Hearing footsteps behind her, she peeked over her shoulder, seeing that Jayce was already standing near her, but Alyse, Rowlin, Xol, and Théodore were now coming up behind him. She looked back outward, taking in every piece of Ilkiz as it showed itself to her.

Alyse began talking with them about what they should do now that they were there, going over details about porting in an abandoned place, which was way over Azahara's head. She tuned out the details of how they'd do it, listening to the sounds beyond the ship. It was like she could hear a civilization of people, and it was as though this place was an island of ghosts.

"Jayce and I can go to shore, and make sure things are safe, then you guys can join us."

Turning nearly immediately, she saw Jayce with his arms crossed over his chest and a wry smile on his face.

Xol, who had commented, glared from him to Azahara, who was trying to keep her heart in her chest and not throw it up as she spoke, "I think you are missing *my* name in that line-up, Xol."

Her expression didn't shift, "No, I said Jayce and myself—"

"And me." Azahara jumped from her position at the head of the ship, Jayce stepping out of her way but watching to catch her if she slipped on the sleek deck.

With a low grumble in her throat, Xol shook her head. "Absolutely not. This ship is the safest place you can be—"

"Do not talk to me about where safety is for me!" Her voice was raised, and behind it, an echo shook the deck below them. Her eyes burned; the anger flooded her entire being, and she couldn't stop the tears brimming in them. "Nowhere is truly safe for me, Xol. Let me choose where I risk my life. Not you, not anyone."

Xol narrowed her eyes, but not with anger. She was reading her and quickly realized she would not back down, so she tore her gaze back to Jayce.

He was laughing, "You already know my feelings on that."

"Do tell..." Xol's tone was dull, and the snarl at her nose indicated she had already anticipated the answer.

Taking a step towards Azahara, he placed a reassuring hand on her back, "She's coming."

As she readied herself to disembark, she reached out to Illyan via the winnox. Their response was swift, almost instantaneous, and she immersed herself in the events of the past several weeks, deliberately avoiding the incident with Goddrick. She understood that revealing what had transpired would only prompt them to breach her defenses, determined to locate and retrieve her.

This was especially true if they told Zhal, and while she couldn't imagine her getting on a ship, she knew she would. There was also the fear that they would do something rash and try and find Goddrick themselves. They stood no chance against a god, and she didn't want to put them in unnecessary danger.

She told Illyan about Jayce and how he had helped her, making it easier for her not to fall into a dark place when they said there had been no changes with Kaed. She wondered how long she would keep him tethered to this realm, or did she have some sick hope that she could somehow save him and bring him back to her?

There wasn't much time to think about that, as both Xol and Jayce were ready to go and were just waiting on her. Bidding Illyan goodbye, she sent her love to them and Zhal and closed her window.

Dressed in pants for the first time since leaving the mainland, and a form-fitted long-sleeve shirt tucked into them, she stepped out of her room. Her hair was tied back into a rubber band, making her realize that her hair was actually starting to grow. Around her hip, loosely fitted to her, was the sword Jayce had given her for the Battle at Sunfall.

According to him, he'd brought it on board when he arrived, but wanted to wait for the best time to give it to her. When she finally saw it, it almost brought tears to her eyes. Not only because of the kindness behind the gesture but also because it reminded her of that significant day and how it had led her to where she was today.

In addition to that, she had one dagger laced around her thigh in its sheath and her long brown riding boots to round up her outfit.

Jayce was adorned with a black-on-black ensemble, with a longsword at his hip. Draped over his shoulders was a long, gray cloak that clasped over his chest. The shirt had a tie at its neckline, which was a shade of gold and had a star pendant hanging from the string.

When he saw her, he took one full look at her, and closed his eyes.

Xol smacked his arm, which caused him to startle and turn to her as if he was ready to hit her back.

"You did this on purpose," he said through his teeth, "you know I can't hit you."

"It was strategic," Relishing that she won in some game with Jayce, Xol smiled widely. "What can I say?"

"What was?" Azahara inquired, injecting a touch of humor into her tone. "Can I be in on the secret?" Her innocent expression, complete with a gentle smile, a tilted head, and fluttering eyelashes, caught both of them off guard.

They both became flustered nearly immediately, "Are you both going to secretly tell me that you are lovers and I've been the third wheel in this relationship?" She continued to stare at them expectantly.

Xol pointed at Jayce, and he blushed—*wait, did he blush?!* She couldn't believe her eyes, it almost felt unreal. His cheeks darkening was both cute and endearing. An unfiltered smile crossed her lips, and a feeling of almost normalcy took hold of her heart.

Jayce and Xol both saw it, which made them both relax.

He crossed the distance to her, taking her hands into his. He looked as if he was going to cry when he said, "No, you just..." One of his hands came to the side of her neck, resting it there as it is his way of showing affection towards her, "You look strong, and I couldn't be more proud of you."

"Same." Xol mirrored, "I just don't get hard—"

Azahara swore the gravity around them dropped, and things became heavier. Jayce had his eyes on Xol, and any moment now, they would pull their swords out on one another.

"Why must you ruin this for me?" Jayce grumbled, though his tone was playful.

Azahara laughed gently, "Let's go before you guys destroy Alyse's poor ship." *And they worry about me...* she commented to herself, "Sheesh."

Day 65
CHAPTER 21
Jayce Latimer

While leaving the ship, Alyse had nearly got on her knees to plead with him to keep his eyes on Azahara, even though the redhead was right beside him scolding her for completely disregarding her as being present. He understood Alyse's concern and nodded in agreement, assuring her that he would always keep Azahara close. With Xol present, he felt confident that everything would be alright.

It wasn't like they would run into a Dragon.

He would be lying to himself if he said he didn't love watching Azahara be in awe of every new place she stepped foot in. From Celadon, when she dove down to see the reefs, to watching the bioluminescent waters of Ilkiz, when her face lit up, he found peace.

He wanted to show her the world, allow her to heal without his Magic being poured into her constantly. She could, in time, learn to live with the horrors that Goddrick had put her through. Maybe after everything was safe for her, he would suggest it. He wouldn't mind asking Alyse to sail around the world, get Kaed, Illyan, and Zhal for her, and show her the wonders beyond the realms she knew.

Never had he thought about that before, but with her, he could see that being a possibility. How soon that dream could be a reality was likely far out, but it seemed they both had plenty of time.

"I think he's daydreaming," Xol's voice barely cut through the haze of his thoughts.

"I've called him like five times," Azahara whispered.

"I can hit him if you would like," He groaned.

"I can do that, too, Xol. It's fine."

Shaking his head, he looked down at Azahara, who was staring up at him with worry in her eyes.

"I'm sorry," he said while watching Xol roll her eyes and refocus forward. Azahara was looking between them but came to focus on him. "Did you say something?"

Azahara stepped to him, "I was just asking what else you knew about this place, and Xol commented that you had firsthand experience."

He was going to kill her.

"How would that be possible?" He asked flatly, staring at the uncolored woman. If she didn't watch it, he would expose exactly who—no, better yet, **what** she is.

Suppose that wouldn't end very well for either of them, and the only one that would be left in the crossfire would be Azahara. She would be the only one hurt by the revelation of who they were.

Still, what a stupid thing to say, putting a target on his head like that.

Xol didn't turn to look when she commented, "From your studies, of course."

Azahara seemed to lower her head, thinking about something.

"We can talk about it later," she said, surprising him and even Xol, who turned and looked at her. "I think we should focus. I'm not sure if it's just me, but I've been hearing things since we came into the harbor."

"And you are just saying something now?" Xol wasn't necessarily angry, and to his surprise, she kept her tone down. Remembering that raising their voice at Azahara triggered a response, he was thankful for her restraint. They both shared hatred for the god that caused her so much torment. Imagining anyone yelling at his girl made him sick.

Xol had her hand on the hilt of her sword.

He didn't say anything, just looked at Azahara, who was coming to a halt. Before them were the large gates that hadn't opened or closed in thousands of years. The elements had reminded the fine onyx metal of who truly had possession of the realm. They still looked sturdy, even to this day, and it truly surprised him.

Watching her, she turned in a full circle, looking up in wonder. "It sounds like civilization is still alive, but it's underwater. Like, they are talking to me, but the sound is muffled."

He didn't hear anything, and one look at Xol confirmed the same was for her. That didn't mean Azahara wasn't, but it made whatever it was a little too mysterious for his liking.

The sound of crackling fire was what he heard before Azahara was moving, even his eyes couldn't capture it, she was so fast. *She can use the dyspoxii?* He thought quickly, not realizing she had that ability from the gods. The flames cascaded over him and Xol as if being redirected from nearly smacking them in the back.

It was Azahara, her body glowing like the sun itself, fighting off **fire**.

His sword was pulled from the sheath, just as Xol did hers. When they turned to stand beside Azahara, before them, stepping from the smoke, two figures approached.

"Looks like we have some visitors, brother," a female voice spoke, flames bouncing between her palms. His eyes widened, and immediately he stepped between them and Azahara.

"Wait, please, we don't want to fight you," Jayce placed his hand onto Azahara, and she looked up at him, "It's fine, they are—"

Before he could finish his sentence, a blast of fire was thrown at him, slapping him in the arm and sending him down to his knee. His cloak seared and he tore at it, ripping it off completely as the flames burst and consumed it. The fire was a mixture of blue and red, and when the blue flickered, the heat was nearly unbearable.

"Shit—Azahara!" He didn't care about himself, but he saw the look in her eyes. "Stop!"

Her body was gone then, as if it had just disappeared, and instantly reappeared behind the girl. With a resounding smack, the fire wielder flew past Xol, crashing into a barely standing building. It instantly crumbled to pieces, flattening her under it.

"Kaen!" The boy screamed, and when Jayce turned towards them, he had water wrapping around Azahara.

Xol was rushing towards her, but he needed to get things under control before she killed them. He turned towards the wrecked building, seeing that there was rumbling underneath, he stood and rushed towards it.

Day 65
CHAPTER 22

"You've made a terrible mistake," Her voice was taut, and even as the water surrounded her, she felt nothing but pure rage. The boy that stood before her had almond-shaped hooded eyes, straight silky-black hair, strong sharp contoured cheeks, and an angered expression across his lips.

With a clap of his hands, the water encapsulated her, and all oxygen was cut off from within its dome. A crazed feeling rose within her then; it was nearly as strong as it was when she obliterated Thall. Seeing that woman attack Jayce, she felt the need to cause pain and destruction, and there was no sedating it.

Xol was rushing towards the boy, but he opened his arms and sent a rocket of water into her, sending her flying upward.

Azahara closed her eyes, and unlike anything she had done before, light erupted from her, swirling and evaporating the water around her. The intense heat from the light dried her instantly. With anger evident in the snarl across her face, she felt the heat gathering in her palm as she charged at the boy.

His hand raised, and another spout of water came towards her, but this time, in the shape of a Dragon. Its serpent-like body charging, its large jaw opening and coming down over her. As though it was going to devour her.

As she raised her hand, her eyes met the beasts, not understanding the pull to do so. As if it were tangible, the Dragon stopped right at her palm.

She tilted her head, and the serpent mirrored her action.

Completely taken out of the battle, she felt the energy around her retreat back inside of her.

The scales, shimmering iridescently, reflected a kaleidoscope of colors in the sunlight. Its eyes were golden, sharp, and penetrating as they stared down into her very soul—the body of a serpent but the head of a dragon. Elegant, powerful, and enigmatic, it would command fear and fascination from anyone who stood before it.

It was a cheap blow, but still a blow, nevertheless. A body slammed into her at full force, throwing her back and onto the ground. It knocked the air out of her, and she groaned in protest.

The boy, who was lithe but tall, tackled her, his legs straddling her waist. His hands grabbed at her wrists and pinned them down at her side. The darkness was gathering in her hands, and she was preparing to annihilate him until she looked up into the eyes blazing like the sun.

"My Little Mouse," when she blinked, she was no longer in Ilkiz. Everything around her was dark, and on top of her was no longer the boy, but Goddrick. "You thought you could run."

Feeling her entire body shut down, she began to shake uncontrollably.

"I told you what would happen if you left," she tried to speak, but her lips wouldn't move. Every part of her went numb, and as he leaned down towards her, she felt the darkness fading from behind her eyes, ready to engulf her and never allow her to see the light. She was suffocating, and soon would be without air.

"N—" *Don't say it... don't say no...*

"Get off of her!" Her eyes blinked rapidly as she struggled to regain focus, attempting to make sense of her surroundings and what was unfolding. It was Jayce, his voice cold and unwavering, "I said get off of her, or she dies."

She was hyperventilating, her body was in shock, and she didn't know how to pull herself out of it. When she looked up, the boy stared off to the side, his teeth baring. Slowly turning, she saw Jayce holding the girl in his grasp, his sword at her throat.

"Get—" she swore his eyes were glowing then, "off—"

"Kill her! We die like warriors, Akua!"

"Shut up, Kaen." He said, looking back down at Azahara, and immediately, his eyes softened.

"Please—" her voice was broken, "not again..." Something seemed to click in his blue and red eyes, making him stand quickly, and release her.

Almost instantly, Jayce was by her side, lifting her up and enfolding her in his arms. Despite his comforting touch, her trembling persisted, and she found relief by burying her face into his chest. Behind her, she sensed Xol's presence, and to her utter surprise, she felt her arms encircle her waist, her head resting against her back.

The two of them cocooned her, and she released silent tears. Their comfort all too needed, and the fear that it would be ripped away made her bring one arm onto Xol's and tighten her hold on Jayce.

He stiffened, "That would be a mistake."

"Kaen, stop it." Akua seethed, "Do not attack them."

"Why!? They come on our land." She had a shrill, teetering-on annoyance tone. It was high-pitched, as though she was trying to whistle at every word spoken.

Jayce was ready to move on them, but Azahara gripped his arm; if he let her go right now, she would fall. Maybe it wasn't good that she came. She thought she was ready, but maybe it was too soon.

Xol stood, "We will leave." Her voice was flat, but Azahara felt the rage behind it.

"I'm sorry," Akua said, and she heard feet shuffling.

"Akua!" Kaen then began speaking in a language she had never heard before, and quickly at that. Everything from her mouth sounded like a mixture of Elvish, Human, and Fae ancestral tongues.

"Kaen shut your mouth," they bickered like Skyy and Mel used to, "I think…" Again, he began speaking in that strange language.

Jayce scooped her up from the ground, holding her close to his chest. Her hands gripped tightly at his shirt, and her face nestled against him. "Breathe, baby, breathe," he urged. The soothing sensation of his hand running through her hair washed over her, spreading from her temples to her toes. "That's my girl. Take deep breaths," he encouraged.

She took an unsteady breath in, the trembling beginning to subside. "I'm here, I've got you." He continued.

"We've got you," Xol said softly, her hand on her arm.

While her heart was still running as though she was sprinting, her head was beginning to straighten, and her vision was returning. Soon, the world would stop spinning, and she could stand without fearing falling.

Akua spoke, "Redhead, who are you?"

Jayce tensed again, turning ever so slightly so that she could see him. He was holding back the fire-bending hot head, nearly pulling her hair out in frustration.

"Azahara." He was looking at her expectantly, "—Starfall." *Why did people expect me to have a full name?*

"Why are you here?" Akua never tore his eyes from her, "And why do you have Rah's power?"

Jayce somehow knew to let her go right then, but not far, only releasing her enough so that she could turn to face the now very apparent twins. Both had the exact same-colored eyes, the same facial structure, exact same hair, and ear shape. The only distinguishing feature that set them apart was that Kaen was strikingly pretty, with sunken tear ducts and bangs; though it didn't take away from how crazed she looked.

"I'm here seeking information from Ilkiz, or about her, rather," She wasn't sure why, but telling them about having Rah's power felt strange, but she, at this point, didn't have a choice, "I was gifted Light by Death, and mistakenly given the power of the gods."

Kaen then was subdued, and her wild eyes shot to her, "Are you the—"

Akua gripped her arm, pulling her towards him. Speaking in their language once again, Azahara looked up at Jayce, who was peering down at her. His hand came up to the side of her neck, brushing his thumb against her cheek. "I should have made you promise not to be reckless."

She swallowed, her eyes moving back and forth between his, "I don't know what happened. Death's power has become exponentially stronger, and I have no explanation for it. When I saw her attack you—I..."

His fingers brushed a strand behind her ear, "You used Death's power, not the gods. Did you recognize that?"

Taking a deep breath, "I guess... not..." While she knew that was Death's gift, she only realized that she hadn't immediately gone to the gods gift like she had done after Kaed was killed.

Jayce smiled and placed his forehead against hers, "And now, your heart is back in place, and you aren't shaking."

"Because of you," she said under her breath. His thumb gently lifted her chin to see him.

"No," at that moment, all she wanted was for him to kiss her, the feeling so strong it was like a slap in the face, "because of you." Knowing it wasn't right to hope for that, she smiled weakly and nodded.

She looked back at the twins, who were bickering still. Xol stepped next to Azahara and whispered, "Should we just take this opportunity to go?"

"Wait," Akua said, seemingly able to hear her, "Azahara—" he struggled to say her name, but she appreciated the effort nevertheless, "Answer my question, and that will determine if we help you or run you out of Ilkiz."

"I'd love to see you try," Xol literally hissed through her teeth.

Kaen, as though she was a snake herself, hissed back.

Fun. So much fun. She thought, shaking her head.

"You stopped my Sea Serpent and made them tangible. What was its name?" Akua asked, and Kaen leaned off to one side, a smirk on her lips. How was she supposed to know the Dragon's name? It hadn't spoken to her.

Or had it?

She took a deep breath and closed her eyes. The darkness around her was palpable, and while she could hear the noise around her, it was drowned out by the weight of her thoughts. *What was your name? Tell me. Please.*

Gasping, her eyes shot open, *"My name is Venruvemi, but Akua calls me Vemi."* As the dragon spoke, its voice seemed to cling to her ears, surrounding her in a cocoon of sound. It was as if she were submerged in an underwater world, the echoes of the dragon's words reverberating in her mind like gentle ripples in a tranquil ocean.

It was like nothing she had ever experienced before. The sound seemed to vibrate through her being, leaving an indelible impression on her very soul.

"Venruvemi, but you call them, Vemi."

Jayce and Xol looked at the twins while Azahara's head tilted backward, her eyes directed at the sky above.

"We weren't expecting you so soon," Akua stepped towards them, his hand coming into a fist and then moving it to his chest. "At least not for a few thousand more years. Things must be bad out there."

Kaen stepped beside her brother, and mirrored his action, "Sorry to have attacked you like that. My bad." She shrugged her shoulders.

"Suppose I'd have done the same," Azahara said, both weary, looking between Jayce and Xol. "We have family back on the ship. Will they be safe?"

It was Kaen who stepped towards them, her hands placed behind her back. She was able to take a moment to soak in her appearance. Taller than she was, she had a lithe form like her brother, which was only made more apparent by her traditional clothing. The jade green and black colors adorn the one-piece head-to-toe shirt and pant ensemble. Her brother wore nearly the same style of clothing.

"We can bring them too since Akua will be your passer here."

Akua rolled his eyes, and she sensed that Kaen was even too much for him sometimes. He found her watching him, and a gentle smile laced the corners of his lips. He gave her a nod. "You can choose to bring them on land or keep them on the ship. We will bring no harm to you and your family."

She looked at Xol, "What do you think?"

"Jayce?" Xol surprised her by directing the question to him, "I think we should all go, but I want to know your thoughts."

"They won't harm us," Xol narrowed her eyes at him, and Azahara squeezed him closer to her, "after all, being descendants of Ilkiz, I think we all have a common goal here."

Azahara looked at Akua, who was staring at her intensely.

Thank you, Venruvemi.

"Call me Vemi, my Keeper."

Day 65
CHAPTER 23

The twins followed them back to the ship, where Kaen the Crazy and Xol walked up the bridge to the Neptune.

It wasn't that they necessarily didn't trust the twins yet, but they were afraid to leave them alone, even for a moment, to go and instruct the crew to deboard. Jayce suggested that one of them accompany the other, and here they were. Xol was ill-pleased but ultimately conceded, considering Azahara and her state. It was appreciated, and while she did feel considerably better for the moment, she didn't want to be away from them, just in case.

Akua stood behind Jayce and her as they waited at the edge of the dock for the rest of the crew to join them. She could feel his gaze on her and wondered if this was a good moment to talk without his crazed sister bombarding him. After resolving her decision, she turned to face him, finding his strong gaze unwavering.

Jayce stayed staring out at the Neptune, but he linked his pinky with hers, reassuring her that he was there and listening.

"Akua," she didn't need to say his name, but she felt in the moment it was appropriate to at least address him. His eyebrows relaxed, and so did his shoulders. "What is a Keeper?" Not only did Akua visibly shift, but Jayce tensed beside her.

"Your people still have that much text about Rah." It didn't feel like a question, more like a surprised statement that he didn't want clarification on. Either way, she shook her head. One of his arms crossed his body as he leaned to one side. "How do you know about that then?"

"Your Dragon," Azahara wasn't sure why, but both of them reacting the way they did made her not want the answer anymore. It wasn't a title that she had ever heard before, and if she was honest, it didn't sound like one that she wanted. "They called me their Keeper."

She was watching for Jayce's response, but he seemed to be less caught off guard or more prepared this time. Akua, on the other hand, had his mouth wide open and was staring harder than he had been before.

"You did hear him, it wasn't a trick."

She narrowed her eyes, "How else would I have known their name?"

"You could be a telepath, or a witch—" *why is it that I have to be a witch? This feels sexist, in so many ways.* "But that is quite the confirmation."

"Great," she didn't want to sound irritated, but it just slipped. "So, what is a Keeper? Do I collect Dragons like the kids collect marbles? Or is it more like a farmer? The Keeper of Sheep." At least she got a soft chuckle out of Jayce, who put his arm against hers, and locking their fingers together.

"Good one."

"Thanks."

Akua was less impressed but didn't fight the upward tug on the corner of his lips. "Not exactly. Someone else is better equipped to answer that. If they don't," he must have seen her about to contest, so he hurried along, "I will answer your question. On Ilkiz, you have my word."

How hard could it be to just explain what that title was? She sighed in frustration, but nodded, she didn't want to argue.

"Also," Akua captured her attention before she was going to turn back around with Jayce, "about earlier."

Her lips part slightly, ready to tell him not to mention it. They were in the heat of battle, and she knew that his intentions were nothing more than to subdue her.

"I am truly sorry," it felt like ice consumed over her, "Water holds many properties, one of which is sight. I saw through your eyes." Her heart was pounding, and a wave of embarrassment flooded her. "You **are** safe. Now that you are here, he cannot enter these lands. Her spirits—"

He raised his hand, and water pooled in his palm, and once again, Vemi, but a smaller version, appeared. It's serpent-like body slithered along his arm and up to his shoulder. The Dragon was made of pure water, unlike when she touched it and saw a fully formed creature of beauty. "They will protect you."

Azahara had stayed quiet the entire time they walked away from the harbor. She had a lot on her mind, mostly Akua's last words and the title of *Keeper*. Thankful as always for Jayce and Xol, they had caught the crew up and asked that they allow her to be in silence. Alyse was the only one that protested, she could see that something was wrong, and immediately blamed the two twins. She wanted to know, from Azahara, what they did because she felt that Jayce and Xol were keeping a secret from them.

Understanding her frustration, Azahara broke her silence for the briefest of moments to give her some peace. While the twins had attacked them, could she really blame them? They were invaders in their mind, coming to their land. It was the same that Zhal and her people felt when her and Kaed were too close to their home. Granted, that had ended a lot bloodier than this did.

Jayce had stayed by her side but refrained from making any physical contact with her. It was what she wanted, she needed to have a clear head to process everything that already happened, while also preparing for what was going to happen. She appreciated him beyond belief because she didn't need to tell him. He took the cue from her tucked arms and slouched shoulders.

Though, now, she wasn't surprised anymore. Not after everything that had happened.

"Oof—" Accidentally bumping into Kaen, as they appeared to have come to an abrupt halt, Azahara looked up. She was turned, looking deep into her eyes, a neutral expression on her face. "Sorry, Kaen."

The fire twin was beautiful, but she was absolutely nuts. For that, she would be directing any questions to her brother, the least hotheaded of the two.

"It's all good, Azahara." She struggled with her name, like her brother, but it didn't seem to bother her like it did Akua. "We are here."

In front of them, was more forest.

They had entered Isis, the massive forest that took over eighty percent of the realm of Ilkiz, a few hours ago. The sun had moved from one side of their shoulder to the other by the time Akua made the proclamation.

The problem was that there was nothing in front of them, above them, or under them. It was just more of the beautiful forest.

"Brother, we should let her go first." There was a smile, unfriendly, lining Kaen's face. She was hoping that this misplaced anger towards her was not due in part to being jealous. She didn't want another Zephyra or Tillin.

Jayce stepped between her and Kaen.

Akua didn't move, just rolled his eyes. Kaen looked Jayce up and down before crossing her arms over her chest. "Such a brute. Can't allow your woman to fight her own battles?"

"I'm not fighting a battle for her." He clarified, "I'm merely getting you out of her face." Her chest tightened and her hands tingled.

"Kaen, back off. Why are you acting like this?" Jayce stepped aside as the twin skipped backward. "If she would like to go first, she can."

"What am I going first into?" Azahara finally asked.

"Beyond the Vail. It is similar to Magic Warding but created with Dragon scales and the elemental storm. If someone tries to enter through without a descendant of Ilkiz, they are –"

"Obliterated!" Everyone turned their head to Kaen, who was wide-eyed and grinning.

"Please excuse her, no, you won't be obliterated. You will be shot back into the sea, right outside the harbor." Akua was just as done with Kaen as everyone else seemed to be.

"Why do you want me to go first then? Since you both are descendants, I should pass right through."

"We will have to pass each of you through individually, but she is suggesting you walk in alone. Only if you would like. I won't pressure you."

"I will." Nearly immediately, a wave of water splashed into Kaen, sending her rushing backward a solid distance away.

Azahara stepped away from Jayce, and he didn't stop or warn her, even if Xol and Alyse tensed toward her. "Where is the border?" She asked, and for the first time, she saw Akua's lips grow to a larger smile.

"Look."

Watching him gesture ahead, she did as instructed. Nothing, all there was in front of her was the forest—nothing out of the ordinary.

"Not with your eyes." Akua stood beside her, his hand hovering below hers, making sure not to touch her. "Power comes from every part of the body. Your eyes can be deceitful, tricked, and blinded—" *I can't see anything, I can't see.* "Allow your body to see what your eyes cannot."

Taking a breath, she closed her eyes and outstretched her hand. She could feel Akua step away from her and then silence. The darkness behind her eyes was heavy, but she had done something like this before. She concentrated on the Light that Death gave her, finding it and bringing it forth to be her strength and the light in her darkness. This felt the same, but instead of grabbing the light that now appeared in front of her, she allowed it to spread—illuminating the darkness behind her eyes.

When she opened her eyes, she found a translucent gate just inches from her fingertips, stretching so far into the sky that it disappeared among the trees. Her gaze shifted from left to right, catching Akua's wide smile in the corner of her eye. The gates appeared jade, but she knew they wouldn't feel tangible if she touched them. They were simply her interpretation of what she believed the wall would look like, mirroring the gate that had brought them to this place.

Her hand was waving and reaching behind her, and she didn't need to wait long for Jayce to take it.

"Can I take him?" Azahara asked, not taking her eyes off the expansive wonder in front of her.

"You can," Akua said, and that was all she needed to step through.

Nothing could have prepared her for what she was stepping into. Within the thick, lush, and dense tapestry of greenery, with towering trees that reached the clouds, was a vibrant, very much alive city. Within the canopies of the trees were houses crafted from an enchanting blend of wood and foliage, perched delicately upon sturdy branches, manmade posts, and some were even hanging with the trees woven fabrics.

Completely losing herself in its beauty, she took another several steps forward. Mesmerizing sights of cascading waterfalls added more elements to the awe that was this place. Some of the homes were even nestled within the glistening precipice of the waterfalls, where she could hear the soft, melodious sound of the water dancing along the rocks.

The trees were towering giants, and while she couldn't see the sky, she knew they kissed it. She had once said that Celadon would be a place she could live, but this place, she wanted to call it home.

As if the trees themselves were a cocoon from the world, she felt safer than she had ever felt in her entire life.

"Incredible," Jayce said beside her, his hand tightening around hers. "I've heard stories of the City of Spirits, but nothing does this justice." His tone mirrored her awe, and she felt the stinging in her cheeks and across her nose. The tears weren't out of sadness or pain but were instead out of happiness, and that alone pushed them forward. They were silent, but of course, he noticed and placed his opposite hand holding hers to her cheek, catching them. She leaned into his touch, the smile still plastered on her lips.

She inhaled unsteadily, "Do you think they would come for me here?" With gentle tenderness, he slipped his hands up to cradle her face, lifting her gaze to meet his.

"They would," he said, and she was thankful for his honesty, "but I will protect you. If you say we stay, we stay. There are no questions."

Their gaze was so intense then, and she wondered if it was the atmosphere around them or simply just because it was him. Her heart raced, yearning to find solace within the sanctuary of his chest.

She had been watching him just as much as he watched her. He had always been cautious with his affection, even before the incident with Goddrick.

"Thank you," her voice was breathy, and whatever resolve he had broke in that moment. He leaned in towards her, and she didn't want to pull away. She wanted him to kiss her, and she didn't care about anything else.

"By the gods this place is beautiful!"

"Wow!"

"What is this place?"

"Aza? Jayce?!"

She could smell the minty scent on his lips; that's how close they were when the outpour of screams echoed around them.

"There you both are!" Alyse called out to the two of them, "Did you guys sprint or something?"

Jayce leaned away from her, a smile adorning his face. Although she could see the hint of pain reflected in the wrinkle between his eyebrows, she appreciated his strength at that moment. The last thing she wanted was to be interrupted when it happened, and despite the butterflies swirling in her stomach, she was determined to find a way to manage them—for now.

"No, Alyse, we didn't." He said, never looking away from her.

One of his hands dropped, and she took another unsteady breath in, this time for a different reason.

In that moment, she realized something which terrified her more than she ever imagined. While she felt the butterflies in her stomach and yearned for him to kiss her, no other feelings came. There was no urge for him to touch her. No heat between her thighs. No desire for anything, absolutely nothing, else.

I fucking hate you, Goddrick. What have you done to me...

Feeling Jayce wrap his arm around her back, she swallowed back the lump in her throat and smiled. "Let's get going. It's already been a long day," he said, and his words resonated within her. She nodded, determined not to dwell too much on that revelation, hoping it was caused by something else.

Don't be naive, he did this...

Day 66

Chapter 24
Jayce Latimer

If she knew all of who he was, he would have immediately taken them to the highest tree and kissed her until their lips were numbed, and even then, he would have fought to keep going. The force that drew him to lean in and kiss her was something he'd never experienced, and no amount of strength he had could stop him. It was as though someone was placing small cuts throughout his body when he stopped. The universe telling him that he was making a mistake by not just going for it.

He felt her need and that it was just as strong as his was. It didn't make it right, and he should have been able to restrain himself. He never wanted to put her into a situation where she would be brought back to the moment with Goddrick. Fear that even kissing her would bring her mind back to the darkness should be enough to keep him away, but the pull was far too much.

His soul finally knew what it was like to be touched by hers, and there would be no going back. The only way he could think of, was to forcefully separate himself from her, try to get himself back in check, and then return with a stronger resolve.

That, however, was never going to happen. He would never be further from her than what was absolutely necessary. He would find the strength to pull away, even if she would make it impossible to do so.

When they arrived deep within the village earlier that day, everyone immediately surrounded them. Thankfully Akua, while still weary of being much better than his sister, was there with a voice of reason—explaining in brief words what had transpired at the port.

He shared their story, explaining that their people had no chief, leader, or king; instead, they were guided by the spirits. After a brief, spiritual interaction with Azahara, the people welcomed the group into their homes. It wasn't surprising at all; they warmed up to the redhead almost immediately. The kids were drawn to her, the elderly bowed to her as was their custom, and the teens gathered around her in awe. Although she despised the attention and had the urge to flee, she managed to keep her composure in those moments.

Again, her strength was something he envied beyond all else.

They were offered a place to stay, and he felt grateful that the grouping of pods hanging from the trees allowed everyone from the crew to be connected. If anything were to happen, they would all be within running distance of each other. Azahara shared the same sentiment, and her joy matched his own.

When they offered one for each of them, he looked to Azahara, not wanting to overstep her boundaries. Even if he had been in her bed every night since the incident, he never wanted to assume.

She looked at him like he was crazy for thinking anything else and later whispered, "Why would you assume otherwise?" It made him laugh, and thinking about it now, had him chuckling once more.

It was clearly past bedtime, but Azahara had requested some time with Carmen, and Jayce couldn't have been prouder. The two of them sat in a cozy canopy designed for lighting a fire and relaxing around it. Xol and some other crew members tried to join, but Carmen promptly turned them away.

He didn't eavesdrop on their conversation but watched them intently, ready to go to her if she needed. Emotions ranged from laughter to tears, from anger to joy. Whenever something brought her to tears, Carmen was right there, offering her hand if she wanted to take it.

Whenever she mentioned Goddrick, he could sense it. Her soul seemed to crumble and scream for help, as if terrified of returning to a cage. It became evident that Goddrick had somehow ensnared her soul, locking it away, and he couldn't help but wonder if that was the reason the god had been able to remain so connected to her.

His hatred for the gods would never be sedated, even after Goddrick was destroyed. How could they have allowed this to happen? How could they hurt her like this? She deserved nothing but love and happiness, never pain and torment.

In that moment, her eyes shifted to him, and he responded with a wave and smile. Returning one back to him, she then turned to Carmen, as if indicating that it was time to leave. They hugged, which was a significant step for her. Xol had been the only other person she allowed to touch her beyond just holding her hand.

He would need to protect Carmen, and all of the crew, from this point on. If she lost them—no, he wouldn't even consider it to be a possibility. They were her family, and ultimately his, so they would be safe.

He watched as she picked up her dress, which was far too long for her, and walked across the wobbly bridge towards him. Everyone had difficulty navigating the high canopy, but Azahara seemed to adapt relatively quickly, as though she was meant to fly.

"Hey," she dropped her dress, kicking it out as she walked. It was being held up by two very small straps, and he wondered how the fabric carried the weight of it without snapping.

"Hey, how did it go?" He watched her take a deep breath and straighten her shoulders.

"Good—mmm, actually it went great. I didn't realize how much I just needed to talk to someone." A gentle smile lingered on her lips, "Not that I don't talk to you, just, she knew the right questions to ask. Knew when to, and when to not ask them. She had a way of shifting the conversation, so I didn't always feel like I was complaining, or always being negative."

He smiled widely at her, "I'm so happy to hear that."

"We talked about Kaed too," she watched him, but she'd get no reaction. Whether he was gone or not, Kaed still had a piece of her heart, if not all of it. He still held to the truth that she had enough love to give this entire realm, which included him, "and I realized that I needed to talk to someone sooner about losing him. It will take some time, and many tears, but I do feel better. Like, I'm not betraying him for trying to be happy."

By the Mother, Sunshine, I am so proud of you. He stepped to her, and with her advancement, he wrapped his arms around her. Her arms came around his torso, squeezing him tightly.

"There is something else," she continued, "but I'm nervous, for once, to talk about it with you." His hand caressed her hair, watching as it bounced back into place as soon as his hand reached beyond its length. "I—" She cleared her throat, stopping her statement in its tracks.

"You don't have to tell me now," he said, watching her lean back to look at him. "There is plenty of time, okay? No pressure." His hand came up, pulling on one of her curls playfully.

A soft pink color filtered under her freckles, and he could have melted right then. "No pressure for anything?"

Realization hit him like a rushing horse causing his eyes to widen, "Of course! For anything—nothing, oh Aza." His head was shaking in utter shock. Had he ever given her the impression of that? "It was what happened earlier, wasn't it? I—I would never expect—"

Her palm covered his mouth, and he took a deep breath, immediately relaxing.

"You have been nothing but a gentleman. As for earlier, I'm only upset it was interrupted," his heart skipped a beat, "I just... what he did to me, it's changed me, and I just hope that is okay with you."

She, of course, was thinking about him, and his feelings. He would never understand, truly beyond the realm of possibilities, how anyone in their right mind could ever hurt her.

Moving her hand from his mouth, she waited, a sheepish expression on her face.

"You could tell me you never wanted to touch another man ever again and that you were switching sides for good—" it got a soft laugh from her, which he'd hoped it would, "and I would stay. I would still give you the world without anything in return just to be in your life."

A tear rolled down her cheek, and he leaned in, kissing it to catch it from falling any further. "Thank you, Jayce."

When he leaned back and looked at her, the light from the torches around them reflected off of her porcelain skin, giving her an ethereal glow. Her mismatching eyes held both the calm seas and roaring flames, drinking in his gaze.

He loved this girl more than his own existence and couldn't wait to share it with her. After Ilkiz, he would tell her who he was, and while it terrified him to think of how she would react, he knew it was the right time.

Her sweet scent was intoxicating; she smelled like honeydew and apricots, sweet but not overpowering, and it reminded him of summer nights. Hints of nectar and lavender that brought him to a garden under the stars.

"Jayce," She ran the back of her fingers down his cheek, "We should get some sleep."

He smiled widely, brought his hand to hers, and kissed it.

"I agree. Tomorrow is going to be a long day." There was wonder in her eyes.

They made their way into the pod, which looked very similar to the shape of a beehive. It had moss adorning the outside, wrapped in vines and purple flowers he had never seen before. They looked like tulips but blossomed outward, and a yellow tail lay between its petals. It reminded him of Azahara's window, and he couldn't keep the chuckle in.

"What's funny?" She asked as he closed the door behind them, and she crossed the small space towards the wardrobe, if that was even the right term for it. It was just a pole hung against the wall where they'd decided to hang the few bits of clothes they had. Akua had mentioned that while they were there, they should wear their traditional clothing. The long flowing dress Azahara had on was something from Kaen. Jayce opted not to change but promised to dress appropriately for the following days.

"Nothing just remembered something, that is all." She was slipping the straps of her dress off her shoulders when he turned away, looking at the walls.

"Can I be let in on the memory?" She pressed, and he heard the dress hit the floor with a resounding thump.

Looking at nothing in particular, Jayce's eyes wandered the circular room, "How this place reminds me of home."

"You haven't told me where you're from, now that you mention it." He could hear her rummaging through her things and would wait for her cue that she was dressed before looking at her.

"South of Avlyrra, near So'ol."

"Such a beautiful place," she commented, "but I'd rather never see it ever again." He heard the frustration in her tone and then shuffling. "Okay, I'm dressed, thank you."

He already knew why, but still asked, "Why don't you like So'ol?" When he caught sight of her, his knees almost gave out. The green silk shirt and matching shorts were beautiful on her, and when she stretched her arms over her head to pull her hair into a bun, he saw her belly button. The thin straps gave him a view of her perfect shoulders that were curved and called for him to kiss.

By the Mother, the things you do to me.

With a resounding sigh, she pulled at the bun and crossed the room, "I won't peek; you can change." He couldn't help but turn to see her backside as she stood looking out the singular window, cracking it open to let some of the crisp outdoor air in. "Fae captured me there and brought me to Höwl."

Turning away from her to get ready, he sighed. He wasn't aware of the circumstances of how she had arrived in Höwl, but when he felt her presence there, it sent him into a frenzy. It was the one place in the entire world that he could not go, at least not physically. He had a connection with a prisoner, an old friend who reached out to him. Thankful that he had placed Magic in her the night they danced at the Idle Fox. His friend, who technically would be the Sam in her life, felt its presence.

"Why..." he was angry, which translated into his tone.

"You don't need to worry about it, really," He **would** worry about it. "It was a misunderstanding. At least I learned of Jaakobai's true intentions with me. What he really wanted, which is why I know for a fact that Thall was all a distraction. A means to begin some plan to either reshape the world as we know it, or simply take-over ruling the realms.

"You know, now that I say it out loud, I guess I didn't learn too much. What a waste..."

He quickly took his shirt and pants off and slipped into loose-fitted pants and a shirt when he saw her looking at him. "You peeked." he said, tying the loop on his pants.

"Thought you could tell when I was lying," she countered, crossing the room to the bed. "It was where I met Sam; since then, he's been around to save me. I don't think I deserve him, truthfully. I'm sure he will get tired of having to step in and protect me at some point." Her fingers were running along the sheets of the bed. "If it hadn't been for him, I would just have been a slave to another tyrant. I would have been curious to see what

Goddrick would have done. Since Jaakobai was ready to risk it all and make me his." She was mocking him by waving her other hand near her face and implementing a jester tone into her words.

While he knew the outcome, it still pissed him off, "I'll kill him too."

"Good," she tore back the blanket and closed her eyes, apparent frustration lining her crunkled nose, "Anyone who has ever touched me without my permission has or will die."

"He—"

"He didn't get the chance." He was prepared to release every Yuul unto him if he had, "Though, honestly, he seemed more interested in hurting me mentally than physically. Which, I guess, is better…" As she sat down on the bed, he crossed the room to blow out the single candle and moved back to join her.

She rubbed at her eyes, "I think I'm tired; I'm talking crazy—"

"You aren't crazy, don't ever think that Aza." *I'm going to enjoy killing that fake Elder,* he slipped under the sheets beside her. The bed was not meant for two people, so immediately, he turned to his side. She was there, mirroring him, but to his surprise she put her back to him.

"Is this okay?"

"Are you asking for my permission to lay a certain way?"

She chuckled, "I guess so." He pulled her to him, her head rested against his bicep, and he wrapped it around her chest, just below her chin. The other lay across her stomach, his grip sandwiched between her hip and the bed.

His head rested behind hers, and he felt her heart racing against his arm. Not that he didn't hear it already, it was pounding against her chest hard enough.

"I do feel crazy sometimes," she whispered, nuzzling her head against his arm. "Which I guess is better than feeling nothing at all. I just want in the end of all of this, to not hurt, whether that's in this world or not." What ached him the most was knowing that she would choose death to get away from the pain. She had made it abundantly clear that she would join her love in the afterlife if it meant being free of her suffering.

If she were to go, he would as well. He would separate himself from his wings and depart from this realm to be with her in the next. If that were what she truly decided in the end, nothing would stop him from going. He had lived long enough without her.

"I'll help you to find that freedom." His head tucked into her neck, and she relaxed more into him. "To the end, no matter what."

"To a new beginning, that sounds happier." Her voice was low, and he knew she was slipping into a slumber.

"Then, to a new beginning, my sweet girl."

Day 66
CHAPTER 25

"You are joking, right?" It was Alyse nearly cawing at Azahara as they walked through the canopies early the next day.

As much as she wanted to sleep longer, locked in Jayce's arms, her nerves were getting the better of her. It was similar to the feeling she had just before the Battle at Sunfall.

Just as the sun was seeping through the trees, she had made her way out of the beehive-inspired pod. Jayce had woken, but she urged him to go back to sleep and that she wouldn't be going very far, except that had been a lie. In her defense, it was technically Alyse's fault. Her ability to talk and continue a conversation was impeccable, and they had both not realized they'd made it nearly past the fall of homes and into a different section altogether.

Azahara had slipped the same dress on from the night before and one of Jayce's black cloaks, which helped shield her from the crisp, morning air.

"I'm not." Azahara finally answered, the pause merely for dramatics.

Alyse was incredibly animated that morning, and Azahara wondered if she had already had her beans for breakfast. Throwing her arms up in frustration, Alyse scowled at Azahara. "You're telling me he hasn't kissed you? And he's been a perfect gentleman even though you've slept together for how many nights now?"

"Alyse, lower your voice," She scolded, "He hasn't, and yes, he has."

"I don't think I give him enough credit," she tapped her finger against her chin, sighed, and shook her head. "No kiss though?"

Azahara shook her head. She wasn't sad about him not kissing her. They had almost done so when they arrived in Isis, but the exuberant captain had cut that moment short. If they had then, she would have been more than happy with that. Last night, that was a different story.

That wasn't to say she didn't want to, that would be wrong, she would have if he had leaned in and closed the gap. It was what she wanted, but not what she needed.

He was so perfect. It was like he was put onto this planet just for her. He knew exactly what she needed when she needed it, and beyond that, he never wanted anything in return but to simply be in her presence. That had always been what she wanted, for over five hundred years, for there to be people in her life that didn't expect anything from her. It was why she loved Illyan so much. She had nothing to offer them but herself. They weren't sexually attracted to her, didn't need her to feed or protect them, they were just there to be with her.

"Goddess to Azahara?" Alyse was waving her hand in front of her face, "Are you okay? Do I need to get Jayce or Xol?"

Shaking away the fog in her brain, she looked at Alyse, a smile lining her lips. "Sorry, I'm okay. I tend to do that a lot these days."

Alyse had a judgement-free, understanding expression on her face, "Don't apologize. I was just saying that he really is one of the good ones." Azahara nodded in agreement as she continued, "Rowlin and I were both suspicious in Celadon, but we are glad he cleared all that up."

"Cleared what up?" Azahara asked and immediately wished she hadn't. Alyse tensed almost instantly and rolled her eyes in another direction. "Alyse." She felt her heart drop, fear rearing its ugly head behind her eyes.

Alyse laughed nervously, "Rowlin saw Jayce send a raven, but he cleared it up—"

"Jayce cleared it up?" Azahara cut her off, "The same way he somehow convinced Zephyra that..."

Closing her eyes, she took a deep breath. Jayce **was** perfect, but he was a liar. She was a liar too, that didn't make him a bad person. *It doesn't make him a bad person,* her mind wandered back to Helgum. She had so much distrust for the people that she loved and cared for. It had blinded her, and it in the end, nearly got Zhal killed. If she had seen what was happening, and not felt suspicious of all three of them, she may have seen right through Illyan's plan. She could have tried to find another way.

With another heavy sigh, she looked at Alyse, "What did he say that convinced you both otherwise?"

Azahara and Alyse separated shortly after that, and she made her way back to the pod to get dressed. The rest of the city was waking, and soon it would be time to meet with the twins. They were going to discuss with her the plan to get to Ilkiz's tomb, where she would find what she was looking for. Akua, whom she was becoming quite fond of, had suggested she wait a few days to acclimate to the different land, whereas Kaen couldn't wait for her to get things going.

After returning to their sleeping quarters, she found it empty, and for the first time, she was happy about it. Speaking with Alyse hadn't necessarily made her mad at Jayce, but keeping herself together and not prying, would not do her any good. She needed to focus, and she knew that with him around, all she would want to do was get to the bottom of things.

That time would come after visiting Ilkiz's Tomb.

When she was cleaned up and dressed, she went down the canopies to solid ground, where Akua had said to meet the day before. Her clothing, it was something else. These were the traditional garments the twins had provided, and she felt strange wearing such high-quality clothing in a forest.

It was a white and gold ankle-length dress, unlike anything she had ever worn or seen. It was crafted from silk, boasting both a smooth and glossy texture, which shimmered subtly in the light. The wide, flowing sleeves elongated her arms, adding a regal aura when she raised them.

The garment was adorned with intricate patterns; all of the Dragons depicted not a battle, but in flight. They were always seen as creatures of destruction, which she ignorantly believed until now.

A broad sash was tied across her waist, which was the most difficult piece. Woven with opulent golden threads, it cinched the dress gracefully around her hourglass silhouette. She knew that her body type was not built for these dresses, which was slightly embarrassing, but it was their tradition. Hopefully, they found no offense to how she wore it.

Being late to the party was her signature now, and she hated it. How had she been the first one up and the last one to arrive?

Surprised to only see the twins, Xol and Jayce, she shuffled quickly to them. Akua caught her coming first, as he had been facing in her direction. His eyes widened, and a blush crossed his nose. Then, the rest turned to see her, and she hated that they all gave her the same look.

She stopped, dropping her arms down her sides. They weren't but feet away from her then, and all of them—*including Kaen*—had their mouths parted, staring at the dress.

"You are kidding me, you guys get to wear pants on this hike, but I have to wear a dress?" She tried to stifle her embarrassment and fight back the urge to run upstairs and put something else on.

"It's tradition, you have no choice," Kaen said, her normal aggravated tone slipping, and a more normal, girly note came forth.

"Ilkiz, save me." Akua was stepping between them and walking to her, closing the distance. "It's twisted." As he reached for her, she felt her skin crawl. Every part of her went into fight or flight mode, and she stepped back. His mixed eyes captured hers, and he must have seen her fear because he pulled his hand back before touching her.

"I'll fix it," Jayce said, coming up beside her, "You have the sash stuck here." He smiled down at her before looking at Akua, "Thank you."

"Yes—thank you, Akua. I'm..." *Don't apologize; It isn't your fault.* "I'm—" She bit her lip and turned away. Jayce untied the sash, adjusted it, and then retied it for her. His hands gently pressed against her waist before he stepped back, giving her some space.

"You are stunning," Jayce had his hand out towards her, and she placed hers into his. The sense of calm that came over her was like a drug. She hoped that it was not an influence and that it was because of her true feelings.

At that moment, she saw his facial expression shift, and for the first time, she saw uncertainty.

"Thank you," It wasn't the time to dwell; she wanted to get this over with.

"All right, now that we are all feeling *awkward*, thank you both for that by the way." Kaen was something else, and Azahara rolled her eyes. It wasn't lost on her as she walked past Jayce, that he watched her with weary eyes. *Good, simmer.* She thought, feeling the corner of her lip curl up.

"It's always like this with them," Xol chimed in but reached out her hand towards Azahara, who took it without hesitation. "You do look very lovely."

"You do," Akua complimented, and an unfiltered smile lined her lips.

"I still don't like that I am going to be hiking in a dress. Especially one as beautiful as this." She placed her hand on her stomach, feeling the embroidery and silk under her fingertips.

Xol placed her forehead on Azahara's hand then, and it took her back. Never had she done that before, and it sent a strange shockwave through her. "We aren't walking," Xol stated before moving her hand down and releasing it. "Akua can open portals using his water."

The elemental magic that the Spirit Riders' descendants used would never cease to amaze her. Her mouth was wide open, staring at him, and he wasn't shy about enjoying her gaze. *Water has many properties...* She remembered back to their conversation just outside of the Neptune.

"That is incredible," she said, pure amazement written on her face. Using wëther portals required a lot of Magic, and for gods, their dyspoxii traversal. To be able to shift water from one place and travel through it to another place just seemed impossible.

Akua placed a hand on his hip, giving her a gentle smile, "I'd love to show you everything that water can do when you return."

"Fire is better," Kaen grumbled.

Azahara smiled widely, "Please! I'd love that."

"Perfect, then it's a date."

Watching Akua shift his gaze to Jayce had her looking up at him. *Today is a day of firsts,* she thought, seeing the expression laced across his beautiful face. Was he jealous? Why? *Yikes.* She took a deep breath and found Jayce's hand. Their fingers lacing immediately, and he settled.

"Let's get going," Akua continued, turning his back to them, and placing his hands in front of him.

"Hey," Azahara was watching Akua, but tilted her head to the side, raising her ear to Jayce, who whispered, "I get my date first." His hand snaked around her waist and pulled her to him. "Okay?"

Turning her head up to look at him, "You can have your date," she stepped from his grasp, surprising him, "After," looking back at Akua, who had water spinning in a cyclone in front of him, "I get my answers."

"Let's go!" Akua called out.

Azahara didn't look at Jayce but reached for Xol's outstretched hand. She watched Xol take Kaen's and jump through, tugging her along. With Jayce taking hers, the three of them followed suit. The water drenched them but felt comfortable, unlike the wëther portals that tore her apart just to put her back together again.

She was immediately hit with heat when they emerged on the other side. It was nearly too much, and she cowered backward, ready to jump straight back through the portal to the comfortable air of Isis.

Jayce was behind her, his hands on her arms.

At first, she thought that Kaen was setting something ablaze, but that wasn't the case. All around them, steam spewed through the ground, the smoke making it a bit difficult to see further than a few feet in front of them.

"This is what is known as the Katsukazan. The Mountain is alive, and while nothing in our texts have explanations for it, it has never harmed us. We believe it is Ilkiz's way of protecting her tomb from those with fear in their hearts." Akua hadn't released her hand, and she slowly slipped it from his grasp.

At first glance, she hadn't noticed any water around them, but upon closer inspection, there were small bouts of water seeping through the ground. It truly shocked her at how little water he needed to bring them here. She was thoroughly impressed.

"Speaking of, there it is." Xol stepped beside them, all three of them drenched but quickly drying thanks to the heat. Following her eyes, Azahara looked up to the towering structure that was crafted entirely from black onyx. It was imposing, radiating both elegance and strength and it made her need to take a breath, as it stole it nearly immediately.

It sat at the peak of one of the mountain ranges that cascaded the distance. There was no greenery here like there was in Isis, but it held its own beauty. The dark rocks and steam added an otherworldly element, as though she had stepped onto a completely different planet.

"Why are there five dragons?" she asked as they began walking up the windy pathway. Five mighty dragons rested on different sides of the structure, all facing different cardinal directions. They seemed to be guardians, all holding an air of protectiveness in their features. Their eyes, made of the same jade used in so many areas of Ilkiz, seemed to glow.

"They represent the five elements: earth, water, fire, wind, and space. Each of them was gifted to Ilkiz children and their children. The five you see here were all her first Dragons, and upon their departure from this realm, their bodies became capsules of memory."

She was smiling as Akua was talking, completely oblivious to anyone else at that moment. It wasn't just the sheer awe-inspiring sight before her that was captivating her, it was its power that was drawing her towards it.

Despite the billowing smoke surrounding the mountainside, the tomb itself seemed untouched, as if shielded by an invisible force. This world truly held wonders that Azahara had not even fathomed she would see, and she wondered what else it had to offer. Knowing a place like this existed and never being able to see or feel it, was a tragedy. She was beginning to wonder if living for eternity would be such a bad thing if she got to see more of this.

Once they made it to the trail's end, which led up a small flight of stairs, Akua and Kaen came to a halt. "This is where we part ways, Azahara." Akua turned to her and gave her a soft bow. Kaen followed suit.

Awkwardly, Azahara did the same, bowing and smiling to try and dismiss the tightening in her chest. "You both will be here when we come back out?"

Kaen crossed her arms with a large grin, "When *you* come back, your little protection detail can't enter with you."

"What?!" Xol and Jayce nearly screamed simultaneously.

Jayce stepped just in front of her but didn't block her view from the twins. "You never mentioned that," She felt the heat radiating off of him, and the tremble across his skin as his hand curled into a fist. "I'm going with her, I don't mean to be rude to your traditions, but I cannot leave her."

Akua began, "Ilkiz would annihilate you if you entered; even her descendants can't—" but he was quickly cut off.

"I don't care," his voice had lowered, but the fervor behind it never faltered, "I made a promise." *"I'm here, I promise I'll never leave you,"* she heard his words from when he held her on the beach of Itotaki, just after she was saved from Goddrick.

"I don't think it's the right time, especially with everything going on. It wouldn't do either of us any good."

He wasn't lying; he was protecting her. Jayce was always trying to shield her, not only from physical threats but also from those unseen.

He was keeping her safe her from the King and Jaakobai, understanding that if he volunteered to find her, he could throw them off her trail. He would protect her from Goddrick because he was the only person that could, and that was what he wanted.

He loved her, and he never needed to say it.

"Jayce," She captured his attention, and he turned to her. The unsmiling face that looked at her was not one she liked to see, but understandably accepted. "It's okay."

He was shaking his head. "No, if you go in there, and don't come back out, I don't know what I'll do."

He was searching through her eyes, hoping that she would concede to him coming. "I can feel her, Jayce." His hands came to the sides of her neck, his thumbs brushing against her cheeks. "She won't hurt me, and he can't get me here."

Still, he didn't smile nor did the fear in his own eyes disappear. "I'll come back to you. I promise." She whispered, trying to settle him.

It may have seemed weird to the twins, but his fear was valid. Along with Xol, who she could feel was hovering closer to her. They both had seen what happened, and if Azahara was right about Xol, they both knew equally what the world could bring down on her and have no remorse for it.

Jayce pressed his forehead against hers, saying, "You better." He pulled her into an embrace, holding her so tightly against his chest that she let out a huff of air. Her own arms wrapped tightly around his torso, not wanting to let go, but knowing it was necessary.

"I will," she closed her eyes, and took in the place that felt like home.

After he finally released her, she gave Xol a hug. "Be safe, call out to me if anything goes wrong." When she stepped back, she looked deep into those sapphire eyes. They were not familiar, but Xol was. Azahara was sure then she knew who they were, and believed that the once monstrous creature turned ally, would come to her as she had in Höwl.

"Thank you," Azahara said, smiling and turning towards Ilkiz's Tomb. With a deep intake of air, she made her way across the courtyard that led straight to the singular entrance that had no door, but a blanket of darkness just beyond its veil.

Before she stepped through it, she looked back at the four of them one last time. Surprised to see Xol grabbing at Kaen, and Jayce wide-eyed staring at her. *What the hell is going on?*

An unspeakable force grabbed her arm and ripped her through the darkness, taking her out of their sight and plunging her into the abyss.

Azahara was not afraid of the dark, and it knew it. It tried to steal her breath, but she only took more of it. It tried to silence her, but instead, she spoke, "Hello?" The quiet that answered her was by no means surprising, but she had hoped at least an echo of her own voice would ring. There was nothing to indicate up from down, left from right. No indication that she had truly stepped into a tomb or was back in purgatory with Death.

Her head slowly turned on a swivel, taking in the abyss that was truly *nothing*. The sounds and lack of anything but darkness was both eerie, yet beautiful. The temperature was comfortable, and she realized that she was completely dry.

Then, just before she was going to take a step forward, she heard a voice.

"Hello," She was right back there, sitting at the dining room table five hundred years ago. "We weren't expecting you for at least another couple thousands of years."

She turned, and standing before her, with an innocent smile that yearned to spew about romance novels and telling's of the world, the wavy red hair that complemented her porcelain skin, and the gray eyes that were seekers knowledge and exuded understanding.

"Mel..." Her voice was shaky, because unlike seeing a spirit or a vision of someone, she was standing right in front of her. Complete, as if she were truly there in the flesh. "Melody? Is that..."

"Hello sister, I've missed you."

Day 66
CHAPTER 27

"How?" Azahara wanted to rush to embrace her young sister, but fear gripped her from doing so. It could be a trap; Mel would have been dead for nearly as long as she had been immortal. Her hand slowly reached out towards the girl, watching her fingers tremble as they felt the cold skin under them.

Immediately she pulled them back and took a step away. "Who are you?"

Mel smiled, "Melody Rothwen, you know, your sister."

Azahara shook her head, looking away to see if there were any other surprises waiting to sneak up on her. "She's dead. She has been for a long time."

Without hesitation, Mel nodded, "You are right. I am dead. For someone so close to Death, you tend to forget that doesn't mean it is the end."

Truthfully, she didn't want to believe that Mel was standing before her. That would mean she wouldn't have been able to move on, step into another life, or live in Paradise where she absolutely deserved to be. She had a heart of gold, and while she would have wanted her to live a long, happy life, she also wanted her to be guided to the next one to bring joy to it.

Except for hearing those words, she knew that at least there was some part of her that existed before her. The burning sensation behind her eyes came quickly, and she stepped towards her. "Are you really her?"

She placed a hand on Mel's cheek, and the girl smiled. "In some ways, and in others, I am not." Leaning in towards her, Mel put her arms around her waist, her head coming to rest on Azahara's shoulder. "I've missed you."

Azahara felt tears streaming down her cheeks as she finally wrapped her arms around Mel's neck. Their embrace seemed to slowly illuminate the circular stone room around them. The only notable structure was a small drinking fountain in the middle.

"I've missed you beyond words, Mel, I'm so sorry." She placed a kiss at the top of her head, stroking her fingers along her ruby hair. "I couldn't protect you and Skyy, I failed you both so much."

Mel let out a gentle laugh, and leaned her head back, "You protected us from the darkness for as long as fate allowed, and in the end, when it was our turn, Death took us peacefully." Her tears didn't stop, and she just looked at her sister who was the same young, youthful spirit as she had remembered. "We were not meant to be in this world, but you are."

"I didn't want to be," she choked on her sobs, "not without you, not without Skyy, and—" her teeth clenched, knowing that Kaed was the line she couldn't cross. Not then, she had to keep her head straight or she'd fall into her own darkness that was out there to hurt her. "How often I had wished to be with you, it transcends time."

There was an understanding smile on her lips. "I know—**we** know. Aza, you will make a profound impact on this world, and that's why I'm here. Not to bring you down, but to help you forward."

She swallowed, staring down into the wisdom of such a young girl. Though, she supposed this version of Mel was not young, at least not in years. "How are you here?"

"The door you were yanked through, sorry about that by the way, that twin—the girl—she's got quite the big mouth." Mel let out another laugh, "I was afraid the muscle was going to run up and grab you—" she shook her head, and continued, "It wasn't a door, but a portal. The structure, while it holds the bones of the once mighty Ilkiz, is not her tomb. That lies beneath the mountain, so deep that it rivals the world's core.

"Mortal and God alike cannot enter, only those that are allowed can pass through. If anyone else had tried, they would have been annihilated. It is why, sister, you are safe. Goddrick cannot get to you in here, nor can the mortal King or the Fae Elder."

Azahara's eyes widened, "You know..." Her voice weak.

Mel nodded, "She has been following you since the thread was laced, and you began walking the path fate set forth."

"When was that?"

A frown etched on Mel's face as she stepped away from Azahara, "I can't tell you that, I'm sorry. There are some things that are best left in the book, and not spoken aloud."

While she wanted to argue, Azahara conceded, watching as this version of Mel walked towards the drinking fountain in the middle of the room and gestured for her to follow.

Mel continued, "For you to see Ilkiz, you must first relinquish your connection with the powers of Death, and the gods." She waved her hand over the fountain, and it began filling with water. "You will need to pass a test, as well. I know you didn't go to school but—"

Azahara shot her a warning glance, and Mel laughed. It truly was her, as she was so many years ago. Feeling the sting of more tears, she took a deep breath and attempted to stifle them quickly.

"What is the test?" Azahara asked, weary of the response.

"Drink, first."

"Why? Why do I need to give up my powers to see her." She stepped to the fountain, looking down into her own reflection, hating what she saw.

"You must go to her as yourself, not what others have molded you to be." Mel gestured down to the water, and while Azahara was hesitant, she leaned down. "It will hurt." She said, just before her lips were to touch the liquid now calling out to her.

With a quick glance at Mel, Azahara said, "I'm no stranger to pain." Taking a sip, she immediately felt weightless as the ground below them crumbled to dust.

Her throat was on fire, and every inch of her skin felt like it was ripping apart. The arrow in her chest tearing through her skin, the cuts from Goddrick slicing across her body one by one, the broken nose and Gorruk toxin, it all came back and destroyed her from the outside in. As she fell further, it only got worse. Each death flashed before her eyes, throwing her mind into a frenzy of what was reality, and what was history.

While she tried to scream, it was silenced under the weight of a hand around her throat. Her head was under water, keeping any words from escaping her lips; keeping her from calling out for help. She felt her heart slowing, as though it was ready to stop and take her back to purgatory.

Every second threatened to pull her into unconsciousness, but she fought to feel it all. She knew passing out would be her body's only means to end the suffering. Except she had to stay awake, she needed to be strong without the powers that were granted to her. She needed to be Azahara, not whatever it was they were trying to make her be.

With a resounding thud, she crashed against the floor, her body feeling the rocketing pain from the force.

Her eyes were closed, trying to gather some semblance of her body before she tried to capture the world around her. Everything felt heavier, and she could tell that she was no longer connected to Death, and the darkness of the gods were not lingering behind the door of her heart.

With a steadying breath, she slowly opened her eyes.

"N—..." *Don't say it. Don't say it...*

Her entire stomach was in her throat, and she was surprised it didn't project right out of her mouth. The sight in front of her was not what she had been expecting. This—this was pure torture.

"So happy you could join us." His voice sent a shrill pain throughout her entire body. The voice of the creature destroyed not only her mind, but her body. He was standing over her lifelines. They were in Isis, and everything was on fire. The smell of ash, blood and death filled her senses.

Around them were bodies, so many of them. She recognized them, and her throat began to close. The beautiful face of Alyse was marred and mangled.

The only reason she knew it was Xol was because of the white skin, there was no head to confirm. The entire crew lay dead at the monster's feet, and she was ready to join them.

On their knees in front of Goddrick was Jayce and someone she didn't quite recognize, their hands bound behind them and gags across their mouths.

There was no darkening rage that pulled from within her, and the light that would have captivated her skin was not there. She reached for it, deep down, and tried to pull it to fight for them, but it wasn't there.

"How easy it was to trick you, Little Mouse. You left them for the picking. The moment you took that portal, it was time for me to destroy everything you ever came to care about." Her hands were trembling so hard that she felt the bones within them. "Aw, I did warn you. You only have made this worse for yourself, Dikos Mou."

She slowly stood, the pain that she felt was nothing in comparison to her heart being ripped from her chest. Jayce's hazel eyes were filled with remorse, while the stranger looked at her with sorrow. His face, older in age, brought her back to the Port of Kortez. A stranger with his hand on her shoulder, wiping away the suffering she was having.

"Don't look at them, look at me." Immediately she raised her eyes to him, as though she were still his property and she had to listen. "Good. Now, come with me—"

Jayce fought against his restraints, screaming, and shifting his shoulders, trying to break free. "Shut it!" Goddrick kicked his back, sending him flying forward, and he hit the ground with a thump. Azahara let out a scream and ran towards them.

He had a sword now pointed right at Jayce's back. The sight stopped her dead in her pursuit, and she immediately dropped to her knees.

"Please, Goddrick, I beg of you don't hurt him—please, please!"

Moving the blade back, he stepped towards her, "I do love it when you beg."

"Please...not him. Not him. Anyone but him."

"So, the other one?"

Azahara leaned her head up, tears streaming down her cheeks, "Me. Take me, I won't ever leave. I promise. I swear it."

Goddrick tilted his head as he stepped over Jayce and towards her, "You are pathetic, you know that?"

"I know," she said, a stream of tears continuing to fall.

"It is quite poetic, you know," His blade lifted her chin to meet his gaze, "I'm going to kill them anyways, your brave Knight, and the Fae that tore you from me."

As though she was snapped out of a trance, she said, "What?"

"Sam— Do you not recognize the one you so clearly have fallen in love with?" Her eyes met his, the same smile she had come to hate laced on his lips.

Azahara began to stand, which surprised Goddrick, "What did you say?"

"You heard me girl, now get back down." He pressed the blade to her throat, "You don't have Death's powers anymore. You're just as weak as you were when I made you mine."

She did not move back down, instead stepped towards him, the blade biting into her neck. Feeling the blood from it fall and soak into the white gown. His eyes were wide, and he dropped the blade, cutting down to her chest.

"You are powerless, Little Mouse." His voice was deeper then, a thunderous sound that rattled her brain. "Bow to me."

Their eyes were locked, and a snarl crossed her lips. "How disappointing," her voice laced with divinity which echoed around them, overpowering his own, "I wish it were this easy to kill you."

When she reached out towards him, her skin was illuminated by a purple flame, flickers of light danced at her fingertips, and she felt at peace. "I will obliterate you one day, for everything you've done to me."

This power was not hers, and she knew she was stealing it. She could feel the being around her attempting to pull it back from her. As if they were playing tug of war, but Azahara was filled with so much willpower that they, whoever they were, would not get it back. Not until she relinquished it back to them.

As his sword thrust through her heart, her fist punched through his chest as if it were nothing more than sand and she were the shovel. Taking hold of the beating organ within him, she easily tore it out, and tossed it to the side. Treating it as he had always treated her: like nothing.

The body of Goddrick fell backward, pulling with it his sword. While her body jerked forward and the pain was immense, she just looked over at Jayce who was staring at her. He wasn't truly there, and this was just a trick—or, the test that Mel had warned her about, but seeing him there, the pain wasn't so bad.

"You are okay, Keeper."

She stepped towards him, ignoring the voice that boomed in her ears. Those hazel eyes took hers in, filled with worry and love, drawing her closer to him. Whether real or not, all she desired was to be enveloped in his arms.

Her hands were trembling, her heart seemingly stopped, and she was moving solely from the power she had stolen.

Unable to take another step, she fell to her knees and looked down at her hands.

"I will protect you, now come to me." The loud, enigmatic voice reverberated in her head. Her arms opened, and she felt a strong, solid mass push against her. The texture was rough, ancient, and with weathered scales. Leaning her head forward, heavy-eyed, she rested it against the snout of a mythical creature that hadn't existed in the realm for thousands of years. Its outward breath through its nose was hot, reminiscent of the fires simmering under the Island below.

Her eyes blurred, and the power she had in her slowly separated from her before she was plunged into darkness once again.

Day 68
CHAPTER 27

"How could you overlook that?" A very distinct male voice broke through the silence that sleep had her in.

"*Excuse me, mop head, how was I supposed to know?*" A booming, deep female inclined tone answered.

"You are literally Ilkiz, that is how. Haven't you been connected to her for months; how wouldn't you have known?"

"*I'm sensing some underlining pain points, is this just about the boy or something else?*"

"Are you patronizing me for your oversight?!"

"*I think you need to nap, just like our girl here.*"

"How could you have stabbed her like that?"

"*She took my power, I let it slip.*"

"I think she's waking up."

"*She has been awake, you are losing your touch.*"

"Please—" Azahara groaned, "Don't stop on my account."

She felt a cushion below her, but it wasn't a full-on mattress or bed. The hard ground under it seeped through, reminding her that she wasn't in the ship's comforts and Jayce wouldn't be there to wrapping her in an embrace.

As her vision slowly cleared, the surroundings gradually took shape. She found herself in what appeared to be a chamber, a spacious and singular expanse. The air carried the distinct fragrance of aged parchment, leather, and the warmth of a crackling fire. Blinking away the initial blur, she focused on the nearest wall adorned with thousands of books. A solitary desk and chair occupied a corner, surprisingly neat. The ambient lighting, dancing from the flickering flames, imbued the space with an ethereal quality, as if she had stepped into the pages of a living history book.

A pair of legs came into her field of vision, belonging to the individual engaged in conversation with Ilkiz. As he stepped in front of her, she instinctively raised her head. He loomed above her, a towering figure that obscured his face from her view.

"Let me assist you up, Azahara." She pushed up onto her arm and raised her hand. Gracefully, she climbed to her feet and met his gaze. "Damn, she was not wrong."

Stepping back, grasping the undertones of his words, she instinctively withdrew into herself. His striking features were reminiscent of a fair-skinned Karver, boasting sharp cheekbones, a chiseled jawline, and a complexion of rich ebony. The sides of his head were cleanly shaved, and his short dreads gathered into a tie at the nape of his neck, their exact length elusive from her particular angle.

"Don't stress, technically I'm dead, so you don't have anything to worry about from me."

She chewed on her bottom lip, "Gods technically aren't alive..."

"Ah, I like this one." The booming voice echoed in the chamber, and while it sent a chill down her back, she didn't cower from it. *"Do not worry, child, he won't touch you unless you ask."*

"Ilkiz, why would you add that last part?!" The man, who looked no older than she did, groaned out. "Please excuse her, she's old and obnoxious."

Her arm curled around her waist, gripping tightly at the fabric, "Who—"

"Am I?" He raised a thick eyebrow, exposing his glowing orange eyes. "I'm so glad you asked," She got the sense he hadn't spoken with many people outside of whoever entered this chamber. "My name is Rahmulous, but you would likely know me as, Rah."

If he hadn't rushed to her, she would fallen to the floor with how quickly her legs went numb. "Wow—" He expressed, placing a hand at her back, the other gripping her arm. Her eyes were open so wide that they began to sting, and tears brimmed at them.

"Rah—" She finally blinked, and having him so close to her, she could sense it.

She could **feel** him as if she were him, and he, her.

He smiled widely, "And you are Azahara, it is a pleasure to meet you, finally—at least as myself. It has been a while since I've had any interaction with someone outside of Ilkiz, so you'll have to excuse me if I'm a bit, out of touch."

The urge was too strong, and she allowed for it. Her arms wrapped around his neck, pulling herself to him as though he were a long lost relative. Someone she knew but hadn't seen for decades. There was no fear that held her from embracing him, and for once, she was happy that the reciprocated response was gentle, and with care. He even moved her from side to side, as she used to do with her younger brother, who never lived long enough to be taller than her.

Her head pressed against his chest, and she let out a silent sob. Rah gently ran his hand against the backside of her head, curving it between her shoulder and neck. "I know," She could feel him smile as his cheek pressed against her temple, "We've got you. You made it."

It was crazy to think how a simple couple of words could cause her to crumble at the seams. Her arms tightened around him, and he held her without consternation or judgment. She was resolute that this world held no one who would understand what she was going through. In her mind, Rah had died nearly seven thousand years ago, the last living soul burdened with such a fate.

Yet, here he was, in the flesh. Or, at least tangible so.

"Don't ruin this, Rah."

"You will be the only one to ruin anything, ghost. Relax." He said, edging her back slightly. The gentle smile on his lips as he looked down at her longingly made her face burn from crying. "She's already been—what do they call it, claimed? Mated—" he shivered, "Sounds so possessive."

"Bonded, you idiot. Or just simply, taken."

Rah laughed, "Sure, I'm just here to help, nothing more. Like I said, I'm technically dead." He brushed his finger against her cheek, wiping away the tear that was falling. "You going to be okay?"

She nodded and took an unsteady breath, "Yes, thank you."

"Good. Now, do you want to turn and meet Ilkiz? I'm fine to keep staring at each other, but time is of the essence."

It was then that she felt a strong wind brush against her back, sending her hair flying in front of her face. The heat from it indicated it was not made organically, but from a creature; a massive one.

"She's been here the entire time?"

"*Well—yes, how do you think I've been speaking.*" Suppose Azahara hadn't thought that through. It sounded like it was coming through her head, and not necessarily within the room. Thinking back, though, it did sound like the voice was echoing around her.

Rah rolled his eyes, and placed his hands on her shoulders, "She's just a large horse, don't be intimidated."

When he turned her, she was not prepared for what her eyes lay upon. "*Did you just compare me to a horse, Rah?!*"

Ilkiz was beautiful and stating that she was huge would be an understatement. She was elegant, and her form was curled upon the ground. The pristine white scales shimmered in the candlelight, and the subtle red undertones lent an aura of both serenity and power. Her size was breathtaking, and while she wasn't bulky by any means, her length rivaled Xlok, who was the oldest known Giant to have ever roamed the realms.

Her fiery-red eye met Azahara, and immediately she felt the same connection she had with the water serpent dragon that Akua summoned. It was as though Ilkiz was looking through her mortal form, delving into the depths of her very spirit. She could see the wisdom in the dragon's eyes, and the fear that had wrapped her just seconds ago, was gone.

Taking a step towards her, she saw the gentle rise and fall of its mighty chest, and that same warm current of air that emanated from its breath hit her once more. A horn, like a polished ruby, rested regally on her head, and Azahara could swear she could sense its life force coursing through her own veins. Ilkiz was the embodiment of strength and resilience, and she wanted people to feel that when they looked at her. Not a body to be touched and prodded.

"*You are much stronger than the others,*" Her head turned, and as Azahara was mere inches from her, she reached out a steady hand. "*You already found the connection, it is profound.*" The size comparison was difficult to comprehend, but when she compared just a single of Ilkiz's eye to her, it still was bigger than she was.

Her hand pressed against her scales, and the texture was both pleasing and strange. It felt like leather, with etched designs across its surface. Each change of the scale was a different feel, and under them, she could feel fur as though she was touching Starlight.

Azahara let out a heavy breath, not realizing that she had been holding it the entire time, "I cannot believe I am touching a Dragon. Not just a Dragon; Ilkiz."

"It is quite incredible." Rah was standing beside her then, his own hand coming up to touch, "Except I'm offended you said she's stronger than me." He pulled at one of her scales, and a shrill hiss came from Ilkiz.

"The truth hurts, boy, don't make me devour you."

"Oh no, I'm so scared." His arm came over Azahara's shoulder and he pulled her to him. "Anyways, I'm sure you have so many questions."

She couldn't bring herself to look away from the massive, slanted eyeball in front of her to really gather what was happening. *"Move your arm, Rah."* Nearly immediately he did and took a step back.

"My bad," he chuckled nervously. The cadence of his speech was disorienting, but suppose he was from a completely different time, so it would make sense.

"Ilkiz," Azahara moved passed the moment, "the Trial."

"You completed the Trial, little one. Not in the way that we intended, but I believe that was my own fault for underestimating you."

"Oh, so you take the blame for her but when I try to do it—"

"I will roast you for dinner, Rah." They fought like Xol and Jayce, but this tension has been built for thousands of years. *"Every one of the four elements of the realm, known as the Veritum, require a trial."*

"I never went through anything like that for Death or the gods' power," she cut in quickly, not wanting to be rude but she had so many unanswered questions.

It was Rah that spoke then, "Technically, you passed Death's test several times. It was showing unconditional love to something that has only known hatred. Death has always gotten a bad rap, you know, the whole reaper thing." Before her eyes, his body morphed in seconds, and standing where he did was Death. Wrapped in their black cloak, a hood covering its fully skeletal form, and a long-curved scythe in hand.

"I'm known as the boogeyman to most," Even his voice shifted, sounding exactly like the Death she had all but come to love. "Boo." He stepped towards her, but she didn't flinch, just stared at him in awe at his shapeshifting ability.

With just a blink of her eyes, he was back to normal.

"Death is one of the harder trials, because it is difficult to change what you are trained to see. It was, at least for me, but I came to understand that it was not a means to an end, but a new beginning." Those words were some of the same that Death itself had said.

"Then, the gods power? I never…"

Rah turned his head away from her, and she felt shame once again hit her. The embarrassment that she felt knowing that these two knew exactly what had happened to her washed over like a wave.

"It will never be okay what he did to you," Ilkiz shifted ever so slightly, enough for her snout to gently push against her back, and she instinctively leaned over and wrapped an arm around, at least in an attempt to do so.

"Goddrick made a mistake and gave you a good deal of his power. For that, the trial was surviving it." Rah crossed his arms, the tone in his voice shifted to disgust, "He lost his title, and became what is known as the people's god; empowered by the might of mortals… Even after losing his title, Goddrick maintained his titled powers, but being in the mortal world strengthened him beyond the threshold of what we thought was possible." She turned to look at him, his teeth clinched, and his hand balled into a fist. "Piece of shit, it was those types of gods I hoped would have never found their place in this world."

Ilkiz huffed, *"Calm, Rah, don't get worked up."* She sounded much calmer than she had before towards him, which seemingly worked to settle his anger.

"Sure—sorry. The only reason gods are as powerful as they are, is because the people worship them. That is their source of sustenance. Even after they are forgotten or have stopped being worshiped, they still retain their power. Goddrick, he had been sealed away in that hourglass for nearly two thousand years, but before that, was worshipped for over three centuries. Besides the God of Might, I would argue Goddrick is probably one of the strongest gods currently in existence."

Somehow, with that knowledge, she felt better. At least she could find some solace in knowing even as hard as she fought, it was useless.

Rah continued, "Back to the trial. He began the Veritum, which brought Ilkiz to you, and pretty much everything that happened afterwards."

"Jaakobai, Thall, the battle? How—Thall had to have been gathering that army for years." She countered.

"Right, he was," he crossed behind her, drawing her away from Ilkiz and she followed, "That battle was inevitable, whether Goddrick screwed up or not. You prevented it from what *could* have been, though." He was making his way towards the lining of tomes, where one stood out amongst the rest.

Bonded in pure white leather, was a large book that rested on its side, drawn around it was a crimson strap, with no keyhole, just tied in a knot.

"You were never meant to be there, and the mortal realm was supposed to lose that battle. But with the shift in your fate, came the fate of the realms."

"That is the Book of Aurora, isn't it?" Azahara asked, stopping as he grabbed it off the shelf.

"Yes, it is." He ran his thumb along the pages, readying to open it.

"Please, don't," Her voice was shaky, and he looked up at her. "I don't want to know anything that hasn't happened yet." His eyes narrowed, and she continued, "Just, tell me what has happened, and what should been."

"Smart girl." Ilkiz chimed in, and Rah shot her a glance. *"Not everything is a jab at you, Rah, relax."*

Azahara could only guess that Rah had read the book when he was in her position but she wouldn't prod to find out if that was the case or not.

"How long..." She continued, swallowing and fearful of the response, "was I meant to be under his curse?"

Rah placed the book back on the shelf, his head dropped and didn't respond. Something ate at her then, as though she were hungry and all she could eat was her own stomach. It felt horrible, and it made her nauseous.

"Another thousand or so years, child." Finding her hand over her mouth, she swallowed the lump in her throat. Her eyes squeezed tightly, and the prospect of that nearly made her faint.

His filthy voice slithered its way into her head, *"I pulled these memories, all seven hundred and forty-three of them, individually—"*

Go away, go away! Please!

"Oh—" Her hand searched for something sturdy to keep her afloat. She was looking for Jayce, to pull away the onslaught of memories that were about to come. The inevitable flashback to those days he trapped her and violated her. Every instance over the last five hundred years that he destroyed the sanity she thought she had.

"You are mine."

"Please—"

Rah was there, his hand in hers, keeping her upright. "You are **safe** here, Azahara. Don't let him in, you have retrieved your soul. You are no longer bound to him. All that is left is his anger and obsession."

"My soul?" She looked at Rah, focusing only on his face, and his words.

"He trapped your soul in his hourglass. But when," he paused, and she pulled her eyebrows together, "Sam—when he came for you, he broke the confinement that he had trapped it in. It was with you where he had you captive."

"You saved your life, but he saved your soul, and broke all ties with Goddrick that remained; including the curse."

I'm safe here, she thought, closing her eyes and centering herself, *he will always keep me safe. No matter what...*

Removing her hand from Rah's grasp, she turned away and began pacing around the room, feeling both a weight lifted and another settling on her shoulders. There were so many questions, she truthfully didn't know which direction to keep moving in. She was grateful that Rah, who was slowly making his way into the center of the space, continued.

"You may have two of the four elements of this realm, but you have received them in a dangerous order. It is why we needed to strip you of them upon entering. Every Keeper before you—"

"We are called Keepers?" Azahara cut him off, looking to find him and seeing he had come to a stop.

"Yes. We are what are known as the Keepers of the Realm."

"They don't call you that," she countered, "they talk of you as a Star."

She wasn't sure what a Dragon would sound like laughing, but the sound she just heard wasn't it. The booming laughter nearly brought her to her knees at how loud it was in her head. It was low in tone, but high in its roar. She quickly covered her ears, thinking that would help; it didn't.

"Rah, a Star? Baha—" Again, the laughter continued, and Azahara regretted saying anything.

Rah didn't seem fazed by the laugh, but he couldn't help feeling hurt by the offense it carried. "Real mature," he retorted with a hint of disappointment in his voice.

"They say," She felt like she was yelling, "The Four Points of Rah's Star, at least, that is how they refer to you. Or just Rah's Star."

Once more, laughter roared, causing Azahara to stumble as the reverberations in her skull became almost unbearable. A persistent headache took hold, one she feared wouldn't relent.

"I've got you," Rah said as he was in front of her, his hands coming up to her temples and placing his palms on them. Immediately she wanted to pull away, run, not allow him to touch her so sensitively. "Oh, is this better?"

When she blinked, in front of her was Jayce. Her eyes widened in shock, the feeling in her stomach not changing, nor did she feel any better.

She shook her head and wanted to run even more than before.

Rah laughed, and even the smile was perfect. It got the completely opposite reaction from her, and she felt angry.

"Don't take his face," she said without any kindness. The realization that he had changed to Mel in that moment also added to her rage. He shifted back, thankfully, without any argument. The smile still on his face.

"You idiot." Ilkiz was coming down from her fit of laughter.

Rah stepped away, "It worked, though, you stopped hearing her." He wasn't wrong, all she heard was ringing from the anger that was writhing throughout her. "Shall we move on? It doesn't matter what they call me, I'm history, you're the present and the future.

"As I was saying, every Keeper before you, they gained the elements Magic, then Power, then Death and Life. Once you receive Power, you can retake the elements of Death and Life." He watched her, expectantly.

"Why does the order matter?" He was expecting that question.

"Magic is the most volatile because it has a mind of its own. It has the control, not you. It is like—"

"I know what it is like, I've felt it before." She didn't want to cut him off, but she was more familiar with Magic than any of the other three and didn't need a lesson in it.

"Right, so starting with that is easier to manage. Power, which is governed by Ilkiz whom the Keeper bonds with, helps contain the Magic, and Death and Life, they equal each other out. It is why you were able to survive gaining them both within moments of each other. If you had received Magic and Life, for instance, you may have been obliterated in seconds."

The thought didn't scare her, so she didn't react, which shocked Rah.

He repeated, "You could have been obliterated—"

"I heard you," she confirmed.

Ilkiz grumbled.

"Okay..." Rah was over his head with that one, so he moved on, "The bonding part with Ilkiz is easy, but—"

"Hold on a moment," Azahara once again cut him off, "Who said I even wanted to bond with her?" Shock, again, laced his expression, and she didn't wait for him to try and continue, "I'm here to ask for help. All I want to do is kill Goddrick and move on with my life. I don't want to be a so-called Keeper." She threw her hands up in frustration, "I never wanted this. I didn't volunteer to be some savior to a realm that currently hates me."

"They don't hate you." Rah countered.

"They fear me. Even if they would have sided with me for what I did on that battlefield, they would run from me given the first sign of trouble."

Rah sighed, "You think I wanted it?"

"You sought out the Mother, so I would say, yes—you did."

It elicited a laugh from him, but it held no humor. Ilkiz, for once, was staying quiet. "You would be sorely mistaken, Azahara. I did not, in fact, want this." There was no pain in his face, but she could tell in his tone that he felt no joy. "I can't tell you about the time before the Reshaping because then I would be removed from this existence without an afterlife awaiting me. I quite like the thought of moving on peacefully.

"What I can tell you is that the world was on the brink of collapse. Great nations were at war with one another, weapons equivalent to those of Dragons and Giants but stronger and more devastating, were ready to destroy everything. It was on the precipice of a global war, and there was no end in sight. Great leaders promised peace, promised change, but in the end, it was only lies. The rich were richer, safer, and more untouchable. It didn't matter what we, the little people, did.

"There would be no one left after the war, none that would create a better world when it was all over, anyways. I had no choice but to find a way to save my people, and I'm not talking about Shapeshifters, but those that wanted peace. So, I knowingly went and sacrificed my life to protect them, with no reward in the end. Other than the knowledge that I had tried to make the world a better place for those that survived.

"So no, Azahara, I did not want this life. I wanted to enjoy my marriage, have children, and be the doctor I had promised my mother I would be. It is what all of us Keepers have in common, unfortunately. We rarely get the choice."

Tears streamed down Azahara's face without her awareness, the sting in her nose and forehead catching her by surprise.

"It's okay. I'm sure the text has misguided many about who I was. Though, I do like being a Star over a Keeper." A Cheshire smile adorned his face, devoid of any trace of anger stemming from the comment she had made.

"I'm sorry..." Her voice wavered, and she brushed the back of her hand over her eyes. "I just—" Both of them displayed patience as she searched for the words to convey her thoughts. In that moment, her heart ached for Rah. Once again, she empathized with his pain, feeling it as if it were her own. "I just want what I want for once, and I know it sounds childish, but even the life before my curse was never truly mine."

"I know, and it won't ever be easy. Your path has not been completely written, so I cannot say for certain if you will ever get what you want." He had read the book of Aurora. "All I can say is, it is possible. To have the life you want at the end of it."

"How? You died after the Reshaping, and I'm assuming all the others did as well." She hated that she was crying, but that feeling of anger in her chest rose, and she knew if she didn't let it go, something else would come instead of the tears.

"You are not taking the path of a traditional Keeper, Azahara. You choose what you do with the powers provided to you. You can choose to Reshape this world as I did or destroy it."

"Is there no other option?"

Rah took a deep breath and looked over at Ilkiz. She followed his gaze, watching as her large red eye shifted towards her. *"No one has tried another option, but that does not mean there is not one."*

With a resounding sigh, she nodded her head. "Can I think about it? Even if not just for a few hours."

Rah seemed to be nervous about the prospect, "Yes, that is fine. Are you hungry or thirsty?" It felt too mundane of a question.

She shook her head and turned away, "No, but if you don't mind, can I just look through the books? Or are they memories of the world lost?"

"Be my guest; they are random books left by travelers when they used to visit." With that, she distanced herself from them, settling on the floor and starting with the book closest to her. She didn't intend to read them, but the pretense might dissuade them from interrupting her contemplation about what direction to take in her life.

It was *her* life, after all.

Not **theirs**.

Day 69

Chapter 28

What felt like several hours passed in slow motion, which was exactly what she had hoped for. It felt like instead she had been sitting on the floor for months, without being hungry or needing anything to keep her alive. Running through her thoughts felt easy in here, and while she could have used a warm body beside her for support, being there alone gave her some clarity she desperately needed.

If she chose to bond with Ilkiz, she would be one step closer to becoming the realm's Keeper. She didn't care to change what was going to happen; who was she to determine the fate of the realm? People died every day, and there would always be terrible people. Rah couldn't speak of what his time was like before the Reshaping but, by the smallest of details he did share, there was absolutely zero to show for his sacrifice. Look where they were now. Nothing had changed; powers sought to overthrow other powers, the affluent continued to exploit the less fortunate, and gods wielded their influence with impunity, thinking themselves above consequences.

Over the span of nearly seven thousand years, they obliterated Dragons and Giants out of fear, and isolated an entire race. The gods forged a treaty with the mortal realm, pledging not to interfere in their affairs—only to shatter it without facing consequences.

History would continue to repeat itself, and there was no amount of Reshaping that she could do to change that.

Then came the prospect of destruction, eradicating the entire population to commence anew with nothing but the bones of this world. While there were moments when she could envision such a drastic act, it was a reality she would never bring to pass. Despite her disdain for many individuals and places, she recognized the presence of good. It wasn't her position to assume the roles of judge, jury, and executioner.

This brought her back to the alternative option. What could it entail? Becoming its protector, perhaps for eternity? The thought felt like an enduring sentence she was unprepared to embrace. Without unlocking the secrets within Aurora, she remained clueless about any other possibilities, and she had no desire to confront what she couldn't comprehend.

It was not within anyone's right to foresee the future, justified or not. Attempting to alter the negative aspects would only disrupt any potential good that could come her way.

"It's okay to be scared; it's not okay to give up." Jayce's words seemed to effortlessly weave into every facet of her life. Regardless of the situation, his expressions were impeccably timed, perpetually serving as a guiding light in her darkest moments. He never belittled her for feeling afraid; instead, he consistently uplifted her, empowering her to summon strength and discover her ability to overcome challenges with time.

Time stretched before her, and in the end, if she were to exact revenge on Goddrick, perhaps she could spend her days with the three elements of the realm, forsaking the pursuit of Magic. As they themselves had acknowledged, she stood apart from the other Keepers. The answer might elude her for now, but with time, she believed she could uncover it.

With a heavy sigh, Azahara closed the book that had not been flipped through since she opened it and placed it back on the shelf.

Coming to a stand, she found Rah ready for her near Ilkiz.

"Thank you both for being patient with me," She said guiltily, "I have never been able to choose what I wanted to do in my life. Now that I have the ability to do so, I find being too hasty will get me in trouble."

"You don't need to justify anything to us, Azahara." There was a smile lining his lips when she looked up at him. "What have you decided?"

Looking at Ilkiz then, she nodded, "I'll bond with you, if you will have me."

Rah prepared quickly, and Azahara wanted to ask what the hurry was, but she didn't want to make him feel self-conscious. It's possible he was afraid that she would change her mind.

As if preparing for some ritual, he drew a large circle in the center of the space and drew symbols within it. The chalk was white, but as time passed, it turned red and began to glow as if it were being lit on fire.

She stood there just watching, really unsure of what to do. Thankfully, Ilkiz filled the quiet with a question.

"Do you want to know the truth about what happened that day you met Goddrick?" There was part of Azahara that didn't want to know. That she wanted to stay ignorant in the hopes that she truly hadn't damned herself to this life. However, there would be a part that would continue to eat at her. That part which would have wanted to know the truth, to try and overcome the trauma and pain that it would inevitably cause.

Taking a deep breath, she nodded her head.

"You did take your sisters up to the tomb that day. They wanted to see the god of legend who helped the lands prosper. When your sister ran in, you chased after her. She had been reaching for the hourglass, and you instead grabbed it before she could even touch it. Once your skin contacted it, your fate was sealed. Your choice to turn it was not your own, and the power that he held, seduced your mind into turning it for him. It pulled your soul from you, and sealed it away.

"You had been very unhappy, Azahara, but you never hated your family, and they never hated you. You were loved, and you loved them. He took more than your life away from you, and I will ensure his destruction."

Hating that once again, she was crying, she asked, "How—how do you know that?" Her words echoed broken and unrepairable, mirroring the shattered state of her heart.

"It was written in the Book," A soft gasp escaped her lips, *"Rah asked to stop it. While I fought with the prospect, we could not change fate. Only the ones that are caught in its thread can do so."*

"Was I fated to turn it all along?"

"You were."

Her hands were trembling, "Can the book be wrong?"

"Wrong, no. However, it can be changed, as we have seen with your fate."

When Rah began walking towards her, his hands covered in white chalk, she sniffled and nodded. "Thank you, Ilkiz, for telling me the truth."

"We will destroy him; it is my promise to you." She believed her and knew that Ilkiz would give her the strength to do so.

"You ready?" Rah said, putting out his hand to her. "This isn't the hard part, and while it may be uncomfortable, it shouldn't be painful."

It had been a reoccurring comment of hers, and it was continuing to hold true. "I am no stranger to pain."

"Let's change that." Ilkiz commented just before Azahara found herself in the center of the circle, on her knees. Rah positioned her hands on her legs, palms up. It was only then that she glanced down at her clothes, still in the traditional dress she had entered with, but now immaculately cleaned—no traces of blood or dirt remained.

The ground rumbled around her, signaling Ilkiz's approach. Without needing to look, Azahara sensed the Dragon moving in her direction. Rah positioned himself in front of her, prompting her to lift her gaze alongside his.

With a majestic stature, Ilkiz's neck extended upwards, revealing the vastness of the chamber designed to accommodate her immense size. Gradually, the dragon lowered her head. Even in this descent, the wind stirred by the motion tousled Azahara's hair, creating a whirlwind that scattered dust outward from their presence.

Rah smiled, "Ready?"

"What will happen to me?" she asked, her voice trembling.

That smile on his face grew wider, "You will become strong."

All she desired was the ability to be strong—both physically and mentally. The idea of possessing the strength to safeguard the people she loved steadied her heart. Those same nerves transformed into a liquid power coursing through her veins.

"She is ready, and always has been."

"Your heart, Azahara Rhay Starfall, will beat with the might of a Dragon. The blood in your veins will burn like the fire in their throats. Your bones and skin will thicken to withstand the Spirit of Ilkiz. Your eyes will see the Realm from new heights."

She closed her eyes and thought only of them. *Jayce, Kaed, Illyan, Zhal, Xol, Alyse—*

"With this bond, you give your everything to protecting Ilkiz and her people; as she will protect you and your world."

They are my world.

Her eyes opened, and she beheld the radiant glow emanating from them. They were ablaze, but not with the threat of tears. They were transforming, much like her body.

"Incredible."

She watched as Rah grinned, baring his teeth in excitement.

Sensing her hands twitch, she directed her gaze downward. She observed the subtle lines in her palms visibly shifting, as if making room for something new. A cold wind shot through her spine, attempting to wrap around her, its chilling embrace intensified by the molten flow coursing through her veins, a threat to engulf her in flames.

Tilting her head back, she met Ilkiz's gaze, her head positioned directly above her. Hunger flickered in the creature's eyes, as if it were ready to devour her. Yet, there was no fear in Azahara's eyes; instead, a serene smile graced her lips.

"Take my Spirit, Keeper."

"As Souls bond, so do Spirits. Never fear falling," Ilkiz intoned with a resounding boom. As the dragon opened her mouth, flames of Power erupted, engulfing Azahara. Yet, she did not burn; instead, the fire stimulated her senses, and her skin absorbed it like the warmth of the sun. The roaring echoed in her ears, but it brought no pain. It resembled the call of a mother bear, beckoning her cub. In that moment, Ilkiz was bringing her home, and Azahara surrendered to the embrace, feeling the profound connection.

There was no pain nor was there any discomfort. It felt right, and as the flames faded and her eyes opened to see a space above her where Ilkiz used to be; a sudden feeling of being whole took over her. It was like waking up from the perfect night's rest, without a dream or nightmare to disturb her. Like after having sex, and not only was she satisfied, but so was her partner. A sense of accomplishment washed over her for doing absolutely nothing, and she allowed it to engulf her.

She blinked before looking down to Rah, who had his arms crossed over his chest. The satisfied grin on his face made her smile.

"You look strong," he commented.

As she began to stand, her eyes drunk in her completely bare body. The flames, they had been real. All of her clothes had burned, and all that was left was dark ash surrounding where she stood.

"Do not fear," Ilkiz's voice reached her ears, now much gentler than it had been in the room. The soft caress to her earlobes was soothing. *"He will not touch you."* She swallowed and met his gaze.

"Turn for me. I want to see your Connection."

For some reason, she hesitated to speak, as if fire might erupt from her throat next. Gathering resolve, she turned, presenting him with the view from behind.

She heard his footsteps approaching, and she stiffened. "Incredible. Yours is dynamic, much more so than mine was," he remarked. The heat from his hand triggered a defensive reaction, prompting her to swiftly turn and grip his wrist. "I wasn't going to touch," he defended himself. "You can speak. Let me hear, please."

"Be kind to him. He did not get to meet the last Keeper. He is in just as much awe as I am of you and your power, Azahara."

Licking her lips, she parted them and spoke, "Creep." While the sound of her voice wasn't too far off from what it sounded like prior, there was a subtle echo that sounded ethereal, naturally gliding her singular word to new heights.

Rah laughed, "Fair enough."

Azahara smiled then, "I want to see it."

He led her to a mirror, albeit broken, but enough for her to catch a glimpse of herself. The sight of her bare body still induced a wave of nausea, the awareness of what had been done to it haunting her. She quickly turned around, stealing a glance over her shoulder.

Stretching from nearly the base of her spine to the back of her neck were black markings resembling wisps of smoke. A singular upward angle, as if she were aflame. The intricate design stayed within the confines of her spine, not venturing beyond the expanse of her back.

"It looks like smoke," she commented, tilting her head to try and see a different angle.

"It looks like paint," Rah said, also tilting his head. "Like someone took a paint brush and dragged it up your back, and just used all the paint until it ran out."

Ilkiz chuckled, *"Everyone will see something different. Even you when you look. Rah loved to paint before he became the Keeper, so while not too far off from its original design, it makes sense that is what he sees."*

"It is weird not hearing her," Rah said, looking at her through the mirror. "I can only tell she is talking to you, by the wonder in your eyes."

"It feels sort of like the winnox, but clearer," she mused, uncertain. Suddenly, a realization struck her, and she turned. "Rah—wait, what will happen to you?"

He sighed, and with a relaxed smile, he said, "I'll pass on."

Her heart thumped against her chest, quickening its pace. He tilted his head towards her, the smile never leaving his expression. "It's time," he uttered, and the burning sensation behind her eyes intensified. "While I'll be gone from this world, you know better than anyone that it is not the end. I will join the other Keepers. From what Death has told me, there is a special place for us. I'm hoping that there are beautiful women there," he chuckled, "maybe I'll be lucky enough to find someone like you."

Azahara smiled brightly, feeling tears brimming in her eyes. "They'd be lucky," she responded. He playfully waved his hand at her and mockingly twirled fake hair around his finger. "Jeez, you are so strange," she teased, eliciting laughter from both of them.

"We will need to go. You will need to summon me and ride before your body begins to feel the pressure of two Spirits."

"It's time to go," Rah said, stepping towards her. "I will see you off, and I'll alert the Spirit Riders of your return." His hands were cold as they pressed against her shoulders.

"Why does it feel like I've known you for longer than a day, Rah?" Azahara asked, her hands coming up to his chest, feeling the tears burning down her cheeks.

"It's because, while not physically, we have always been connected. Along with all the other Keepers," he placed his hand onto her cheek, "Miss me just a little bit, though, it makes me feel like the Star that I am."

His lips pressed against her forehead, and she laughed through her sobs.

"Ilkiz, give the girl some scales! By the skies above, you are testing a man's resolve not to look!" Azahara swung her fist, but he swiftly transformed into a mouse and scurried a few feet away. Upon returning to his original form, she felt a peculiar sensation, as if something were moving up her body.

"These are scales and should really be worn over clothing. I would normally tell you to embrace yourself, but Goddrick ruined that for you."

White and red scales, intricately layered, adorned her skin—spanning across her breasts, down her stomach, and raising from her flesh. They continued over her hips and down between her thighs, eliciting a gasp from her. The sensation was akin to ants crawling across her skin, and every second of it was an experience she despised.

"Those will stop nearly any man-made weapon," he grinned, and as she looked at him, he began to fade.

"Rah!"

"Ah, shit—" He looked at his hands, clearly able to see beyond them, as though his body was becoming translucent. "That happened fast."

She ran over to him, asking urgently, "Where do we go?"

"I've let them know you are coming out, but you must ride first. No matter what, do not go to them. As you exit this temple, you will regain your other gifts—it won't be as bad as it was when we took them." Her hand reached out to his cheek, still able to feel him. A handsome smile adorned his face. "Do me a favor, hmm?"

"Of course," she said as he slowly continued to disappear.

"Call me Rahmulous, just once."

Azahara laughed through a few droplets of tears. "You are such a weirdo, Rahmulous."

"I'll see you later, cutie." With a wink, he grabbed her waist and pulled her to him. A bright light engulfed her, and before she knew it, she was free-falling, nothing but the solid ground ready to meet her in mere moments.

Day 69
CHAPTER 29

Her scream was so loud that it cracked in her throat. Her arms waved as she frantically tried to stay flat and not tumble in a circle. The air in her lungs was stolen away as the sheer speed at which she was falling was far too great for her to fight against.

"*Relax, he just loves the dramatics.*"

"Ilkiz!! Help!!" Again, she screamed, and she swore something flew into her mouth because she began coughing immediately.

"*Call to me.*"

"**I JUST DID!**" The ground was becoming closer and closer, and in the corner of her eye, she could see water spinning as it had when they first arrived.

"*Through your Spirit, girl, and hurry or else—*"

The least Rah could have done was tell her how the heck to speak through her spirit. She was still getting used to having her soul back, *How the hell?!*

Closing her eyes, she delved into the darkness, seeking a glimmer of light that could guide her toward what she needed to do. The freefall sent her stomach plummeting so deeply that she felt on the verge of vomiting, and her head spun out of control. The ground loomed closer, and instinctively, she reached her hands out, as if attempting to halt her rapid descent to the ground.

It was then that she saw the palms of her hands. "Where did these come from?!"

"*Place them together, now!*"

Without hesitation, she clapped her hands together, and a powerful force propelled her forcefully backward, causing her to ascend instead of continuing the descent. The moment was fleeting, and as her body felt gravity pulling her back down, she spun and braced herself to resume the descent.

Her eyes locked onto Ilkiz crawling up from the ground below, shooting straight up at her. The dragon's massive wings generated a hurricane of wind on either side, obliterating boulders and the nearest cliffside.

While Azahara continued her dive fairly straight, her arms and legs wobbled in an effort to prevent another spin. The fear that gripped her just moments ago vanished as she witnessed her powerful protector approaching. Now, she could discern that Ilkiz had only two feet, and her arms were integrated into her wings, which spanned beyond her own eyesight.

Ilkiz was incredible.

A smile etched on her face as she saw her reflection come into view within the Dragon's massive red eye.

"I've got you, little one."

Got her, she did. As they collided, Ilkiz enveloped her in her grasp. The handoff wasn't painless, yet the ache in her bones didn't feel as severe as it should have. It was as if she had been thrown against a wall and bounced off without a scratch.

Ilkiz lifted her up to her neck, a harrowing experience. This was nothing like riding a horse. When she barely straddled a few scales on her neck and found nothing to hold onto, she instinctively leaned forward, embracing the massive beast as if she were at risk of slipping away.

"It will take practice, and I won't do anything crazy. For now."

Trembling, she groaned, "Very reassuring."

"I'll slow down. Enjoy the view before we have to go back to the ground. I know I am, it has been too long since I've stretched my wings."

Taking a long, deep breath, she leaned up and tightened her legs as though holding on for dear life. When her eyes absorbed the surroundings, her breath was stolen. The sky adorned itself with a beautiful hue of pinks and oranges, and she sensed Rah watching her take her first flight before disappearing beyond the veil.

Her heart swelled with awe and wonder as she gazed at the scenery below. Slowly, and as promised, Ilkiz descended gently, bringing her closer to the marvelous trees that stretched across nearly the whole Isle of Ilkiz. With lush greens on one side and the vast sea on the other, she felt embraced by the beauty that flight bestowed upon her.

She could smell the fragrances of the forest below—the scent of damp dirt, blooming flowers, and the sweet aroma of ripe fruits that grew only in this part of the world. Even amid the rumbling of Ilkiz's heart, she heard the wildlife below, a natural orchestra of sounds. She wondered if it had anything to do with her newfound body.

Fire began to flicker over the forest as the sun prepared to bid goodnight, and the moon would soon illuminate their way. She felt a perfect connection between herself and Ilkiz, as if they had coexisted within each other for years rather than minutes.

"I find myself feeling a profound sense of belonging for you. It has never been this way. It is a strange sort of possession." Ilkiz confessed, *"Death spoke of your uniqueness. I do wonder if it is how you came to us, or just that you truly are the light that this realm needed."*

Azahara sighed, her head dropping as she stared down into the seams of her scales. "I don't know about the light part," her voice was soft, and she feared Ilkiz wouldn't hear her, "but I strangely feel the same with both you and Death. It may be that I welcome you as you are, with no expectation of change. It makes bonding to me easier."

"It could be."

Feeling a sudden drop, she lifted ever so slightly off Ilkiz, before gripping onto a scale for her life. "I'm getting you a saddle."

"You will do no such thing."

"Stirrups?"

"I am not a horse, little one."

"Reigns?"

"...Possibly."

Ilkiz slowly began to descend, and as they did, she could see a small group of people waiting not too far from where she had entered the temple just yesterday. Her eyes focused on one person above anyone else: Jayce.

"Be careful not to—" Ilkiz flapped her massive wings, sending rocks and dust billowing around them, "not to do just that."

As they approached the ground, she started to slip from Ilkiz's neck. Immediately regretting it, realizing she was not close at all, she desperately tried to stop. Thankfully, Ilkiz must have gone through this exercise a few times because she extended her wing, creating a makeshift slide.

Her feet felt good on solid ground, and her toes dug into the warm dirt. "How do you go back?"

"*I eat you.*"

She narrowed her eyes, "That doesn't make any sense. I should eat you."

A harmonious laugh escaped Ilkiz, and it boomed. "*I am going to love you. I already know it.*" That made her smile. "*Just think about me returning to you, like a ball bouncing off a wall. It is the same concept, different execution.*"

She moved under Ilkiz, shadowed by her presence, and placed her hand onto her belly. *Come back.* While she figured there was no need to ask or think of directions, it may help in the meantime. Her massive frame slowly dissolved into smoke, which didn't fly away in the wind which picked up her hair then, but instead came flying into the palms of her hands.

"Interesting," she said, watching as the symbols returned to her hands.

Running her hand through her hair, she brushed it back. Sensing something different, she pulled it in front of her and realized it was significantly longer than when she entered. It now reached just to her collarbone, whereas before, it had been at her shoulders.

"Aza? Aza!" Pulling her from her random finding, she searched through dust and smoke around her.

"Jayce?!" She called out and began running down the small incline towards where the voice was echoing from.

"*You must be careful.*" Ilkiz warned, "*You are much stronger than you were when you entered, especially when our Spirits are connected as they are right now.*"

A figure was coming into view, and she picked up speed. "*Slow down, he will get to you.*"

Heeding her warning, she returned to a jog. Moments later, she caught sight of his face, and her eyes widened. A bright, unfiltered smile beamed across her face.

Uncertain of what to expect—perhaps a smile, a witty remark about her speed, or even a playful comment on her strength that made the journey shorter than anticipated—she approached with a mix of curiosity and anticipation.

"I will explain—but I couldn't tell you in there, or else you would have only thought about getting back to him." Her eyebrows furrowed in confusion.

The expression on Jayce's face nearly knocked her out. Anxiety and pain were written all over it, prompting her to stop moving and look down at herself. She wasn't bleeding, and she didn't feel injured. Why was he looking at her like that?

As he reached her, she could tell he was shaking, and before she could question what was wrong, he slammed into her. His entire being engulfed her, urgently pressing himself against her. His arms tightened, as if he were searching for confirmation that she was truly there.

"Jayce…" His desperation was palpable, making her own need in her grip on him just as urgent. She clung to him as if he, too, were on the verge of disappearing.

He pulled back, both of his hands coming to her cheeks and looking into her eyes; *why does it look like he is going to cry?* "Jayce, you are scaring me. What's wrong?"

His eyes were sharp, and they pierced right through her.

"You—" She felt like crying and she didn't know why, "You were gone…" Those tears lined her lids, "for nearly three months, Aza."

She released a single huff of air, "What?"

~~Day 69~~
Day 162

"What—?!" Azahara shook her head, her hands trembling as they came from around him. "It's been... not even two days!" She was arguing with air.

"He is correct," Ilkiz confirmed, causing her vision to shake, *"I'm sorry. In the chamber, time works differently. For you, it was merely two days, when in reality, it was months."*

Jayce was placing kisses across her forehead, down to her cheeks, and then along her jaw before tucking his head between the curve of her neck. His arms encompassed her once again, his shoulders trembling. She could feel his lips pressing against her neck, the sensation hitting a particularly sensitive spot.

Her arms moved around his neck, and she held him to her.

"Jayce... I'm here..." While feeling his trepidation, she needed to calm him down; his entire being was rattling. Her words weren't enough—he was completely lost to his fear, for the first time. The symbol of strength for her was crumbling to pieces in her arms.

She placed her hands at the sides of his neck, as he would do to her, and with her thumbs, pushed his head up. There was force needed because he was not giving up.

He lifted her off the ground, and she stared down into his eyes, "I'm here, Jayce, it's okay." Remembering when he had asked her to tell him something to calm him down. It had seemed to work then, and she knew him well enough to know it would work again. "I've always had this thing with the moon."

Surprise lined his expression as he took a deep breath.

"There has always been something about it that has drawn me to it. It always irritated me at how mysterious it was," a smile graced his lips as he pressed his forehead to hers, "like it had a secret it wanted me to know, but right as it was ready to tell me, the sun would come up and take the opportunity away."

Jayce placed kisses tenderly across her face, "I never had enough time with it, but somehow," his fingers laced between the coils of her hair, "I always fall in love with it." Then his lips met hers passionately. Her body succumbed to his, allowing them to melt together as one.

Locked in each other's embrace, his hand moved to cradle the back of her neck while the other lovingly wrapped around her waist, drawing her closer. Their lips entwined in a soft and careful kiss, he had always been tender with her. It felt like an eternity of yearning had led to this very moment, and now they were finally savoring the sweetness of their connection.

The layer of bristly hair on his face was silky, and not at all itchy as she once thought. His lips were inviting, and as they turned their heads to deepen the kiss, she could taste him. The taste of strawberries lingered, and she wondered briefly if he had consumed them daily while she was gone. When his lips parted, she dared find out for herself. Allowing herself a moment of further weakness, she slipped her tongue between his lips, tasting the sweet berry and peppermint.

Feeling him stiffen, she retreated to a gentle, innocent kiss before leaning her head back.

"I apologize; that was my influence," Ilkiz commented, and she sounded sheepish.

It's okay, I'm not mad.

An elongated smile crossed his lips, and its infectious nature caught her, causing her to smile just as widely.

"I'm happy to have my girl back," His voice breathless against her lips.

"They say the heart grows fonder with distance." She was slowly being put back down to her feet when the clatter of footsteps echoed toward them.

Jayce shook his head and brushed his hand against her cheek, "I think we have been away from each other for long enough. I don't need distance or time to tell me of my fondness for you."

Day 163
CHAPTER 30

"You are lying!" Her shriek came out a bit louder than she had wanted, "You are telling me you were born with it?"

The hearty laughter from Akua filled her with joy, but also concern. Was what she said really that funny? Hopefully, he didn't find her accusation of him lying to her hurtful. She had even jumped out of her seat at his proclamation and slowly resettled herself in the lounger that sat adjacent to him.

"Yes, Azahara, all descendants that are blessed with the Spirits, are born with them already attached." His gaze was hard focused on her, never once taking his eyes from her, "Why is that so hard to believe?"

Inhaling deeply, she released a heavy sigh, leaning her elbow onto the armrest and cradling her chin in her palm. "It just feels off, you know? It's like you're not given a choice about becoming a Spirit Rider."

Another chuckle resounded from him as he responded, "We don't have to answer the call, or rather, receive our marks. While we have connections to our dragon's spirit, if we don't receive their mark, we don't complete the bond."

She remembered the marking on her back and glanced over her shoulder. Not that she could see it, she wore a dress that covered her completely, from neck all the way down to her ankles. After being naked in front of Rah, and then slapped with scales around her private areas as if that did anything, skin was the last thing she wanted to show off.

"I'm not talking about your Connection," he continued, "I'm talking about the one on your palm."

Opening her hands and looking down, she could see the yellow lines that created two separate symbols. Neither of them meant anything to her, and if she had to describe them in any way, she'd say one looked like an "L" with lines through it, and the other, a "T" with the same sort of scribble. They were interesting, to say the least.

"May I?" He was leaning towards her, and she nodded.

When he leaned in, she outstretched her hands to him. "Ah, I should have figured."

"What?" she quickly asked.

"I bear only one symbol, while my sister carries the other." He extended his palm, revealing a symbol distinct from hers – an "A" embellished with tails on every point. Closing his hand and gently placing his fingers over her symbols, he explained, "These are Ilkiz's portals to this realm, manifested through you." Tracing a line up her wrist and pressing onto her veins, he continued, "It courses upward, connecting to wherever your Spirit resides within you. My conjecture is, it's likely nestled within your heart."

"He doesn't need to touch you for this story, little one," Ilkiz hissed.

Azahara slowly pulled her hands away and placed them in her lap. "What do they say, the symbols, that is?"

Leaning back and casually crossing his legs, Akua remarked, "Mine stands for Acquiescence." Her assumption for that would be subdued demeanor, yet evident readiness to take action.

"Oh, so they are letters."

"Not necessarily. Kaen's is a swirl, with a line through it. I attributed it to her crazy personality, but don't tell her I said that." He winked.

It elicited a chuckle from her, and she nodded. "Noted."

"If I may be so bold," his almond-shaped eyes slanted at her, revealing a depth of insight, "Considering your history with time—" it seemed that in her absence, the crew had divulged more about her than she had anticipated, "one of them symbolizes that. As for the other, I would venture to guess it possibly represents love, or even, beauty."

Her eyebrows furrowed, but before she could voice her thoughts, Ilkiz interjected, *"He has been diligently studying. It doesn't excuse his insufferable flirting, but he is accurate."* The shift from irritation to surprise was swift enough to bring a wide smile to Akua's face. "Your markings indeed signify time and beauty."

Ilkiz had advised Azahara to engage with a Spirit Rider to gain insights into their experiences and knowledge, given her newfound Power. The caution about not depending too heavily on Ilkiz for historical information lingered in her thoughts. She had been warned that inadvertent revelations from before the Reshaping could potentially fry her brain.

Azahara emitted a soft groan and nodded, "You've hit the nail on the head."

Akua seemed proud of himself, and ran his fingers through his silky black hair, tossing it over to one side. "I didn't spend so many years in the Academy for nothing."

She noticed his gaze trailing over her shoulders, and curiosity got the better of her, prompting a daring glance. It was Jayce who held his attention, casually propped against a post, absentmindedly dismantling a leaf. Despite her request for a private conversation with Akua, she had offered him the choice to linger nearby, a choice he willingly accepted.

After their kiss, Xol, Akua, and Kaen swarmed around them, practically pulling her back to the village in a flurry of excitement. Xol had covered her after prying her from Jayce's arms, scolding him for being a weak male and not being decent. With the irony of it all, she couldn't help the laugh that had been brought to her lips.

The festivities were confirmed for today, a celebration marking the union between a new Spirit Rider and their Dragon. It wasn't exactly a tradition for an outsider to undergo such a ceremony, let alone the ensuing celebration. Her markings were already a part of her, eliminating the need for the customary process. The revelry would extend over the next week, honoring Ilkiz and, by extension, Azahara.

Her attempts to protest the attention conferred on her were met with resistance, especially from Kaen, who bluntly advised her not to be selfish. The celebration, she clarified, wasn't solely for Azahara but for the people. Ilkiz, in stark contrast to Azahara, reveled in the anticipation of being celebrated, showcasing their striking differences in their appetite for attention.

"Is there anything else you'd like to know about us?" Akua redirected her attention back to him, sensing her momentary distraction while she was lost gazing at Jayce, momentarily forgetting her surroundings.

"Hmm?" Slipping back into her seat, she looked at him, "Oh—sorry. Do you have a, what did you call it, Connection mark?"

"It's just simply called the Connection and we don't have them." Her eyes widened. "The mark, it is specific to those that are blessed by Ilkiz, and her alone. The Connection is not meant for the two of you, but for those that look upon you.

"Your kind has held many titles, but the Keeper has always held true to its name. The Keeper holds the balance in their hands for what will be the future of this world. When the people look upon you, as they will, what they see matters. The Connection was created for people to see themselves in you. While not everyone is as beautiful, or as short—" she narrowed her gaze, "or as smart, or strong, as you, they will see something of themselves when they see the Connection."

She shifted her gaze away, focusing on her fingers as they idly picked at her nails. With a slight groan, she mused, "That sounds like a lot of attention I really don't want."

Akua sighed, "Even without seeking it, their eyes would find you. Whether you desire it or not, you've stepped into the light, and their gazes will follow."

She closed her eyes, acknowledging how right he was. Ignorance wasn't an option when it came to her appearance, and although attractiveness naturally drew stares, now, with this newfound power, the looks directed her way would carry a different weight. *Witch. Whore. Succubus. Seductress. Manipulator.* These were the labels she braced herself to confront in the inevitable conflicts that lay ahead.

"You should live here, when everything is said and done." Akua suggested, gently pulling her from her contemplative thoughts.

"Why?"

"You would truly belong here. We would embrace you, and treat you as one of our own," he expressed with a sheepish smile, his cheeks tinted with a blush. "You know, that family stuff everyone yearns for."

With her own smile, she said "I appreciate that, but I'm not sure where I'll end up after all of this. Will I even be alive?" Her words carried a breathless laugh, "Will this world still stand? I haven't even thought about the ending; my focus has been on figuring out what my next move will be."

"I think I can speak for all of us here, when I say that we would accept you if you decided to stay."

"Thanks, Akua," she expressed, feeling a warmth rise at the back of her neck as her smile broadened, "This place would make a wonderful home."

"Good."

"Here it comes." Ilkiz presented both an intriguing sensation and a touch of annoyance. She realized she would need to establish clear boundaries with her.

"So, the celebration tonight. You will need to have a partner for the sealing process."

Sealing process? She asked Ilkiz.

"It is their tradition; I didn't realize they still did it." The response was swift enough that she was able to refocus on Akua without missing a beat.

"I can stand with you for that, if you would like."

"No, you can seal yourself." It was akin to navigating two conversations simultaneously, attempting to concentrate on one without overlooking the other. Her head was starting to spin from the effort.

She laughed nervously, "Akua, I'm not even sure what the sealing process is. Can't I do it myself?"

"It's painful, and the person standing with you can take half of it from you." As Akua explained, she could feel Ilkiz sigh so prolonged it felt like her body was vibrating. "It is no problem, really."

Taking a deep breath, she put a weak, very nervous looking, smile on her face, "Ilkiz says I need to do it alone, but thank you."

"Your friend is likely going to kill me with the look he is giving me," Akua murmured, a hint of nervousness creeping into his tone. "By the skies above, why is he so intimidating?"

She laughed, leaning forward, and remarked, "You're flirting with his woman, what do you expect?"

Akua shot a quick glance in her direction. "Ah, I do apologize. Alyse said you and he weren't—"

"I like you Akua," she interjected, rising to her feet, "So please take this with all the respect in the realms." Her smile was gentle, devoid of any animosity. "I'm unavailable, other than as a friend."

Awkward interactions weren't her forte, and had this occurred before Ilkiz, the expression on his face would have likely prompted her to fold, followed by profuse apologies as if she had committed some grave error. However, to her surprise, he took the initiative to apologize, bowing his head and almost pleading for her forgiveness.

After what felt like an eternity, he eventually relented. Akua reassured her that he would be on his best behavior, emphasizing his commitment to serving her as the Keeper and avoiding any actions that might jeopardize their relationship.

Once she was satisfied that the air was cleared and there were no lingering reservations between them, she bid him farewell. It was time for her to start getting ready.

Having been awake for the past day since her return, the realization that she hadn't slept in over three months loomed over her. Despite the lack of fatigue, the prospect of maintaining this energy throughout the ceremony that night was daunting. There was a nagging concern that her body might suddenly give out in the midst of it.

As she contemplated this, a sinking feeling settled in, and her head dropped with a groan.

"I wasn't eavesdropping or anything," his voice was always a savior to her souring emotions, "but that was the smoothest rejection I've ever witnessed."

As Jayce sauntered over, hands tucked casually in his pockets, their eyes instantly connected. Her heart leaped to her throat. Nerves gripped her, and the sting of anxiety knifed right at her stomach. The need for a conversation hung in the air, but she wasn't quite prepared for it. Earlier emotions had been intense, the rush of realization that he hadn't seen her in months, even though it had only been days for her, had clouded her thoughts completely.

Not that she regretted the moment—she wouldn't have changed it for anything. However, that didn't alter the fact that Alyse's words to her, right before she left, still lingered.

"Nervous?" His ability to read her so effortlessly made her curse herself.

"I did mention that before, you know?" As he approached, she gently bit her bottom lip, tilting her head to maintain eye contact. "You overheard, then?" His hand enveloped hers, which had been slowly picking at her nails, on the verge of tearing them off.

"I was trying not to eavesdrop, I should say." His thumb brushed the back of her hand, "Don't worry, I don't think I heard anything important. Just that you were unavailable other than friendship."

By the Mother, why are my emotions on the fritz right now. I feel sad, mad, happy, upset, nervous, confident—Ilkiz!

"While I am enhancing them, this isn't my fault."

"Azahara?" Her heart thumped so forcefully against her chest that it bordered on painful. "I just wanted to say I'm sorry."

"Huh?" Attempting to refocus, her tone turned breathy, eliciting a squeeze from him on her hand. "For what?"

"When I saw you, after being away for so long, I—" He sighed heavily and dropped his gaze. "My head, I had just gotten you back, and then you were gone again. The circumstances around this time were much, much better, but it didn't make it any easier. When you came back, by the Mother, I had forgotten how to breathe. I didn't believe it was you—"

Placing her hand against his cheek, she lifted his gaze to hers, "Jayce, it's okay. I would have done the same thing. You got the short end of that stick. I only had to miss you for a few days."

He leaned into her hand, turning and kissing her wrist, sending an unexplainable pleasure shooting down her spine. "I just hope I didn't force you into that kiss because you felt it was the only way to pull me back."

Her cheeks ignited with warmth. "Oh, you... are sorry for that?"

"Only if you weren't ready." He looked at her cheeks, and it elicited a smile from him.

"I was, Jayce." His hand came to the side of her neck, "If I hadn't, well, it wouldn't have happened."

Never again would she allow someone to take advantage of her. Without a shred of doubt in her mind, she was determined that no man, woman, or other would touch her without her consent.

His face softened, and the laughter that emanated from his throat sent a lightning bolt through her chest, straight down to her stomach. "Good to know," he remarked.

Taking a step toward him, she noticed the surprise once again flicker in his eyes. "I need to get ready, or Kaen will kill me. I can feel her eyes bearing down on me," she groaned. Looking up, she spotted a very angry Kaen within the canopies, standing along a wobbly bridge. She had promised to be with her before the sun cascaded towards the horizon, and unfortunately, it was already kissing its edge.

"She's scarier when she's mad," Jayce commented, also looking up. It looked like Kaen was saying something, but she was drowned out by Azahara humming a gentle laugh. It brought his attention back down to her.

"Before I go," she said, pulling out a piece of paper from the pocket sewn into her dress, "this is for you." Jayce took a step back, accepting it into his hand. "The only stipulation to you opening that, Jayce Latimer—look at me," he was staring at it longingly, and when she called out, he redirected his gaze to her. "Actually, there are two. One, you can't open it until I'm getting ready. Alyse won't let anyone see me until the celebration starts. She says Kaen is adamant that I don't appear until it's time." There was annoyance in her tone, and she did air quotes to emphasize it. "The second, I just want to ask you something, and I want the truth," her hand quickly shot up and stole the letter from him. The pure shock on his face charged her confidence.

"It's about Xol," his eyes focused on her, "did you somehow bring her to me, or did she come on her own volition?" There was no shift in his expression, and he was searching for something behind her eyes.

"Both. I had an influence, but she didn't need convincing," she replied, and the edge of her lip curled upward.

"Okay," she handed the letter back to him, "once you read it, we will talk in the way we know best." She spun around him and skipped towards the ladders that led to the canopies above.

"How is that?" He called after her.

"You'll know when it's time."

Day 163
Chapter 31

The amount of nerves that were running through her body was teetering on unhealthy, maybe even life threatening. It had been a few hours since she left Jayce with her letter. A wave of queasiness rolled through her, a constant unsettling churn in the pit of her stomach. Was it a cowardly move to put that into a letter instead of just telling him? *Probably*. Was it easier? *Yes*. How was she supposed to just, bring that up to someone? This situation was far too unique, and it had been plaguing her for weeks—well, months now.

She tried her best to sit tight while Alyse and Kaen worked on her hair. They griped about her coiled curls making it a real challenge to do anything fancy. There would have been no complaints from her, but alas, neither of them was going to go down without a fight.

They'd wet it, and immediately got to work. Nonetheless, this was the reason behind her prolonged preparation time. Kaen had focused on adorning her facial markings, a customary ritual for them. In light of her fair complexion, red paint was chosen over white, a decision she justified by noting that white wouldn't be visible. Alyse nearly burst into laughter, the irony of the sun denying her any hint of color adding a playful sense of defeat to their jest.

Kaen delicately traced dots beneath her eyes, gently arching them until they seamlessly reached her hairline. Continuing from the midpoint of her brow, she sketched a line that extended gracefully down to her chest, concluding precisely where the dress would commence. Taking her preference into consideration, a crescent moon was artfully drawn at the focal point of her forehead.

They finished almost simultaneously, affording Azahara a moment to appraise her decorated face and styled hair before donning the dress. Ordinarily, she would have staunchly resisted wearing anything even remotely as revealing as the ensemble they had crafted for her, but its beauty was undeniable. When they revealed it to her, she was left speechless, and the revelation that Kaen had personally designed it only heightened its sense of awe.

The silver dress was a breathtaking sight, its allure heightened as candlelight danced across the crystals intricately sewn beneath the lace that adorned the silk fabric. Although the neckline was cut entirely too low between her breasts, a detail she wasn't entirely pleased with, the customized sizing ensured there was no risk of any nipple slips. Despite her reservations, she opted not to ask how Kaen had precisely determined her measurements, particularly in the chest area.

The dress's second key feature, and perhaps its most captivating, was the back – a straight, downward plunge that revealed the small dimples of her spine, drawing attention to her Connection. Akua, along with Kaen and Ilkiz, emphasized the significance of this design element, as it would be the focal point during the sealing ceremony with their eldest descendant.

Despite the revealing aspects of the dress—the low-cut chest, the silk barely reaching her thighs, and the lace fabric comprising the rest—the standout feature was the inclusion of wings. Crafted from silver metal, meticulously bent, melted, and shaped, the wings adorned the shoulders acting as the dress's straps. They gracefully curved over her collarbone, traced down the sides of her chest, encircled around her breasts, and descended to her stomach, forming a captivating wing-like structure. Acting almost like a corset, they accentuated her already slender waist. The wings enveloped her shoulder blades, with the scapulars terminating just shy of the connection point.

"You look incredible," Azahara turned to see Xol standing in the doorway, admiration in her gaze.

"Hey!! We said no one is to come in here!!" Kaen was preparing to burn the damn place down.

"Kaen, it's fine. Xol is escorting me down, remember?" Azahara feared that woman. Not because she didn't think she'd win in a fight, but with just how destructive and unpredictable she was.

Almost instantly, Kaen lowered her hands. "Oh, yeah, that is right." She turned to Alyse. "I think our job is done here anyways. We should go get ready." And with that, they vanished, leaving behind the rattling of their pod as they hastily retreated.

"I thought the men were insufferable. Women are just as bad." Xol groaned, closing the door behind them before stepping further into the pod.

Azahara put her hands together in front of her and laughed nervously, "I would have to agree, but less so than men. You'll come to learn that, in time. I have a feeling we will have a lot of it together."

A gentle smile lined the colorless woman before her, "When did you figure it out?"

"I always had this strange feeling around you, not a bad one, just—like I knew who you were, but I didn't at the same time. As though we had this crazy adventure, but I didn't know your name, what you looked like or anything."

Azahara walked over and settled onto the bed, crossing her legs at the ankle, and leaning forward. The absence of the familiar sensation of her hairbrush against her shoulders felt peculiar, almost making her unwittingly disturb the crown of braids Alyse had meticulously crafted for hours. Fortunately, Alyse had thoughtfully left a few strands around her ears for moments like these, providing a comforting source of diversion when nervous.

"So, then, your kind don't seek out Fae wings to destroy the realms?"

"No," Xol crossed the room and settled beside her. "We seek them to be released from our immortal forms. Typically, it takes the Magic of an Elder, but thanks to being released into Höwl I was able to feed on enough wings to suffice. While I'll still live an eternal life, my body is no longer that of a creature that cannot be killed. Or as hideous."

They shared a harmonious laugh.

Azahara smiled, not at the fact she inevitably killed Fae, but in the confirmation that Xol was indeed the Yuul who had rescued her from captivity. A peculiar sense of relief washed over her, as if a lingering uncertainty had been lifted, and now she could truly move forward with her relationship with Xol.

"They hurt you, don't feel bad for them," she said, placing a hand onto Azahara's leg. "They deserved what they got."

"I know," she looked into her sea blue eyes, "trust me, you don't have to convince me. I suppose I am curious though. Your connection to me, was it built just off me being the means to your salvation? Or was there something else?"

Xol grinned, letting out a soft chuckle, "You were the reason I was released, whether you brought me there or not, I owe you that. However, it was when you grabbed me just before you went through the portal with your Fae friend."

Thinking back, she wondered where the courage had come from to grab a Yuul like she did. As if it couldn't effortlessly shred her to pieces with a mere flick of their wrists.

"You disregarded all fear of what I was for someone you loved. While I had no mind to understand at that time what it meant, when I was reborn into my eternal self, that act of kindness molded me to be sane." Xol placed a cold hand against her jaw, holding her with a gaze filled with gratitude. "My kind feared release from our immortal bodies, not for death, but if their minds would allow them to succeed. I thought only of you when I came to, and it guided me."

Azahara felt the familiar sting in her eyes, "I'm so glad…"

"Don't cry," Xol gently pressed a finger beneath her eye, physically pushing back the tears.

"They will try to kill me if you mess up their work."

"Sorry—" She took a deep breath and centered herself. "Your eyes, and your appearance—was this who you were before?"

Xol shook her head, "I modeled them after you, for the most part. Time was much different than what it is today when I was mortal. Returning to my original form would have been, I believe, too much for this world."

Azahara would not ask; she refused.

"Now it's strange calling you beautiful," she quipped, placing a hand down onto Xol's thigh, which was dressed in fine leather. "But you are. Thank you, it's very flattering. Maybe too much so."

They both let out a hearty laugh.

"I didn't mold everything after you though," Xol had a quirky expression on her face, "I know why you see me as a female, but since I basically created myself, there was no point in picking just one."

A dense fog enveloped her mind, rendering everything blurry. The strength of the heat that gathered in her face made her start to sweat, and she feared ruining the paint on her face. Swiftly averting her gaze from Xol, she withdrew her hand, apprehensive that she might soon discover precisely what Xol was alluding to.

"W-Wait—should I—wait, then, are you—?" The heat intensified, prompting her to spring to her feet. "Oh jeez, I need some air." Xol found herself almost rolling on the bed with laughter, while Azahara, flustered, paced back and forth.

Only after a moment of digging a line into the floor, Xol grabbed her hand and stopped her from fainting. Her other hand rested gently on her shoulder, the coolness from her palm permeating through the metal against her skin. "Don't worry, I only told you because I knew I'd get that reaction." Azahara lifted her gaze, watching those dark lips smile widely. "Thank you, Aza, for setting me free."

Her anxiety shifted, and she smiled in return, "Thank you for being here with me."

They shared a smile, savoring a moment of shared silence. She had many questions about her life, and she knew they had plenty of time to do so. Azahara was so thankful for her, and the thought of never meeting her or setting her free tugged at the strings of her heart.

"Let's go." Xol said, beginning to step towards the door, when Azahara pulled her back. "What is it?"

"First, about Jayce. Do you know who he is?" she asked, and the surprise that washed over Xol served as a sufficient response. Lowering her gaze, she groaned, "My intuition really is shit."

"Don't say that," her voice held a note of pain. She knew that Xol having to lie to her or, just not tell her, had been tough. "It wasn't as if it was that obvious, at least not to you." Xol paused, waiting to see if Azahara would respond before continuing, "Did he tell you?"

She shook her head.

"When did you figure it out?" Xol remained at a distance, giving her the space she might need after stepping away.

"I knew before we got to Ilkiz; Alyse sort of confirmed the rest of my suspicions," Xol's expression held a mix of understanding and concern. "I should've let you kick his ass when he couldn't fight back." A hint of laughter lingered through her following statement, "Now, I'll have to do it."

A mischievous grin slid across Xol, "Oh, I am excited to see that. Please, allow me the honor to watch him suffer."

"I'm sure he is currently simmering," she stepped towards Xol and put her hand into hers. "Especially after the letter I gave him."

Opening the door, Xol raised an eyebrow, "Oh, do tell."

Day 163
Chapter 32
Jayce Latimer

He was simmering.

For the past several hours, the unopened letter had remained in Jayce's hand. He had found himself concealed from the rest of the crew and the citizens of Isis. His eyes were fixed on the letter bearing the words "To: Jayce" in her handwriting. He wondered if this was some form of karma, given that he had asked for more letters to be written to him shortly before the Battle at Sunfall.

He cursed himself once more, feeling his heart leap into his throat at the mere thought of opening the letter and discovering its contents. Perhaps he was overreacting, and it was merely a harmless joke. *"You can have your date, after, I get my answers,"* her words lingered in the recesses of his mind, just before she vanished into Ilkiz's Tomb.

It wasn't a joke, and as he recalled the story of the moon, it struck him how eerily similar it was to the situation he had entangled himself in with her. Repeatedly, he had approached the precipice of revealing the truth to her, yet each time, some intervening force or a surge of apprehension caused him to back down. He convinced himself, time and time again, that it was for her own well-being.

Receiving this letter the day after her return was torment. The most agonizing, yet strangely satisfying part, was that she knew precisely how it would affect him. This was why she strategically handed it to him just before he was no longer allowed to see her, knowing that the next time he did, there would be hundreds of eyes on her.

She was going to make him suffer and truthfully, he deserved it.

After taking one more deep breath, he unfolded the paper. What took him by surprise was the first word. He hadn't even read further down the page, but he already knew that his worry was entirely justified.

Sam,

That was a dirty little trick you pulled on me. I expect you to apologize profusely, and dare I say, beg for my forgiveness. I won't take no for an answer on this one.

Tonight, I want you to know that I know who you are, who I'm dancing with. Whom I stare at all night. Whom I'm likely going to strangle.

When you take me away from this place because I am tired and overstimulated from all the attention, I want you to know, I know, who I'll be leaving with.

Then, and only then, will you tell me the truth. You will tell me everything because I deserve that. I trusted you that it was not time and allowed for it.

I want to know to whom I am willing to give my entire soul to.

I want to know who I have fallen so hard for that it hurts.

I deserve to know who you are, Jayce.

See you soon.

Love,

Your Sunshine

He couldn't contain the unfiltered laugh that escaped him. His heart was racing, not from nerves or fear, but from relief. *That's my girl,* he thought as he folded the paper and tucked it into his shirt pocket.

He rushed back to where everyone was waiting for the celebration to begin, a whirlwind of thoughts racing through his mind. How had he not noticed that she knew? When had she found out? Could Ilkiz have known and told her? Amidst these countless questions, one fact was certain: it was time. He had already planned to tell her after the ceremony. Knowing she was aware of who he was and seemed ready for him, he felt a wave of emotions he wasn't prepared for.

As he reached the focal point of the celebration, aglow with hanging lanterns and towering torches, people danced to the melody that resonated through Isis. Some engaged in lively conversations, but the crew, who all gazed in the same direction, held a different air. Alyse wore a mischievous grin, and Kaen seemed far too pleased with herself. His eyes landed on Akua, whose expression hinted at intense anticipation, leaving only one conclusion.

Steadying himself, he took a deep breath and followed their gaze.

"By the Mother," he said aloud, not addressing anyone in particular, "You are beautiful." He might have assumed she wasn't real if it weren't for Xol walking beside her, holding her hand as they approached the final ladder. *Dress or no dress, look at that smile,* he thought, stepping in her direction.

She hadn't noticed him yet, her focus on navigating the ladder in her form-fitting dress. She lifted her head and glanced around only when her feet were safely on the ground.

A little to your right, he said through the winnox. Watching her slightly jump and shift her eyes just a bit to the right, he smiled when they met.

Her eyes narrowed at him, trying to act mad, but the smile she was fighting betrayed her. She raised her hand and pointed at him, *"I should be so furious with you."* Even her voice sent a chill down his back.

I know... You can punish me later. For now, you are stunning. A blush was growing on her lifted cheeks as she approached closer. *I may have a surprise for you after everything is done, as long as you promise not to hurt me.*

"I promise." She babbled through the end of his words, making him laugh aloud. *"Thank you, save me soon."*

Always, Sunshine. Knowing that she was aware of who he truly was and that he didn't have to struggle to avoid accidentally using his favorite nickname for her, he felt as though a weight had been lifted. Seeing the joy on her face, which brought forth a bright, toothy smile, made him fall in love with her all over again.

The crew congregated around her, and Kaen left no room for doubt that touching her was off-limits. There would be repercussions if they marred the masterpiece she and Alyse had crafted. She set her palms ablaze to heighten the drama, causing Azahara to take a nervous step back.

"You'll set her hair on fire!" Akua shouted, sending the group into a fit of laughter.

Azahara laughed in unison with them, her shoulders bouncing with mirth. He had never seen her with her hair up, aside from the occasional messy bun, and he had to admit it suited her. Observing the graceful curve from her neck to her shoulders unobstructed, he marveled at every detail that whoever had brought her into this world had taken to craft such perfection.

You are perfect, he said through her window, watching her cheeks turn red like flames.

"Let's see, do a spin!" It was Carmen, and with Xol's help, she did as she was asked. Not because she really had a choice, of course. Though he wasn't upset that she did.

The marking on her back was new, and it wasn't something he was familiar with. No other Spirit Rider had *that,* and it took him entirely by surprise when he saw it. In black and dark blue ink, starting at the center of her spine, there stretched beautiful raven-like wings. They extended up to her shoulders, cascading down her back and disappearing beneath the dress. He could almost swear they moved as she completed her turn.

He focused on her face, and although she seemed preoccupied by something Théodore was saying, she appeared to sense his gaze. Her eyes briefly flicked toward him before swiftly returning to the ongoing conversation.

"Are you excited?" Kaen was practically bouncing with enthusiasm, which was somewhat concerning.

Azahara questioned, her smile tinged with weariness, "You mean for the Sealing, right?"

"Yup! The sooner we get it done, the better," Akua groaned which made Kaen quickly add, "I mean, the sooner we can start the celebration."

Jayce approached the group, and they made way for him.

Azahara continued, "But what exactly is going to happen during the Sealing? Nobody has provided any details, and of course, Ilkiz is..." She noticed him approaching and choked on her words, "remaining silent." He could hear Alyse giggling beside him, and Xol, who hadn't moved from Azahara's side, stared at him.

"Fae out of the bag," her toothy grin elicited an eye roll from him. He was thankful that everyone was too engrossed in Azahara to overhear their exchange.

"Yuul out of the bag too," he retorted, and she seemed nonchalant about it. There had been no concern from his side when Azahara found out. They had been mortal enemies for as long as he could remember, and overcoming that enmity was a challenging feat for him. Yet, here he was, doing just that for his girl.

Azahara looked back and forth between the two of them, her expression changing as understanding dawned. "It all makes so much sense now," she exclaimed as if a light had suddenly turned on, and she tilted her head back. "I've been so blind."

Xol and he shared a laugh while the people around them appeared bewildered.

Kaen had no reservations about inserting herself between the three of them. "Alright, listen up. We are going. Come on, you can suck everyone's face later."

"Why would I do that—ah!" Kaen pulled Azahara away with a forceful yank, not even allowing him the chance to embrace her. It was probably for the best; he might have smudged her face paint, and he wasn't sure he wanted to challenge Kaen while she was in such a volatile mood.

He didn't like her leaving, but watching her go was something else. Especially that mark on her back; it stole his soul from his body.

"It's her Connection," Akua commented, probably noticing him staring. "It's what will link everyone to her. Each person will see something unique. For me, I see a water lily." As he began to follow Azahara, Akua remained at his side.

Kaen was pulling her like she was some animal on a leash. He wanted to get to them and stop her—but he knew better. Azahara was more than capable of controlling the crazed twin if she wished to. He knew what she needed from him: to allow her to be her own support. It was why she came to Ilkiz in the first place.

"What do you see?" Akua asked, and while it would mean nothing to him, he answered honestly.

"Raven wings, they take up nearly her entire back—" Akua stopped, and Jayce instinctively did the same, stopping and looking back at him. "What?"

Akua animatedly waved his hand in front of him and followed back into step, "Sorry," he cleared his throat, "you said her entire back?"

"Nearly," he muttered, glancing again just as she was led up onto a small platform. Kaen was basically yelling at her while addressing the ever-growing crowd around them. He couldn't help but feel sorry for Azahara; she looked incredibly uncomfortable up there. The desire to rescue her was overwhelming.

"Then I am even more sorry for flirting with her," Akua said, slapping Jayce's arm. "I thought she was only telling me she was your woman to ease the pain of the rejection." He narrowed his eyes at Akua, which made him laugh nervously.

His eyes went back and forth from Azahara to Akua, "What is the significance that it covers her back?"

"It isn't obvious?"

"Apparently not," he said flatly.

"It means that your connection with her is extraordinary. That's what the legend suggests, at least. Only two people saw the mark that significantly for Rah: his wife and Ilkiz. The only one that can confirm that would be Ilkiz herself now."

Jayce nodded, "I suppose that makes sense." Not that he needed any more confirmation of his belonging to her, but it was nice, nevertheless. "How big is yours?" he asked, driven purely by curiosity.

"Maybe the size of a gold coin."

With a heavy sigh, Jayce smiled so widely that his cheeks hurt. "Thanks for letting me know, Akua."

"What's that look for? Hey—where are you going?!" He was walking away from Akua, not because he disliked the guy, but because his attention was required elsewhere. The ceremony was commencing, and Akua would talk his ear off, given the opportunity. Perhaps later, he would indulge, but for now, it was Azahara's moment.

As he made his way through the crowd, he overheard the eldest descendant speaking to Azahara. Her voice was hushed, and he wondered how anyone other than him could hear anything.

"We welcome you to the family, Keeper," she intoned. *There was that title again,* he thought, "Ilkiz has blessed us all. Sealing, while painful—"

Hmm... He didn't like the sound of that but continued to listen. "Signifies a great deal to our people. It symbolizes the blood you will shed for us, and we for you.

"While our Spirit Riders have partners during their sealing, you have chosen to journey alone."

"I have. It is my pain to bear." Her voice held an unmistakable air of confidence and a hint of raw, unfiltered power, sending a shiver down his spine.

Desiring a more precise view, he navigated through the crowd, finding a spot off to the side. Although there were still people around, he now had a better view of her face.

"These are searing rods forged with natural elements, dragon scales, and the fire of Ilkiz. Place your hands together."

His eyebrows pulled together while Azahara did as commanded.

"Stand your ground, pretty boy." It wasn't Azahara who leaned into his window; instead, it was the commanding voice of a Dragon. *"If you go to her, I'll eat you."*

His eyes widened in surprise, and he asked, *How are you in her window?*
"She allowed me through, knowing exactly what you would try to do."

He observed her as she closed her eyes took a deep breath, and a profound silence enveloped his ears. The only sounds were the gentle rhythm of her breathing and her heartbeat.

What is this for?

"This will demonstrate to them that she embraces their traditions. She could have rejected it, and they would have respected her decision," Ilkiz said as he watched the searing rod placed over Kaen's flames, the tip turning a bright red and yellow. *"However, she insisted on it, asserting that her strength would be derived from those around her. If she couldn't prove her worth to them, she believed she didn't deserve it."*

The piercing sound of flesh made him tremble, but he never looked away. There was shock on her face at first, the pain registering instantly. He expected the scream to come then and would have to fight to not go to her. Every fiber in his body tingled, ready to physically restrain himself. Except, it didn't come. He just watched her back straighten, the expression on her face pained.

"As you bleed for us, we will bleed for you, Keeper," the elder proclaimed.

The rod was removed from her hands, and her legs trembled as she bit down on her lower lip. She gingerly pulled her hands close, making sure not to touch her dress. Blood poured from them, and he took a deep breath.

"Ah, love." Ilkiz crooned.

Oh no, not another one. I beg of you, Ilkiz—

"Shh—just accept me, as she has." He threw her out, hearing a booming laugh as he did.

"You are now a part of us as we are a part of you." The sounds around him came back, and cheers and excitement roared through the forest around them. Kaen put her hands onto Azahara's shoulders, turning her to the Ilkiz descendants, and she smiled out at them. Sweat pooled at her forehead, and she was visibly as uncomfortable with that as she had been with the rod through her hands.

"Now it's time for you to summon her, come! Come!" The crowd parted as Kaen pushed Azahara down the stairs and through them. *Damn it.* He couldn't help but roll his eyes. The need to chase after her felt ironic, like another consequence of what he had done to her.

He made his way around, watching her being shuffled through by Kaen, and when they turned toward his direction, he stopped. As the last of the crowds parted, he crossed his arms and watched her face flush at being stopped directly in front of him.

She laughed nervously, "It's a lot."

"Do you want saving yet?" he asked, raising an eyebrow.

She shook her head adamantly, "First, summoning, then dancing, then my surprise." She stepped past him, her hands held in front of her, blood dripping down her wrist. She was so casual about what had just happened that he would have thought he had dreamt it if it weren't for the blood.

"You may want to back up," It was Kaen, who was standing right next to him, unmoving. "It's about to get windy."

He swallowed and stepped away from her, but not from where Azahara stopped. The circle was expansive, but he had seen Ilkiz, and it didn't appear big enough. When they returned through the portal to Ilkiz's Tomb, and he witnessed her falling, his wings were readying to take him to her. But when the Wyvern Dragon emerged from the ground to catch her, he felt like he was losing his mind. It transported him back to the War of Ilkiz, and the sight of seeing her in the flesh again felt almost unreal.

"Alright, how do I do this again?" It was Azahara, and he shook his head, knowing that she was talking to Ilkiz through herself.

"I have holes in my hands... what do you mean clap them... fuck you, I know what clap means... Ilkiz, I swear on the Mother." Jayce laughed, his hands in his pockets as he leaned slightly. Watching her was heartwarming, and witnessing her come from such a dark place to this, was a happiness that had not been tapped into for many, many years.

"I'll put a saddle on you," she laughed, and before him, her skin began slowly turning to lavender flames. He could feel the heat even from where he stood, but she didn't seem fazed. "Come on, enjoy the attention you so desperately crave while I indulge in my own fun." He observed as her hands moved downward to the ground, and with what appeared to be a gentle push, the ground cracked beneath her.

Then came the quake that shifted the ground, and for the descendants of Dragons, they came to witness their Keeper bring alive their guardian: Ilkiz.

Day 163
CHAPTER 33

Azahara couldn't fathom the overwhelming happiness she experienced in those moments. From the understanding gaze of Jayce to the exhilaration of summoning Ilkiz before her descendants, eliciting roars of excitement, she felt a profound sense of purpose for the first time in her life—something beyond mere love and a body. Perhaps amid all the pain and suffering she endured until that point, there was a possibility that it would amount to something meaningful.

This realization brought tears to her eyes as she gazed directly into Ilkiz's eyes, the massive entity emerging beneath her feet. She was something to be loved and adored, never to be feared. If not for herself, she resolved to uncover the events of that day and understand why Kuraid had flown Zuru into the Kingdom with malicious intent.

"Enjoy your night, Azahara," Ilkiz spoke aloud, and she wondered if everyone present could hear her Spirit. Gently placing her hand against the Dragon's snout, and as the magnificent being shifted, the ground beneath them trembled.

Without hesitation, the children and even the adults rushed toward Ilkiz. Azahara turned away, confident that Ilkiz would enjoy the company of her people, and decided it was her turn to do the same. As she beheld her family, wide smiles and excitement painted across their faces, she couldn't have envisioned this scene nearly half a year ago—a feeling of belonging to those who truly saw her. The tableau before her would only have been made more perfect if Illyan, Zhal, and Kaed were standing there. Though the thought made her stomach turn, she held onto the belief that one day they would be here, in one form or another.

Approaching them, Azahara could hear Alyse and Kaen roaring and jumping as though she had just won an award. The rest of the crew seemed more reserved, offering neutral smiles and winks, undoubtedly pleased to see her as happy as they were. Xol, standing beside Jayce, wore a bright smile with open arms. Their emotions seemed to surface more each day, and Azahara pondered if the prolonged time apart had softened Xol toward her. Perhaps the once protective nature had transformed into something deeper—love.

Accelerating her pace, she hurried into Xol's arms, holding her tightly. No worry lingered about causing harm, but she remained mindful of her newfound strength; the last thing she wanted was to accidentally snap someone in half.

"I've seen men twice your size cry to a paper cut. You took that searing rod like a Yuul." Xol squeezed her just as tight, and when she released Azahara, she took her hands. "Ah, and you are already healing them. Incredible."

Azahara experienced a sense of exhilaration as she realized her body was growing stronger. The open wounds in her hands were seamlessly stitching themselves together, and although she could feel the sensation, it didn't bother her. It felt akin to someone gently scratching at her palms, a perception she would admit felt more like a tickle than anything else.

"You did wonderful," Jayce chimed in, and for once, Xol conceded and passed her over. He didn't grab her right away, just held her gaze. His eyes were glistening as he took her in. "I am beyond proud of what you did tonight, and have done over the past months, Sunshine."

Her cheeks burned as he stepped closer. "I know I'm in trouble, as I deserve, but—" He didn't get to finish before she launched herself into his arms. He didn't even stumble, enveloping her so intensely that she knew he'd never let her go. "Never mind." His heart raced, and she'd be lying if she said she wasn't happy to feel it so.

A plastered smile adorned her lips, and it showed no signs of fading. He had a lot to tell her, yet she wasn't genuinely angry with him, even though she had every right to be. She truly believed that he had kept it from her because he thought it was for the better.

He gently placed his hand under her chin, lifting it to make her look at him, "My Sunshine."

"My—Fae?" She chuckled, never imagining a day in her life that she could have ever fallen in love with a Fae.

"Your overbearing man is fine too," he said, leaning down towards her. She lifted herself to her tiptoes, meeting his lips halfway. It felt right to kiss him, as though her soul was complete when they were connected.

One of his arms wrapped around her neck, pulling her closer and deepening the kiss. He consumed her entire being, both physically and mentally. Jayce would be one of two that would have full claim to her. The only other would be Kaed, and she had enough of herself to give them both.

His hand came up to her cheek, and chills ran down her arms. As she had done to him outside of Ilkiz's tomb, he brushed his tongue between her lips and tasted her. While small, a jolt of lightening shot through her stomach, and she instinctively moved her arms up and around his neck to pull herself closer.

It was only when she felt hands on her backside that she was brought back to where she was. Quickly pulling away from Jayce, she shot her head around. It was Alyse, sheepishly smiling and blushing. "I hate to interrupt, but—"

"YOU ARE MESSING HER FACE PAINT UP YOU FOOL!" Kaen was on fire; literally.

Azahara's face was hot, and she stared at the pyromancer as though she was ready to end everyone's existence over a few lines of paint. His hearty laugh behind her made her even more worried that it would send Kaen into a frenzy.

She licked her lips, tasting the peeled paint. When she gazed at Jayce, he had a red smear across his face, and he grinned, well aware of what she was observing.

Kaen grabbed onto her arm and dragged her away, "It's time to drink and dance, you guys can suck face later. I told you—" her voice disappeared as Azahara looked back at Jayce who was in tow, along with Alyse, Xol and the rest of the crew, who was chatting amongst themselves and showing excitement for the rest of the night.

Azahara was excited, maybe not for what they were going to do, but knowing at the end of the night it would end with knowing *who* Jayce was.

Though, it was slightly agonizing that she would have to wait till Kaen was satisfied with her presence enough that she could slip away peacefully.

The agonizing feeling she had been worried about vanished the moment they had a few drinks and started dancing. She felt beyond elated that they had wine, offering a welcome escape from the bitter ale that seemed ever-present. She didn't indulge heavily, only savoring a few glasses with her family and the people of Ilkiz.

The music resonated as both beautiful and distinct from anything she had heard on the mainland. A fusion of gentle instruments, such as the flute and harp, juxtaposed with the more robust sounds of drums and violins, all harmonized seamlessly to create a rhythm that she believed even moved the trees. Someone was singing songs—tales as ancient as Ilkiz, and some from Rah. They portrayed him not as their Star but as their Keeper. She pondered, if he were watching then, would he be contemplating that.

To her, he would always be a Star.

She devoted a significant amount of time dancing with everyone, from Lucala and Zayne to Carmen and Yelena. At one point, she discovered all of them dancing together in a large circle, the effects of the sweet wine and ale beginning to make their presence felt on most of them.

At a certain juncture, she found herself wondering if it was just her mind playing tricks, but she could have sworn she saw Tessa and Broan dancing among them. Tessa, her smile genuinely illuminated by her eyes, and Broan, the excessively large, gentle-hearted bear, relishing a moment of happiness in such a darkened world.

Perhaps, one day, she would seek out their souls. Venture into Oblivion, scour for them, and bring them back from solitude. She had no clue if it was even possible, but for them, she was willing to try.

Jayce gently wrapped his arm around her waist, drawing her undivided attention, and she willingly responded in kind. Amid the lively dance with everyone, he focused solely on her. Laughter and smiles abounded, and in that moment, she discovered the peace and happiness she had fought so hard for. While she was fully cognizant that this wasn't the culmination of her journey, and challenges still lay ahead, she recognized that this particular moment deserved to be permanently etched into the pages of her life's story.

Happiness is fickle, but she was determined to strengthen its presence around her.

After what felt like days and not hours, Jayce lean down and whispered, "Can I save you now?" Her heart was racing, and while she had always said he made her nervous, now truthfully, she was.

"Yes," her cheeks began to burn under the intensity of his gaze. His hand gently brushed over her cheek, then slid down to hers, lacing their fingers together.

Gently but with fervor, he led them around the crowd of still dancing people. When they exited, she let out a heavy sigh. It had felt like she had been holding her breath the entire time they were in the pit of dancers.

He brought them to a stop, and she glanced around. Ladders were leading up towards the canopies, but they weren't close to their pod. "Not that I was expecting anything specific," She said with a sheepish smile, "but we can go up to the canopies at least to talk."

The smile on his face only widened, "Do I not strike you as a romantic, Sunshine?"

Her entire body flushed with heat. "I didn't say that." she quickly interjected, taking a deep breath, and letting out a heavy sigh.

She observed as he raised his hand and effortlessly sliced open the space in front of her, tearing apart a wëther as if flipping a pancake. Beyond it, she caught a glimpse of dark wood, but he promptly covered her eyes. "Ah, no peeking. Jeez, you are so bad."

Her laughter echoed, and soon she felt her back against his chest, his arm around her waist guiding them forward. She took another deep breath, acutely aware of the unique sensation these portals invoked, mentally preparing herself.

Yet, the only indication she'd passed through was the absence of dirt beneath her feet, replaced by the sound of wood creaking under their steps. It had been the smoothest portal she'd ever experienced, raising her excitement. Just how strong was Jayce?

His hand still lingered, but she caught the scent of the sea and, perhaps, flowers or candy—she couldn't quite place it. Alongside the aroma, a soft violin played a gentle melody, harmonizing with the calm water that ebbed and flowed around them against what she now could recognize as the Neptune.

"Dance with me first, just me, and then I will tell you everything."

She bit her lip, heart racing as his hand lifted from over her eyes. "Okay."

Almost instantly, the urge to cry welled up within her, prompting the contemplation of whether this surge of emotion mirrored the essence of true happiness—a profound feeling cascading beyond the boundaries of her being.

Lanterns adorned the ship's hull, their exquisite paper casings casting a mesmerizing play of lights that gracefully pirouetted across the vessel. Artfully arranged flowers and vines adorned the posts and were scattered throughout, thoughtfully positioned around a circular clearing where he led her.

Turning toward the music, she expected to discover someone on the ship playing the violin. However, she found the wëther still ajar, just slightly, allowing the entrancing notes to slip through while maintaining the mystery of what lay beyond.

"Jayce..." His name escaped her lips in a breathless whisper.

"I think you're missing the best part," he remarked, gently lifting her chin. Her eyes widened as she beheld the nearly full moon, its brilliance undimmed by any veiling clouds.

His arm enveloped her back while the other tenderly clasped her hand. "Is this a good start?"

She fought back tears, managing to ask, "A good start to what?" Lost in a state of euphoria, she missed the essence of his question. Her eyes drank in the beauty of each lavender bloom and the seemingly infinite vines. The scent transported her back home, evoking memories of waking up with her window slightly open, the fragrance of the nearby forests wafting in.

"Your forgiveness," he responded. Her head turned at last to meet his gaze, finding the warmth in his eyes. As the music swelled and they moved closer, their bodies blending in a graceful rhythm, igniting a dance of passion.

"I've already forgiven you, and honestly, there's nothing to forgive. I just wanted you to simmer for a bit," she said with a smile, prompting a sigh and a shake of his head. "What?"

"You." He released her to twirl her before reclaiming her back into his arms. "I've kept asking myself how anyone could hurt you. You are kind, beautiful, understanding—and have quite the fire on that tongue of yours."

Sheepishly chewing on her bottom lip, she shifted her gaze downward, focusing on his hand holding hers. "You should have seen me when I first boarded the Neptune. I'm surprised they didn't throw me off immediately."

He laughed lightly, "Oh, I saw." She shot him a look of surprise. "What? Are you really shocked?"

Suppose she wasn't, and the longer she thought about it, it would have been stranger if he hadn't been there. Nonetheless, she eyed him, and he laughed again, this time with a touch of nervousness. "You promised not to hurt me."

"Physically," she clarified, stepping out from his embrace, twirling under her arm, and releasing his hand. Coming to a halt a few feet away, she regarded him with veiled eyes and a gentle smile gracing her lips. "I have other ways to hurt you."

The feigned devastation on his face as he gazed at her stirred a hunger in her stomach, causing her resolve to falter. Her hand extended, but he quickly seized it, pulling her back. With her now facing away from him, he wrapped one arm around her waist and the other across her chest, his hand resting on her shoulder.

"Thank you," she murmured, her head nestled against his chest, sensing him lean down to rest his cheek against her temple. "For everything."

He chuckled, "You never have to thank me. I want to give you the world, and I don't plan on stopping there."

Her eyes closed, surrendering to his embrace as he guided them in their soothing dance. She realized she had been mistaken; the way he moved them against the melody was almost too perfect. He knew how to dance, leaving her to ponder on what else she could tease him about.

"I hope I can give you everything too, Jayce. The world, love, affection, protection." The hand on her shoulder shifted, gently tilting her head up to meet his gaze.

"You have already give me everything I've ever needed. Anything more is just a bonus."

She pressed her lips together, not accepting that. Nothing was going to stop her from giving him her everything, whether he asked for it or not. At the very least, she was determined to try. After everything that had happened, she hoped she could.

"Can I ask," he inquired, turning and drawing her close, his hand snaking up her back as he dipped her down, "When did you know?"

While she anticipated the question, she felt nervous about answering, and she swallowed before responding. "I guess I'm not as bad at lying as you thought I was." Her fingers ran through his hair as she looked up into his patient eyes. "I saw you."

He drew her back up to him, holding her close yet maintaining enough distance to see her face.

"When you saved me from Goddrick," she confessed. His eyes widened, and the genuine shock etched on his face added to her nervousness.

Everything had happened so quickly, and when he burst through the portal and separated her from Goddrick, she thought she was hallucinating. That, or, Sam, in an effort to ease her discomfort, had somehow made her perceive Jayce instead of a stranger.

It was when she saw her soul, as though she was a ghost of herself, moving towards and pressing against him for comfort that she knew.

"I—" His hand rested against the side of her neck, his forehead gently meeting hers, providing comfort for her frayed nerves. "I was hoping you'd tell me the truth then, the times I would bring up Sam, that you would crack and just be honest with me. Except, your words about it not being the right time resonated."

"So, you knew it was your soul reaching out to me when you spoke through the winnox," his voice, soft and gentle, brushed against her heart.

"I did," her voice equally as soulful.

He chuckled, "My girl."

"Then, there was Alyse—" She playfully pinched his side, causing him to jolt. "Who told me about the letter in Celadon, and that you had convinced Rowlin that you weren't trying to ship me back to the King..." He planted a kiss on her forehead, a soft laugh escaping from his chest. "Through shared memories between us, and your words, the ones you told to Rowlin in the room while you thought I was sleeping."

"You are my everything. Always have been, and always will be," he echoed the same words, now directing them at her. The sensation, much like it had been before, surged through her like a whirlwind of love and care.

"While difficult, I played ignorant. It was when I began to do a lot more connecting. That, and it helped place the pieces together regarding Xol."

He shook his head, exhaling a sigh of relief. "You never cease to amaze me." His hand traced down her arm, a sheepish look on his face. "Thank you."

An unfiltered grin adorned her lips. "You're welcome, but now I never want to hear you call me a bad liar again."

With a conceding shrug, he kissed her nose and gently guided her away from him. She hadn't even realized the music had ceased, and the portal was now closed.

Feeling her heart quicken once again, she gazed at him as he casually put his hands into his pockets. "Man, I've thought about this day so much," he admitted, his nervousness evident in both his smile and his tone. "But before I tell you everything, there's one last thing. It played the biggest factor in me not telling you sooner."

Damn it, now I'm even more nervous. Her heart lodged in her throat as he advanced towards her, eventually dropping to his knees.

He gently took her hands into his and looked up at her. "I know what you've done for Kaed." It wasn't at all what she was expecting, and she felt her eyes welling up. "Keeping his soul tethered to this realm, hoping he wakes up. Xol told me." Her vision wavered, and she sensed her stomach tightening. "Azahara, I want nothing more than for him to wake up and return to you."

Feeling her knees weaken, she leaned against his hands for support.

"No matter what, I know you love him and would die for him. There's no place in this world you wouldn't go for him, no depths too endless that you wouldn't dive to bring him back. When he comes back, Azahara—" *When...* The word hung in the air, and tears welled in her eyes, but she refused to blink, preventing them from falling. "I will love and protect him just as fiercely as you do. And if it becomes too much for you, if you wish me to leave, I will. As long as I know you'll be happy and safe."

Her tears fell, despite her efforts to hold them back. "I may be too late to be your first love, but trust me when I say, I'll do everything to just be one of them."

No amount of strength could have kept her standing then, and she collapsed into his waiting arms. His grip on her remained steadfast, and she clung to him as though he might disappear, fearing he was too good to be real.

"You idiot," she mumbled through her tears, nestled in the crook of his neck. "Why'd you say that? Now my face paint is really messed up."

Jayce chuckled, his arms embracing her even tighter. "Don't tell Kaen."

"I'm telling—" she sniffled, rubbing her eyes against his shirt, observing the red paint staining it. She pulled back, meeting his patient gaze. "Okay, I won't," she hiccuped, "she scares me."

"Terrifying," they both quivered in mock fear, leading to a shared moment of laughter.

"Jayce," she found his hands in hers. "My world wouldn't exist today if you weren't here. The mere thought of not having you in it is like losing Kaed. There will never be a time when I don't want you with me."

He wore a smile that reached his eyes, and she pressed on, "Ilkiz told me that you saved my soul, imprisoned for five centuries," His smile slightly faltered, "breaking the curse and Goddrick's grip on me." A revelation crossed his eyes, not so much surprise as a sudden clarity. "When you came for me, you freed me. My soul, Jayce, didn't want me. It wanted you. If it were a tangible thing, I'd have had to wrestle it to keep it from attaching to you.

"But I didn't need my soul to know of my true feelings for you. It merely confirmed my heart was leading me in the right direction." His eyes brimmed with tears as he leaned towards her, and she drew him in to close the gap between them. Their lips met, and he leaned over her, cradling her head and gently lowering her onto the deck.

His entire weight rested upon her, careful not to smother her beneath his frame, but he enveloped her, nonetheless. Their kiss deepened, becoming passionate, and she was willing to forsake everything that led them to this moment just to keep him close. Drawing him nearer, she locked her arms around his neck, feeling his body respond to the dance of her tongue against his. His arm slipped beneath her, fingers gripping the fabric of her dress, and she sensed him trembling, fighting every urge not to tear it apart.

"Let me show you," he pulled back, breathless, "just how long I've waited for you." Another kiss followed, accompanied by a magnetic pull on her mind. The force was so intense that no amount of strength could have anchored her to that ship. Before she knew it, her eyes flickered open, and she found herself no longer in Ilkiz. Instead, she stood on the outskirts of a village, surrounded by trees and people, with Jayce passing by as though she weren't even there.

~~Day 163~~
111,986 Days Prior

CHAPTER 34

Azahara was aware of their location, but that knowledge didn't diminish the shock of being there. Particularly as she observed Jayce completely bypassing her, weaving through the crowd. Taking her first step, she felt a firm hand wrap around her wrist, halting her movement. Her gaze traveled down to the hand and followed the arm, discovering it belonged to Jayce.

Whipping her head around, she caught sight of his back as he walked away, only to find him standing beside her when she turned back. "What?"

A soft laugh escaped him, and he pulled her close, his arm encircling her shoulders. "This place exists only as a memory, so you're seeing me nearly three hundred years ago." Her heart leaped to her throat. "We are in a small village at the most southern point of Zibbema, and it's the day that I met you."

She turned as her eyes followed past-Jayce as he navigated through the crowd, drawing the admiration of those who watched. He was gorgeous, she didn't blame them, but he seemed lost. The infectious smile she had grown to cherish was absent, replaced by a persistent frown that etched his face. It pained her to feel the sorrow that enveloped him.

"You are truly something, feeling my emotions even in my memory," he remarked, prompting her to lift her gaze to meet his.

"You're not smiling, it isn't hard to see you are unhappy." Watching him shake his head, she narrowed her eyes. "Seriously, you're almost always smiling."

"I wonder why," he quipped, steering them in the direction to follow past-Jayce. "I had just left Höwl, which is a story for another time, and was lost. This was my first time back in the mortal realm since, well—" He laughed, likely realizing he hadn't actually mentioned his age. "Thousands of years."

Her back straightened, and she looked up at him. "How old are you?"

"A little over six thousand years old. I was born not too long after the Reshaping."

Nothing could have prepared her to hear that. She had been expecting him to be maybe a thousand years old. Although she hadn't gotten the best view of his wings, they were substantial. That was what led her to believe he was old, but not that old.

"Is that a problem?" he asked, a playful grin on his face. "I think I'm pretty spry for someone that old." She swatted his chest, and he gasped.

"It isn't a problem, I'm just... taken aback a bit. My goodness." Her head dropped, contemplating everything he had witnessed and the stories he held. The reminder of Xol's comment about his firsthand experience with Ilkiz lingered, and she knew she'd be pestering him about that later. "I like older men; it's fine," she added with a laugh.

He kissed her head, joining in her laughter. "Silly—let's get back to it. I'm about to run into you."

She turned her head quickly, easily spotting past-Jayce. "As I was saying, I felt lost, not really sure what I was supposed to be doing with my life, and at a breaking point. Until I saw you, selling bread as though it was your duty in life."

In an instant, the two of them stood just feet from past-Jayce, and to their right, past-Azahara. She looked unchanged, save for slightly shorter hair. She wiped her hands on the apron around her waist, smiling and waving at a couple who had just purchased a loaf from her.

"I nearly died when I saw you, and while I could attest it was because of how beautiful you are, my damn soul was ready to leave me high and dry," he chuckled, though she could sense the pain beneath his furrowed brows. "I didn't want bread, but damn it if I wasn't going to talk with you. This beautiful human, who had stolen my breath and almost my soul, in that moment, you were the sunshine to my endless nights."

"*Hello!*" Past-Azahara said with a wide smile, and past-Jayce stepped forward. "*Would you like a loaf or just a few slices?*"

"I—uh—" He stumbled over his words, *"I'm Jayce."* His hand was extending towards her, and she looked down at it.

She placed her hand into his, and smiled, *"I'm Aza, loaf or slice?"*

"You didn't care who I was, and when your soul didn't react as mine did, I knew then that it had to have been just a feeling in the wind. So, I bought your bread and left." Stepping them back, they vanished from the scene, descending into the night. Clouds filled the sky, threatening rain, and the once bustling village now lay at rest.

"Of course, not for long. You stayed on my mind the entire day, and I had gone back at least six times." Jayce laughed at himself, but her heart ached, and she couldn't quite pinpoint why. "After almost walking away from the village several times, I had concluded that I would just ask you out on a date. What was the worst thing you could do, say no?" His grip on her shoulder never wavered, his hand gently rubbing her arm. "So I came back through, looking for you."

She could hear it in his voice, the downturn in his joy, and she sensed what was coming. "I remember this night," she said, her voice low.

"I knew you would when you saw it." He pulled her to his chest, his hand cradling the back of her head. "You don't have to look. I can tell you this part without you seeing it."

"Wait—" She responded so quickly his expression jumped in surprise. "I want—I need to see. I'm fine."

His hand delicately brushed the single strand of loose hair behind her ear, and he pressed a kiss to her forehead. "While it is sad now, it's probably my favorite story I'll ever tell." He turned her and wrapped his arms around her shoulders.

Spotting a figure in the distance, confirmed to be past-Jayce, running from the town square up the hill and out towards the fields, he shifted them closer. "I had come back looking for you, but you'd already closed up shop. I was ready to knock on every door to find you when I smelled copper in the air. There was so much of it, it was nearly blinding. I didn't know it was you right away, but something told me that I needed to check whoever it was and see if they needed help.

"When I approached, your curly red hair was what came into view first. I didn't know pain until then, and I've fought in battles where I'd lost limbs and nearly died. But this, no, this was not pain; it was agony. My entire body, spirit, and soul were in writhing agony, and I had only just met you. Seeing you there, on the brink of death, it tore at my reality."

She watched past-Jayce then, falling to his knees and gripping his chest.

"Though I may have been able to save you, I wasn't sure. You were so close to death then, and I knew too much about fate to intervene. So, I watched you, I suffered through it, and as your hand raised towards the sky, I wanted to take it into mine and hold it till you found peace." His voice was raw, and even though she stood there right in front of him, reliving this moment hurt him. The grip he had on her was beyond strength but pure need. Even then, he was afraid she would disappear, never to be seen again.

"I was reaching for the sky," she said, realization hitting her like a horse pulling a wagon, "and then—"

"I parted the clouds because that was what you were telling me you wanted. You wanted to see the stars in your final moments." She was crying, and there was no holding them back. "Then, I pulled a star for you, dropping it just low enough so that you could feel as though it were coming right at you."

Her mouth was open, and she was sobbing; pure, unhindered tears that fell like a waterfall down her cheeks.

"And then, your heart stopped, and so did mine." He held her up, her body curling into itself like she was crumbling to nothing.

The memory of that moment was vivid, leading to her changing her name because she felt it was meant to be. While there was no memory of Jayce she could see, this moment lived on within her books and memories as one of the single happiest, even if driven from the darkness. In that moment, he had become a part of her life without either of them realizing it.

"I left immediately after, unable to see you like that and not knowing if you had family or friends that would come for you." He pulled her up, kneeling down onto the ground, his arms tucking under her legs and setting her in his lap. "Truthfully, I didn't know what to feel. Your soul didn't call to mine, but it felt like I had lost my own, so I wandered. For nearly three hundred years; well, two-hundred, and ninety-five to be exact."

He brushed her cheek, and she looked up at him. "Jayce..."

"It's okay, Sunshine. You can imagine how I felt when I heard Alyse call you Starfall, and when you confirmed my suspicions, I could have cried right then." He was gentle, caressing her cheek with his hand, brushing away the tears.

After a few minutes, she took a deep breath. "I'm sorry."

"Don't apologize. I've had many years to come to terms with that moment. You've had seconds." He leaned in and kissed her closed eyes one by one. "You okay to move forward?"

All she needed to do was nod, and they shifted to another point in time. They were in the Kingdom, and she recognized the square as though it were yesterday.

"I ended up joining the Order but found myself rising to Commander with the White Cloaks quickly. I had no real desire to be there, but I didn't have much else to do with my time. I had fought in wars, had my fair share of lovers, both in men and women," she wasn't surprised; the subtle but not-so-subtle indications of his preference in partners was never hidden. That honestly made her more attracted to him. "—and was just bored. It was the best way to consume my time.

"I'd never ventured to the Idle Fox before," he motioned to his past self, donned in the signature White Cloak uniform, eyes fixed downward, and once again, carrying an air of discontent. The downturn of his lips, the furrow between his brows; he was in pain without even understanding why. "I can't recall if I was drawn to show up there this day or if it was just coincidence, but when I walked in," he took her hand, and their perspective shifted, landing them in the Idle Fox, "to my astonishment, a beautiful redhead was there to greet me."

"Hello! Welcome to the Idle Fox!" It was past-Azahara, with an ear-to-ear smile, and bright-eyed expression.

"Little bee, you don't have to greet people like that." Her heart sprinted as Broan called out to her.

Past-Azahara giggled, a girly one that she wondered if it was forced, but the joy on her face didn't depict it being that way. *"Oh, but I love to."*

Past-Jayce stood unblinking, staring at her.

"I couldn't believe my eyes," she looked up at him, the smile on his face wide, a gloss covering his eyes, "at first, I thought I was dreaming. You'll see as I go from shock, to disbelief, to reality. You were standing there, after so many years, as though you hadn't aged. That... and you were alive." He took a deep, healthy breath in.

"You were alive," he repeated.

"You are alive..." Past-Jayce said aloud and went to touch past-Azahara.

"Hey, hey—keep your hands off the lady. Do you want something Commander?" Broan said pointedly. He was protecting her, and she felt her heart swell.

"I obviously got myself together, but you were so kind that it hadn't mattered of my awkwardness. You waited on me, and I stayed there until you were done for the day. You were living there at the Idle Fox at the time, and I went to Broan for who you were. He was skeptical about telling me, but he let me in with a little magical influence."

Meeting his gaze with an unexpected calm, she acknowledged that, given the circumstances, she would have done the same thing.

"You had been working there for almost a full year at that time and said that you were looking for an escape from your reality. I asked what your name was, and he told me it was Azahara or, Aza, for short; I knew then that it was you. While it could have been a coincidence or reincarnation, that unique name was not something I could ignore. I was getting my second chance, and I wouldn't let it go."

He leaned in towards her and smiled, "We obviously know I somehow messed it up."

With furrowed brows, she frowned, "I probably did that."

His hand came up and rested at her neck, "Let's see, hmm?" He kissed her forehead and the room around them shifted, but they stayed in the Idle Fox. She observed as if days lapsed over seconds.

"If I had known then I would have only had a few weeks, if even that, I would not have waited. I'm not even sure why I did, to be completely honest. I came every single day, sat at the same table, and spent the entire day with you. Even though you acted the same way you had before, as though I was just another person."

Past-Jayce remained seated, his unwavering gaze fixed on her every second. Although one might consider it unsettling, realizing his soul longed for something unrequited, she empathized with his yearning. She wondered if he could see the change in her each day because she could. The way she would immediately look for that single table to see if he was there. Her smile was always brighter when she saw him. She'd loved seeing him there, and even if he couldn't feel her soul yearning for him, she could see that *she* was. The subtlety of her desire lingered, as she acknowledged the impossibility of having him, even as her heart truly wished otherwise.

She almost began to break down again at the sight of a chessboard coming into play. Past-Jayce had brought it and offered to teach her, quickly discovering that she was a natural. Witnessing him intentionally lose, just to elicit the victorious cheer from her, nearly brought her to tears.

"I tried to get to know you, but you were so elusive, and obviously, now I know why. However, then, I thought maybe you were hiding something. At first, I thought you were a Fae, and while you had connections with Magic, it wasn't strong enough to come from wings. I also saw your back several times, and there was nothing there. I went through every possible scenario, and all of them were wrong.

"I was gaining the courage to just straight up ask you to have dinner with me, when someone came looking for you."

"The redhead, where is she?" The voice was unmistakable; she didn't need to turn around to identify it as Goddrick. A shiver ran through her body, and Jayce swiftly pulled her away, snapping them out of the memory and depositing them outside the Idle Fox.

"Broan shared this memory with you, and I refuse to make you watch it. I'm sorry for even letting that moment slip." He lifted her gaze to him, and to his surprise, she had a neutral expression. "That's my girl."

A smile graced her as she gently bit down on her bottom lip.

"When I came in, I couldn't expose who I was. Not in front of everyone, especially not you. So, with a little Magic—"

"That was you!?" Her voice nearly shouted, shock threading through every word.

"You did the punching, I just applied the pressure," he said, slipping his hand behind her neck, pulling her towards him. "Then, of course, you left."

Once again, they moved just outside the Kingdom, and she saw past-Jayce running. Past-Azahara, who was just crossing the gates and moving beyond the borders of the Kingdom, oblivious to his pursuit.

At least, until he called out to her, *"Wait, Aza!"*

"I ... remember this moment." She swallowed and took a step away from his grasp. "I don't understand why I don't remember it being you... or any of this really..."

"*Hey, Jayce!*" Past-Azahara said, turning and greeting him as he approached her.

"*Where are you going?*" He asked, and she smiled.

"*I'm heading home, for my birthday. I'm going to celebrate with my family.*"

"I could tell that you were lying, but I didn't understand why. It was such an innocent answer, yet it felt like you were running away from something. Hiding." He was so candid with his feelings, and she felt them deep in her soul. "It wasn't until your next words that I realized I might never see you again."

"*I'll be back.*"

"You lied straight through that beautiful smile of yours." He shook his head.

"I can protect you, Aza," he stepped towards her, "I can keep you safe, if you'll stay with me. I know you don't know me, but—"

"*Jayce, thank you but I'm fine.*"

"You were going to cry," He didn't need to tell her that, because as she watched her former self begin to buckle, she felt her turmoil. Those words, **keep you safe**, were all she ever wanted to hear. That was all she **ever** wanted. "So, I didn't pressure you."

"*Thank you, but really, I'm okay. I need to go. When I get back though, I'd love to have dinner. If you'd have me.*"

"The pain I felt then was near at a breaking point," he confessed.

"*Then it's a date,*" Past-Jayce said to her, and without another word, past-Azahara left.

Turning to him, she asked, "Can you see my memories?" He nodded, putting his hand on hers.

"Just think about where you want to take me, and we will go." When she took his hand, she brought them merely a few minutes into the future of his memory of her walking away.

When he saw her past self, Jayce began trembling.

Beneath the sheltering branches of a tree, past-Azahara sat with her arms tightly wound around her legs, tears streaming down her face. The intensity of her emotions caused her entire body to tremble, and she dug her nails so forcefully into her arms that blood started to seep through. With a heavy heart, she lifted her gaze to the sky above.

"I hate you. I hate you! I fucking hate you! I hate you! Please let me go! Let me go! Please!" As past-Azahara screamed, Jayce grabbed her and pulled them from the memory, falling into darkness.

He held her close while she whispered, "Hate was never a strong enough word."

"I'm sorry I didn't see," His tone gentle against her ear, "If I had seen, if I had just noticed that your soul was trapped... I would have saved you right then."

"I was protecting you," her voice carried a note of anguish, "at least, in my mind I was. I was going home to prepare to forget the happiest year of my life. I didn't know **that** at the time, but now I can attest it to be true. It had been the time with everyone at the Idle Fox, feeling normal, and just enjoying every bit of freedom." She emitted a gentle, amused exhale, "You may not have felt it, but I wanted nothing more than to get to know you. I wanted you to know me, but the true me. Not what Goddrick had made me."

In the darkened space around them, they stood together, his arms encircling her torso, his forehead pressed against the back of her head. She could sense his heart racing against her back, and while hers also pounded, his surpassed in urgency. The weight of his prolonged pain bore heavily, and the knowledge that it wasn't the end added an indescribable ache.

He planted a tender kiss on the top of her head. "Do you want to stop? We can finish another time."

She shook her head with determination. "I want to see."

His embrace tightened, and in an instant, they found themselves once again in the square in front of the Idle Fox. Though things hadn't altered significantly, time had moved forward. He pulled her along, fingers interlocked with hers, guiding her up the stairs toward the front door.

"I never left the Kingdom after that, and came to the Idle Fox every day, even just to pass and ask if you had returned. It wasn't until five years later, that you showed."

"It's been what, five years?" "Where have you been beau!" "My god you haven't aged a day!" "I've missed you!"

"I could feel your panic. I didn't even need to see your face to know something was wrong. You couldn't breathe, and you were screaming for help. I could hear you through the winnox and swore you were calling me."

It was as though there wasn't anyone else in the Idle Fox but past-Azahara and past-Jayce. He surged through the crowd, a resolute determination etched on his face as he made his way towards her.

They observed as he guided her towards the rear of the Idle Fox. When he turned away from her, the emotions playing across his face were a tumultuous blend, too intricate to dissect in that fleeting moment. Shock, fear, joy, happiness—all were inscribed on his features. Only when he gathered himself did he turn to be strong for her.

"Did they hurt you?" Maybe it was because it was his memory, but his tone had shifted. What once sounded like mere concern now carried an undertone of pain.

"I saw the scar on your face, the change in your eye, and nearly destroyed everything around me. It was why I had no restraint to lift you to look at me. I knew it was stupid," he laughed, "especially when you immediately shrugged away from me. A fire like I'd never seen from you was there, and I knew right then that this time was different.

"Your friend came to save you, and I couldn't believe it, but you had a **friend**– a travel companion; you weren't alone. Then to find out you had the Elder Fae's great-grandchild traveling with you and a half-elf who was obviously madly in love with you, just as I was. Man, was I way over my head." He laughed again, shaking his head, and pulling her from the memory, bringing her to the King's castle.

"Karver, she's here." Past-Jayce was pacing back and forth, and right beside him, was Karver.

"Brother," A smile on his flawless ebony face, *"this is wonderful news."*

"Something is wrong though," past-Jayce was flustered, and she could see a purple glow slowly rising from his skin, *"something happened to her. I don't know what, but she's..."*

Karver put his hand on his shoulder, stopping him with force. *"We will figure it out. Did you speak with her?"*

"Barely, she isn't alone this time."

Karver smiled, *"That is wonderful news. Maybe whatever was ailing her before has now—"*

"No, it's still there, but I feel it again. That power that lingered in the realm after Rah—"

She felt her eyes widen, and she trembled.

"Jayce, that is a bit of—"

"I know what that feeling is, and it isn't just that. Someone has her soul. It's why I couldn't feel it, it's why she never felt our connection, and it's why I cannot leave her ever again."

Karver furrowed his eyebrows, *"How did you find out?"*

"When I touched her this time, it called out for help. She called out for help." Without hesitation Karver embraced his dearest friend, his brother.

"Let's protect her together then."

The moment shifted, and as he released his grip, she stepped back, casting a questioning gaze at him. "You knew?" His expression turned sheepish. "I did call out for help, but I didn't realize I had shot it through any form other than in my head."

Jayce was shaking his head then, "No, what I meant by you calling for help was your life force, your heart, your body, your mind—it was screaming for its soul. You were never complete without it, and when you gained Light and Devilite, you realized it was missing without consciously knowing it. The closest soul to yours, was mine."

"Why?" She asked, "Why yours? Why not Illyan or Kaed?"

She saw him taking a deep breath, "A story for another time, let's just say it was fate. My soul was ready to save yours in that moment."

She conceded with a nod, her eyes scanning the grand archways of the King's castle enveloping her.

"When you appeared before the King, I nearly lost it, **again**. Seeing the way he was speaking to you, and Kaed not saying anything—" he paused, taking a quick breath to steady himself, "I understand he couldn't. The only thing I fault him for is bringing you, although, to be fair, you were probably too stubborn to sit it out."

She narrowed her eyes, "I didn't want to come in the first place. I told him to send a raven."

He laughed, "I know, you told the King that, which I thought was... quite hot. That tongue of fire." His hand was outstretched for hers, and she took it. "Let's move on—"

"Wait, can I ask you something first?" She stepped to him, "You were drawing your sword; I think I know the answer but were you—"

"I was prepared to kill all of them for even entertaining the thought of harming you. The sword was just a formality; I could snap my fingers and reduce them all to nothing more than memories in an instant." The revelation of his strength sent a shiver down her spine, and a selfish desire welled within her to witness it, especially when it came to a particular god.

"You weren't afraid of me then," her cheeks igniting, and an almost embarrassed expression wrapped around her.

"Never," she couldn't stop the smile forming, "and I'll never fear you. Even in the end, when you are stronger than I am."

She chuckled, "Me? Stronger—pfft." It wasn't that she didn't wish that were true, but the idea of him effortlessly snapping his fingers and causing someone's demise compared to her, who had to lose control for even a semblance of that power, didn't quite match up.

He drew her closer to him, "Yes, stronger. Strong enough to kill Goddrick. Strong enough to only need yourself, which is all you have ever wanted." His lips met hers, capturing her in the intensity of the moment. She closed her eyes, surrendering to the depths of his kiss.

Being the gentleman he was, Jayce didn't linger long. He pulled away after a moment and smiled. "That night," as her eyes opened, they found themselves back in the Idle Fox, "I was determined to tell you everything. I ran through portal after portal just to gather the courage, searching for some semblance of myself strong enough to reveal everything. However," his hand gently rested against the side of her neck, lifting her gaze to meet his, "you had been drinking, and you were so against me even being there. Which, truthfully, I couldn't blame you for. I conceded to dance with you, and even that turned out to be a mistake.

"I was hopelessly in love with you and having you that close was blinding. I forgot who I was and what I was there for. All that mattered in that moment was that I had you in my arms, and I never wanted to let you go. It was stupid of me to even try and kiss you then, but after waiting for so long, it was torture. I couldn't believe myself and was thankful that Kaed came to save you."

She avoided scanning their surroundings, focusing solely on his eyes as they absorbed her presence. Part of it was to avoid catching sight of Kaed. The fear that it might be too painful weighed heavily on her.

"It would have likely made things worse, and when I left, I left the Kingdom. His decision to go to the balcony, while hot—"

"I think I'll just go now," she tried to pull away, but he held her in place. Embarrassment flooded through her, her entire body ablaze with discomfort, and all she wanted was to escape the moment.

"Oh, no you don't," he wrapped his arms around her, grinning and burying his head in her neck. "Don't be shy or embarrassed."

She groaned, realizing they were no longer in the Idle Fox but elsewhere in the Kingdom. "I'm pretty sure he did it on purpose." Her voice carried a hint of anxiety. "I'm so—"

"Don't apologize," he cut her off, tilting her backward. "As I was saying, while it was hot, obviously I was envious. I just didn't want to watch; I wasn't angry at him or jealous. I was jealous at first but for a completely different reason."

"And that was for...?"

He brought her back up, her head craning to meet his gaze, "They were making you happy and I wasn't."

"Gods be damned, Jayce." How could her heart hurt more? She dropped her head to his chest, and she could feel the rumbling under her as he let out a hearty laugh. "How is it that I can be happy, and sad, at literally the same time?"

"Because you are the epitome of a good person, Azahara Starfall."

Grumbling, she asked, "Where are we now?" Determined to press forward before her heart chose to depart and never return, she leaned back and surveyed her surroundings.

"That night, before I left, I put some of my Magic inside you. Right—" he placed his hand over her chest, "—here. So that I could always find you if something were to happen. I was resolved that I wasn't going to be able to leave with you. The King had your name laced on his tongue and I'd be damned leaving it there. While Karver was fully capable, the best place for me was here, keeping you safe from afar. You had the great-grandchild of the Elder Fae, a Væragi, and a man that loved you. Who else could better protect you?" He groused, "My judgment was lackluster, to say the least."

Somehow, she laughed, "Trust me, I felt the same. It was never my plan, none of this. Never to see the King, never to go find the Yuul—that was the King's doing, ordering Kaed to find out who killed the Elder Fae."

"He did?" He cut in, "I must've missed that. I thought you suggested the Yuul, knowing your history with Death."

Shrugging, she sighed, "Nope." A shiver went through her, *too close, too close...*

"Helgum?" He continued, brushing his hands up and down her arms. He must have noticed the chill that ran through her at nearly saying the word 'no'.

She shook her head, "Illyan lied about sending us through the wëther to the nearest Outpost, and instead sent us to Helgum. Jaakobai, before the Rite, told them that the wings of Helio were likely there. They were convinced bringing them back would clear not only their name, but mine."

"You never needed to clear anything up, that piece of shit conned his father into believing you were using black Magic to get yourself there." His anger radiated around him, and its raw strength was something that sent bumps up her arms. This was merely in his mind, too; imagining what it would feel like in the real world was thrilling.

She never stepped away from him, feeling the dark purple aura around him consume over her like a blanket.

"When I felt you in Höwl, Azahara, I **did** lose it. I was in So'ol instantly, and let's just say, it isn't in the same geological location as it was before."

She swallowed.

"Putting my Magic in you was the best thing I could have done. Being banished from Höwl, I couldn't send any Magic in or out, even using the winnox was risky. With everyone on high alert because of you, and the loss of their Magic, it was not a good time. Thankfully, the prisoner known as Sam," he winked, "is a dear friend of mine. When he sensed my Magic in you, he reached out, and allowed me the privilege of his vessel to see you and try to protect you.

"He was too weak to break you out, so I merely spoke with you, but when I saw you, Sunshine, I knew that Höwl was going to suffer. I didn't care that I had friends there. What they did to you, it would not go unpunished." She felt his heart slow, and that anger turned to rage. "When Jaakobai took you, and I couldn't see you, I went to find the Yuul. It hadn't been hard because who did I find fighting it?"

"Zhal and Kaed." She answered, even if she didn't need to.

"They subdued the Yuul, with a little bit of assistance, and I spoke through its mind. Gave it the image of a beautiful redhead that needed to be saved, your scent and name, with the promise when they were done, I would allow them their feast and safe passage back to the mortal realm." Jayce had knowingly killed his kind for her, and she felt the weight of that.

"Were you the one in my cell?" She quickly asked before that same pain raptured her again. "When you said—"

"I want to take you away from this place, but I can't. Yes, I had broken the law for a mere moment of weakness, but in the chaos they would never know."

"Why didn't you take me away then?"

"Because you would have hated me, and you needed Kaed, Illyan, and Zhal. Not me. Not Sam. Them." He was intimately linked with her emotions even before their souls connected. "Then, you were in Helgum, and I couldn't go there without completely exposing myself. There was also a damn Fae ward around you for some time, and I nearly lost it again. It was like the Mother was testing me, telling me I had made mistake after mistake when it came to you."

He laughed without humor, "If I were human, I'd have had wrinkles and gray hairs from all this."

Drawing his hand from her temple down to her jaw, he released a soft sigh, "I watched everything else unfold from afar, all without being too far. I wanted to be by your side, and I hate myself for making the wrong decisions every time."

As she took a deep breath they shifted once more. "I should have taken you away in this moment," He moved her to stand beside him, placing his hand at the back of her neck, leaning her against his arm. Her arm snaked around his waist, curving into his embrace.

Past-Jayce stood concealed behind a tree, just outside the Outpost, and she sensed it was the night preceding the Battle of Sunfall. The perpetual tension in the air was etched into her memory. In the distance, Karver and past-Azahara approached, and she could discern the rhythm of his heartbeat. As Karver tried to offer words of relief, a forced smile adorned his lips, but the agony etched across his face was unmistakable.

His magnificent raven wings were unruly, quivering as though he were cold.

"My entire body was out of control, terrified for you, that I was unable to keep my Magic in check. It was why I couldn't allow for you to see me." He pressed his lips against the top of her head. "Karver told me where you two would be, and I had only come to see you, not talk. Except, I'm completely weak for you. My need to hear you speak to me was far greater than I could fight."

"You are pretty bad at that, you know, metaphors, Officer Cross." His hand trembled against the tree, looking at past-Azahara, who jumped up. The conversation was muted from there, but she watched as past-Jayce smiled when she spoke to him.

"At this moment, when you placed your hand on the tree, I sent my Magic through to caress you. I wanted nothing more than to take you into my arms and ensure your safety. To tell you how much I loved you." She looked up at him, the gloss over his eyes threatened to expose just how painful this moment had been for him. "Karver knew how hard I was fighting myself, so he returned quickly to get you."

The breeze caught past-Azahara's hair, swirling it around her face. It dawned on her that it was caused by him. Past-Jayce was twirling his fingers, conjuring a gust of wind with his Magic, reveling in the smile that graced her features.

"My soul was ready to tear me apart for not keeping you. It was agonizing, watching you walk away. I swore I had a dagger through my own heart then."

She stepped in front of him, "Jayce…" her voice a whisper as she placed her hands against his chest, "You speak of my strength but completely ignore your own. You knew what I needed and sacrificed so much to give it to me. By the Mother, I don't think I could have done it."

She enveloped him in her arms, drawing him close. He obliged and cupping his hand behind her head and placing a tender kiss on the top of it. Gradually, the surroundings faded away, and the scent of the sea returned to her senses. They were emerging from his memory, and she could feel her back firmly against something.

"You made me strong, watching you fight so hard for the ones you loved constantly. Never giving up even though I knew how badly you wanted to. But, even as strong as you were, I was done not being by your side." His words hung in the air, and as her eyes blinked, she found herself back on the ship, lying on the wooden planks, gazing up into his illuminated hazel eyes.

"It was why when Jaakobai and the King were ready to send the Fae army after you, I volunteered to get you myself. I had done enough to protect you from the backline, and now it was my turn to fight beside you. Except, I still somehow allowed Goddrick to get a hold of you. I was trying to play it all by the books, trying not to start a war with myself, the mortal King, and the Fae.

"That was stupid because I would destroy this world for you. I'd protect the ones you wanted but burn the rest for ever harming my girl." His forehead pressed against hers, lifting her from the floor.

Seated on his knees, she wrapped her arms around his neck, her legs mirroring the same action around his hips. "I promise you, from this day forward, I'll never leave your side unless you tell me to. I've made enough mistakes to last a lifetime, but no more."

One of his hands rested against her hip while the other gently held the side of her neck, "Now you know everything. Do I still need to beg for forgiveness?"

Pure wonder filled her eyes as she gazed at him, and a soft laugh escaped her, though it was accompanied by a gentle sob. "No, you don't." Sensing his hand at her hip move up her back, traversing the Connection to her neck, she bit gently at her bottom lip.

"I love you, Azahara, and will do so for the remainder of my days, from this life to the next." His eyes remained locked onto hers, and she could sense the depth of his emotions in his declaration. "I will stand with you but never in your way. You choose your life, and I only ask to be a part of it. In whatever way you wish, it is just that. Yours. I am yours."

A peculiar sensation enveloped her, as if her soul had discovered solace and could finally find rest. In that moment, if Death finally decided to take her, she felt she would be at peace. It would have been a satisfying way to go, cradled in his embrace, experiencing absolute love without compromise. She had always been his priority, above all else.

She had never stopped smiling, but somehow, it grew even wider as she molded her body against his. "I love you, Jayce, with all of my being. I want to give you my all and make you as safe and happy as you've made me."

The space between them vanished, and his lips met hers. This kiss was a fusion of passion and yearning, coursing through her to the core. Previous kisses had been amazing, but this one transcended realms. Ecstasy lifted her entire body, and for a moment, she feared she might float away.

Yet, that fear was unfounded because Jayce held her tightly, anchoring her to him and to this existence. For the first time, she truly felt safe.

Jayce was everything she needed and wanted, and she knew that if she were to ever fall, he would fall with her. There was no duty or call he would answer that wasn't for her. She was his world, and she would give it to him without hesitation or restraint.

Day 164
Chapter 35

In Jayce's strong embrace, he swung open the door to the quarters that had held both love and trepidation for her. It was a space marked by turmoil yet brimming with genuine care and compassion. This was where she envisioned spending the rest of her days, sailing within the embrace of the family she had grown to cherish, until there was no more sea to traverse.

Her heart raced, but it wasn't because of Jayce. Instead, it was her own fear that gripped her. She didn't want to ruin this moment by being afraid, but she knew she would.

Not that she needed to say it, because as the door closed behind them, he gently lowered her to the ground. "I told you there was no pressure for anything," his hand pressed against her chest, "settle your heart, please; I'm afraid it'll go running." A shared laugh lightened the atmosphere, and she was grateful for it.

"I know," her veiled eyes met his, and his darkened cheeks eliciting hers to blaze. "But I don't want him to own anything of me. I want it back. Just as I got my soul, I'm going to take my body back, too."

He grinned from ear to ear, leaning down to plant a quick kiss on her lips. "That's my girl." Whenever he said that, it felt like a flame burning around her heart—a claim, but not in a possessive way.

"I'll just need help, and time," she said, her voice unintentionally breathy. The way he looked at her then made the room feel starved of air.

"Tell me what you need, and it's yours," his voice was silky, gently lifting her gaze to his. How could she even breathe right now? Her entire body was ablaze, and she just wanted to be free of the dress that constrained her.

It felt strange, having to be so careful. She had never been shy about her sexual desires and knew what she wanted when it came to pleasure.

Stepping away from him, she moved with unspoken cues, and he watched, prepared to respond. With shaky fingers, she unclasped the metal shoulder pieces of her dress and tossed them aside. Their weight became apparent as the floor vibrated from their impact.

Her arms clung tightly to her body, supporting the dress to prevent it from falling. It wasn't as though he hadn't seen her naked, but that had been a completely different scenario. Aside from glimpses of her back in the shattered mirror in Ilkiz's Tomb, she had not seen herself naked since Goddrick had her. Since then, she had actively avoided looking at herself. Now, with him standing there, awaiting her decision, she felt the weight of millions of eyes on her.

Before she could crack under the pressure, she felt his embrace.

His hands touched her back, running gently up and over her shoulders, his skin soft against hers. As his hands moved across the curve of her neck, she leaned her head back to look at him.

"I know where to start," he said confidently, making trusting him so easy.

They walked together step by step toward the wall, where a sheet covered the only mirror in the room.

"You're absolutely beautiful, and healing will take time," he slipped the sheet from over it, and she observed the two of them standing there. Before she could ask, he turned around, pressing their backs together, and laced his fingers into hers. "The only eyes that matter are your own. Look, and I'll be here to support you, and if you fall, I'll catch you."

She took an unsteady breath, closing her eyes momentarily. *You can do this,* she encouraged herself.

Refocusing on the mirror, she stared at herself for the first time, her eyes trained directly on her face. Her flawless skin, uniquely red freckles scattered from ear to ear, and her full, pink parted lips all felt foreign. Her widened almond eyes showcased a singular crystal blue eye while the other had red and orange cascading outward from the iris, the once vibrant blue trying to hold its dominance. The tip of her nose seemed highlighted in the flickering candlelight. The red paint smeared across her cheek and down her neck drew her attention to where the problem lay.

Squeezing his hand, she loosened her grip on the dress, and slowly, it fell to the floor. Immediately, her eyes closed, feeling the sickness in her stomach ripple through her. She didn't want to see his hand marks—the ink that no one else could see but herself. The rough trembling in her hands seemed to vibrate throughout her entire being, and she wanted to run. She didn't want this.

"What happened will never go away," Jayce spoke softly, his gaze lifting so that the top of his head would rest on her own. "Overcoming them will be difficult, but you can do anything, I know you can."

He was right, she could do anything. Taking a deep breath, she opened her eyes.

Terrified, she took in her bare appearance. The façade of perfection was all a lie. The bruises, cuts, and destruction he caused were all still there, just blanketed with false security.

Observing her chest rise and fall, witnessing the seemingly untouched body that she should love, had the opposite effect. She could still perceive what it went through—the suffering it had endured, only to be seen as a *blessing*. The familiar sting in her nose pierced through her eyes, and she swallowed roughly.

As her gaze moved down to her hip where his hand held tightly to hers, a sense of calm enveloped her. It made her heart slow, and her trepidation began to dissolve.

Her breathing quickened as she looked back up at herself. "I genuinely hate looking at myself. I know, for someone who looks like I do, it's stupid."

"It's not," he quickly intervened. "You have every right to feel that way."

She leaned her head back against him. "What do you see?" Her body turned away from the mirror, her hand pulling him to look at her.

When he looked down at her, she took a step back. Her cheeks burned, and she trained her gaze downward, not wanting to watch him take her in. Every part of her skin tingled as she could feel his eyes, and yet again, she wanted to run. The sense that she was breaking into pieces like a shattered mirror, ready to litter the floor with fragments of herself, was nearly overwhelming.

His fingers gently came under her chin, directing her eyes towards him. His gaze was reverent, and his cheeks were flushed. "Through my eyes, I see nothing but beauty and quintessence. But through yours, I see the invisible scars. I see someone forced to appear okay, but truly isn't. An illusion of perfection involuntarily placed on you while you suffer from bruises and scars that no one can see."

She wanted to be okay, but never wanted to pretend to be. They always saw perfection when she was anything but.

"I'll help you heal so you see the beauty I see when I look at you. No matter how long it takes."

"Stupid tears," the onslaught of heat rose to her eyes, and they welled with emotion. "I don't want to cry."

Before the tears could pour from her eyes, his lips pressed against hers roughly, and his hands were at the sides of her neck, thumbs at the contours of her cheeks. "—Jayce," she gasped through the kiss, feeling his body tremble. Her body reacted as it would have before, and butterflies fluttered around in her lower abdomen.

His hand came up to her hair, and with a groan, dropped it to the back of her neck. "Damn those girls," he cursed through bated breath, sucking in a healthy intake of air before reclaiming her lips as his own.

She moved her hands down his chest, tugging up on his shirt and pulling it from his pants. When her fingers contacted his skin, the sound that escaped his lips made her legs tremble. He was quick to grab her hand, "Mmm, shit—" The sheepish mutter and huff of air that came from him surprised her.

"Did I—"

"No... no..." He smiled and released a sigh, "Give me a moment." Her hand was against his lips then, and he was kissing down her wrist, gently biting it. It sent her head back and her own gentle moan to leave her throat.

"What—" she bit her lip, his lips moving further down her forearm, "What happened?"

She could feel his smile against her skin. "I have control touching you, but obviously, I have none when you touch me." He guided her hand over his neck as he kissed up and across her collarbone, and with care, he bit down on her shoulder. The shock it sent through her made her back arch, and she clutched his hair for dear life.

The gentle suck accompanying his bite made her melt against him and let out a soft, barely audible moan. Resisting the urge not to touch him was becoming nearly impossible for her.

His arm swiftly tucked under her leg, lifting her into his arms. Their lips met as he carried her to the bed. The mattress sunk in as he let her down and moved on top of her. One of his arms propped him up while the other traced a fine line from her chin down her body, following the red paint that was now smeared and blotchy. Every part of her skin tingled with fire, and small bumps rose.

"Jayce..." His name escaped with an unfiltered moan, impossible for her to keep tamed.

He cursed under his breath before his lips were on hers again, immediately intertwining their tongues. He placed his hand under her breast, and she felt her body ready to explode. As she attempted to spread her legs, she realized that he had straddled her.

It dawned on her then that he was doing everything right: keeping his hands from venturing beyond her stomach, keeping her legs closed so she wouldn't feel self-conscious about it moving too far, and checking himself any time he felt he was losing control.

The depth of his strength knew no bounds.

She wasn't sure what her limit was, and truthfully, she was afraid to find out. She wanted to give all of herself to him, free from the constraints of her fear and anxiety that held her back.

Her hands settled on his cheeks, gently pushing him back so she could see him. Both were breathing heavily, and she could discern the desire in his eyes. At that moment, she wondered if he could see and feel her longing as intensely as she could sense his.

With her newfound strength, she pushed him over and rolled on top of him. A look of shock spread across his face as she swiftly wrapped the sheets around her waist, concealing her lower half while straddling his hips. Her hands clutched the sheets, and the blush returned to her face, both heating and serving as a reminder that she didn't need them, except to cover herself.

"Take your shirt off," she said while diverting her gaze.

He laughed softly, "Demanding before a first date."

She sucked in a deep breath and shot him a glance. That breath was stolen right back as he had already slipped the shirt off, revealing his bare chest.

Her fingers traced the curve and lining of his muscles, drawing a line down his stomach as he had done to her. He trembled under her touch, and she yearned to do more. His hands were under the sheet at her legs, gripping with every movement of her nails against his skin. The look on his face was driving her crazy. His powerless attempt to keep it together was evident everywhere. She wasn't trying to make him suffer, but knowing she had that effect on him with a simple touch made her feel powerful.

It wasn't until his hands moved up from her legs that all that power was lost. His hands at her hips, thumbs pressed against the bone, sent a shock of ecstasy and fear through her. He didn't move her or shift her in any way; he just put them there, and it was driving her to lose the hold she had on the moment. Nearly sending her mind back to—

"Aza..." He sat forward, her head leaning up as their chests pressed together. "This was a strong start." His voice, a blend of love and desire, resonated, "Let's stop here."

Love wasn't a potent enough word for what she felt in that moment. Even on the precipice, ready to dive deep into the waters without considering the monsters that awaited, he chose to save them both with a decision that was far from easy.

"Jayce—" she began softly, but he leaned in, kissing her needy lips. She wrapped her arms around his neck, pulling herself to him, and her legs encircled his waist. His hands ran up her back, snaking around her. "I love you," she uttered between their lips breaking. He smiled, reclaiming her, and they tumbled back down to the bed.

Day 165
CHAPTER 36

In the hush of dawn, a dense mist had settled upon the vessel. Azahara, with a blanket gracefully draped around her shoulders, stepped out of her quarters, leaving Jayce still in the embrace of slumber on the disheveled mattress.

Gazing over the ship's edge, she became entranced by the enchanting panorama of Hydrox Port. Her mind painted vivid scenes of the bustling harbor, teeming with a diverse tapestry of people and travelers converging from every corner of the world.

The previous night lingered in her memory like a breathtaking dream, leaving her wondering if she would wake up to find it all wasn't real. Unexpected revelations had woven themselves into the fabric of her joy. The only way this moment could have been better was if Kaed, Illyan, and Zhal were there with her. Sharing this moment with them would have made her feel complete.

A gentle melody escaped her lips, a soft hum echoing through the ship. The rhythm, felt in the depths of her throat, reverberated off the deck, encapsulating her in a soothing cocoon. It was a simple tune, evoking the memory of the violin's tender strains from the night before.

"Don't tell me you can sing too," she gasped, startled by his sudden appearance behind her. Swiftly turning, she watched him saunter out of the room towards her, shirtless and seemingly unaffected by the cool air enveloping them.

Shaking her head, she replied, "I don't sing."

"You sounded lovely just now," he complimented. Her arms opened, inviting him under the blanket, and he embraced her without hesitation.

Leaning in, he whispered, "You can sing to me anytime you'd like." She smiled as he kissed her, his hands securing her arms, as if ensuring she wouldn't slip away.

Pressing his forehead to hers, he grinned, revealing a toothy smile. "It was worth the wait," he said, lifting her and placing her on the railing, standing between her legs.

Resting her head on his, she shyly smiled, her cheeks ablaze. "Stop, or I'll melt into the sea."

"I'd come to collect you."

As his fingers traced a path up her side, a playful laugh bubbled from her lips, accompanied by a delightful shiver as his arm gently shifted the blanket from her shoulder. The tips of his fingers grazed the small dip between her collarbone and shoulder, sending a thrilling sensation coursing through her.

"Can we stay here all day? Just the two of us?" she asked, reminiscing about the times when all she desired was to linger in bed with Kaed, only to be constantly on the move for one reason or another.

"Your wish is my command," he murmured, his fingers continuing their journey down her arm, and she couldn't help but grin.

"Music to my ears."

True to his word, they remained on the ship for the rest of the day, enveloped in each other's company. She opened up to him, sharing more about her life before the curse. Delving into the details, recounting the final moments and explaining how she found herself at the Temple, inevitably turning Goddrick's hourglass. Though the truth brought a sense of relief, it wasn't the outcome she had hoped for. From the very beginning, he had deceived her into releasing him from his prison.

Transitioning to the events involving Ilkiz and Rahmulous, Jayce was astonished to learn that Azahara had encountered Rah's spirit. She delved into every intricate detail; recounting Mel's involvement, Rah hurling her skyward from the Tomb, and the summoning of Ilkiz. Jayce, surprisingly, had no questions, and she spoke almost uninterrupted for hours. Even the trial was covered, in which he said he'd have a word with the ghostly Dragon for doing that to her.

As the conversation shifted to Azahara's varied lifetimes, Jayce was captivated. From seeking simple adventures like climbing the Veesilka mountains for fun to serving as a house mother at a brothel, each story left him eager to ask more. Although she now acknowledged the year at the brothel as a fun one, it paled in comparison to her time at the Idle Fox.

When the focus turned to Jayce, the barrage of questions began. At six thousand two hundred and thirty-three, barely three hundred years after the Reshaping of Rah, he astounded her with his age and grounded demeanor. He explained that there had been so many changes and shifts throughout his lifetime, from the Conquering of Parádeisos to the Wrath of the King, that it had kept his mind level.

However, he emphasized that, despite the longevity, there had been only a few couple hundred years of actual peace between each significant event. It was why he left the mortal realm and returned to the Höwl, seeking some semblance of it, but it was short-lived.

Jayce had desired to be the Elder Fae when Helio was selected. She didn't understand their politics and asked him not to dive deep into it. It wasn't something she was interested in unless it truly affected him. Which it didn't, so he digressed.

After the Rite, and although he had been selected, the outcry from Helio's children accusing him of cheating led to a near war within the houses. Despite Jayce having the majority vote, the more powerful voices compelled him to step-down due to baseless accusations.

Imprisoned for over a thousand years without evidence, he harbored no resentment toward Illyan, as they hadn't been alive during those tumultuous events.

Karver, who he said was like his brother, finally had the opportunity to get him out. His newfound strength enabled him to rupture the cell wards, setting him free into the Mortal Realm. Aware that remaining there would result in his sentencing, Karver chose to accompany him.

In a moment that wasn't exactly humorous but carried a certain irony, he quipped about the fortuitous timing of her being captured, occurring when there was an absence of Magic around Höwl. If the prison had been fortified with their impenetrable Locke Wards, without question, he would have had to decimate the place he once called home, to get to her.

The surreal realization that he would have sacrificed his home and people for her felt unreal. Then again, if the world or anyone in it tried to take him from her or anyone she loved, there would be no mercy. Even if it meant becoming the villain. For the sake of them, she was willing to embrace that title.

Throughout the day, they engaged in ceaseless conversation, punctuated by brief bouts of sleep that never diminished the precious time they spent together. As the sun set, they both observed the encroaching night.

"Another question," she sang, leaning over the ledge. "The connection on my back, what do you see? I haven't been able to ask anyone, and I'm a bit nervous to... I'm not even sure why."

He laughed, mirroring her posture. "I see raven wings that span your entire back from shoulder to, I believe also to your butt, although I didn't get a good enough view last night to confirm."

"Wow," she looked up at him, eyes wide and cheeks flushing. "That big? I'll really have to find out more about this thing." Her face reflected excitement, as if uncovering this mystery was simply another desire, not an obligation.

Jayce slid his hand around her back, fingers slipping between her arm and torso. "Akua shared some information about the Connection with me. He says the stronger your bond with someone, the bigger it is." Anticipating her surprise, he added, "I was just as stunned, though not displeased by the revelation."

She chewed on her lip, stealing a glance out at the sea. "Can I see your wings?" Her voice held a subtle hint of shyness. "I mean, if that's—" The soft flutter and gentle rustling of feathers reached her ears, prompting her to spin around. Witnessing them already unfurled in their full splendor behind him, her heart quickened, and her eyes widened in absolute awe of their magnificent display.

They appeared longer than she had remembered, their sheer force leaving her breathless. Not only were they beautiful, but they also exuded strength. Their color resembled midnight black, yet upon closer inspection, an iridescent sheen revealed itself. Hues of blue, purple, and even a hint of green emerged from the tucks and folds of the glossy feathers. The alluring beauty of their appearance tempted her to reach out and touch them.

"Are they heavy?" Her voice was soft, as if speaking too loudly might startle the feathers that twitched and fluttered at random.

"No, surprisingly."

"I'm okay to touch them?" She heard him laugh.

"Of course, they are just like another part of—" Her fingers glided gently along the surface of the wing, confirming that they were as smooth and silky as they appeared. The tightly packed feathers overlapped neatly, reminding her of the moment he had wrapped her in them—like a cozy blanket enfolding her in comfort. "me..."

Shifting her gaze, she saw that he was blushing. "I swore you said they weren't sensitive."

She could see his throat bob. "When anyone else touches them, apparently. Maybe they longed for your touch as much as I did."

"That is a thought," she ran her fingers along them, feeling the tapered shape, watching them shiver at the simplest of attention. "They are huge, by the Mother." They towered over her, and even as she looked to her left, they felt endless. "Do you know how long?"

When she didn't get a response, she looked at him, and his gaze turned away from hers. "Jayce?"

"Hmm?" He still didn't look at her. "I haven't measured in a while. Twenty-five, maybe thirty feet." His voice was husky, and she narrowed her eyes at him.

Deciding to play dumb, she walked down towards the tip of his wing, and as she had done before, took it and wrapped it around her. "I think I'll take my next nap right here."

Almost instantly, his wing shifted and gracefully scooped her up, gently cradling her within its curved shape. Surprised, she let out a soft yelp. As her gaze swiftly met Jayce's, she noticed him walking towards her, simultaneously drawing her closer with a tender gesture.

As they drew near, his wing gently guided her to her feet and pressed her against him. Her hands rested on his chest, and as she looked up at him, the sight of his flustered face caused her own cheeks to blush.

"You're willing to make me risk death for you, do you know that?" His voice, silky and tempting, sent a shiver down her spine. When his thumb brushed her chin, she released the breath she'd been holding.

Burning up, she asked, "What did I do?"

"My wings are hidden at all times through a glamour," he explained, wrapping them around the two of them. "But if you keep treating them that well, Sunshine, I may keep them out for further affection."

Biting her lip, she raised her hand over his shoulder, gently brushing her fingers along the feathers. "Then only bring them out to play with me."

The shock on his face quickly gave way to pure, raw lust. His hand was behind her head, fingers through her hair, gently pulling her back. "Never in my years have they been out for someone, even another Fae." The prospect sent shivers throughout her body, and he felt or saw them because he let out a soft, throaty laugh. "A first for even me, that is quite the feat."

She swallowed, feeling his lips at her throat, finding it fit to press a kiss. A low, needy moan escaped her, and she felt his smile. When he bit down, rougher than the night before, she gripped his shirt and arched her back.

"Ah—" The grumbly moan she released only enticed him more. His opposite arm wrapped around her waist, pulling her closer. His tongue flicked across her skin, igniting her entire body with euphoria. She knew he was sucking, and her body moved without guidance. In a feeble attempt to wrap her leg around his hip, she settled for his thigh; she cursed her short stature or his towering height.

It didn't faze him. His hand slipped under her leg, lifting it, and inevitably, her. Taking it as an invitation, she wrapped both legs around him while his lips trailed down to her collarbone, kissing and running his tongue along her sensitive skin.

The night before, they had barely ventured beyond him touching her stomach and back, leaving small marks across her shoulders. She had expressed her fear of going too far and ruining the moment. Jayce, a true gentleman, assured her that she'd never ruin anything. He promised to always watch and feel for her cues, whether through her words or her soul.

Her soul yearned for him, and she feared that it would betray her body.

He turned so he could sit her on the ledge, his hands slipping under the sides of her shirt and she put her arms up for him to remove it. There was no hesitation, and she felt her muscles tense as his eyes, full of desire, took in her own. The moon's light now overtaking the sleeping sun, illuminated those beautiful iridescent colors in his feathers. The absolute need to touch them was something she could not explain, and it was like he felt that radiating off of her and tucked them closer so she could fulfill the desire.

"Remember," his lips were mere inches from her, "stop me if it is too much." With a decisive nod, he placed a kiss on her lips before leaning back down, trailing the central line down her chest. Her breathing was choppy, and she curled her toes in anticipation of him finding her breasts.

One of his hands was keeping her steady, while the other was slowly moving around her waist, his fingers dangerously close to the underside of her breast.

Her hand reached around his shoulders, finding her fingertips brushing downward against the silky feathers. They quivered under her touch, and she felt the need in his lips cupping over her nipple. The rapture that overtook her body sent her head flying back and an unadulterated moan escaped.

The vibration from his own groan against her skin sent another wave of pleasure that shot straight through her stomach and made her legs tremble. He shifted to her other, and ran his tongue around her hardened bud, before encapsulating it with his lips and sucking gently. His hand that had been slowly moving to grasp one, took it into his hand, massaging it with gentle, yet needy, motions.

As she leaned back, instead of the sea beneath her, his smooth wings served as a cushion, supporting her, and keeping her upright.

As she gazed down at him, he met her eyes, and whatever he perceived sent tremors through her entire body. His eyes widened, and she drew in a deep breath, suddenly aware that one of her hands was entwined in his hair, and the other rested against his wing. "W-what..." Her voice came out breathy, and she swallowed, a mixture of confusion and anticipation lingering in the air.

In the span of a single blink, the light hazel eyes she had come to associate with him transformed into the more notable ones of the Fae. They turned into a vibrant amethyst, more intense than any she had ever seen, glowing in the darkened night. "I realized that I was seeing who you were, but you weren't seeing me," he confessed with an intoxicating smile, causing her to bite down on her lip and shift. "Only for you, though."

He moved his attention back to his previous efforts, but instead of going to her breast, he kissed down her stomach. A world-shattering vibration rolled through her body.

"Jayce—" She had shorts on, and undergarments, but that was her most feared place. While her entire body healed, she never wanted to look between her legs. The sheer terror that gripped her made her hesitant to discover whether he had caused any permanent damage. Although it likely healed like everything else, the knowledge that that part of her was both a traitor and the focal point of his pain kept her in the shadows.

He didn't look up at her, but lingered at her belly button, "Tell me when to stop." He whispered against her skin, and she pressed her lips together. Slowly, he moved down, his lips finding her hip bone, kissing, and leaving gentle bites as he did. There was no physical sensation as he lowered her shorts and kissed the curve between her thigh and pelvis.

He looked up at her, and she was breathing heavily, burning with both desire and fear. Torn between wanting to confront her fears and the urge to make him stop, tears brimmed in her eyes.

Jayce immediately stood and wrapped his arms around her shoulders, pulling her close. "I'm sorry—I'm sorry—" She found herself apologizing, feeling she had ruined the moment. "Damn him, damn him—" Rubbing her eyes on his chest, she brushed away the fallen tears.

"Shh," his gentle hand stroked down her hair, placing kisses along her head. "Don't apologize. You're making incredible progress, remember, one step at a time." His encouraging words began to calm her turmoil, and her body ceased its trembling. "Look at me, Sunshine."

She sniffled, leaning back and sheepishly looking up at him. "Tell me, "his caring voice was filled with understanding, "what I can help you overcome."

Her lips parted slightly, watching as he looked from her lips back up to meet her gaze. His shining eyes, both strange and alluring, made her body vibrate with ecstasy. "I haven't looked or touched since then... I'm afraid of so much. Did I heal? Will it feel the same? Do I even get aroused..."

He grinned, "I can answer that last one," making her blush. "I don't even need to touch you to know that you are..." he let out a throaty groan, making her heart flutter, "quite aroused."

After placing a gentle, quick kiss on her lips, he continued, "Do you want to stop?"

She shook her head, and he kissed her again, lifting her from the railing. Notably, he placed one hand under her butt and gave it a playful squeeze. She smiled, appreciating that he considered her feelings while also reigniting the mood.

Before she knew it, he was tossing her onto the bed, his wings tucked behind his back, their grandeur unaffected.

"How does it ... work, the glamour?" she asked, watching him effortlessly tear his shirt off.

"Ah, it's complicated. Magic sometimes has no limits, and let's just say this is one of those things that defies what should and shouldn't be possible." She recalled Kaed's initial comment about Magic, causing a shiver to erupt down her spine—not out of fear, but intrigue. "I'm one of very few who can, along with shifting my appearance."

He was moving to her then, his fingers lacing under her shorts, but minding to keep her underwear on.

"And your ears?" Her breathy tone barely audible.

"Pointy," he lifted her legs to remove her shorts. He kept one of them, kissing at her ankle, "I keep those as human as possible, though. Since those are a telltale sign of being Fae." He was moving further up towards her knee.

She was blushing, her hands cupping one another in front of her mouth as she watched him slowly crawling up her body, "Jayce..."

"Hmm?" He gazed up at her, his eyes filled with pure love.

"When I'm whole again," she covered her face, embarrassed about what she was going to say, "I want you to take me without reservation. No holding back. I want—"

His speed propelled the bed against the wall, the headboard cracking beneath his hands. He was over her in an instant, his wings vibrating as they had when she touched them. The room seemed to buzz, as if gravity itself was being lifted, and the air around her became thinner and cleaner. His Magic was unlike anything she had ever felt before, its raw strength could instill fear in everyone but not her.

"You aren't easily broken, Sunshine, but I will not be testing your limits until I am certain you are okay," he whispered, his warm breath caressing her skin. "But, one day," he gently brushed his lips down her neck, "you won't have to ask for me to go harder."

Her soul departed her body, and the room became unbearably hot. He must have sensed her desire because he slid beside her, took her hand, and pressed it to his lips. Kissing her fingers before moving them down her body together, he kept his hand over the top of hers, bringing them under her panties.

She gasped, pulling back and looking up at him.

"You first," his arm wrapped around her neck, drawing her close, and he claimed her lips with his own. While her hand trembled, she released the strength she was fighting against his advancements. He laced his fingers between her own and slipped them between her thighs.

The shock at how wet she was, translated to a soft gasp that barely escaped through their kiss. His finger pushed hers between her slit, and she took a deep breath, closing her eyes tightly and deepening the kiss.

The feeling of touching herself while he guided her was like an out of body experience. Only after he guided her through the precipice did he refrain from going any further, allowing her to find the piece of herself she was so afraid to feel. Everything was as it was before, a comfort she needed, yet also a source of pain. *Was my fear even valid?* She thought, feeling a wound in her heart as she began to slide her hand out from her undies.

"Yes," he broke their kiss, capturing her gaze, "it is." Taking her hand into his, he laced their fingers together and pulled her on top of him.

She spread her legs and straddled his hips, her body molding into his, relishing their skin-to-skin connection. "Do you always hear my thoughts?" She felt a twinge of embarrassment at the prospect, wondering if anything could remain a secret.

"You... said it through your window."

"Of course I did," she groaned, "I've had a mental block for so long, it's strange keeping it open. I should probably close it..." she eyed him, all the while he kept the cheesy grin on his face.

"You should, I enjoy coming and knocking." He pulled her up, placing a fleeting kiss against her lips.

"Jayce, how the hell—" She bit the corner of her lip, suddenly realizing that something was missing given their position. "How do you have so much... restraint?!" Not once had she felt his arousal against her.

"Oh, Sunshine," his fingers laced through her hair, the other brought her hand up to his lips. He kissed her fingers, inhaling deeply through his teeth. "I can promise you it is difficult. However, I don't want to push you, and that is what keeps me sated."

"I know, but I haven't even—" she began to scoot down slightly, and his hand slapped her butt so hard that she let out a cry. He hadn't meant to slap it, caught up in the quick movement. "J-Jayce!!" she whimpered.

He let out a laugh, "I'm so sorry, but please, Azahara, why would you even test my strength like that?" His hand massaged her now stinging cheek, lifting her up off of him. "By the Mother," he released her and brought his hands up to his face. "The things you do to me."

She was blushing intensely, and she knew both of her cheeks were the same shade of red. "I just haven't even felt it once, I'm innocent, I swear." Her mock whimpering fell on deaf ears as he shook his head in consternation. "Do you glamour that too?"

His eyes went wide, "No, you didn't just ask me that."

"Why are you looking at me like that?"

"Do you want to touch it?"

"Oh, by the Mother, don't ask me that!"

"Well, now you have to—"

"JAYCE!"

She was so, so happy.

Day 165
CHAPTER 37

"You look tired," Azahara said with a chuckle, noticing Ilkiz slouching near the harbor's shore closest to the ship. She had slipped from Jayce's grasp, leaving him asleep, when she felt her Spirit calling out to her. "Did you party for nearly two days straight?" she playfully asked.

The Dragon grumbled, huffing a heavy breath of air in her direction. Thankfully, with the newfound strength from Ilkiz, she was able to hold her ground, preventing herself from being launched hundreds of feet into the sea behind her.

"Don't be crude," Ilkiz's voice boomed, "but yes, I did."

Azahara let out a hearty laugh, placing her hand onto the large snout and giving it a gentle pat, "It's fine, no judgement from my side. My days have been filled with nothing but wonder."

"You are radiating, Azahara. I'm happy he finally found the balls—"

"Ilkiz." She eyed her Spirit, "Be nice."

"You deserved to know." It was warming to know that Ilkiz had her best intentions. This close to decamillennial creature who has seen countless wars, and the eradication of their own kind, cared about this measly little human. "While I've never been a fan of the Fae, he is one of the few good ones, I'm only messing around about his balls."

Azahara rolled her eyes, but kept a playful smile on her lips, "I'd be inclined to agree. About the good one's comment. Not about his balls."

They both shared in a laugh, and she could feel Ilkiz ready to be returned and rest.

"I need a favor before I pull our Spirits back together," her subsequent request would not make either of them happy, Jayce or Ilkiz, but it needed to happen. She paused while walking towards the water, "I need to see Death."

"Then summon it." It was obvious to her then that the four powers didn't know much about one another, which was oddly surprising to her.

"I can only summon Death when there is death close, I've tried to just simply request its presence, but the only time I could was during the Battle of Sunfall, when it arrived on my request to take the souls I had killed, along with Thall. My connection isn't like the Yuul's."

She could feel Ilkiz tense and see her scales tremble, "What are you requesting that I do, little one?"

"Throughout this year I have..." Somehow saying it out loud felt more shameful than she expected it to be, "Only have been able to see Death upon my own death." She could feel Ilkiz trembling, and she took a deep breath.

"How often have you visited its presence?" There was pain behind the tendrils of her words.

"More than a dozen, or so, times." She admitted with a sincerity that felt almost unnecessary. Ilkiz's turmoil at that moment nearly sent her to her knees. "You have to understand that I was in a dark place after losing Kaed and what I did at Sunfall."

"I am in no place to judge you..." she assured, though her lack of conviction did little to ease the overwhelming wave of emotions she projected.

"I begged Death to take me, every single time, but I'm not going there this time for that. I'm set in my fate and now understanding that it isn't time for me to leave this life. I just need to thank them for their part in saving me from Goddrick. If not for Death, I would likely still be trapped." She confessed, placing her hand tenderly on her mighty snout before gently kissing her. "It will be the last time, I promise."

"You ask me to kill you and expect my heart to not shatter as I do?" Again, she shot her a heavy thrust of air that would have sent her flying if she were the same Azahara from six or so months ago.

"I will not permanently die, Ilkiz. I'm simply going to sleep—"

"Your heart will stop," she cut in.

"I am asking that you put your tail into the water and hold me down, pretend we are playing a game." She tried to laugh, but Ilkiz was not having it. "I heal too fast now and would just suffer more if I tried another alternative. If you would rather, I can tie my foot to something and sink."

"Are we seriously debating your death?!" Ilkiz was angry, and she would have feared her if it would have gone anywhere beyond her scolding.

"You will know when I'm ready to come up." She said, walking into the water.

Ilkiz moved with swift grace, her elongated form blocking Azahara's path effectively. Her massive frame loomed over, making the thought of climbing seem futile. Instead, Azahara met Ilkiz's large crimson gaze, "Please, before Jayce wakes up. He will also need to be held back; I really would rather only do this once."

"You would make me fight the Fae, by the Sky above Azahara..." Feeling her contemplation, Azahara took a deep breath. "You won't let me convince you otherwise— Why not talk through the Yuul?"

"I've never feared death, nor Death itself. I do not plan to start now. As Rah was with you, I am with Death," she spoke with a gentle and understanding tone. "Ilkiz, thank you, but it will be fine. Mere moments of suffering will bring me happiness in the end. Sometimes, the toughest choices are made not for the betterment of others but for oneself."

Ilkiz, as if laboring against invisible resistance, slowly cleared a path. The ground quivered beneath, and she was keenly aware that Jayce must have sensed or heard the disturbance. With that realization, she briskly entered the frigid water. As it crept up to her chest, she met Ilkiz's gaze, and the Dragon brought her tail over.

"You'll know when I'm ready, but not before."

Ilkiz didn't say anything, and just narrowed her eyes at her. Delving into the experience of death wasn't something she desired, but it became a necessity. It was the only way to speak with Death, and it might be the last opportunity she'd have for quite some time.

Without taking a breath, she sunk under the water and watched as the massive tail of her Spirit swiftly moved over her body and rested her down to the sea floor. That itself could have killed her, the weight of it stealing all the oxygen out of her lungs, and she knew that this would be the quickest, least painful way to go.

Her body began shaking, the immediate need for air took hold, and she began fighting to get loose. It was her body's natural reaction, even if she was conscious of her actions. Killing herself had always been difficult but hoping it would be the last time she would do it, always drove her to try. Now, she wanted to live, so the pain of her lungs shriveling and her throat closing as water drowned her was harder to overcome.

"*Azahara!*" The voice in her head was not her own, but Jayce, "*What are you doing?!*"

It's okay, I'll come back.

"*What does—AZAH—*"

The encroaching darkness behind her eyelids veiled her vision, and the struggle and pain ceased. All that remained was the familiar warmth that always awaited her on the other side—the space between realms and embers, where love and compassion enveloped her.

"My love." Drawing an unnecessary breath, Azahara opened her eyes. The dim room around her familiar, and the echo of her dearest love's voice in her ear brought a sense of home. "My Light."

Death stood above her, a joyful expression gracing its face. Golden tears welled in its eyes, on the verge of spilling down its cheeks.

"Death..." Sitting up, Azahara noticed the inch of water beneath her was no more. The bony fingers of Death lightly brushed her cheek, guiding her gaze upward. They affirmed her presence, assuring it that beyond Purgatory, she was safe.

Death embraced her then, holding her close to its frame and shrouding the cloak around them both, engulfing her in warmth. Her own arms gripped tightly at Death, never wanting to leave its side even though she wasn't ready for death itself.

"My Azahara, you did it." Its voice was pained but also filled with relief. "I am so, so proud of you. Thank you for not giving up."

"Thank you, Death, I... I don't know what would have happened if you had not given me hope." There was no sign that either of them ever wanted to release their embrace. Tears of pure joy pooled in her eyes being back with Death.

"I have not known pain like that since my creation." Death leaned her back slightly, placing a kiss on her lips, and then settling its forehead against hers. "He will suffer. This I promise you."

Azahara nodded before resting her head against its chest, feeling the silence and calm that lay below it. This was the place she had yearned for, the rest she so desperately desired to have. It felt like so long ago that she desired to stay and never return.

"The Underworld rejoices with me, my Light." Death's fingers ran through her hair, "We have so much to catch up on, but it appears we do not have much time together. Your Fae is demanding your return." Death shook their head, "Threatening to remove the tail of my longest, dearest friend, Ilkiz. Shame on him."

"Overbearing— but I do love him..." She laughed, not upset at Jayce, but was hoping for even a few more minutes.

Looking up at Death, she had a bright smile lacing her lips, "I wanted to let you know that I'm better, and healing, and that when things are done and it is my time to depart that life, I want to be with you, just as Rah was with Ilkiz."

Death was smiling. Those soft pink lips trembled lightly as golden tears drew down their cheeks. When its hand came up, it was no longer skeletal but wrapped in the same soft, silky porcelain skin as its face.

"You would choose me—"

"Every time." Azahara took its hand into hers, lacing their fingers together. "In every version of my fate."

Death placed its other hand behind her head, drawing her in. "My name— it is Anastasia." She placed her hand onto its cheek, a surprised expression on her face with Death's admission. "You bring me to life, Azahara."

Anastasia leaned in and placed gentle kiss on her lips. Though fleeting, its tenderness left lingering sparks, igniting a sense of warmth and affection.

"Speaking of life," she said sheepishly, "I probably should go."

"He is physically removing the tail from on top of you as we embrace." Anastasia commented with a short chuckle, "Before you go though." It took a step back from her and stood with its hands together. "Call me, and I will come. You do not need to come back to Purgatory to see me. Be damned the laws of man and gods. If you need me, I am there. No matter what."

Azahara nodded with a shaky smile, not wanting to leave but knowing she needed to. "Thank you, Anastasia. I love you."

"I love you, my Keeper."

Coming back from Purgatory was always easy. The realm was not ready to separate itself from her and welcomed her with open arms. It was always colder, and while she could have chalked it up to being soaked, it wasn't because of that. Death had never been the cold, dark place that text and scholars warned about.

"Jayce..." Her throat felt raw, a consequence of swallowing saltwater during her drowning.

"Aza?! Azahara Rhay Starfall. By the Mother, what the hell!?" Jayce, visibly upset, scooped her up into his arms, his embrace so tight that she had to exhale to create some breathing space within her lungs. "Why? Why would you do that?!"

"You didn't instruct me to tell him, " Ilkiz commented.

"How could you do that, Ilkiz?" He nearly shouted.

"Azahara, he threatened to take my tail!"

"I should have—"

"See! See!" The ground beneath them quivered as Ilkiz edged closer. A deep growl emanated from her, and as Azahara finally opened her eyes, she witnessed Jayce baring his teeth defiantly at Ilkiz.

"Stop, both of you," she managed to force out, bringing her hand up to her head. "It was always so quiet when I came back before..." She groaned.

Ilkiz tilted her head so she could look straight down at her, along with Jayce, who gave her a bewildered look. "Please don't..."

"Oh yes, the dozen or so times before, right?" Azahara's mouth fell open in disbelief. Had Ilkiz just openly told on her as if she were a child?

"That was—get in here," Azahara slapped her hand against Ilkiz, feeling the peculiar tugging sensation at her palms. The colossal form of her Spirit Dragon began to disintegrate into smoke, withdrawing amid the tendrils of her marking, seamlessly melding with her own spirit.

Strength like she had forgotten soaked into her, and the sluggish soreness of death dissipated entirely. When she attempted to sit up, Jayce restrained her, his expression revealing a rare anger directed at her. There had been numerous instances when she longed for him to scold her for recklessness, but now, she regretted ever desiring that.

"I—" She cut herself off.

His chest was raising and falling quickly as he tried to catch his breath.

"Do you understand why I'm upset?" He asked, his grip tightening.

"Because I just killed myself?" It was so matter of fact, it only seemed to anger him more.

"No," His eyes closed and he shook his head, "Well yes, but no, you didn't tell me. Why? I would have listened—"

"Jayce, I wasn't killing myself to die." Her voice was gentle. There was no reason to fight. His being angry at her was rightfully placed.

"I know... you weren't. You didn't tell me because you thought I would stop you."

Her eyes widened, "You would have."

"No, I wouldn't have. I would have been right here, sucking away the pain for you to sleep and see Death. Instead, you chose to assume I would not support you and ended up sending me all your pain as you died. At that moment, I had no idea if it was voluntary or if he—"

"Oh fuck..."

Jayce was pulling her up then, his head buried between the crook of her neck.

"I did not think about that..."

Ilkiz, go to sleep.

"Sorry—"

"Gods be damned, Sunshine!" The arms that had been trembling slowly began to calm, and she wrapped her arms around his torso and molded into him. "I beg of you, just tell me. You don't have to do it all alone anymore."

She snuggled her head against his, her heart racing in her chest and feeling his pound against her. "I'm so sorry, Jayce... I didn't even think—"

"No, you didn't," his hand was at the back of her head, gripping her soaked hair, lacing his fingers through it, "As much as I'd love to stay angry at you, I can't because I understand why you did it. You didn't want me to hurt, even if it had the opposite effect."

She had hoped to be in and out before he realized she was gone, but of course not. Their souls were interlocked in fate, and the other will strike when one fate is threatened. She hadn't even considered what he might feel if he had not sensed her anymore. His turmoil was unmeasurable when he shared that he couldn't feel her when Goddrick took her.

"Just promise me, next time, you'll tell me." He pulled her back, pressing his forehead to hers.

"I promise," she released a sigh before continuing, "though there won't be a next time."

He hummed in question.

"Death, they told me its name," Jayce's eyes went wide, "and said I could summon it whenever I needed. Damned be the laws of man and gods." She repeated Anastasia's words back to him.

His anger had vanished, or at least been concealed, replaced by the absolute shock etched on his face. She allowed the moment to linger before inquiring, "Why are you surprised?"

Jayce shook his head, letting a minuscule laugh come from his throat, "You know Death's name. Try to tell me it."

Her eyebrows furrowed, "It's–" When she opened to speak it aloud, she couldn't. It was as though her tongue was stuck to the roof of her mouth. "What? Its name is–" Placing a hand on her throat, she rolled her tongue around in her mouth. "What the?"

"I'm still upset with you," he promptly threw in before adjusting them, allowing for her to sit up and out of his arms. "But knowing Death's name has more significance than you think." She was looking down at her soaked-through clothes, taking in his words. "It has never been known for anyone to know Death's name beyond Death, or the Grim Reaper, which is such an outdated title."

"I wish I could share it, it's beautiful."

"Death gave it to you and only you. It means the two of you belong to one another, beyond the scope of what any mortal or immortal deem being together forever means. It's not like a belonging between, say, you, Kaed and I. It's deeper than that. You and Death will be forever interlocked when this world ends, and another is created. Death will never allow anyone to take you from them, not I, not Kaed—no one."

The prospect of having Anastasia never allowing anyone to take her, made safe not feel like a strong enough word. While she understood that meant her life beyond death was safe, it still gave her sanctuary knowing Jayce protected her life and Anastasia her death. It was a strange sensation, and she felt her skin tingling under the prospect.

Jayce ran his fingers through his hair, clicking his tongue against his teeth. "You are incredible, but also incredibly frustrating."

"How can I make it up to you?" She asked, her eyes drooping, her lips pulled downward. "I really am sorry."

A smile slowly lined his lips, "Oh, Sunshine, don't look at me like that." He grabbed her under her arms and pulled her back to him. "I can think of one thing, but afterward, you are going to help me fix Alyse's ship."

She gasped, "What happened to—"

"It's not **that** bad," He said pointedly.

She was a bit nervous to see the damage but would take full responsibility for it.

"What do you have in mind? Don't say lose at chess because I'd rather walk naked through Isis than do that."

He threw his head back laughing, and like a plague, she was infected with it, joining in on the hysteria.

Day 165
CHAPTER 38
Jayce Latimer

After their fit of laughter, he swept Azahara into his arms and unveiled a wëther. As they emerged on the other side, he relished the audible gasp he elicited from her—a reaction he had hoped to cause.

During her three months in Ilkiz's Tomb, he found himself with an abundance of time. Remaining with the crew only heightened his anxiety, and he had been cautioned multiple times that attempting to retrieve her from tomb would result in his confinement. They clearly had no understanding of his capabilities, and while he could effortlessly escape any mortal prison, he preferred not to earn enmity.

Most days, he roamed the Isle of Ilkiz, discovering several noteworthy places he intended to share with her, and this was one of them.

"Welcome to the Floating Mountains of Xi," he announced as cascading mountains suspended in the air surrounding them, moving so gradually that they were nearly imperceptible to the naked eye.

Hundreds of towering mountains with jagged cliffs jutting out from their sides, adorned with veils of waterfalls that shimmer and sparkled like liquid crystals in the sunlight.

"Xi was one of Ilkiz's first five children, and his element was Space. For fun, he would often lift the entire island from its place and move it effortlessly. Ilkiz, being the concerned mother she was," he gently set her down, watching the wonder in her eyes expand and her mouth widen. It prompted a chuckle from him before continuing, "She granted the southernmost part of the Isle of Ilkiz to Xi, allowing him to create and play as he pleased. These mountains are suspended with his Spirit, serving both as protection and a warning to those who dare to harm his people and Spirit Riders."

"By the Mother..." He watched her take a step, and outstretch her hand as though she could touch the towering mountains that were hundreds, if not more, feet above her. "This place is unbelievable."

For Jayce, there was no greater joy than witnessing her excitement about exploring the world. As he observed the spectrum of emotions crossing her face—from astonishment to a beaming smile, and then back to awe—he couldn't help but hum. While he might not have experienced everything the world had to offer, he had seen enough to usually be immune to the thrill of discovering something new. Yet, with her, everything in his life felt refreshed. He looked forward to experiencing it all anew through her eyes.

Approaching her, he lifted her once more into his arms. She gasped in surprise, clutching his shirt. "You are a marvel, my love." A tingling sensation ran down his spine, accompanied by a gust of wind bursting from behind him. His wings unfurled, stretching to their maximum without any constraints.

"Wait—Jayce..." Concern laced her voice as she wrapped her arms around his neck.

"You flew on Ilkiz; what's the difference?" He flashed her a toothy grin.

"She's a Dragon."

"I'm hurt. Do you fear I'll drop you?" Leaning in towards her, she bashfully sunk below her arm, attempting to hide her blushing face.

She shook her head. "That's not it," her voice was so gentle that his heart leapt to his throat. "I was just going to ask you to go slow, that's all."

Slow my beating heart, jeez, he chuckled while shaking his head. "As you wish." Placing a quick kiss on her forehead, he bent his knees and launched them off the ground. The takeoff would be the fastest part, but as soon as they were in the air, and he could allow for a slower speed, he did.

He focused on avoiding the smaller rocks that had, over time, broken off from the floating mountains. They were not merely lifeless formations; they teemed with energy and power. The air around them hummed with a vibrant aura, and the wind that drifted around them carried them higher, without him needing to exert much effort. Brilliantly colored vines dangled from their cliff-sides, while flowers of all arrays of colors bloomed, casting a feeling of home inside of his chest.

Azahara was in awe, and while he didn't risk looking down at her, he could hear her soft bouts of astonishment. He could feel her heart, and the fact she never felt fear.

While he would still need to work on her being more forthcoming about certain aspects of her life, he felt she did trust him. She always tried to protect him, even when he didn't need it, and that just melted his heart.

As they were coming up to his point of interest, he slowed, his wings shifting to push backward and slow their descent until his feet landed flat onto one of the many floating mountains. He placed her down, but she gripped onto him for dear life.

"Is it safe up here?" She asked, tapping her foot around to ensure the ground was solid.

He laughed. "You think I'd put you up here if it weren't?"

"I suppose not," she moved away cautiously, "Though you could be messing with me because of what I did. Was showing me this place what you had in mind?"

Moving forward, he laced his fingers into hers and tugged her forward. "Yes, but more specifically, this mountain." Before them was a crystal-clear pond of water that was being overfilled with a cascading waterfall. It smelled like nature had been untouched, and the surrounding greenery infused with the crisp water created a refreshing aroma around them. The air was tinged with the slightest hint of minerals, a testament to the pristine nature of the water source, and just how clean it was.

The might of Dragons that once ruled the skies never ceased to astonish him.

Inhaling deeply, he felt the warm mist on his face. "I thought you could wash up here," he said, looking at her as she turned to him, "From your dip in the salty sea."

Her cheeks were turning pink. "There was a bath..." he stepped to her, and her head tilted all the way back, his fingers against the bottom of her chin, "in the room..." When she spoke so breathlessly, he felt his resolve wavering. The want in her tone, as it had been the last couple of days, was fighting with him.

"I can join you here; the bath, it's a bit of a tight fit." His eyes wandered to her lips, which parted slightly, and then back between her mismatching eyes. "Is that okay? I don't have to join—"

"Yes—I want you to." She was quick to cut him off, and he watched her bite down on that damn bottom lip. He took a deep breath, his eyes rolling back.

She turned away from him, beginning to slip her shirt up and over her head. The Connection mark on her back drew his eyes and demanded their attention. Her pants, still damp, stuck to her backside, making removing them a bit more of a challenge for her. She was fumbling around, embarrassed at her own doing, likely cursing herself for not removing her clothes before going into the sea.

The full view of her bare back was incredible, and he was shocked to see that the wings moved down its entirety, and the tips curved around her butt to her thighs. He leaned his head to the side, watching as they seemed to quiver with his gaze.

She was looking over her shoulder at him. "Are you going to come in clothed, or..."

"No, absolutely not. Not after you asked me about glamouring my—" The yelp that escaped her lips as she ran made him laugh jovially.

As he watched her gracefully splash into the pool of water, he couldn't help but feel a rush of affection. Seeing her rediscover that carefree side of herself and bringing her back to the light filled him with indescribable joy. He cherished the moments when he could make her feel this way and would be content with just that, without ever touching her physically.

Slipping off his shirt and then his pants, he joined her in the water, which was much warmer than he had expected. It likely had to do with its elevated position above the clouds, being much closer to the sun than the sea. Its warmth felt akin to a bath, prompting a grin and a sigh of relief.

He watched her for a moment, her back still turned to him as she stared up at the waterfall, the cascading waters tracing lines down her back.

"Mind sharing what's on your mind?" he asked, resisting the urge to reach out and take her into his arms.

Her shoulders rose and fell with a sigh. "Just that I wish I could share this with them." Finally turning towards him, he could see the neutral expression on her face—not upset, but not exactly happy either. "Kaed,

Illy, and Zhal. I miss them, and I know that they would love this place just as much as I do. Okay—" he watched her as she rested her arm under her chest, feeling his cheeks burn. "Maybe not Zhal. She would say something like 'This is unsafe, how could this even be possible?' It's even possible Kaed would say, 'Magic has no limits. There are plenty of waterfalls on the ground.'" She laughed, and that beloved smile graced her lips. "Illyan would just be happy to look at you."

Rolling his eyes, he crossed his arms over his chest. "Too young for my liking, sorry, Illyan."

Her mouth dropped in utter shock, making him throw his head back and laugh.

"I think Kaed is younger, if I'm not mistaken," she said, her pondering eyes calculating.

"There are always exceptions," he shrugged. "But let's be honest, his taste will likely only be for you, anyway. Which, I'm fine with." She watched him, assessing his truth. "I'm possessive of your safety and your happiness. You have plenty of love to give, and that body was not meant to belong to just one."

She dipped so quickly under the water that he swore she used the dyspoxii to disappear. He chuckled, seeing her pop up, eyes simmering.

Standing back upright, she took a step towards him, "You really do feel that way, don't you?"

"Yes, I do. I've lived long enough to understand that monogamy is a lie. It only leads to heartbreak."

"What about Akua? The way you—"

"Don't confuse that with jealousy, please, I beg. If you genuinely wanted Akua, then I would be fine. You don't—and him insufferably flirting with you and taking your words beyond their meaning was frustrating." Especially with everything that happened with that god, anyone that took anything she said or did beyond the truth of them would have no kindness from him. He never looked away from her, keeping eye contact to ensure she understood his true meaning. "I promise. There is a difference."

With a soft nod that nearly seemed sheepish, she conceded and continued, "What if, selfishly, I didn't want you to be with anyone else?" Her question, while pointed, didn't faze him.

"You don't need to ask me that. Like I've mentioned before, I've had enough lovers to last me plenty of lifetimes." She was a mere foot away then, but he still kept his arms crossed.

"In five thousand years?"

"Infinitely," he said decisively. "But you wouldn't ask that of me."

She grinned, "Oh, but I was jealous of Zephyra—"

"No, you weren't," his hand came to the side of her neck, his thumb brushing against her throat and running across her jawline. "You aren't ever jealous because you know that there is no one that can compare to you." Her cheeks were brightening. "That doesn't make you vain. My soul belongs to you, and you can feel it."

Watching her lick her lips and bite down gently at the bottom one sent a chill up his back. "Jayce?"

"Yes, my love."

"Thank you," she closed the distance between them, her chest pressing against his torso. "For seeing me." Her face was turning further red, creating a boyish grin on his face. "I love you."

Feeling his own face burning, he leaned down to her. "And I love you, Sunshine, for our forever."

Her lips were the essence of life itself, and they truly brought him to pure bliss. She tasted like summer nights under the stars, eating fruits and drinking sweet wine until standing was no longer possible. When she turned her head, deepening their embrace, he mirrored her.

His arm wrapped around her waist, pulling her up above him, where her hands came to his face and held him. Their eyes met as she looked down at him, the sparkle in them casting a spell immediately on him. Her smile was bright, as she said, "Can I see your eyes?" He blinked, and they would shift, which was indication enough by her biting down on her bottom lip.

"I know why you hide them," she whispered, wrapping her arms around his neck, "but, around me, you don't need to." He placed her legs around his waist and lowered them down into the water, leaning her backward and dipping her hair in, getting a giggle from her.

He placed kisses down her chin, and her neck, "As you wish," his lips lingered along her chest, brushing his tongue against the curve of her breast. It caused her to moan softly, and her legs to tighten around him. He was excited to elicit more of those noises.

This mountain wouldn't survive if they were to go further than they already had, and keeping that in mind, he slowly made his way back up to her neck.

"Jayce..." She whispered, and lifted her head, the curly hair lying flat across her shoulders. There was a deep blush across her nose, "Don't stop."

A shiver ran through his entire body, imagining those words coming out of her mouth in the heat of the moment broke his resolve. She was leaning forward, staring at him. When she bit down on her lip and simply rolled her hips, he was done for, and whatever restraint he had, depleted.

He slowly moved them to the edge of the pond, resting her back against the soft moss. Her fingers ran through his hair, "I want to keep trying... I want you..."

"Sunshine, the things you do to me," he leaned down to her chest and took her nipple between his teeth. Its nub became harder then as rolling goosebumps crawled across her body. The sounds that she made drove him wild, and even as she placed her hand over her mouth to stifle them, they were clear as the water below them. He wrapped his lips around its entirety and sucked gently, flicking his tongue, and causing her hips to lift.

Trailing his fingers up her thigh. He was paying mind to her cues, and as her legs slowly opened, he continued. Her breathing was getting heavier, and he could hear her heart pounding in her veins.

Releasing her breast, he moved up to her lips, placing his against hers just as his fingers found her slit. She gasped into his mouth, and he paused briefly. Enough for her to tell him to stop, or move his hand, but when neither came, he ran two fingers along her clit. Her arms gripped onto him for dear life, and as his fingers moved in a rhythmic motion, she threw her head back and screamed out in unfiltered pleasure.

He leaned in and kissed her neck, and with more force, he bit down. Feeling her nails dig into his shoulders only drove him to suck on her silky skin, lifting a mark just as he moved further down her shoulder, rinsing and repeating the action until he found his lips back on her breast.

Her knees were buckling, and she was writhing under him. Never had he remembered being this turned on and it was blinding him, making his body tremble. His wings, which had been tucked behind him, were extended and quivering at each moan and roll of her hips.

"You are fantastic," he was breathless, and she hadn't even touched him nor he himself.

She called out another loud cry, mixing his name between the spurts of groans and moans. His fingers pressed ever so harder, and finding the movement that made her squirm the most, he focused on that.

"Y-Yes—right there..." He wanted so badly to taste her, slide his fingers inside of her, remove the god from being the last person to have ever done so. "Fuck! I'm—" Except, he knew that it wasn't time, and just being able to make her come would be enough for now.

"Come for me, Azahara." Taking her opposite nipple back into his mouth, he felt her reach the pinnacle, and let out a cry that trembled the mountain around them.

"Don't stop! I'm—Ah!" Her body was lifted so high that she completely came out of the water, and as her body vibrated and her legs crossed, he lifted up and kissed her with passion, finding her tongue already coming for his, he smiled. Her gasps and breathless moans muffled by her inability to release him.

Her body quivered under him, and only after she was complete, did he move his hand up to the side of her neck. His thumb brushed down her bottom lip, which was trembling. Her breathing wild as she swallowed and squeezed her eyes shut.

"Mmm," he purred, leaning in, and kissing her neck.

She sucked in air through her teeth, "Jayce..." the breathy way she said his name made him groan and lean down to the curve of her neck.

"You drive me crazy," He put his hand behind her neck and lifted her, and she placed her hand onto his stomach, her eyes at half mass. She was slowly trailing her fingers down and would soon find how much power she truly had over him, when he quickly grabbed them. He laced his fingers with hers, bringing them up to his lips and kissing them.

"No, sweetheart." He smiled down at her.

She scowled at him, "Why..." her attempt at catching her breath was cute.

He raised an eyebrow, "Because," she opened her hand, and he placed it against his cheek. "I'm happy just pleasing you."

"For now." She said, pressing her lips into a fine line. Her arms moving and wrapping tightly around his neck. "How did you know?"

"Hmm?" He pulled them back into the water, rubbing his nose against hers. The look in her eyes and the deepening red across her cheeks in answer to his question. "You are still asking that after everything, Sunshine?" Getting onto his knees where the water would be at his shoulders, he had her lifted over him again.

"I guess so..." She placed kisses across his face, "I may also like to hear it."

He chuckled, "Your lips don't need to move for your body and soul to tell me what it wants and needs."

Day 166
CHAPTER 39

She found herself unable to shake off the thoughts, every reverie leading back to him—his lips on her breast, fingers exploring her most sensitive places. The mere touch of his hands had left her feeling so overwhelmed that walking in a straight line seemed like a feat.

After spending hours amidst the Floating Mountains of Xi, Jayce brought them back to the ship. It wasn't just for sleep but also to address the collateral damage he had caused: a few broken boxes and half of the wall in her room. Surprisingly, the door's hinges had managed to stay intact.

Although the desire for continued intimacy lingered, the day's events had taken a toll. From conversing with Death to the enjoyable moments they shared, the exhaustion hit her hard. The moment her head hit the pillow she began snoring—no doubt about it.

The next morning, they decided it was time to return to Isis, at least for a while. Jayce told her if she wanted to come back when they caught up with everyone, he would be more than happy to oblige.

He had his fingers laced with hers, and she was staring down at them as though they were going to slip between her pants and once again please her till she came. There was more satisfaction to what he had done for her than just the pleasure, Goddrick was no longer the last person to have done that to her and would never again. She found solace in that simple fact. That the tainted feeling she had when she thought of releasing, would begin to associate with Jayce, or anyone **but** Goddrick.

Aware that her emotions were in turmoil—shifting from pleasure to anger, satisfaction to rapture—Ilkiz even grumbled, though she didn't voice anything.

"Jayce to Azahara," he said, pulling her closer, his fingers unlocking to put his arm around her shoulder.

Lifting her head, she blinked away the thoughts plaguing her. "Sorry, did you say something?" Her lips curled upward, but his expression remained neutral.

"What's wrong?" He slowed their pace just before reaching the threshold of the City of Spirits. "You've been a bit quiet this morning. Are you sure you wanted to come back? There is no rush. We can spend some more time alone." Concern laced his tone, and she felt her heart swell. "Also, if I went too far yesterday, you can tell me. I can—"

She shook her head vigorously. "Not at all!" She nearly yelled, "I'm sorry, that definitely isn't it. Sheesh, I think you know what my body needs more than I do."

He let out a hearty laugh. "When you are ready," he brought her in front of him, placing a hand at her cheek, "I will give your body everything it wants, needs, and desires."

Her face was burning. "Jayce..." she felt flustered and hid her face against his chest.

He hummed. "I love when you call my name." His fingers fluffed out her hair. "I do enjoy making you flustered, but sweetheart, what's wrong?"

"It's embarrassing," her grip on his shirt tightened, a pit forming in the center of her stomach. "It's not bad. I'm just thankful that I was able to... finish, and I can begin associating it with pleasure, and not pain."

He was silent, and his hand had stopped moving down her hair. She didn't want to look at him, maybe saying it out loud was too much. Ready to begin apologizing, she felt his arms move and tightly pull her to him. His arms were trembling, and she felt his heart racing.

"I should have killed him." Her body stiffened. "I swear on my life, no one will ever touch you without your consent ever again." Pulling her back just enough so she could see him, tears immediately filled her eyes upon seeing him look the way he did. His handsome face was pained, and when he closed his eyes and bared his teeth, she felt her breath hitch in her throat. "I will help you destroy him and anyone that wishes to bring you or your family harm."

"I..." She blinked, and tears fell from her eyes, her hands coming to cup his face. "I do not deserve you. Thank you."

That drew a smile from him, and he leaned down. "You do. You deserve peace, love, and happiness. You deserve the entire world; it is they that do not deserve you. Everyone is lucky that Death won't take you." His violet eyes bore into hers, the passion in his words tangible, wrapping around her. "They are also lucky I won't just take you. I could bring us somewhere safe and beautiful, wait out whatever shit is coming for this world, and we would survive it. I'd make sure of it. Then we would help rebuild whatever was left. Always know that is an option."

Her heart felt so full and light that it was impossible for her to stop crying.

His thumb brushed across her trembling lip while she sucked in a deep breath. "I want that so much." She wrapped her arms around him. "I want to run away from this responsibility."

"Say the word," Jayce leaned down to her, his lips kissing her cheek. "Tell me to take you, to take our family, and we'll go. We will get Illyan, Zhal, and Kaed."

She choked and put her arms around his neck. "You would bring them to me?"

"I would, the three of them. I'd bring them right here to you."

Her arms were trembling then, every bit of her elated at the prospect. "Four. I want Karver too. I don't need him there; I need him here. Fuck the King."

He lifted her up by her hips, his hand pulling her head down while his lips took hers. His smile caused her to do the same, feeling the strength in his emotions rip through her.

"Let's get them here—" she said through their kissing, "then—" he grinned, taking her again, "we can—" and again, "talk about running away."

There would be nothing better to look at than his smile.

"Let's bring them home," he said, pressing his forehead against hers, giving her one last kiss.

Illy... Illy?

Once they made it to Isis, through the Veil and surrounded by their friends and family, she attempted to reach out to her best friend through the winnox. In the past, they had always responded immediately, but this time, all she encountered was unsettling silence.

Jayce was beside her, reaching out to Karver. He had been so happy that she thought of him. He who was like a brother to him. Karver had no reason to stay with the King, and they would deal with the fallout later, together.

Illyan? She tried again, only to be met with a hollow silence that filled her mind. Looking at Jayce with growing concern, she asked, "Don't tell me. Silence?"

"I have never been unable to contact him," Jayce admitted, his voice laced with concern. "Even if he couldn't speak at the moment, he would still acknowledge me and ask to come back later."

Xol approached them, accompanied by Alyse and Rowlin. Noting their distressed expressions, she inquired, "What's wrong? You both look… well, distraught. Not at all what I would have expected after a few days alone." Alyse was grinning ear to ear.

While Xol knew about Jayce's true nature as a Fae, the rest of the crew didn't. Jayce had preferred to keep it a secret until they departed Ilkiz, considering that Fae weren't the most beloved, and he felt more comfortable sharing this information with the crew alone rather than all of Ilkiz's descendants.

Azahara sighed, "I'm trying to reach Illyan through the winnox, but there isn't anything on the other end. It's like their window is gone…"

Jayce rested a reassuring hand on her shoulder, "Let's not assume the worst. There might be something going on with the Magic, or Ilkiz itself could be influencing this. The wards in this place might be blocking your ability to reach out."

Nodding, Azahara took a deep breath, her gaze shifting down to her hands.

"Do you think we could—" Her sentence was abruptly cut off by a searing pain that coursed through her body, akin to being struck by an arrow directly through her head. Her legs gave way, and as her knees met the ground, Xol was there to catch her. "Aza?!"

Her arms felt immobilized, as if bound to her body with an unyielding force.

"Hello, Princess." The unmistakable voice echoed in her mind.

"Jayce, it's... Jaakobai. Wait, don't—Ah!"

Darkness, her unwavering ally, embraced her tightly. Standing in its presence, she found herself in a void with a solitary window. It remained featureless, offering neither light nor warmth. The frame, white with gold accents, stood flawless in a world marked by imperfections.

"You truly are something else," Jaakobai's voice sliced through the silence as he approached. "What do you think of my window?" His sudden appearance seemed surreal, challenging her mind's inclination to deny the unfolding reality.

"What do you want, Jaakobai?" Azahara's voice dripped with venom as she watched him circle her, his gaze sweeping from head to toe.

"Not even a 'hi'? You completely forget my kindness. I fed you and clothed you after my father left you in that cell."

Rolling her eyes, she laughed without humor, "Doing something for someone, and expecting something in return, is not kindness."

Not to mention how you touched me...

A laugh escaped him, "Oh, you missed out on me really touching you. The offer still stands; if you ask me to take it off, I will." He gestured toward her, and when she looked down, the same lacy dress he had forced her to wear adorned her body. Clenching her jaw, she met his gaze through lowered lashes.

"I suppose this is the winnox; my thoughts are my voice. I'll tread carefully." Her voice echoed, drawing on Death's power to break through his hold on her mind.

"Please, you won't escape from here." A brief pause made her narrow her eyes. As though thoughts were consuming his means to speak, his eyes wandered about. "Hmm, interesting..." he pondered something before laughing again, his hand running through his silk gray hair. "It looks like you found those who can actually protect you. For now."

Her nose curled as she snarled, "What—do—you—want?" Her voice was raised, keeping her thoughts to herself, trying not to overthink and bring up things that had transpired beyond leaving the Kingdom. Keeping everything a secret would be difficult, especially if she wanted to break free from this.

"You need to come back for your justice for what you did in Sunfall and now in Itotaki." He stepped towards her, "That commander of the King's, I knew he was incompetent."

"You think," she cut in, "We were leaving today. The Commander convinced me to plead my innocence, especially after Itotaki."

Jaakobai laughed, a full, throaty sound. "Oh yeah? How convenient. I know you haven't left Ilkiz. Do not play me as a fool."

"I said we *were* leaving until you started playing this game of yours."

His nose twitched, "Months in Itotaki... and the day I come for you..."

"Ever heard of a coincidence?" Her tone mocking.

He took another step toward her, his hand reaching for her. Even though she knew this was in their mind, the connection between the winnox, she spat, "If you would like to keep your hand attached to your body, I would not touch me."

He must have felt the threat because he hesitated, "You are different." His voice was low, lacking remorse as he grabbed at her throat. "Still weak and unworthy of the powers gifted to you. Your threats are flimsy, at best."

You have no idea, she grinned.

"Jaakobai," she said, her voice hoarse as he squeezed, "You cannot kill me here."

"I like watching this," She tried to swallow, feeling the air being ripped from her lungs. "This is my realm. You think you know Magic, but you don't. It will kill you, and I will enjoy watching it."

Taking her hand up, she grabbed onto his wrist and was ready to squeeze when she stopped, remembering he couldn't know. Feeling the lightheadedness of the loss of oxygen, she felt her knees give out, and her skin heat.

She needed to be weak, one last time.

"Please—" She choked out.

She needed to find out why.

"Beg." His voice raw with destruction.

"Please—" Her body was trembling beyond this place, and she couldn't stop it. "Jaak—obai..."

As his grip loosened, she sucked in a breath of air, gulping it down as if it were water after walking through the desert. "Good, princess. Now listen. Tell that Commander to hurry up. A portal will be waiting for you in Itotaki."

Her hand was at her throat, rubbing at it, feeling the divots where his fingers had gripped. "Where is Illyan?"

He smiled, "Smart; it's incredible. How you can understand why I'm here yet be so stupid as to play into my son's lies. Though, I'm not surprised since you allowed the Commander to seduce you into coming back here."

Narrowing her eyes, she slowly stepped away from him, "Where is Illyan? I won't ask again."

"Here, with me."

Goosebumps rolled down her neck, all the way to her toes.

"Along with your dead Elf," she felt anger rise, "and that big woman, the one that bargained with the Yuul and killed many of my people."

"You don't care about your people."

"Don't I?" He seethed. "They are the reason I do this. We're kept isolated from the world due to the hate and fear that people have towards us."

She had no sympathy for them. They had done that to themselves, and in the end, hated everyone else for their isolation. Helio was the best Elder they had, and it had taken a long time to mend the bonds, and here Jaakobai was, ready to tear them right back down.

"Why did you take them?" Her voice was low.

He walked around her, and while she followed him to the edge of her vision, she didn't turn to keep sight of him. "To hurry and get you back here. I don't believe the Commander got through to you, and honestly, you probably seduced him and brought him to your side. Dirty little whore," she felt his body mere inches behind her, "lucky the King favors him, or he—"

"Choose your words mighty carefully, Jaakobai." Her voice boomed in the room, as if she were speaking through Ilkiz herself. His hand rested at the crook of her neck, squeezing, "I also told you not to touch me."

"You have a lot of resilience in the winnox, princess. I cannot wait to watch you break when you arrive." The resemblance in his voice to Goddrick's made her stomach churn. "You have fifteen days to get to

Itotaki, or I will kill Illyan, the Væragi, and remove that seal around your lover boy, releasing his soul—quick enough it obliterates."

Every part of her vibrated, and she was losing her will to hold back.

"You should have come with me when you had the chance," His hand moved up her neck and turned her to look at him, "Now you will be ash in the wind when I create the new world." He jerked her away, but she didn't stumble. "Such a waste of a good body. Hopefully, you are reincarnated into a more willing host."

She laughed, "I can't wait to watch you beg for me to let you live."

Their obsession with slapping her was getting old, and when the contact hit, she stepped to the side. She once again laughed, "But not before I rip your wings from your back." The anger radiating off of him fueled her, and she grinned through the casted shadow over her eyes, "I will enjoy killing you while he watches."

The force with which he threw her out of the winnox made her back nearly snap. She gasped, her body feeling foreign, and her eyes so dry she couldn't blink.

She found sunny eyes, those that brought life into this world, staring down at her. They were familiar, and she wondered if she had snapped her back and died once more.

"Death," she felt her throat clear, and when she was able to blink, she could see that they were shrouded in darkness. However, it wasn't from being pulled to Purgatory, or by Death's cloak. Instead, raven wings sprawled across them, a very angry Jayce at the epicenter.

Anastasia spoke, "He may have grabbed your mind, but I was not going to allow him to rip you from here." They had come for her, "He tried, and failed." She looked down at her shoulder, seeing the porcelain skin of her love, Death. "Your Fae here allowed for it by shielding me from your mortal family's eyes."

She looked at Jayce, his eyes were closed, teeth clenched.

Feeling her body returning to itself, she stood slowly, with the assistance of Anastasia. Taking a deep breath, she wrapped her arms around Death and was reciprocated with one. "Thank you." The persistent hum of bees in her head pricked at all the wrong nerves.

"I am yours to summon; remember that, but be cautious, those that lay their eyes upon me will not see who you do. Fear is a terrible thing, and ultimately, may lead them to death." Anastasia leaned down and kissed her cheek, "Until I see you, my Light, and..." It looked at Jayce, "I find if I had a heart, it would beat anew with that one."

When Death disappeared, she charged at Jayce, her arms wrapped around his waist and he gripped tightly around her shoulders. His head tucked between the crook of her neck and kissed at her skin.

They took a moment, embracing one another with no words. When he pulled away, which felt far too soon, he looked over her. His amethyst eyes were glowing, and it lit the space around them. Soon, his fingers were brushing against her neck, and she hissed, feeling a slight tinge of pain. When his hand came to her cheek, it burned.

"Which hand was it?" His voice hissed with rage.

"Right." She looked up at him, her anger laced between the unfriendly down curve of her lips. "I warned him."

"I know," his hand was glowing, and she felt the pressure at her throat release, and the warmth in her cheek dissolve. "I heard everything and will be taking his tongue for the things he said to you."

Her nostrils twitched, "I had to be weak one last time."

Jayce leaned his forehead against hers, "You exuded nothing but strength in there, and you got everything you needed for it." He took a deep breath, "We need to go, and honestly," he pulled his wings around, curving them behind his back, "I have some explaining to do."

Xol was behind her, putting her arms around her waist and pulling her into a hug. She could feel her trembling, and if it weren't for her own physical strength, she may have just cut her in half with how hard she was holding her.

Beyond her and Jayce, stood the entire crew, eyes widened and staring. They would have to make a choice then, which would be theirs to make.

Day 166
Chapter 40

 Xol and Jayce stood beside Azahara as the crew deliberated after only briefly asking what had just happened. It was abundantly clear that Xol had chosen her path no matter what Jayce was, or her, for that matter. While she could assume that Alyse wouldn't care that she had literally brought Death physically to this existence, she wasn't too sure about the rest of the crew. Even if Alyse liked her, now feeling death in its incarnate around her, that is something completely different.

 While they couldn't see Death, thanks to Jayce, they could feel it. It would have brought fear and a sense of dread to them. They could see her as a living embodiment of Death, capable of summoning her lover from the afterlife at any moment to ferry their souls to the underworld. It might have been a tad dramatic, yet not entirely implausible.

 Amidst this tension, the sound of approaching footsteps drew Azahara's attention. Turning around, she saw Kaen and Akua walking towards them, each offering a closed-fist gesture to their chest accompanied by a subtle nod.

 "Aza, could we have a word with you? Preferably in private," Akua requested.

 Xol and Jayce peered at one another, but Azahara nodded and stepped away with them. The palpable tension in her protectors did not escape her notice. It seemed odd that they desired a private conversation with her, almost as if they assumed she wouldn't share the details later. Moreover, the notion that Jayce couldn't hear even the slightest sound from another realm added some amusement.

Kaen stepped behind her, blocking them from view—at least she tried. It wasn't like Jayce couldn't see over her, even from this distance.

"Akua, Kaen—what is it?"

"We want to come with you," Akua got straight to the point. "We want to serve our Keeper, but beyond that, we want to keep you safe."

His statement left Azahara taken aback. "Both... of you?" As Kaen crossed her arms over her elevated chest, she grinned toothily. "Yes—I can protect you better than Akua anyway. It only makes sense for me to come."

A chill ran down Azahara's right side. "I—I didn't think you guys could leave Ilkiz. I can't ask you to leave your family."

Akua placed his hand on her shoulder, while Kaen mirrored the gesture on the other side. The sensation wasn't one of urgency to pull away; instead, she thought of Jayce and the unexpected progress he had helped her achieve. A sharp burning sensation gripped her nose and eyes, and she fought to swallow back the surge of emotions welling within her.

"Let us be your family, and we will protect you with our lives," Akua said, smiling.

Kaen added, "I'd kill lots of mainlanders without your word, but doing it in the name of someone or something, makes my tummy tingle."

By the Mother she is so strange, she thought with a gentle, cracked, laugh.

"They will be strong allies, little one, and you will need them in the battles to come." Ilkiz slipped through.

I don't want anything to happen to them, Ilkiz.

"Be more confident in those around you. Look," She felt a tug on her head, as if she was being forced to look over at Jayce and Xol. *"You have a Fae that holds enough Magic to destroy armies in an instant for even looking at you wrong, a creature that's sole purpose is to keep you safe, Death itself, an ancient Dragon that is pretty strong—if I do say so myself."* She couldn't help but laugh, which got caught with a sob. *"You will have two Spirit Riders, and their people, behind you."* She was pulled once more, prompting her to turn her gaze back to Akua and Kaen, who stood side by side, patiently awaiting her response. Beyond them, the descendants of Ilkiz observed with bright-eyed anticipation. They must've known what they would ask of her, and anticipated the response as they were.

"Don't worry about what may happen. The what-ifs are inevitable. People will die, no matter how hard you try. Allow them to make the choice how they go." Ilkiz echoed her own words back to her. All she had ever wanted was the power to make choices in her life—deciding whether to embrace life or face death, but always on her own terms.

As a smile graced her lips, tears traced their path down her cheeks, "It would be an honor to have you both fight beside me."

In a burst of enthusiasm, Kaen leaped into the air, throwing her fists up in triumph, while Akua simply beamed, acknowledging her with a nod. The people behind them erupted into cheers.

"Actually," Akua hesitated, rubbing the back of his neck with a hint of nervousness. "There's one last thing. Technically, we can't leave, and neither can you."

"Oh yeah..." Kaen halted her celebratory jumps, her shoulders aflame with contemplation.

Azahara's eye twitched, "Explain, please." There was no anger in her tone, but deep inside, she was boiling. Every second that ticked by, the closer those fifteen days got. While they could arrive early with Jayce's portal, if Jaakobai was watching, he'd feel or see that Magic. She didn't want to expose him, not yet at least. Them being ignorant to who he was would play into her favor.

"Ligrok." Akua responded.

Was that name supposed to mean something to me? She immediately went to Ilkiz.

"It is the Kraken that the gods cursed the people on Ilkiz with. They are unable to leave this place because of it. You will need to destroy him."

Azahara grinned, "You mean I get to release some of this anger right now?"

"I love you, by the Skies, let's kill the beast that has trapped my people for thousands of years."

Kaen lit herself ablaze, her entire body, including her hair, engulfed in flames. "Yes."

For the first time, Azahara felt a deep connection with Kaen. Her eyes mirrored scorching flames, a shared intensity signaling their readiness to charge into battle.

"Jayce," the moment his name slipped from her lips, he was beside her. He was accompanied quickly thereafter by Xol. "I need to go," his eyebrows pulled together, "Ligrok, some Kraken thing. We need to kill it, and honestly, if we do get back on Alyse's ship after this, I need to blow off some steam. If I don't, I fear what I may do accidentally."

With a low laugh, he nodded, "Do you want me with you?"

She smiled, "Always, but I need you here. Let me know their decision," she peeked over his shoulder by means of jumping, "If they choose to allow us to stay—"

Jayce cut her off, his hand on her cheek, "They will always choose you. They are deliberating something else."

Shaking her head, she placed her hand on his elbow, "If they won't allow you on, that is not choosing me either." His near-bashful smile prompted him to pull her towards him. "I'm serious, Jayce. I'll throw Xol onto Ilkiz with us, and we will fly to Itotaki for all I care."

"I know, Sunshine, but that isn't what I was implying. They are trying to find out how they can help you, and not be a burden." The surprise on her face led him to place a kiss on her forehead and laugh. "Get going, I'll let you know when we are at sea."

Lifting herself up, she brushed her lips against his, and turned to Xol, who gave her a nod.

"Let's go," she said to the twins.

"Wait—us?" Akua rushed after her as she started off to a clearing. "Having three riders on Ilkiz would only slow you down."

"I don't expect you to ride Ilkiz," she heard Kaen sprinting up behind her, "I intend to summon Vemi, and—uh, Kaen, what is your Spirit's name?"

"Fury." *Simple, and fitting,* she thought as they came to a stop.

"*Azahara, I am not sure you can do that.*"

I did it before, she rolled her head around her shoulders, feeling her neck pop in several places.

"*When? I do not recall this.*"

Before we bonded.

There was a moment of silence, and she glanced between the twins. "Akua, summon Vemi as you did before when we first arrived here in Ilkiz. Kaen, do the same." She observed as both twins exchanged a look, with

Akua showing hesitance and Kaen emanating readiness to burn the world down.

A smile adorned her face. Before her, flame and water spiraled, and the sea serpent appeared alongside a pure red Knucker Dragon—it had no legs but large wings spanning at least a dozen feet across. They were a sight to behold, and as her hands raised, both spirits placed their elongated heads into them. Their bodies swirled, and just like Vemi had done before, they both solidified. When their frames hit the floor, the ground shook.

Fury, with its shimmering brilliance, captivated her in that moment. The light cast a fiery glow in every direction, reflecting off its vibrant crimson hue akin to that of molten lava. Its serpentine neck coiled with elegance and grace as it shifted towards her, adorned with several horns that swept back like fiery flames themselves. When Fury spread its wings wide, their span shadowed her, whistling air in her direction—just as powerful and slightly out of control as its owner.

Vemi, equally brilliant, leaned towards her as though they were old friends. His bluish tint held magnificence and intelligence, impressing her with the impeccable alignment between rider and spirit.

With a clap of her hands slamming into the ground, the world below her parted. Gathering the hate and anger for Jaakobai, she held it in her chest. Ready to destroy, nothing was going to keep her from unleashing her wrath. He would suffer, and unfortunately for this Kraken, it was about to feel her fury.

Day 166
CHAPTER 41
Jayce Latimer

"I'm proud of you," Xol's tone was condescending, even though she was smiling. "You permitted her to leave." It wasn't as if she wasn't inclined towards Azahara's departure. The Yuul was probably just as uneasy as he was about allowing it.

"We are never going to be in her way," He said, crossing his arms over his chest and taking in a deep breath, "To be honest, I felt her anger in there, especially when…" Shaking his head, he wanted to laugh, "he was about to threaten **me,** and I swear the world shook."

There was a laugh that came from Xol then, "I felt it, that, and Death."

He didn't want to say the word fear, because Death was much more than what awaited one when they passed from this realm. They were the life beyond their existence as they knew it then. However, to say that he did not feel the rapture that was brought when it arrived, he would be a lie. Knowing that Death was coming, only by Xol's warning, he had to think quickly to protect not only himself but the crew, and people of Ilkiz. It hadn't been an easy decision to expose who he was to them, but it was for their good, and ultimately, Azahara's.

Witnessing her in that state was also no easy ordeal. He could have forcibly extracted her from Jaakobai's mind, but when she signaled him to stop, even without fully articulating the words, he had to trust her instincts. The way Jaakobai treated her made restraint nearly impossible for him. Then, when he attempted to seize her, behaving as if she were trapped and defenseless, everyone sprang into action. Alyse, Rowlin, and Xol were on her, poised to intervene. They were unwilling to let him take her, likely believing it was once again the god at work. It wasn't until Xol turned to Jayce and pleaded for his help that he overtly repelled them, shielding Azahara, and ultimately, Death.

Pulling him from his own darkening thoughts, he heard not one, but three dragons calling out to the sky. Glancing at Xol briefly, he lifted his head and witnessed three dragons soaring across the sky. Both Akua and Kaen were visible, their smaller dragons evident, with their arms raised straight into the air as they screamed in joy. Somehow, she had made Akua and Kaen's Dragons into solid, tangible creatures.

Although he couldn't see her, he knew Azahara rode Ilkiz, her silence carrying the anger and hatred she felt in that moment.

"Incredible," Xol said, "I watched the war against Ilkiz. I never hated mortals and gods more than I did then. Dragons were meant to rule the skies."

He nodded, "I agree."

"Did you fight in the war?" She asked while he kept his gaze on Ilkiz as they crossed over the tree line.

"I did, unfortunately. It was when I was preparing to become the next Elder successor. However, and this never needs to be spoken beyond us and Azahara," he turned his attention back to her, "I never killed any of them, but placed memories in random Fae's minds to believe that I had."

"Why does it matter who knows that?" Xol countered.

"It is one thing to use our Magic against mortals, but another to use it on another Fae. I'm already in hot water with my own kind, I don't need more." He sighed, and shook his head, "Not that I care what they think of me, it's more for the sake of Azahara. If she needs to call on the Fae to fight with her, in any capacity, it will affect how they look at her. With me standing by her side, they will see a traitor more-so than someone who attempted to overthrow the Rite election."

He watched her, noting the disgust that crossed her expression, "Fae are weird," she commented, and despite being one of them, he found himself in agreement.

"Hey," Alyse's voice interrupted their conversation, drawing both of them back to the present moment. Jayce dropped his arms and straightened, keeping Alyse in his line of sight as she approached. "Where did Aza go?" Her neutral expression was a promising sign.

"She and the twins are off to deal with a Kraken," Xol replied. "We'll inform her once we set sail, and she'll catch up with us."

Alyse crossed her arms and narrowed her eyes. "Who said you're setting sail with us?" Jayce struggled to contain his smile; her attempt at projecting toughness was both endearing and amusing.

"You guys talk so loud," Xol interjected. "We heard you."

"I—" Alyse deadpanned, dropping her head. Jayce couldn't help but laugh, and soon, Xol joined in.

"How could you guys trick me like this?!" Alyse stomped her foot and swung both fists at them. Jayce allowed it, while Xol sidestepped. "You both have so much explaining to do while we walk to the ship." She emitted a loud grunt and turned around. "Let's go."

We are heading to the ship, Sunshine.

"Is it safe for you to be here? In the winnox with me?"

Jayce rolled his eyes as they started walking behind Alyse. He could hear Xol beginning to explain her side of the story, but he redirected his focus to Azahara. *You would be concerned about me. Yes, I've locked your window and my own.*

"How are you here then?" Her curious voice, though adorable, was tinged with anxiety. She was upset, angry, and prepared to unleash her frustration on something. Truthfully, he wanted to witness it. Observing her—or rather, listening to her tell Jaakobai that she would relish killing him while he watched—sent a strange chill up his spine. The "he" she was referring to was him.

I'm just inside your window. He said, and for a moment, he could hear her thoughts fluttering through as though passing his own mind, *think of it as I'm visiting, and you closed the door behind me. Same thing, basically.*

"Fascinating." Her tone conveyed little enthusiasm, but he understood.

"Thank you."

For what? This time, he had no idea what he did.

"Do you want specifics, or can I say everything?" He laughed aloud, earning a questioning look from Xol and Alyse. They inquired, but he waved them off, explaining that he was talking with Azahara. While Xol understood, Alyse looked around in confusion.

Specifics, but will accept everything for now, and you can tell me later.

"I'll tell you later, Kaen is signaling we are about to break through the cursed—I have no idea how to say what she said. It's like a barrier or some sort, once we cross it, the Kraken shows. Have you ever seen one?"

No, he confessed, *but I've heard a great deal about them. They were monsters created by the gods thousands of years ago, and the Kraken is one of three that remain. Soon, to be two.*

"Your confidence in me turns me on."

He stifled the laugh that was ready to spill from his lips but, instead, just coughed. His chest tightened, *I do like you turned on, and angry, as long as it's not at me.*

Somehow, he felt her laughter, and he wondered if it was their souls. He acknowledged that he would need to tell her about that at some point. It didn't really make too much of a difference whether she knew about the bond or not. It wasn't what drew her to him, or him to her.

"I can tell you I am quite angry." Her admission wasn't necessary because he could feel it, and he sighed in frustration for her, "Don't forget, it was his right hand."

Oh, Sunshine, I will not ever forget that.

"I need to go now; by the Mother that thing is fucking huge. You know, Ilkiz—wait, this is the winnox, how do I swap? Shit."

There was no holding back his laughter then. Placing his hand over his face, he looked up at the sky, *Good luck, be safe please.*

"Okay, funny guy, your turn. Spill the story, or I'll snip, snip those wings," Alyse declared. She was amusing, and while Jayce wouldn't typically find humor in someone threatening his wings, it was fine. She meant him no harm, and he had no problem explaining to her his and their story.

Day 166
CHAPTER 42

To say that Azahara wasn't even slightly terrified would be a blatant lie. Ignoring the tightening in her stomach, the unmistakable grip of fear would be plain stupidity. The sheer magnitude of Ligrok was nearly impossible to comprehend, and as her mind closed the window with Jayce, the resonating presence of Ilkiz poured through.

"Allow the fear to meld with your anger, little one," Ilkiz thrummed, her scales trembling as sheer elation ran through her. *"You ride me, the mightiest of beasts to claim the skies. You have nothing to fear when I am with you."*

Ilkiz's size was grand in comparison to Vemi and Fury, but it fell short of the colossal entity before them. As Ligrok breached fully through the surface, the sea around it convulsed and churned, creating tumultuous waves that echoed the magnitude of its presence. The heavy mist they had broken through clung to its colossal body, adding even more to its imposing aura.

Immense tentacles, housing strength that likely decimated ships, stretched out in all directions. Each of them lined with suction cups that could grip and pull anything in their path. The mere movement of these tentacles created whirlpools and currents, contributing to the chaotic scene surrounding Ligrok.

Its massive mouth, with razor-sharp teeth glistening in the falling sun, resembled a dark abyss ready to consume anything in its path. Each tooth was a formidable weapon, capable of rending ships and tearing through the toughest materials—enough to instill fear within Azahara for Ilkiz if she were to get too close. Its eyes, piercing white like snow, glinted with malicious intent.

Ligrok was a nightmare leviathan, one that she was determined to destroy.

"Kaen!" Her scream resonated, pushing her throat to its limits. "Go for its eye! Akua, follow Ilkiz!"

Do I just tell you where to go or...? Azahara asked, tilting slightly to the right. As if responding to an unspoken command, Ilkiz immediately began fanning downward.

"No, we are connected in more ways than just our minds. Place your mind into my body, and I will know what you would like to do."

With a deep breath, she steered Ilkiz straight down towards Ligrok. Although it had already spotted them, it refrained from attacking. Only when they closed in did it assume a poised stance. Several tentacles lifted from the water and shot straight at them. Their movements seemed to be in slow motion, but as her mind directed Ilkiz to dive, the magnitude of the force behind them was anything but sluggish.

Straightening, she focused on Kaen, who guided Fury straight into one of Ligrok's eyes. Its claws latched onto its lid, and a blast of fire shot into it. The resulting cry was a haunting blend of a resonant tone and a high-pitched wail. Its piercing shrill created its own wind chill, compelling her to put her hands against her ears.

Go for its neck, Ilkiz, she instructed, leaning forward and grabbing hold of any scales she could. The descent was rapid, but as her wings flapped them forward, she was surprised she was able to hold on. The wind in her face forced her eyes closed, and the water felt like daggers against her skin.

As Ilkiz closed her wings and made contact with Ligrok, she latched on with a tight, unforgiving grip. The sudden stop in momentum made Azahara shift, but her newfound strength kept her settled.

Looking up, she saw Vemi circling. "Akua! Help Kaen!"

Just as her attention shifted to Ilkiz, her mighty Dragon clawed at the grotesque, rough, slimy, and rubbery skin. It seemed she was having a difficult time grasping, as a thick, mucous-like slime coated it.

After a brief moment of struggle, Ilkiz tilted her head back, a surge of Power gathering in her throat. The anticipation was palpable as Azahara sensed the impending release. Then, with a resounding roar, streams of purple flames with sparks of lightning erupted from Ilkiz's mouth, colliding with the Titan and eliciting yet another thunderous cry.

As the ominous feeling of an imminent strike loomed, their quick thinking kicked in, and Ilkiz wasted no time. They gracefully toppled backward just as a barrage of tentacles violently struck the space where they had been latched onto just moments before.

Azahara couldn't stifle a startled scream. In the midst of the fall, she desperately reached out, but the distance proved insurmountable, and they separated.

"Ilkiz!!" Her desperate cry resonated through the chaos, and attuned to her distress, the mighty form of her Spirit swiveled as the scent of the encroaching sea filled the air. With precision, it employed its colossal talons, securing her within its grasp.

"Too bad you don't have a set of wings yourself, little one," Ilkiz joked. While Azahara wanted to banter in return, reigning in her racing heart took precedence. *"You aren't going to like this, but just trust that I will catch you."*

The ominous statement didn't sit well with her, and as Ilkiz unfurled her wings, soaring into the sky, Azahara's unease grew justified. In a toss that felt like she was merely a plaything, she was hurled upward while Ilkiz spun. Breaking through the clouds, Azahara swore every inch of her body clamored for survival, convinced she might suffer a heart attack mid-air.

As the ascent halted and gravity took over, she entered a free fall. Arms outstretched, she kicked to maintain some semblance of control. Emerging through the clouds, Ilkiz swooped in to catch her. Bouncing roughly on the center of her back, Azahara rolled to a stop.

"Fuck—" She grasped her head, quickly rising to her feet. "We really need to work on that." Grumbling, she hurried to find her proper position at the nape of Ilkiz's neck.

"You okay?" Ilkiz inquired, her concern evident in the cadence of her words.

"Sure, did that cause any damage?" Once the turbulence subsided, they angled back downward. As Ligrok came into view, Azahara spotted Fury and Vemi circling the Titan.

"Doesn't look like it. Somehow that doesn't surprise me." Approaching closer, the confirmation resonated that not even Ilkiz's formidable Power had breached the Titan's thick skin. It had only managed to break through the barnacles and coral formations that had clung to it during its enduring

existence in the harsh sea environment. *"It was placed here to keep my people and my children from breaking through."*

"Maybe I should have brought Jayce," she bit her lip. "Let's keep it distracted. We can allow the Neptune to get through, and then we can fly past it."

"It will likely chase, but I suppose that works."

"Okay then—" she was abruptly cut off.

"Set us free," Azahara's eyes widened. That voice was not Ilkiz. *"Please, set us free. Don't leave us here."* The same voices that had greeted her upon her arrival in Ilkiz, like echoes from an underwater civilization, resonated once more.

As more voices inundated her mind, threatening to overwhelm, there was a shift and they gradually began melded into a soothing cadence of prayers rather than desperate cries for help. Tears welled in her eyes at the collective hope for freedom, and a realization struck her. Ligrok wasn't merely a barrier preventing Ilkiz's people from leaving; it was stifling their growth, hindering them from living.

"Set us free."

"Ilkiz, fly over its head." Uncertain of what she could achieve, Azahara couldn't turn away from the call for help. She refused to ignore the pain and suffering of the people, determined not to be like the King who disregarded the pleas of the common folk—like the farmer striving to safeguard his land and family.

Without a moment's hesitation, Ilkiz executed the command, lowering them overhead as they faced the looming obstacle.

Can you speak with Vemi and Fury?

"I can, what are you going to do, little one?" Her tone held worry, but an undercut of intrigue.

Probably something stupid, she released an exasperated sigh, *tell them to fly as far away as possible but to still stay in view. You, come find me when I call.*

"Don't die, I don't want to have to deal with Jayce."

They shared a chuckle as they glided over the Titan's colossal frame, and as they reached a pivotal point, she rose to her feet. A peculiar sensation settled in her stomach, a premonition of what she was about to undertake. Deliberately plunging into the gaping maw of a Titan—undeniably an act of audacity. Jayce would likely be infuriated, but what had she fought for if not to wield the strength bestowed on her? Was she destined to perpetually depend on others for the very purpose she was called to fulfill?

No, she refused to be confined to a mere title; she would be more than that. Fueled by resolve, she sprinted to the edge of Ilkiz's neck and propelled herself forward. The initial freefall felt normal, but as her gaze fixed on the Titan below, normalcy metamorphosed into regret. An unsettling flip in her stomach clamored for her to retract her decision, to summon her Spirit back and ensure her safety. The instinct for self-preservation nearly triumphed, yet, as she clenched her jaw tightly and drew upon her inner strength, her power surged.

The Titan's mouth yawned open with a screech that reverberated through the skies, marginally slowing her descent due to its ferocity. An overpowering blend of noxious and briny odors assaulted her senses—seaweed, salt, and the stench of decomposing matter threatened to overwhelm. The pungency nearly rendered her unconscious, but she stood resolute.

Passing the initial lining of the Titan's mouth, she closed her eyes and sought the Light. Yet, instead of grasping for it, she reached beyond. Delving into the malevolence thrust upon her without consent—the painful reminder that no matter where she fled in the world, *he* would persist. It served her in that she still had a long road ahead for her healing, but equally for her revenge.

As the light surrounding her faded, and she descended into the twilight of the Titan's body, she clung to the darkness, succumbing to thoughts and feelings of annihilation.

Day 166
Chapter 43
Jayce Latimer

Alyse cried throughout the entire recounting of their story. While Jayce couldn't necessarily blame her, especially when it came to finding out why her name was no longer Rothwen and now Starfall, Xol had to practically carry her the rest of the way.

He felt bad, but she had asked about who he was to Azahara, after all. It wasn't enough that he practically spelled out through their history together how madly in love with her he was, she needed further proving. Especially since at first, Azahara held no interest in him. Alyse was convinced that he had used his Magic on the poor redhead, tricking her into loving him, as he had influenced them to thinking the crew had known Xol for months longer than they had. Along with him being anything other than a shipmate that was looking for work. The frustration stemmed from feeling played and tricked into getting him, and Xol, on the ship.

By the time they reached the Neptune, Jayce had concluded their story. The entire crew had gathered to listen, and while some maintained a neutral expression, most were moved to tears, especially Carmen, Alyse, and Rowlin.

"Guys, it's okay." Jayce tried to reassure them as they prepared to get to work, now fully aware of the urgency they faced. "I'm honestly unsure of what you're crying about, but it'll be okay." He let out a nervous laugh, and Carmen turned to look at him, wiping away tears with the back of her hand.

"She knows everything now?" Naturally, her concern was for Azahara, and he loved that.

"She does."

"Good, that is all that matters. She deserves it." Carmen looked at Alyse then, who nodded her head in agreement. The depth of unconditional love they both had for Azahara filled him with affection for them.

Alyse's command echoed through the air, prompting the crew to spring into action. Before he knew it, they were hoisting the anchor and unfurling the sails. The ship shifted and set into motion at a speed he had never witnessed before. They understood the urgency, and although they would temporarily part ways in Itotaki, the crew made it clear they would eagerly await their return.

As time passed and the Neptune navigated through the misty fog on the outskirts of Ilkiz, he noticed Rowlin gazing into the sky. Was he awaiting her? When his eyes shifted to Alyse, she too was looking upward.

He found himself casting his gaze to the sky, where hues of pink and orange painted its vastness. The sun was preparing to bid farewell, ready to make way for the moon's appearance. A sense of calm enveloped the surroundings, as if the world itself were finding a moment of peace. It was strange, even for him, sensing that something in that exact moment was shifting. As though their reality, its own timeline, had veered onto a completely different course. This one didn't feel ominous; instead, it brought a sense of relief, even as they sailed toward uncertainty and into the lion's den.

It was then that he heard the calling of three joyful Dragons. Around him, the crew scurried to the ledge, just as Akua came into view. His serpent dragon skimming the water with ease, even going as far to cast water across the deck, splashing half the crew along with it. He maneuvered out of the way to stay dry.

Following closely was Kaen, her dragon a vibrant pure red, mirroring her wild demeanor. The dragon swooped and dove, executing spins that seemed like attempts to throw the fire user off, but it only fueled the crazed twin's enthusiasm.

There was no sign of Ilkiz, which was peculiar given her much larger size compared to the other two.

Suddenly, two loud thuds behind them jolted the deck. Jayce turned to see the twins brushing their hands against their Dragons. Vemi, Akua's Dragon, slipped back overboard, leaving a snail-like goo across Alyse's ship.

Kaen's Dragon flapped its wings and ascended, narrowly missing the white sails but leaving a significant crack in the floor.

Alyse screamed at the twins, and Jayce shook his head in mock disappointment, stifling the laughter that threatened to escape.

Momentarily taken aback, *Wait, did they just leave?*

"She did it," Akua said breathlessly.

"I mean, we kind of helped," Kaen groaned, both of them completely ignoring Alyse. When Kaen caught him looking, she skipped over, "That woman of yours is crazier than I am. I don't care what anyone says."

Akua, who had a smile painted on his face, followed right behind her. "Don't call her crazy, Kaen. That title is yours alone."

"Where is she?" Jayce asked, trying not to sound concerned.

"Above us." Akua said, pointing straight up.

When Jayce looked up, *by the Mother*, there Ilkiz was. Her sheer size outstretched the Neptune, and it was a wonder that someone as small as Azahara controlled something that size. There would be no way for her to land, so he wondered what they were doing.

Do you need me to come pick you up? He reached out to her, but only silence met his inquiry. He was about to pull his wings out and fly up when Ilkiz began to turn to the right and drift downward. Walking to the side of the ship again, he watched as she swiftly glided to the water's surface, making sure to stay far enough so that her wings wouldn't graze the side of the Neptune. She was staying steady, and when he looked up at his girl, his eyebrows pulled together. She was covered in blood, from head to toe.

"Is she injured?" His voice was taut.

"No," Akua responded.

Jayce kept his eyes out towards her, she was leaning forward, and laying down onto Ilkiz. The Dragon's eyes closed, and he could swear she was beginning to cry.

"She released them," He turned to see Akua, and to his surprise, Kaen, crying. "The Dragons. We had no idea, nor did Ilkiz." Akua was choking on his words, and Kaen was wrapping her arms around her brother.

"What?" He was surprised by his own voice breaking.

"There was a rune on the Kraken's heart, it was keeping us from summoning or breeding them. We thought it was because Ilkiz was gone," Akua had always been this strong presence in the wake of his crazed sister.

To see him fighting tears and holding onto his twin as he did, it nearly made him begin to cry. "But when it called to her for freedom, she dove straight into its mouth, and from within she released them. Released them all!"

"I can hear her Jayce, she won't hurt me." Her stunning voice recalled to him, *"It's like a civilization is alive, but under water. It's calling to me."*

He released a breathy laugh, his eyes teeming with the urge to cry and rejoice.

He turned back to her then and confirmed that Ilkiz **was** truly in tears. Azahara was hugging her, and it was a sight to see. This tiny girl, comforting a nearly ten-thousand-year-old Dragon.

"They are back." He said aloud, and with a resounding smile, he leaned onto his forearms and observed her. *You are beyond comprehension, Sunshine.* She shifted her head to look out at the ship, *Come here, I promise I'm not usually needy, but I find myself being so in this moment.*

"I could use some neediness from you if I'm honest," her voice carrying that silky nature in it. He wondered if he was making it that way or was, she purposefully doing it.

What else could you use?

She sat up from Ilkiz, her mouth moved, and for the first time, he couldn't hear her. The sounds of the ship, the sea below, and Ilkiz herself completely masked it.

"A bath."

Mhmm, done.

"New clothes..."

Mhmm, or none, but whatever your preference.

She laughed, *"Maybe some food."*

Is that all, my sweet girl?

"There is something else." She resumed talking, and he observed as Ilkiz straightened out her wing, and she stood. The poise and sheer calm she exhibited as she walked across the full length of Ilkiz's outstretched wing was awe-inspiring.

Approaching the tip as it began to rise, she wobbled slightly but managed to maintain her balance. As she neared the ledge, he leaned out, extending his arm to her. She grasped it, positioning one foot at the ship's edge. Grinning down at her, he took in the sight of her completely covered in Kraken blood, while she smiled her pearly whites up at him. Here was this five-foot-something woman who didn't appear as though she could beat up a training dummy, climbing from the back of the mightiest Dragon to ever roam these lands. She had just taken down a god-made beast, as if it were just another everyday task.

Cheers erupted behind him, but all he focused on was her. When she stepped up onto the ledge and stood over him, she lifted her gaze out at the crew. The smile on her face was beautiful, but the aura she radiated was Magic. Not the Mothers, but the kind she created.

"The skies belong to us!" Akua bellowed out, and Kaen let out a howl that cracked the space around them.

"As it will be!" he called.

"Be as it will!" Kaen followed.

Azahara was laughing through shed tears that left streaks down her blood covered cheeks. "On my life, they'll stay that way," she whispered under her breath, so quietly that no one would hear her but him. When she looked down at him, he was blown away by the beauty of her. It wasn't just the setting sun behind her that made her seem as though she were on fire, nor was it the sparkle in her eyes that seemed to be its own sunrise. No, it was everything that she was.

"What was the other thing you needed?" He put his hand up, and she took it. Jumping from the ledge, he guided her feet to the deck. She stepped to him, only needing to bite her lip in response, and he knew. He hummed while placing his hand at the side of her neck. "The things you do to me." She lifted herself up on her tiptoes as he leaned in and met her lips, bypassing the sour blood and going straight to her sweet, intoxicating taste.

Day 167
CHAPTER 44

"Have a good night," Azahara was desperately trying to escape from everyone. They had allowed her to take a quick shower in Alyse's quarters, but apart from that, they wanted every single detail of what had happened, especially concerning Death. Jayce had thankfully provided their story, sparing them from an all-night interrogation. She understood their need to know what they were getting into, so she obliged by sharing the necessary information. However, when the questions shifted to the fight with the Kraken, she was ready to call it quits. That story could wait for another day.

Alyse groaned, "How are you even tired? I'm hyped up on so much adrenaline I can feel my blood pumping in my veins." She had been hanging around Kaen for too long, and that made Azahara nervous.

"She imploded a Kraken, what do you mean how is she tired?" Thank goodness for Akua, who became her voice of reason. Xol was also right there, but she knew the urgency to retreat into her room. It had nothing to do with her being tired.

With just fifteen days to reach Itotaki, it would be a close call, but they were confident they'd make it. They decided to delve into the specifics in the morning.

After a few more minutes of banter, they conceded and allowed her to leave in peace. Jayce had already departed several hours prior, and when she inquired, he mentioned trying to break through whatever wards were placed around Karver and her family. He said that while he was strong, Jaakobai held enough Magic that could contest him. It didn't make him stronger, just capable of it. Jayce had his Magic his entire life, whereas

Jaakobai was new to wielding that much. It would be difficult for him, but Azahara didn't want to underestimate his pride. It was also his family's Magic, which could make it easier to consume and use. This was new territory for Jayce.

Inhaling deeply to calm her nerves, she swung open her cabin door and stole a glance inside. Jayce occupied the lone chair, facing outward, engrossed in the view beyond the open window. For a fleeting moment, she imagined Kaed standing beside him, engaged in a discussion about what their next move would be. The need for his presence was paramount, and she felt fortunate to have Jayce, who understood the significance of it. *I will love and protect him*—his words resonated with her on a level he could never fully comprehend.

"Massage for your thoughts?" When he met her gaze with his captivating amethyst eyes, her smile broadened even more.

"I'd tell you without the massage but if you are offering…" The potent, feral urge she experienced earlier, though subdued, lingered.

She observed him rise and motion toward the bed. Without hesitation, she slid out of the gown she borrowed from Alyse and settled onto the plush white bedding. Crossing her arms under her head, she rested a cheek on her forearm. Noticing him gazing at her, she raised an eyebrow, turning slightly for a better view, "What?"

He shook his head with a smile, a soft, husky laugh escaping, "Just enjoying the view." Rolling her eyes, he continued, "I'm serious—" He walked over, the bed dipping as he crawled towards her, "It's like every angle of you is perfect." She felt her cheeks flush. "It only compliments everything that you are."

"And what is that, exactly?"

"Flawless." Before settling over her, he kissed her temple.

"I have plenty of flaws," she admitted, feeling the first of his hands against her lower back.

"Okay, name one, then we'll get to what was on your mind."

Biting her lip, she confessed, "Quick-tempered." His thumbs hugged the sides of her spine and pushed straight up, eliciting a groan. "I also have this internal distrust for people, even if it may not seem like it on the outside." His hands came to her shoulders, wrapping around them, a reminder of where they had been just the night before. She buried her head into the sheets to stifle the sounds escaping her.

"Well, I'd say the distrust in people is warranted. I don't think anyone would fault you for that." Whether that was true or not, she hated it. "Your quick temper, I'll concede to that being your only flaw." It made her chuckle; thankful he wouldn't try to fight her on it. She knew her temper had become difficult to deal with since Höwl.

He moved back down to focus on her hips and the small of her back. "Now, your thoughts."

Taking a deep breath, she sighed as he applied pressure to the rolling of his thumbs, "I was imagining you and Kaed when I walked in, talking about what our next move would be." There was no hesitation in his attention, and she smiled, "Life would never exist without the sun and its moon. That is exactly how I feel. While I know his life is uncertain, I still hold onto the hope that I can be as lucky as this world to have both of you." Her fingers gripped the sheets.

His hands moved under her arms, wrapping over her chest to her shoulders, and hugged her. Taking care not to put too much pressure on her, his chest pressed against her back and his forehead to her head.

"I hope for the same," he kissed the back of her neck, "You deserve us both, and I will do everything in my power to make it happen." She turned her head, seeing his eyes filled with strength and determination.

He would do it, even if it meant his life, and that wasn't what she wanted. If something were to happen to him, and she lost them both, there would be no world to reshape. No realm to protect. It would all be gone, and in the end, if it were just her alone, she would make sure no life existed to feel the pain that she had.

"Overthinker..." He turned her to lay on her back, "Why do you do that?" There was no condemnation in his tone, just pure curiosity.

She sighed, "I tend to see the underlining words people don't say, and in them, the truth behind what they mean."

"What did mine tell you?" He parted her legs and settled between them, his hand reaching to the side of her neck, his thumb brushing against her jaw.

"That you would sacrifice your life for my ultimate happiness, but I don't want that."

He shook his head, "I'm..." he paused, as if weighing his words, and deciding that wasn't what she needed to hear, "I said you deserve us both, which includes me in that, so I won't be doing anything stupid to endanger that. I promise."

Her arms were wrapping around his neck, "Promise again."

"I promise," he leaned towards her.

"Swear it."

"I swear to you: my world," his hand wrapped around the back of her neck, and she ran her fingers through his raven hair. "I'll always come home."

Before her mind could take her to a place where it didn't need to be, he locked his lips to hers. He snaked his other hand around the small of her back and lifted her hips to his. Every part of her buzzed, especially when he pushed against her groin, and for the first time, she felt his arousal against her. It made her gasp involuntarily, and immediately caused his lips to curl up into a smile.

He broke the kiss and bit gently down on her bottom lip, her eyes rolling back in response, "I can put the *glamour* back over it," he joked, her heart thrumming against her chest, "if it's too much."

She felt her face burn in both embarrassment for ever making the comment, and the complete, sexual excitement. "I mean it is a **lot**," she pulled him closer, "but, that isn't a bad thing."

He let out a throaty laugh, "That wasn't what I was implying, but" he leaned towards her ear and whispered, "thanks." When the sensation of his lips pressed against her neck, another jolt of pleasure ran through her. One of her legs curled over his, pushing herself up against him, and a groan escaped from his throat. "I will stop, Aza, you just say the word."

"I know you would," her hands were pulling at his shirt, moving the fabric up to his shoulders, and feeling him shift to help it come completely off. "I don't want to stop, not now." Again, his lips were on her neck, and soon his teeth, nipping and sucking along her skin. One of his hands moved down her body, slowly taking in every inch of her. From the curve of her waist to her pear shape hips, down to her legs, he meticulously touched with gentle measure. It made her body shiver, and bumps rose from head to toe.

He trailed his lips down her collarbone, to the curve of her breast, "This body deserves to be worshiped," his tongue rolled over her nipple.

"—Jayce..." His name came out mixed with a gasp.

She felt his fingers moving between her thighs, "I plan to do that for eternity." His lips clasped around her hardened bead, just as his fingers slipped between her slit and ran the length from her soaked core to her clit. Her hips lifted and she let out moan, which she quickly slapped her hand over her mouth to stifle. They were no longer on the Floating Mountains of Xi, or alone on the ship.

Her heavy breathing broke through her hand as his thumb applied pressure and in a circular motion, rubbed at her bud. He bit down gently on her nipple, before moving further down her body, his lips drawing a line to her belly button and to her hip bone.

Daring to look down at him, he was moving his hands and placing them around her legs. Before he lifted his gaze to meet hers, he kissed her inner thighs. She bit down on her lip, nervous beyond belief. Even after so many times bathing, she never felt clean of him. Would he still linger, and if so, would Jayce know?

Before she could allow the fear to take away the moment, his hands gripped her thighs and leaned forward. His tongue breaking between her petals and taking his first taste. Feeling his lips wrapped around her bud, she forgot anything and everything else. It raptured her entire being, and as if he knew it for himself, he brought her closer, his tongue flicking in perfect, seamless motion. As though he had been pleasing her for centuries, he knew exactly how to run his tongue back and forth, and flick at the right time that made her sing a song of rapture.

She fought to keep control of her noise level, "Please—yes—" her words a muddled mess between bits of moans and gasps.

A chill ran down her as he moved ever so slightly and slid his tongue inside of her. It was so quick that she had no time to overthink the action, and an unexpected force shot through her. She was going to drown in the pleasure he was giving her, and she didn't want the comforts of air. Every inch of her was on fire and she bit down on her arm, trying to keep from telling the entire crew just how much elation she was in.

He moaned against her, the vibration another added element that made her body release its ownership, "You taste like what I imagine Paradise to feel like," as he finished his comment that sent her stomach to do flips, he rolled over, taking her with him.

"W-what—Jayce—"

Now with both of her knees on either side of his face, she leaned back and looked down at him. Her eyes widened and he briefly looked up at her, before taking his eyes back to her flower.

"Sit, my love," his tone a purr in the silence.

Without hesitation, she obliged. His attention back on her bud causing her back to curve. With trembling legs, she did her best to hold herself up; never having sat on someone's face before. This was on another level of intimacy and pleasure she didn't know existed.

Afraid he couldn't breathe with her smothering his face, instinctively, she began lifting herself. He forcefully pulled her back down to him, his teeth gently biting down on her clit. She clasped her hand over her mouth and half stifled the mixture of a scream and moan, the other hand reaching back and supporting herself against his chest.

"—but—ah!" She struggled to articulate her thoughts, as though her mind could form the words but her mouth could only release fragments. It elicited moans of his own, and again, that added vibration against her already sensitive clit.

"Jayce!" She was panting, her hips instinctively moving, without guidance. "I can't—" Feeling the tightening in her stomach, she leaned forward, one hand gripping at his hair and the other at the headboard. "Yes—" Her voice breathy, and she wasn't going to last, there would be no way with how his tongue devoured her.

"Fuck!" She cracked the headboard in her grasp, causing it to bend towards her. "Jayce—wait—"

His hands released the hold he had on her thighs, and she lifted slightly off of him, her breathing out of pace. A tremble rolled through her as he spoke, "Yes?" He gazed up at her, his eyes brimming with desire. She let out a breath, attempting to catch it, but the flustering sensation made it seemingly impossible.

"I—" *Holy fuck, I can't think straight,* "I want you to take me, right here, right now."

As though she was nothing more than paper, he leaned up effortlessly with her on his shoulders. She gripped at his hair, but hadn't needed to worry for long, as he slowly brought her down to his lap. The glossiness on his lips prompted her to exhale the breath she had just taken in. He licked his lips, noticing her gaze.

Leaning in towards him, she shared a smile, and he kissed her. Tasting herself on his tongue was euphoric, and in that moment, she tasted only the both of them. There was no trace of a third being, and the fear that had nearly spoiled the moment before drifted away like mist over the sea.

Feeling him subtly shift beneath her, she wrapped her arms around his neck and deepened their kiss. The soft sound of fabric hitting the floor reached her ears, indicating that Jayce was standing and removing his pants. His hand supported her weight, and she tightened her legs around his waist for added stability.

He momentarily broke their kiss, gazing into her eyes and running his free hand up her back to her hair. After a brief moment, he leaned back in, capturing her lips once more.

Jayce then sat down at the edge of the bed, holding her up with her head slightly lowered, their lips still engaged in an intimate embrace. Nervousness tinged the air, but there was no trace of fear. The distinction was unmistakable, providing clarity between the two emotions for her.

His arm came around her hips, and she lowered herself. "Remember, you are here with me. Safe, and loved," he said against her lips. She felt him press against her core, causing her to lean into him.

There was no doubt in her mind this was what she wanted.

"I know..." He allowed her to lower herself onto him, and as he broke through her, she let out a moan of relief. She heard him let out a groan and his hand grip at her hair and hip.

While she had expected his size to be grand from feeling it through his pants, she hadn't been prepared. When he filled her completely, he leaned down and kissed her passionately. She could feel his struggle to just hold her there, and she too, was fighting her own battle.

As though Magic was involved, the feeling of him inside of her was like nothing she'd experienced before. All of her emotions were heightened and the familiar feeling of free-falling came over her. She wondered very briefly if this was because of their souls' connection.

His tongue intertwined with hers, and in that moment, she lost the little bit of control she had over her own body and rolled her hips. Her legs lifting and dropping her slowly on top of him causing him to tremble and moan into her mouth.

With each rhythmic movement, her body gradually became her own again. Beyond physically, her soul found solace, and the protective cocoon he provided allowed her to blossom in the intimacy they shared.

One of his hands moved to her breast and grabbed its entirety, kneading at it while his opposite arm wrapped around her waist. His lips trailed down her jaw to her neck where he bit down, sucking on her sensitive skin. Feeling him begin to put pressure down on her, and thrusting up into her, she let go of any trepidation she had, and relaxed.

He had been waiting for that moment and burring his head between the crook of her neck, pushing her down onto him. Her wall protested, unable to completely take him, and as her head leaned back to scream, his hand gently clasped over her mouth. Her legs were trembling, and he smiled against her skin, "You feel divine." His breath sent chills up the back of her neck, and she moaned, his hand moving from her mouth. He kissed her neck and rolled them over, placing her on her back and lifting one of her legs over his shoulder.

Staying inside of her he began a rhythmic motion with his hips, sliding in and out of her. His hand found hers and laced their fingers together, placing their arms together over her head. The surge of pure pleasure that wrapped over her made every inch of her body tingle, and she threw her head back, biting her lip and fighting with stifling her calls of pure ecstasy.

"Fuck—Jayce—" Her opposite leg that wasn't being held wrapped around his hip, bringing them even closer together.

His moans were pure enchantment, and they would have put a spell on her if she wasn't already under one. "Good god—Azahara—" The sound of her name on his tongue felt too good, as if it belonged to a realm beyond this one.

Never letting her hand go, he brought his other hand up to her neck as his lips captured hers. Her tongue entered his mouth, flicking against his and dancing with it. His thrust into her became stronger, his desire pouring into her.

She put her hand behind his neck, only to drag her nails across his shoulder. He groaned into her mouth, and as she opened her eyes, through the haze, she could see his wings were spread. Though it might not have held the same significance for others, the fact that he allowed them to be out during this moment made her entire being thrive.

His hand moved to her leg and lifted it over his shoulder. The action caused her eyes to widen. There was only a smirk on his face as he leaned slightly back from her and moved back into motion. She swore his girth thickened, and she felt a pressure like never before building between the sky above and ground below. Everything was coming to the center, and she felt him hitting that spot that would send her over the edge.

He felt her need and sat up completely, pulling her to him with force. His lips pressed against her ankle, and a strange feeling came over her. There was no stifling her moan, and as it came from her mouth it made him vibrate all over, and his form faltered ever so slightly. "I should have taken you elsewhere to hear you sing without restraint," his voice breathy.

"I can't—" she whimpered. Her eyes closed, and she rubbed her head against the bed, finding her body elevating, "Jayce—I can't hold on—"

His thumb found her clit and rolled it in a perfect circle, sending her straight over the edge of the cliff she was hanging over. Her back was lifted off the bed and her toes were gripping and pulling at the sheets. Coupled with his drive, and their mixed sounds of pleasure, she was finding the point of climax rising and there was no stopping.

"There—don't stop! Yes!"

"Fuck—baby..." Jayce called out.

With both of them crumbling, she let out a moan that came from deep within. Every part of her shook as she came so hard that it nearly overthrew his own climax, which both doubled her own and filled her to the brim. She could feel the pressure as his vitality began seeping out of her.

Trembling under him, he pressed kisses down her ankle to her calf before gently laying it down beside him. As he drew closer, she reached her arms around him, fingers stroking along the silky feathers of his raven-like wings. They quivered, and he let out a throaty moan.

He slipped out of her and placed his lips against hers. Their breaths were labored, yet neither seemed to mind. Exchanging smiles, they found joy in their shared exhaustion.

His fingers entwined with her hair, delicately curling a few strands around his finger. A shiver ran down her spine, and goosebumps adorned her arms. He gently brushed his hand across her forehead, wiping away the beads of sweat that had gathered, before placing a tender kiss.

Meeting his gaze, she bashfully uttered, "Thank you."

He turned them onto their side, wrapping his arms around her. "There's no need to thank me, trust me," he whispered, planting a kiss between her eyebrows. "It was my pleasure," a slight tremor ran through him, as though remembering that exact *pleasure*.

For some inexplicable reason, as his wing descended to rest over her, she felt a surge of elation. "You wanted specifics, remember?" Her breath finally steadying, she continued, "I couldn't have done this without you. I know I've thanked you for saving me, but it wasn't just from him that you did. You've saved me from myself. I just want you to know..." Her fingers traced the sharp contours of his jaw, up his cheeks to his temple, feeling the unexpectedly soft bristles of his hair that should be prickly, but wasn't. "I'm only here because of you. So, thank you."

He pressed his forehead against hers. "Then we both should be thanking each other for that." Her eyebrows furrowed, and his hand caressed her cheek. "You saw me; before meeting you, I was lost. It was you, and only you, that pulled me to safety."

A sense of peace enveloped her heart and soul. He continued, "That's why I say this," pausing briefly to place a kiss on her lips, "If you go down, then we go down together. If you fall, I'll fall with you. This world, I'm tired of living in it without you."

Overwhelmed by emotions, tears cascaded down her cheeks. "Jayce..." His name escaped her lips as a whisper. "Damn it." His thumb gently brushed away the tears from one cheek, and he chuckled.

"I know, Sunshine." He kissed her again, pulling her closer and tightening his embrace. "I know."

Day 168
CHAPTER 45

The air crackled with tension as the entire crew, except Jayce and her, engaged in a heated argument. Even Xol, to her disbelief, had joined the fray.

"We shouldn't even be discussing this," Xol's frustration echoed in her tone. "There should be no debate; she cannot go back."

"I'm inclined to agree, but what other choice does she have? And we have to stay on the path to arrive in less than fourteen days," Alyse, standing beside Akua, nearly screamed at her first officer. "It also sounds like this Jake person is somehow watching us—"

"I don't think so," Jayce interjected, his arms crossed over his chest as he slouched against a stack of boxes. "I've got wards around the ship."

She took a deep breath. Jaakobai had tapped into his grandfather's wards and had been watching her for nearly two hundred years. However, Jayce insisted that these wards weren't the same as the ones around her home. She found comfort in knowing he wouldn't give her a false sense of security, especially since their plan would involve them being enemies.

Xol grimaced, "So what, we just let her walk straight back to them?" There was a touch of sensitivity in her words. "Jayce, can't you wëther us into the Kingdom, and we can sneak into the Keep and get her friends?"

Carmen and Théodore both nodded their heads, "We can all go, use our anonymity to sneak—"

Kaen laughed, "You would only get captured and make Aza have to work even harder."

Most of the crew turned their heads towards the fire user, who didn't flinch. Her raised eyebrows silently dared them to try.

Bless him, Rowlin stepped into the circle of the crew and waved his arms to gather their attention. "Aza," he addressed her, "What do you want?"

Taking a deep breath, she glanced at Jayce, having already discussed her idea with him that morning before crawling out of bed. He wasn't a fan, but with limited options for a safe return, her proposal seemed like the only viable choice. When she looked back at Rowlin, everyone had their eyes fixed on her. Xol, above all else, pleaded with her not to make the already decided choice.

"Jayce will take me in as his captor," she watched as Xol shook her head. "Jaakobai still believes him loyal to the King. I won't be going in alone, and that is what matters. We have no idea, absolutely no clue, where my family is being held—or if they are even in the Keep. Our only indication that they are somewhere in the Kingdom is that we are unable to locate Karver." Jayce had informed them about his involvement, saving her from the need to explain. "Once we have located them, Jayce will open a wëther for the twins and Xol to assist."

Shock rolled over Xol. "They will know who you are then," she said, directing the statement to Jayce.

He shrugged his shoulders, a cheeky smile on his face. "It doesn't matter anymore. Plus, this is bigger than my itsy-bitsy secret."

"You are likely the oldest Fae alive; I don't think that is an itsy-bitsy secret," her tone was not playful.

Azahara rubbed at her eyes in frustration. She had already thought about that. Knowing that he would be ultimately starting war with his own people, and their relaxed pursuit of him would begin once again. He was adamant he didn't care, but it still left a sour taste in her mouth. Jayce owed nothing to Kaed, Zhal, and Illyan, and yet, here he was, risking his safety for theirs.

"I'm sorry, Aza." Xol's voice came from beside her, a tinge of anxiety evident. "I'm just...worried."

Offering a grateful smile, Azahara nodded, addressing everyone around her. "I know you are, and I really appreciate all of you. That's why I won't actively put you all in danger. This time..." She watched as Alyse linked her arm around Rowlin's, continuing, "Once we get my family we are going to leave. I don't want to fight, not there. I could summon Ilkiz and level the entire Kingdom, but..." She shook her head, releasing a heavy sigh. "I don't want to be the monster in my story, given the choice. They may not know that," referring to the people of Naverra, "but I do, and so will you."

Her gaze shifted to Rowlin, "You once asked me to tell you my story. You wanted to know the truth." Before continuing, she took a deep breath, "The Battle of Sunfall was all a front, and we—I, played right into Jaakobai's stupid game. It ended up getting the one person in my life that had given me hope, someone I love, killed. When I saw his lifeless body, I lost control. When warned that I would start a war, I didn't care—because they took him away from me." Sorrow etched their faces as she continued, "It was my family, Illyan, who pulled me from the darkness. If it weren't for them, I would have likely destroyed this world."

"Ladybug, I'm here—please!" The memory of Illyan's desperate plea echoed in her mind. *"Please, I love you, don't do this. Let me help you. We will try to figure this out."* She had yelled at them, told them to leave and never return. Instead, they wrapped their arms around both her and Kaed. *"I'll never leave you!"* She hadn't ever deserved their friendship or love. *"I've made mistakes, but the one I never made, was staying by your side over these past two hundred years. You were the one good thing in my life. I beg you to stay with me. Don't destroy yourself. I love you so much."*

"The truth, is, yes I did the things they say I did. However, I didn't know that I would kill thousands in a matter of seconds, and I don't know if knowing that would have made a difference." She paused, seeking support from Jayce, who smiled proudly at her. It was all she needed to continue, "I will kill people like I did at Sunfall, both willingly and not. I... will not be the hero that Rah was, and I don't want to be.

"What matters most to me is my family, and that includes all of you. Alyse, you and everyone on the Neptune have done more for me than I can fathom thanking you for. You waited for me after Goddrick took me, never knowing if I would come back." She hadn't intended to make Alyse cry, but here she was, doing so. "You didn't throw me overboard in those first several days of being onboard, and I definitely deserved it." A few laughs rang out, and she noticed more of them shedding tears. "Your survival until the end is my only priority. The best way to ensure that is for you to leave Itotaki and go back to your lives before ever meeting me." The thought pained her beyond belief, and she felt as though her heart was ready to punch her brain for forming the thought into words.

"However, I'm not going to take the choice away from you, but I don't want you to feel obligated to follow me into the unknown, risking your life for—"

"Oh, shut up—" Alyse crossed the hull so quickly that when she crashed into her, they both stumbled and nearly fell. They embraced, and for the first time, her skin didn't tingle or react negatively to the contact. "We are family, damn it, Aza."

While she knew that was how they felt, Azahara understood that sometimes making the right choice was not the easiest.

"I'd leave the Neptune if Alyse felt any differently," Carmen said, moving towards them and wrapping her arms around them.

"I second that." Théodore joined them, and soon the rest of the crew had embraced them in a warm, almost suffocating, embrace.

Giving into the moment, Azahara closed her eyes and felt their unconditional love. It was difficult to come to terms with, but in that moment, it all felt deserved. None of them owed her anything, and they never would. They had come to care for her over their time together. These people would strengthen her and give her a reason to be better, and find the control she so desperately needed.

"Thank you," it was like a cue for everyone to begin moving away, "really. All of you." When they had all backed away, and their eyes were back on her, she nodded. "Alright then, so it's settled."

It was decided that once her and Jayce were dropped off in Itotaki, they would immediately turn back and head for Ilkiz. Akua, Kaen, and Xol would keep a vigilant watch for the portal Jayce would open. Once everyone was safely collected, they planned to return to the ship. While that outlined the basic plan, Azahara knew from experience that nothing ever unfolded exactly as anticipated. Hence, she braced herself for every conceivable scenario, even those leading to the darkest imaginable places.

Ilkiz had returned, prompting everyone to gather at the ship's side to witness her graceful glide across the water's surface. Smiling, Azahara approached the ledge and leaned over, extending her arm in an attempt to touch Ilkiz's wing. A strong arm gently steadied her, ensuring she wouldn't lose balance as her fingertip brushed against the leathery skin of her Spirit.

At that moment, a familiar smoke enveloped Ilkiz, gathering at Azahara's palms. Power surged through her veins, and she rolled her head, feeling the energy course through her as she stood tall.

Welcome back. How did it go?

"My home is filled with Dragons, as it should have always been." Ilkiz's tone resonated with pure bliss, and though her mighty voice still echoed powerfully, a sense of calm permeated through it.

I'm so glad, she sighed, turning around to see Jayce wearing a warm smile as she continued to lean over the ledge. *I'm scared, Ilkiz.* Rising to her feet, she approached him, and he enveloped her in a comforting embrace, his head resting gently atop hers. *I can't lose them.*

"I know you are, and we will do everything to protect them. You have the might of Dragons behind you."

At that moment, Jayce sensed her unspoken desire—to find solace in his arms. He remained silent, understanding her need for comfort. With a tender touch, he traced a soothing path up and down her back as they swayed gently with the motion of the ship. The steady rhythm of his heart, echoing in her ear, brought an overwhelming sense of peace and tranquility, enveloping her in a profound sense of calm.

I need you to do something for me, her eyes closed, and she took a deep breath through her nose, savoring his worldly scent. *If things go badly, and I have to summon you...* She rubbed her eyes against his chest, and he placed his hand behind her head, running his fingers through the spirals of her hair. *Kill them all. Every last one of them. For what they did to you, your people, and your kin. For everything they've done to me. Destroy the Fae for what they did to Jayce. Destroy the mortal realm for what they did to Kaed. Destroy the gods for doing nothing while their people suffered. Reduce them to ash and return them to the ground from which they came."*

As her eyes fluttered open, she sensed a subtle transformation. It was as if her pupils were expanding and contracting, forming a captivating, razor-thin line. The warmth in her chest surged as she sensed Ilkiz's power intensifying within her. It felt as though she were developing scales and flexing wings that, in reality, didn't exist.

"I never wanted war," Ilkiz uttered, and she could feel the palpable excitement in the words, *"but they forced my wing—now, I shall not show the same leniency. For you, my little one, I will destroy them and feel nothing but elation while doing so."*

Jayce gently guided her back, his hand cradling her chin to lift her gaze. His amethyst eyes gleamed with a bright smile. He understood; she had emphasized that his safety was paramount. Ensuring the return of all of them to safety was her foremost concern. While her ultimate aim wasn't to annihilate everyone in Naverra, if circumstances demanded it, she was prepared to take that measure.

"I've been alive for a long, long time," he whispered, his thumb tracing the delicate curve of her jaw, "people have always tried to draw a clear line between heroes and villains." With a gentle stroke, he caressed her lips. "The eternal struggle of good versus evil, the lost versus the saviors of the realm." Pulling her closer with his other hand, he leaned in, pressing his forehead against hers. "But having witnessed both sides of this tale, I've come to realize it's all a matter of perspective—dependent on who writes the story." He paused, looking deeply into her eyes. "So, my love, don't confine yourself to either of those classifications because you are beyond them both."

For reasons unknown, she sensed power emanating between her fingertips, his words echoing in her soul. He was right; she had never conformed to the mold of good or evil.

A smile adorned her lips as her arms encircled his neck. "To the ones between the lines," her words whispered against his lips.

"To you, Sunshine, only to you." His lips were on hers, and while the uncertainty of the coming days still lingered, there was one thing that wasn't; if they didn't survive, no one would.

Day 180
CHAPTER 46

In the following days, she sought refuge in various training sessions, engaging with the twins, Xol, and even Jayce. Each of them excelled in their respective disciplines, and she was grateful that they didn't go easy on her. The training sessions resembled those with Zhal as they traversed Shubae—demanding, but not necessarily for the same reasons.

The time spent with Kaen proved to be both mentally and physically exhausting. Her goal was to comprehend how Kaen controlled fire, a skill closely tied to the element she drew from Ilkiz. While strength remained the primary aspect of bonding with Ilkiz, the accompanying element, known as Power, but often mistaken for fire, intrigued her. Kaen explained that, although it shared properties with fire, it wasn't crafted from the same construct. Instead, it originated from pure, raw energy, manifesting as flames in both appearance and effect. The released heat, once unleashed, could obliterate wolfram in a matter of seconds.

While the element radiated around her, it was just hot, and wouldn't burn unless exuded further beyond her skin. She had demonstrated this back in Isis. Jayce mentioned that even he could feel the heat, and while not afraid, he wouldn't actively go and touch it.

Training with Kaen was challenging but immensely beneficial. With Akua present to control any flames, practicing the summoning and release of elements felt secure. The synergy between the twins was evident, and she appreciated the balance they provided.

Akua focused on mental training, emphasizing the importance of understanding the truth behind the elements. He delved into the history of the five elements, with particular emphasis on Space. It had been the first she had ever heard of it, and that surprised him, considering Jayce's Magic was that of the same existence. Akua explained that it was taking the force around them that kept them from floating to the sky and warping it to the users will.

He chuckled when she recounted Jayce pulling down a star, but it wasn't a lighthearted laugh. In fact, he seemed more nervous, subtly shifting away from her. He went on to clarify that manipulating something so distant was beyond his comprehension. Dragons and their spirit riders manipulated Space for levitation and matter bending, while Jayce's Magic seemed to defy the gravity laws that governed their world.

During her initial training sessions with Jayce, she brought up his Magic. While he provided detailed explanations, it was clear that he seldom expelled its full potential. The scarcity of Fae his age raised concerns for her, enough to refrain from revisiting the topic. She wasn't afraid of him, but was afraid of what others would do. The mere thought of Jaakobai wielding Jayce's Magic sent shivers down her spine, it was a truly terrifying prospect.

Jayce, always generous, offered to teach her how to fly. He explained that riding something with wings was distinctly different from having wings oneself, but learning to navigate the skies would be beneficial. Surprisingly, it became her favorite training among the four of them. Not because she enjoyed listening to Jayce talk or watching him enthusiastically recount how he learned to fly, or even the way his smile brightened when he caught her staring and not entirely tuned in to his lessons.

The lessons proved fruitful, and by the tenth day, she was getting the hang of summoning Ilkiz on command. While she still believed reins might make things easier, the fact that her hands didn't need support was a confidence boost. Acquiring the comfort for aerial acrobatics akin to Kaen on Fury would take time, but she was confident that she had ample time to learn.

Azahara had gained valuable insights from Zhal in hand-to-hand combat and short sword usage, but training with Xol was an entirely different experience. Xol neither tired, nor took it easy on her. This training drew the most attention from the crew, and Azahara found the scrutiny more manageable than before.

With a dagger strapped to her thigh and her hair tied back, Azahara gracefully sidestepped a heavy swing. Beads of sweat from her forehead cascaded across Xol as she lunged forward again. She swiftly dropped, sweeping her leg across the floor, forcing Xol to leap back. The Yuul cracked her neck and popped her fingers, steadying herself for another charge.

"Come on, you got this!" Carmen called out.

Exhaling, Azahara observed as Xol forcefully pushed off the deck, swinging out a fist. Instead of evading, she extended her hand and caught it, the sheer force sliding her backward a few feet. Another fist struck her in the stomach, prompting a gasp of air. "Lucky for you I only have two fists now," Xol commented with a laugh.

Grinning, she retorted, "It's too bad." She spun swiftly, turning her back to Xol, who hadn't time to pull her fist away. Azahara used her shoulder to toss the Yuul over onto her back. A grunt escaped Xol, and instead of allowing her to stand, Azahara took her wrist, turning it enough to elicit another groan. With one foot pressed against Xol's shoulder, Azahara crouched down, her dagger between her fingers. "Multiple hands sound fun."

Xol bared her teeth in a smile, saying, "Bold words, Violence."

Azahara winked and stepped off of her. "I'm not violent; I don't know where you guys get that from." She spun the dagger between her fingers, flipping it up, and once she caught the hilt, she tucked it back into its sheath.

"I beg to differ," Jayce said, and when she shot him a glance, he threw his hands up. "See, don't harm me, I'm fragile."

She rolled her eyes and shook her head.

As the sun set on their final day, Itotaki came into view, and they slowed the ship for a precise arrival. Nervousness had accompanied her throughout the journey toward their destination, but now, with only a single night remaining, her stomach threatened to release every bit of food she'd ever eaten.

"Alright everyone, let's set up dinner on deck tonight," Alyse called out, and without hesitation, they all began getting to work. "Aza, can you do me a favor?"

"Of course," she said.

"Take a bath, relax."

She pulled her eyebrows together and turned her head down to sniff herself, "Do I stink?"

"No, you don't," Jayce stood beside her, his head close to hers as he wrapped his arms around her waist. With a gentle tone, he whispered, "They want to make it nice for you, kind of like a surprise, but shh, just go." He kissed her cheek and swatted her butt.

"Hey!" She squealed.

He quickly stepped away from her, saving his butt from her own assault.

She did as he said and retreated back to her room. The last thing she wanted was to be alone, but she understood why they didn't want her to help.

This was beyond anything that they had signed up for, and for them to continue to go out of their way again for her, she couldn't help but wonder how she had become so blessed to have them.

Come get me when it's time, she slipped through Jayce's window. The tingling sensation of him reaching through hers was answer enough that he would.

The tub was large, but the water didn't stay warm. Attempting to use the Power of Ilkiz to keep it so proved ineffective. After a very quick bath and dressing, she sat at the window, gazing back at the sea they had traversed. The sky displayed a beautiful blend of orange, blue, and pink hues. It reminded her of the sky just after she bonded with Ilkiz, evoking memories of Rah. Hoping that Death took care of him, she smiled and leaned against the frame.

She needed to keep her thoughts clear for the day ahead and stop dwelling on the countless "what ifs" that could happen.

"Ilkiz," she spoke out loud, feeling that the silence around her would soon drive her insane.

"Yes, little one?"

"When we go, I need you to allow my emotions to run rampant. I've asked Jayce to do the same because I need them to think me weak."

"Have you seen yourself? It will be hard to think that."

They both shared a chuckle, "They will see a short, frail woman, especially the King.

"Do you really think Jaakobai is taking you back to the King? Have you thought of the prospect of him taking you back to Höwl?"

"I have," she swung her feet, "He is playing a game with the King, and taking me to Höwl would ruin whatever he has spent all this time building. I have this feeling it has to do with the Book of Vespera, and the Book of Aurora."

"Vespera was destroyed."

Her eyebrows pulled together, and she felt a lump in her throat, "What?"

"I would know, I destroyed it." She gasped and slumped down. *"Unless they found a way to create another one, which would be impossible, because Rah wrote it himself and has been with me since his death."*

A strange sense of victory washed over her. "How did you destroy it?"

"I ate it, along with the one that held it."

"Oh, I hope that is what he is after, so I can crush all of his hopes in one, swift—"

"Violence is a good nickname for you."

She almost slipped forward into the sea, swiftly leaning backward instead, and tumbled to the floor. The loud thud echoed, and she groaned. "Ow," she muttered, leaning her head back and seeing Xol shaking her head. "My tailbone."

"How did I even sneak up on you? I said your name like three times," Xol rolled her eyes and crossed the room, leaning down and giving her a hand back up to her feet. "While I have you alone, if I may?"

A bit of surprise lingered on her face, and she nodded at Xol, "Everything okay?" Barely getting the question out, she let out a soft gasp as she was wrapped in an embrace. Her body trembled, and Azahara felt heat behind her eyes, and quickly put her arms around the Yuul.

"What's wrong?!" Concern laced her tone.

"I..." Xol mumbled, burying her head in the crook of her shoulder, taking a deep breath.

"Xol..." Her embrace tightened.

"I don't know." The firmness in her hold remained unwavering, and Azahara placed her head down onto her chest. "I've never felt this before. When Goddrick took you, I was angry. That was the only emotion I had.

Now, knowing you are going on your own volition, I've been feeling this strange—"

"You are nervous, sad, upset... worried..." Azahara closed her eyes, feeling her own tears trailing down her cheek. "I am too."

Xol gently placed a hand on Azahara's head, running it down her hair and settling it at the back of her neck. "To others, you are just a beautiful human girl blessed, or cursed, with a burden you never wanted. They see just another person in the crowd of millions. Not me, I don't."

Azahara leaned back, gazing up at Xol's colorless face, her striking eyes glossed over as tears trickled down her cheek.

"I see the reason I am here. To me, you are my goddess, my version of Death." One of Xol's hands came to her cheek, and she leaned into it. "I don't understand the concept of love, but if it is anything like this, I don't like it." That made her smile because she understood. Love was both beautiful and painful. It was the source of her greatest turmoil, but at the same time, the happiest pieces of her life. "You better not do anything stupid, Violence, or so help me, this world will not survive what we will do to it."

"I won't—" Xol's lips met hers, catching her so off guard that she let out a gasp. The taste of salt and lingering nectar filled her senses. Once she moved past the initial surprise, she returned the pressure, reciprocating the embrace. It wasn't something she had ever imagined, kissing Xol, but it was beautiful. A sense of protection and love enveloped her as she was pulled closer.

It hadn't lasted long, and when Xol pulled away, she sighed, "I mean it." Her stern tone and complete disregard for the moment beforehand made Azahara laugh. "Also, why do you smell and taste so good?"

Throwing her head back, she groaned, "I don't know. I did just get out of the bath."

"No, that isn't it," her eyes narrowed on her, "I thought maybe Jayce was exaggerating."

Azahara felt heat flow to her face, and her hands tingled as though going numb. "He... what did he say?" There was no way he was flaunting that around.

With a slight chuckle, Xol shook her head, "No, no, no." She paused, watching as Azahara turned every shade of red she could. "I think this is a conversation for another time, but he does not speak of anything that happens between you two. He merely asked me when I first met you on the ship if I had smelled your scent. I never—well, tried, to not pay attention." Again, she swore she saw her cheeks somehow form color on them, "I could only hold my breath for so long."

That would explain why she didn't speak to me... she thought.

"Now that I've tasted you I—"

"Xol! Please don't say anymore, I am going to die of embarrassment." Azahara grumbled.

"Do not die," Xol seemed concerned.

"It's just a saying Xol."

"Why would you joke like that?"

"Just—never mind, please don't talk about how I taste." Her voice was strained, and she felt further heat building everywhere across her body.

"Can I speak with Jayce about it?"

"Why?!" She nearly screamed.

"So... we can compare."

"Compare what?!" She screamed.

Jayce mercifully entered the room, rescuing her from the awkward conversation they were having. Xol admitted to Jayce that she had kissed her, causing her face to turn an even deeper shade of red, a hue she feared might be permanently replaced with the pallor of a tomato. Jayce chuckled and bid Xol farewell.

"Come on r—" he cut himself off so quickly, she almost didn't realize what he was about to call her. *Red.*

"It's okay," She reassured him with a gentle smile.

He shook his head and put his hand out, "No, that isn't for me to call you. Come on, it's time to eat."

The evening unfolded perfectly, with the moon casting its gentle glow upon them. Laughter and tears flowed freely as they indulged in a hearty feast, although Azahara and Jayce refrained from partaking in any liquor, well aware of the importance of a good night's sleep before the challenges of the following day. They briefly discussed the plan, only to ensure everyone was on the same page.

As the night progressed, Jayce signaled that it was time to retire, and surprisingly, Alyse didn't protest, urging everyone to follow suit. A thick silence enveloped them as they cleaned up, each person burdened by their individual anxieties. Azahara anticipated a sleepless night for all, mirroring her own restless nerves.

Once the hull was cleared, everyone parted ways. She and Jayce retreated to their quarters. She drew in a long, heavy breath, releasing a sigh of tension. Allowing her shoulders to drop, she reached for the crook of her neck, squeezing tightly down her shoulder, and pressed her lips together in a fine line.

"Do you want another massage?" Jayce, ever attentive, asked as he was crossing the room, removing his shirt and kicking off his boots.

She lifted her shirt over her head and unclasped her bra, tossing them to the corner and slipping her pants off. Shaking her head, she expressed a simple desire, "I just want to hold you." Her confession got a soft hum from him. Before sliding into bed, she slipped over her night gown and curled under the covers. He was there, shirtless, waiting with open arms.

As they settled between the sheets, she held onto him for dear life, "Fuck, I'm so nervous."

His hand ran through her hair, brushing it with his nails and rubbing gentle circles at the nape of her neck. "I know, your leg was shaking nearly the entire evening," he remarked. She buried her face into his chest, emitting a groan that earned a laugh from him. "I am too, beyond words. This isn't like Sunfall, this feels like a trap more than anything."

"It is a trap," She said with confidence, "It's why I'm going in with the knowledge that everything we have planned for, is likely going to go wrong."

"We will get them and come home. All of us will come out of this."

She looked up at him and nodded, "Honey..."

The look of surprise on his face made her laugh through her nose, "Yes, Sunshine?"

"You said that Jaakobai brought up the Book of Vespera," he nodded, his hand that had been playing with her hair moved to her shoulder, and gently massaging it. "Ilkiz says *she* destroyed it." He didn't seem surprised about that fact, "Do you think he knows that?"

"Likely, but desperation can be a powerful emotion." He placed a kiss on her head, relaxing into her, "Rah wrote it, if my memory serves me correctly." She nodded, and he continued, "They would have to play God with time, and while I'd say that is impossible, I wouldn't hold it against Jaakobai to attempt it. Though, it won't matter after tomorrow."

Her head was tilted up towards him, watching as he closed his eyes, "Why's that?"

"Can't turn pages in a book without hands," he said it so casually that she couldn't help but let out a soft laugh. "I'm serious. Boy will be lucky to come out alive, which I plan to be his best-case scenario."

Biting her lip, she took another deep breath, and closed her eyes. "Allow me the honor to remove his tongue."

He chuckled, "All yours, baby."

Day 181

For the first time in what felt like forever, she took a seat and gazed at herself in the mirror. The day loomed ahead, and she wasn't prepared for it in any way. Desiring a moment of solitude with just herself, she sat in silence, Ilkiz receded to the furthest part of her, respecting her need for uninterrupted reflection. Every past circumstance had been thrust upon her, and although she lacked a choice in the matter, she was still choosing to face it head-on.

Regardless of whether they believed it, Illyan was her best friend, and she would go to any lengths for them. She should never have left them in the first place, and when Illyan shared with her that they were going after not only them, but Zhal and Kaed, she wished she'd told them where she was.

But Goddrick...

She didn't conceal her face as tears started streaming down her cheeks, leaving a glistening trail along her skin. These tears weren't just about her pain but also for everyone she loved and cared for. It was time to place blame on those who had hurt them—whether it was Goddrick, the King, or Jaakobai. Tessa, Broan, Kaed, and others had suffered, and these tears were an acknowledgment of that collective pain.

Her eyes seemed to come alive, constantly shifting hues of red and orange amidst a sea of blue that never rested in one place for even a moment. In contrast, the other eye, a steady crystal blue, seemed to emit a constant glow. This juxtaposition was almost like a metaphor for her life—a representation of the stability she craved, the normalcy she yearned for, and the life that had been thrust upon her, one she never wanted.

Just like her eyes, this moment was here, and there was no turning back. The ship was now docked, and they eagerly awaited her presence. The time had come to face whatever lay ahead, embracing both the life she had and the one she never asked for.

They were waiting for the *monster*.

Adjusting her top, she stood. The dark blue and black ensemble was stunning, and she had to thank all of the ladies onboard that assisted in putting it together. It was simple, but held a lot of subtle importance. The color was a call to Jayce and his raven wings, and with the gold accents along the arms and shoulder cuffs, a nod to the Neptune. The boning under her breast was a curved golden metal, and between it, a red stone, for the flames of Ilkiz.

She was finishing the braid in her hair when the door opened, and Jayce stepped in. The pain etched across his face nearly convinced her to retreat to bed. To tell the crew to turn them around and forget all about this stupid plan.

"Everyone is doing busy work and will do so as we exit. It needs to appear as if they don't care you are leaving, for their safety." His voice was low, broken, "They—" He stepped to her, "We aren't okay."

Extending her arm toward him, he grasped it and tenderly drew her close to his chest. Adorning the distinctive cloak of the White Cloaks, he wore standard clothes beneath. Absent of any armor, it stirred a hint of unease within her, but she held firm in the knowledge that he possessed the means to defend himself if needed.

"I'm not either," she enveloped him in her arms, intensifying her embrace. "Remember what you said," she clung to him tenaciously, "If you go down, we go down together. If something happens to you—" abruptly, he maneuvered her against the wall, his fingers beneath her chin, directing her gaze to his.

"We're going to get them, and all of us will come home." His hand caressed the side of her neck. "Then I'm going to let you beat me in chess," she chuckled, her heart aching, "and take you diving again, but in the Reefs of Ilkiz." He brushed away a falling tear. "And make love to you every night, hold you till you find peace and never let go, even then." With one arm propping him against the wall, she felt safe, as if he were her sword and shield. "We will come back, Azahara Starfall, and yes, it will be difficult, but we will do this together. I'll be by your side the entire time. Remember, I serve my world: you."

With the lump in her throat refusing to dissipate even as she swallowed, she nodded, "I know, thank you—" she took a deep breath, and he sealed her lips with his. This kiss wasn't gentle; instead, it brimmed with unspoken longing and power. He consumed her, leaving no room for anyone but him in that moment. How she yearned to remain entwined like this, to forget everything and let him carry her away.

After a fleeting moment, he withdrew, running his thumb down her lips. "I love you, Sunshine."

"I love you, Jayce."

"Remember our roles." She knew why he was reminding her, "Don't forget."

With a deep breath and a determined nod, she locked eyes with him. "Let's go get them."

Day 181
CHAPTER 47

Jayce had a firm grip on her wrists, keeping them securely behind her back as they emerged from her quarters. Time lost its relevance as he guided her across the hull, and the busy crew kept their eyes focused on their tasks. Although she hesitated to look at them, she knew that stealing one last glance before leaving would serve her well. Their faces would be a reminder of what she needed to come home to. As Carmen, Rowlin, and Alyse came into view, she witnessed their resolve breaking, glossy eyes meeting her own. Her strength to withhold a smile or offer reassurance seemed boundless.

Xol, busily tying a rope near the deboarding dock, didn't lift her gaze. However, the visible strain in her clenched teeth and the struggle to contain her emotions sent a pang straight through Azahara's heart. This was the painful side of love that remained unspoken, the aspect everyone preferred to ignore; it wasn't always sweetness and roses.

Itotaki appeared veiled in a darkened aura for her, and it wasn't because of the absence of sunlight but rather the solitary figure at the end of the dock. A familiar rippled portal stood behind them.

Jayce forcefully moved her in front of him, nearly causing her to stumble. With a quick recovery, she steadied herself.

"You know how to walk," he remarked, his voice devoid of warmth.

She bared her teeth and hissed through them, "I told you I'd come willingly." She attempted to shift, but his grip on her wrists remained unyielding. "Is the grip on my wrists really necessary?"

Closing the distance between them and Jaakobai, Jayce chuckled without humor. "Can anyone truly trust anything you say?" They both knew Jaakobai could hear them, and though hearing Jayce speak to her in such a way wasn't ideal, the necessity of it kept her tongue sharp.

"You're just sour because you failed in getting into my bed," she added, feeling his hand twitch. "Now you'll never get the chance."

"I'm sure the last several months have been quite fun, Commander Latimer," Jaakobai said with a throaty laugh. He wore their signature gold and white fitted armor, featuring a compass on its chest plate. His hair was braided into a half bun, exposing his face without obstruction. The singular scar across his nose was his most recognizable feature, and she couldn't help but despise how similar he looked to Illyan. While all Fae were beautiful in their own right, he was hard to look at.

"Insufferable," he thrust her forward, causing her head to bow and her arm to nearly pop from its socket. When she looked up, Jaakobai was hovering over her. "Hello, Princess."

Her nostrils flared, "Hey, Jaak-ass." Seeing his eyes widen, she relished in his surprise and fury. "Miss m—" The slap was so strong that even Jayce was taken by surprise and unable to keep her from falling to the ground with a loud crack. Her entire face went numb, and she felt like her vision was going to give.

Jayce remained unmoving, showing indifference in her struggle to rise. A soft groan escaped her lips as her hand instinctively reached for her face, the lingering sting palpable.

"I've been waiting to do that for fifteen days," he declared, crossing over to her and seizing a handful of her hair. "Get up." She staggered to her feet, still reeling from the impact. "It seems Ilkiz didn't yield what you sought," his opposite hand finding the freshly struck cheek. A cruel combination of a slap and a pinch made her inhale sharply. "Good, because that would have made things a bit more difficult, and whilst I do enjoy a challenge—"

"Elder Fae," Jayce cut him off, "I appreciate you showing dominance, however, I'm sure the King is waiting. I have also been away for some time, I would like to go home."

Jaakobai shot his eyes at Jayce, and she *hated* the way he was looking at him. Those eyes would suffer the same fate as his tongue. In that moment, a calculating expression flickered across his small-minded countenance, his grip on her hair unyielding. "You are right, the King is waiting." He tapped at her cheek, the pain blinding—he had to have put Magic behind that slap. It lingered far longer than it should have.

"I'll take her," Jaakobai asserted, his arm encircling her shoulders as he guided her toward the portal. With Jayce at her back, they traversed the wëther. "Tell me, Princess, feeling as strong as you did in the winnox?" Upon emerging, she was caught off guard to find themselves not within the King's palace but standing at the entrance of the Kingdom, ascending from the Port.

Jaakobai observed her bewilderment and chuckled. Surrounding them were numerous guards, one of them holding chains in their hands.

"Put your hands out," the guard instructed. She fixed her gaze on the handcuffs, and an instinctual reaction compelled her to take a step back. *If you think I'm removing your restraints, you are wrong, Little Mouse.*

"Your hands girl!"

*Please...*She couldn't willingly be locked back up, she couldn't, *I can't... I can't—*

Strong hands glided down her arms, lifting them into position, and she sensed Jayce pressing against her back. In their eyes, they'd see a Commander assisting in restraining her, but in her heart, she knew he was taking this moment to remind her that he was there. No chains could bind her for long, and the unspoken assurance lingered that if she called to him, he would break her free from any constraint.

It still didn't stop the trembling as the metal locked, and the burden of the chains pulled down on her arms. Jayce distanced himself, leaving her vulnerable as another officer approached. A harsh shiver ran through her as a cuff encircled her neck, connecting to a chain that linked her wrists together.

"Is this necessary?" Jayce inquired, his voice devoid of emotion.

"Oh, yes." Jaakobai affirmed, seizing the relatively short chain and tugging her forward. "Let me tell you a story while we take a stroll, hmm?" His words were directed at Azahara, diverting his attention away from Jayce.

As they began walking up the stairs towards the Kingdom, the White Cloak soldiers stepped outward, giving as much space as they could to the two of them. She couldn't see Jayce, but she knew he was behind her, just unsure of how close.

"I dislike this realm as much as you do," he admitted, her eyebrows knitting together. "When you unleashed, whatever that power was, on the battlefield, you made my job so much easier than I could have imagined." Her gaze swept over the surrounding White Cloaks; there was no doubt they were catching every word. "Killing my father in the chaos, it was too easy. Pinning it on you, and my son, even easier. The King, pfft—easiest to manipulate." His admission triggered a full-body tremor.

She turned her head to fully face Jayce, who steadfastly gazed ahead, avoiding her gaze. Was it possible they weren't registering the gravity of the conversation?

"Princess, they can't hear me. Only you can, for now." Turning back to him, he was smiling down at her, "I just wanted to thank you, and while I had hoped we could have ruled together, watching you die will be satisfying enough. Unless you are having second thoughts?" His hand moved to the small of her back, and across her hip.

"I'd rather give myself to the Yuul," she hissed, shrugging as far away from him as the chain permitted. When his hand dropped, she asked, "Why? Why are you doing all of this?" They approached an archway, and beyond it, a crowd of people came into view.

"You wouldn't understand my reasoning, child, so I won't waste my breath."

"Where are you taking me?" The 'why' of him doing all of this fell secondary at that point. Why was she here? Why were there so many people? Why weren't they already in the presence of the King?

He looked down at her, "I'm illustrating a point and showing you just how hated you are. Ripping away any hope you have to be seen as innocent." Every bone in her body trembled, and as her gaze focused ahead, she witnessed the White Cloaks moving forward, beginning to part the crowd of people going about their day.

As he leaned in, she attempted to step away, but he pulled the chain, forcing her back toward him, "I do hope you lose control."

A chilling sensation enveloped her chest, akin to the sharp prickling of needles. She was hardly aware that he was propelling her forward; all she could sense was an overwhelming wave of fear and anxiety coursing through her entire being. Ilkiz, now relegated to the deepest recesses of her, hissed and writhed. Azahara had pleaded with her to amplify her emotions, to appear weaker deliberately, but in this moment, there was no need for pretense—she was weak.

Numerous eyes bore into her, yet she adamantly avoided meeting a single one of their burning gazes. She felt the intensity of their collective stare, poised to set her ablaze, and she accepted it. The likelihood that some among them had lost someone at the Battle of Sunfall was so profound that she could practically sense the waves of hatred directed at her.

"Is that her?" "That is—" "That's the murderer—" "The killer." The whispers surrounded her like a cacophony, drowning out her own thoughts. "They got her." "Justice!" "Kill her." The crowd was right to be furious, and she couldn't blame them. Regardless of whether they would have acted similarly or not, she was the cause of their profound grief and pain. It wasn't Jaakobai, Goddrick, or the King; it was her. They perceived her as the monster, and now they had the opportunity to unleash their pent-up fury.

"Kill her!" The hushed murmurs escalated into shouted demands. "Lock her up!" Her shoulders quivered, their shouts more piercing than the sudden pain that shot through her head. As she instinctively raised her hand, Jaakobai yanked down the restraints. "Murderer!" Another pang, this time against her arm, prompted her to finally survey her surroundings, where she noticed a rock rolling on the ground.

From the vantage points of buildings, through windows, and lining the roads, a sea of people confronted her. Some clutched rocks, hurling them in her direction, while others merely pointed and unleashed guttural screams. "You killed him!" "He was only a boy!" "That was my son!"

Her resolve was crumbling, and she desired to beg Ilkiz to help. These people didn't understand her pain, they had no idea what she had been through.

"You've found restraint," Jaakobai remarked, stepping beside her. As rocks and filth were flung their way, they bounced off an imperceptible barrier, likely created by his reluctance to be pelted. "Sad for me, but good for these insignificant mortals."

"You are a monster!" "Monster!" "Witch!" "Succubus, straight from Death herself." "Enchantress!" "Evil incarnate!" "Fuck you!" "Burn, witch!"

Jaakobai withdrew, and she observed a man walking past, defiantly raising a fist. Her eyes widened as the man abruptly froze, and she felt the rage inside her intensify. All she desired was to reduce him to ash, and everyone else with him. This Kingdom and its people would crumble into nothing more than dust by the time she was finished.

Yet, that was precisely what Jaakobai desired. He hoped for her to lose control, making his life that much easier.

As quickly as she had reacted to the approaching man, she stopped and turned her head downward. Instead of lashing out physically, he resigned himself to spitting on her.

"Humiliating." Jaakobai commented with condemnation. "Such a powerful woman, reduced to this." The desire to obliterate him, and all of them, surged within her. If she unleashed Ilkiz, no one would survive. They would all discover the true monster they were creating.

Numb and emotionless, she fixed her gaze on the stone floor, deliberately avoiding their accusatory eyes. Yearning to retreat into a different reality, she closed her eyes and inhaled deeply. A surge of hatred coursed through every inch of her being, and she relished it. There would be no saving Jaakobai when this was all done. *Fuck his hands, I'm going straight for his heart.*

"How does it feel?"

"Enlightening." She answered honestly.

"She's innocent!" She let out a gasp. "Give her a chance!" "She ended the war!" "Our Savior!"

Her head lifted as she scanned the crowd, searching in every direction until she fixed her gaze on those who were hollering for her. "Give her a fair trial!" "Let her go!" "Don't silence her!" "Free her!" Calls in her favor now echoed everywhere, as if they had been stifled before and were finally unleashed. No longer confined behind a locked door, they reverberated freely.

"She's a monster!" "You have no room to judge!" "Kill her!" "Save her!"

Her chest rose and fell rapidly as she struggled to catch her breath. Jaakobai, visibly trembling, emitted a frustrated groan.

She didn't need everyone on her side, but the realization that even some wished to see her find innocence brought a steadying calm to her heart. Sensing hands on her arm, she turned to Jaakobai, who wore a mask of anger. "Witch, how did you—" Her eyes narrowed, and though he left his statement unfinished, she deduced that something had occurred.

It came as no surprise when he forcefully tore open another wëther right there in the middle of the streets of Naverra and tossed her through it. The impact was strong enough to send her stumbling down to her hands and knees. Beneath her, a polished floor reflected her image.

A serene silence cocooned her, tempting her to linger on the ground and embrace its tranquility. However, the cold reality of the marble floors beneath her hinted at what would unfold next. She was acutely aware of her surroundings.

"Stand." It was Jayce, his hands firmly gripping her arm, coaxing her back onto her feet.

"Ah, Commander Latimer," As she raised her eyes to see him, bumps lifted across her arms. "Elder Fae, thank you both for bringing this wanted criminal back for her justice." The King occupied his throne, flanked by Karver and several Fae soldiers. She also noticed the Order's Commander, Olaniyan, and a woman adorned in armor reminiscent of what Kaed had once worn—an elf, like him as well.

"Miss Rothwen," Theon, the King, crossed his legs and leaned forward, "Welcome home." Since she last saw him, he had grown a beard, but otherwise, he remained unremarkable with his brown hair and brown eyes.

"Theon," she said, well aware of the folly in addressing the King by his given name alone. Savoring the moment and reveling in his heightened anger and rosy cheeks to his ivory skin, she felt Jaakobai's firm grip on her arm as he forcefully pulled her away from Jayce.

"No need to be disrespectful, Princess." He flung her forward, and to her own surprise, she managed to stay on her feet. "Bring them."

Her heart pounded, assuming that the "them" he referred to were Illyan, Zhal, and Kaed. The prospect of seeing them after so long was both overwhelming and exhilarating. Once they were present, she could set the plan for escape into motion.

However, much to her shock, another set of restraints was presented. These looked different but familiar, and as they unlocked the ones around her wrists, she regarded them with a discerning expression.

While the King addressed Jayce, her focus remained fixed on the cuffs about to secure her. "Commander Latimer, thank you for your service to me. I understand through Jaakobai that this one is quite the handful."

As they were fastened around her, something felt amiss. Her knees grew weak, and the ground approached rapidly. As if her body were being drained of life itself, she struggled to breathe, her forearms resting on her legs to prevent her from collapsing outright.

Please... not again...

"She was your grace. After Itotaki, I had to step back, as she was becoming suspicious. It is why it took so long for an update." His voice was firm as he continued, "However, I was able to convince her after she wasn't able to locate what she was looking for in Ilkiz, to come forward and proclaim her innocence."

Theon merely chuckled.

"Seduced the seducer, hmm?" Jaakobai spoke, his tone tinged with an unsettling uncertainty, as if he harbored doubt about something.

Jayce stepped forward, positioning himself beside her. As she glanced up, her gaze locked onto Karver, who stood unaffected by the unfolding scene before him.

Her body ached, and now she comprehended the nature of these restraints. Even in the twilight, she would recognize these cuffs — gold-plated and pulsating with his power. As she looked up at Jayce, his eyes never strayed down to meet hers.

"Please..." she uttered, a feigned plea that she wasn't entirely convinced was insincere. Did he recognize these restraints as much as she did? Could he no longer sense her window? Was he aware that these were the same chains Goddrick had once used on her?

"Look at me, girl, not him. He cannot help you." Her widened eyes trailed back to Theon, his smile wide. "The people want to see you on trial, but there is no need for that, let's be honest." A laugh echoed, not only from him but from his surrounding subordinates, including Jaakobai and the two Commanders. Karver and Jayce, however, refrained from indulging in the laughter.

"I want to see them," she said with fervor, "allow them freedom, and you can do with me as you see fit."

Ilkiz, she watched Theon deliberate her words. *Are you there?*

"Yes, little one. These restraints do not work on my Power."

It was all she needed to know and did not communicate further with her. The last thing she wanted was for something to slip, and Jaakobai catch on to whatever she was doing.

"You are going to die here today, Miss Rothwen, why does it matter what happens to your friends?"

"It is your choice," she said, settling back onto her legs, her restrained hands resting in her lap. "I can fight, or I can concede. You choose." Despite the strength in her words, her body betrayed her with unmistakable tremors.

"Your grace," Karver intervened, "Let us heed the words of the Goddess."

"I do not believe that she is unkillable, do you see her? She is smaller than most of the whores that aid my desires, and the way she shakes out of fear. With those restraints—"

"Please," she cut him off, "at least, let me see them. Allow me this **one** thing." Her body tilted downward, her forehead pressing against the cold marble, a chilling sensation coursing through her entire being.

A little more suffering, just a little.

Theon let out a disrespectful laugh and snapped his fingers, "They can watch her die then, if that is what she desires."

Mother, if you can hear me now, I pray to you that you keep them safe. Allow for those that I love to live a long, happy life. They deserve peace, and love, and joy. They do not deserve this evil wretched life that I've put them through. Take my strength as your own to allow for them to be protected if I fail, as I have done so many times before. They are the reason I breathe; the reason that I fight; the reason I want to live. Please do not allow for them to be taken from me. Or this world you hold dearest, will be gone. That is a promise.

Footsteps interrupted her prayer, and as she glanced up, Illyan emerged from around a group of Fae soldiers, accompanied by Zhal. Both were gagged and had their arms bound. Zhal had several chains around her, nearly sending Azahara into a frenzy upon the sight. When their eyes met, they started screaming through the folds in their mouths. Seeing them after so long, her body vibrated with pain and rage. The tears streaming down her cheeks were real.

"Illy—Zhal—" Calling for them, and knowing they both could hear her voice, it had her choking on her words. Every part of her itched to get to them, hold them both close and to never allow them to be further than arm's reach. "I'm so sorry…" Her words carried the weight of truth and ache. Despite anticipating this moment, she found herself unprepared for the overwhelming onslaught of emotions.

Especially when she heard his voice call out, "Azahara?"

It was as though her heart ceased to beat, all the air left her lungs, her brain ceased to function, and the blood in her veins drained away, never to return.

As her gaze followed the sound, she found him. His honey-gold hair framed his face, and those emerald eyes, which had captured her from the first moment, once again stole her breath away. He stared at her, as if she were unreal, and it was the first time he had ever laid eyes on her in the flesh. The look on his face resembled shock, and though confusion should have taken over, her own shock overwhelmed all other emotions.

He was alive.

"Kaed—" His name escaping her lips opened the floodgates of her emotions, and she knew that if she had been standing, she would have crumbled instantly. Her body collapsed as her stomach churned and tightened with pure, unfiltered happiness, a sensation so overwhelming that it made her feel sick.

As happiness has always been, it was too fragile to stand against the all-too powerful thing called life.

Don't do this to me… Why…

Just as Kaed had seized all of her attention, now, standing in front of her, was the one person who brought her the most pain. The one who, despite all her fighting and strengthening, always dragged her down to the lowest point. The one who consistently tore away hope and choice from her. He would always be there, and that had been the only constant in her life for the past five hundred years. "Goddrick…" The name sounded frail on her tongue.

"Hello, *manipulator*."

Day 181
CHAPTER 48

A suffocating sensation of drowning overwhelmed her, and she felt as if the room itself was closing in. The cacophony of voices became deafening, and she couldn't escape his haunting voice. *Little Mouse.* She had prepared for every possible scenario, even considering the unlikely event of Kaed being alive. However, she could never have fathomed seeing Goddrick standing just a few feet away from the King.

Her body quivered, driven by the low, rumbling hiss emanating from Ilkiz. He turned to converse with the guards nearest to him, who seized Kaed before descending the few steps that elevated them.

She had to fight, to somehow find clarity in the fact that she was not the weak little girl he had forced to turn his hourglass five hundred years ago. She was not the same person. Yet, as he approached her, towering over her, she felt like the mouse he had made her out to be.

Fear does not discriminate; it comes when she wants it the least.

Ilkiz... Her own thoughts seemed distant.

"*I will kill him.*" Ilkiz seethed. The raw power seared her, and she lurched forward, her chest feeling taut. *"Release me so that I may—"*

Wait... Her eyes turned towards Illyan and Zhal. *Allow me to fight.*

"Elder Fae, I must say, I am not disappointed in your tactics." She detested his voice, and the way it sent ripples of fear through her. When she raised her gaze to him, her lips curled into a snarl. "They don't understand you can't be killed." He halted a few feet before her, and she finally saw Kaed, who was staring at her with an angered expression.

"Look at me." Finding the strength quickly, she looked up at him. "You will never lay as little as your filthy eyes upon him again." His gaze shifted to Jayce, and her body trembled. "Sound familiar—?" She shifted her gaze to him, and as though sensing what was about to happen, her legs were in motion, placing her body between Jayce and Goddrick.

His blade, previously concealed behind his back, now extended toward her. As if it would have pierced Jayce's stomach, it collided with hers. However, instead of penetrating her, scales crawled across her, enveloping her waist and extending up her arms. The blade shattered, crumbling to the floor.

"Karver!" Jayce shouted, and in an instant, the once loyal second-in-command to the King was beside them.

Goddrick gazed deeply into her eyes, and as she felt Power envelop her, she effortlessly pulled apart the restraints at her wrists, as if they were tied with paper. Scales cascaded across her entire body, molding to her frame and granting her a full set of Ilkiz's armor. The white iridescent sheen matched the brilliance of the white marble that surrounded them.

She held Goddrick's gaze, and in those moments, everything around them bled from existence. Only the two of them remained, and time stood still.

"You will pay for what you did to me," she seethed, and with her words, the boom of Ilkiz's roar shattered the room around them. The painted glass of the Keep rocked and cracked.

"My Little Mouse," his teeth bearing as he towered over her, "you will suffer by any means."

The corner of her lip twitched, "I'm going to enjoy ripping you apart."

As the marble crumbled from her sheer force, screams emerged, but those that mattered stayed steadfast. The familiar sounds of fire and water now cracked behind her, accompanied by the smart remarks of Kaen. "Smells like shit, looks like shit. Must be Naverra."

Jayce stepped beside her, and she could feel his wings wrapping around her, his body emanating power. Goddrick took a step back, and she felt the urge to charge after him but knew that her family's safety was above all else.

"Filthy traitors!" Theon rose, his entire being quivering with the intensity of the unfolding scene before him. "I didn't want to believe it, but now that I see the truth with my own eyes, it is undeniable!"

Azahara surveyed the enemies before them, mindful that they were reciprocating the scrutiny toward her family standing beside and behind her.

Jaakobai and his Fae soldiers stepped between them, blocking the King. "Ah—I knew you looked familiar, but those wings, there is no mistaking. The traitor."

She advanced with purpose. "Eyes on me." Jaakobai, caught off guard, quickly shifted his gaze to her. "Good boy." Her family chuckled behind her, but she maintained a stoic expression. "I have no desire to destroy this place and the people of this Kingdom, but I will. Without hesitation. Give me my family, and we can settle this, all of us, beyond these walls, where the only casualties will be you."

The Elder laughed, and even Goddrick chuckled. However, the King did not find humor in her words. "You fucking witch! Weak minded souls easily seduced by your..." He loomed tall behind his guards, flanked by Fae warriors and a god.

As he stumbled over his words, she narrowed her eyes at him. "By my what? Hmm?" Her gaze shifted to Kaed, who seemed to be staring at Goddrick, anger etching his beautiful face. Then she glanced at Illyan and Zhal, who were looking at her in pure awe.

"Seduced by the succubus herself." Jaakobai took a step towards her. "All of them, weak—"

Jayce moved to step forward, but she placed her hand on his chest, momentarily halting him.

"Call me what you will: whore, witch, succubus—*manipulator*." She shook her head and moved her hand down. "It won't make a difference when you are all dead."

"Kill them all," The King said, and that was all she needed to hear.

Goddrick reappeared in front of her in an instant. With a smile, she observed as Jayce grabbed his arm, which was reaching for her neck. With nearly indiscernible strength, Jayce squeezed, and the oily blood she'd come to hate spattered across her face. The god retreated as quickly as he had lunged at her, one of his hands severed and held tightly by Jayce.

"I thought I made myself clear," Hearing him made her body thrive. "You will never touch her again."

With anger lacing his face, Goddrick shook out his arm, the tendrils of his skin and bone pushing through the marred, severed limb, reconnecting a new one in a matter of moments.

She looked to Karver, "Get my family, please." Without hesitation, he vanished. She caught a glimpse of him at the corner of her eye, behind Illyan and Zhal, opening a wëther for them all to jump through, safely returning them behind her.

"Akua, take them back to the Neptune. Xol, Kaen—" She glanced at the Yuul, then at the Spirit Rider, who was pleading with her entire body to fight. "Ready to do some dancing?"

"Fucking finally!" Kaen screamed—literally—and engulfed herself in flames.

"I've been ready." Xol cracked her knuckles.

"On me." With both powerful women beside her, they rushed towards Jaakobai.

A rocketing boom sounded beside her, and she glanced over to see both Karver and Jayce engaged with Goddrick. When she turned back to Jaakobai, his wings were outstretched, those same dragonfly-style wings having grown exponentially since the last time she'd seen him, spanning further than Jayce's. As electricity sparked through his fingers, he threw it at them.

Digging deep, she found the shield that Death's power provided. Just as she had done against Akua, it wrapped around the three of them, the lightning shooting to the ceiling, cracking through the marble. The pure shock across Jaakobai's face would have been satisfying enough, but as they reached him and Xol connected her fist with his cheek, she rejoiced internally. His head nearly tore from his body with the sheer force, and if it hadn't been for his wings, he would have gone straight into the King and his guards.

Kaen was surrounded by flames, and as she tossed her hands outward, the fire engulfed the space around the Fae soldiers. Even with Magic of their own, unless they wielded water, they would burn.

Jaakobai stood before Azahara, his curved Fae blade swinging outward, surrounded by a purple hue. Dropping to her knees, she narrowly missed the blade. With a forceful kick to his shin, he cried out, but to her surprise, his bone didn't break.

Narrowing her eyes, she disappeared from the floor just as Jaakobai's blade came down at her. When she reappeared, the three of them were circling Jaakobai, while the Fae soldiers pulled their own blades, their gazes shifting between them.

Sensing Azahara looking towards her, Xol narrowed her eyes. "Go, Kaen and I got this."

He remained her priority, and she appreciated Xol for understanding that. With a nod, Azahara turned her attention beyond the ongoing fight. Searching quickly in the sea of soldiers, she called out, "Kaed!" Her heart swelled at the sight of his eyes on her, filled with life. Suppressing the urge to let her emotions take over, knowing that crying now would only hinder her in saving him, she pushed back those emotions and enveloped herself in Ilkiz's Power. The purple flames caused the soldiers surrounding Kaed to seize up.

As she took the first step toward him, Azahara sensed a powerful strike coming from her side, prompting her to disappear once again. The resounding crack of the floor shattering in the place where she had just stood sent a tremor crawling up her legs.

"Using our dyspoxii against me, Little Mouse?" Goddrick roared.

She honestly had no idea it was that she was using, but it made sense. The instances where she found her mind and body placing her in a different location at that exact time, she was tapping into the dyspoxii. "Here I thought I was just really fast," she quipped. The instant transition from one place to another—it was that at work.

As she stood, standing mere feet from where he had attacked, she bore her teeth, "What are you doing here, Goddrick?!" She dared look for Jayce, wondering what had happened, only to see him pulling Karver from a pile of rubble.

"Bringing a murderous witch to justice."

"You sound bitter, did someone hurt you?" Her nostrils flared as she readied herself.

He roared in frustration once more. This time, she had no chance to evade; with a resounding crash, her body slammed against the wall, nearly twenty or so feet away. Slithering across her cheek, Ilkiz's scales receded. Thankfully, they had absorbed most of the impact, preventing her from losing her entire jaw to his massive punch.

"What did I say?" On his left, Jayce extended his hand, and had Goddrick not evaded, she could only imagine the devastation he would have faced. Utilizing the dyspoxii, the space around his former position collapsed entirely upon itself. The floor trembled, and even the air was transformed into sparks of crystallized elements. He had obliterated the space into nonexistence, leaving behind a scooped-out depression in the marble ground.

At the sound of a cry, both she and Jayce turned to witness Jaakobai's hand gripping Kaen's neck. Just as they prepared to intervene, water enveloped the Elder Fae and his soldiers. The heat surrounding Kaen began to boil the liquid, and though they couldn't hear their screams, the agonizing contortions sent a shiver down Azahara's spine.

As Jayce stepped beside her, she felt the reassuring brush of his arm against hers, bringing a much-needed sense of calm. While anger had fueled her determination, the knowledge that he was okay and prepared to fight by her side provided a renewed strength. Goddrick inhaled deeply, and an ominous black aura enveloped his skin, a sight all too familiar.

"Why..." She asked him again, "Why are you aiding them?"

He held no title, like the Goddess of War or the God of Might—holding no connection to the mortal world beyond its people. Though he might have once been worshipped, he meant nothing to these people now, particularly once her voice echoed the truth about who he was and what he had done to her.

"You will find my previous kindness better than what is coming for you, Azahara." The shrill feeling that traveled down her spine upon hearing her name was worse than being called a little mouse.

Jayce took a step to him, "Keep her name out of your filthy mouth, boy."

Goddrick looked at him, and the pure, unfiltered hate in them was like daggers.

"Keep your fucking eyes on me," she said, moving forward and stepping in front of Jayce. "Those eyes, I want them to watch me as I send you to the Oblivion."

With his power pulsating off of him, he looked back at her, and smiled, "Az—"

He didn't even get the first syllable out before Jayce was slamming him to the marble below, his body crumbling below the pressure.

The smile that crossed her face, it was crazed, and she felt as though she was embodying Kaen in that moment. Even as Goddrick used the dyspoxii to retreat back, she found humor in that second, he was *retreating.*

As satisfying as the moment felt to embrace, her smile faltered as she observed him. Goddrick had the power to obliterate this entire structure, to annihilate most everyone in mere moments. The question echoed in her mind: Why hadn't he? He hadn't hesitated in Itotaki.

Jayce once again attempted to collapse the space around Goddrick with his Magic, but the elusive dyspoxii was too swift. While she knew he was frustrated, he didn't flinch, just turned his head to the god to see him.

"Let me," she rubbed her hands together, "Get the Fae's hands for me." He regarded her with a devilish smile before disappearing.

Her outstretched hand conjured a ball of liquid power, following Kaen's teachings. With precision, she hurled it directly at Goddrick, who underestimated the intense heat of Ilkiz. As he raised his arm to swat it away, the molten liquid clung to him, devouring his limb like a relentless disease, spreading rapidly.

"I want to see you suffer for all eternity for the things you did to me!" Despite the echoes of pain in her voice, it carried the power she had endured torture to obtain.

Hearing him scream would be the single most powerful feeling she would ever desire to have over, and over again. As he struggled against the encroaching fire, she materialized in front of him, all the armor shifted to her fist as she delivered a powerful blow to his face. He was propelled backward with such speed that even her own eyes struggled to track his trajectory amidst the billowing dust.

A second scream, Jaakobai's, echoed in the background. While she pressed on to deliver the final blows to Goddrick, she glanced at Jayce who was standing over a bleeding Jaakobai—both hands now removed from his arms.

She was overtaken by pure, unfiltered joy as she catapulted herself over a pile of rubble toward Goddrick, a broad smile etched on her face. As much as she aspired to exude the strength and stoicism of Xol, she couldn't deny the sheer happiness that surged within her at the sight of their suffering – a joy she had longed for.

"Please!" A voice unfamiliar to her reached her ears, prompting her to swiftly shift her gaze and turn toward the source. A scream, an urgent plea that stirred a sense of urgency within her. "Someone! It's—" She cursed under her breath, hastening toward the pile of rubble. As it gradually cleared, she spotted a hand peeking out from beneath two pillars, and her eyes met those of the female elf who had once stood beside General Olaniyan.

"Shit—" She picked up her pace, and when she reached her, she put her back against one of them and began lifting. The weight wasn't limited to just one pillar; several other pieces of the ceiling had collapsed, putting her strength to the ultimate test.

Shifting her stance, she engaged her legs and exerted all her strength to lift the pillar overhead. A primal scream echoed through the room as she hurled it, the clash against the floor sending tremors across the space. Without hesitation, she moved on to the next. While it wasn't as heavy, her body strained to maintain the exertion, her arms trembling as she lifted it above her head.

"Move! Now!" She screamed, to only watched as the Elf looked beyond her, "Move!" She said again, confused at her immobile body.

"Kill her! Now!"

"What?" She said, her arms trembling, "Move damn it—" A searing pain rocked through her chest, and though the sensation was all too familiar, she was still taken aback when she glanced down to find an arrow lodged between her breasts.

"What..."

"Again! Hurry!" Confusion ripped through her as another arrow attempted to pierce through her, but her scales reacted in time, sending it ricocheting across the room.

Looking down at the woman, Azahara stared deep into her green eyes. She had tried to save this person, and still, she sought her death. Feeling pain beyond the arrow, her body trembled, and her expression hardened. Without a single bit of remorse, she shifted the pillar forward, watching as the Elf looked up at her with pure terror in her eyes, and let it go. Her cries were silenced nearly immediately, and the sound of flesh and bone being crushed under its weight didn't even faze her.

"No!" The voice that screamed, however, shattered her resolve. When she turned to find her assailant, all her strength and willpower were drained away.

Standing there, with his bow cocked, was Kaed.

She blinked, her body fighting for ownership with an external force trying to take her down. Was it the arrow? Was it the pain in her heart? *What is happening...*

Kaed released the arrow, and just as before, scales slipped across her skin, sending it flying elsewhere. He had attempted to hit her neck, to silence her.

"You monster!"

She released her breath, "What... did you say?"

Day 181
CHAPTER 49

The space around them constricted, bearing down on her senses. *This can't be happening,* she thought, a surreal tableau that seemed ripped from the fabric of a nightmare. The arrow lodged in her chest tightened its grip, a tangible reminder of the harrowing reality. His gaze, laden with a venomous blend of hatred and fear, pierced through her, inflicting a deeper wound than the physical pain she was feeling.

Her face contorted in anguish, a portrait of suffering, but he remained indifferent. Preparing another arrow, his intent was clear. With a cold detachment, he unleashed the projectile, his eyes never leaving hers. She raised her hand, intercepting the lethal trajectory just as it grazed her forehead. The arrow's tip traced a crimson line down her nose, staining her parted lips with the bitter taste of her own blood.

"Kaed," her voice barely a whisper, trembled with a mixture of confusion and pain, "Why..."

He cast his bow aside, a metallic thud echoing in the charged silence. From his hip, he drew a sword with a golden hilt that gleamed in the sunlight streaming through the windows. The radiant glow momentarily blinded her as he charged forward with an intensity that matched the escalating tension in the air.

She shook her head, an indescribable pain tearing through her heart like never before. Her legs betrayed her, and she crumpled, helpless, watching him approach step by step. The once beautiful face, the one that had brightened entire rooms with his smile and chastised her for her recklessness, now contorted with pure rage. The symbol of bravery that had been her anchor was now nothing but a vessel for fear, all directed at her.

As his blade descended, her hands instinctively clamped over it, halting its deadly trajectory just inches from her chest. Her fingers bore the sting of the blade's edge, its tip menacingly close to piercing her. He aimed directly for her heart—the very heart that had beaten for him, the one that had killed thousands for him, the heart he had sworn to protect and love for eternity.

"Why," she asked once more, desperation lacing her words.

"You did this to me!" His voice felt distant, a far cry from the gentle, caring Elf she had come to love. It resonated with a bitterness that echoed through the space between them. "You took my life from me!"

"I don't—" Heat welled behind her eyes, and though she was on the brink of tears, he showed no remorse for his words or the actions he took against her. "—understand."

"My life! You took my life! You filthy witch. You destroyed it." The accusation hung heavy in the air, each word a searing indictment that shattered the fragile connection they once shared.

She released the blade gripped in her hands, the pressure he was applying allowed for him to cut right through. He flinched, visibly taken aback by her unexpected compliance as the steel pierced her. With hands bloodied and trembling, she reached for his cheeks before he could withdraw.

"I'm so sorry—" Tears streamed down her cheeks, her words choked with emotion as the blade cleaved through her heart, causing her to cough. "I never meant to hurt you... I only ever wanted to protect you."

"You are a monster," he spat out, turning the blade in his hands.

"Please... don't do this... I love you—" she looked down at his hands, which were stark white, attempting to carve her heart from her body.

"You deserve to die for what you did!"

Shaking her head, her entire body vibrating with a mix of fear and regret, she whispered, "You were always afraid of me..."

As Kaed prepared to use all his might to silence her, she uttered a faint, desperate plea, "Jayce..."

The air reverberated as Kaed vanished from her sight, replaced by Jayce who swiftly enveloped her in a protective embrace. His wing cocooned around her, his face etched with pain. Blood was scattered across him, but it didn't look like his, *thank the skies.*

As approaching footsteps echoed, Jayce shifted his gaze from her to Kaed, who was regaining composure and heading back their way.

"Kaed, come on, we need to go—" Jayce's urgent call hung in the charged air. However, as Kaed stooped to retrieve his bow and cock an arrow, Jayce's expression morphed from concern to bewilderment. "What..."

When the arrow was released toward them, Jayce deftly swatted it away with his wing, narrowing his eyes at Kaed.

Jayce... We need to go, she slipped through his window.

"*Kaed—*"

Leave him.

As she said the words, Goddrick appeared beside Kaed. They were **both** rearing to attack again. Side by side, they stood, an unsettling image of an unexpected alliance that cut deeper than any physical wound. The sword lodged in her heart was not the only source of pain; seeing her tormentor and rapist standing beside the man she loved, as though they were allies, that inflicted wounds on her soul.

"Kaed, please. Come with us," Jayce pleaded one last time.

She coughed, blood filling her mouth. The blade, still wedged in her chest, preventing her body from healing through it. With a feeble hand raised toward Kaed, Jayce mirrored the gesture.

Goddrick extended his arm, as if shielding Kaed. A smirk played at the corners of the god's lips, signaling her defeat once again.

"Jayce, please—" her words were muffled by the blood welling in her throat, and in that moment, they vanished. The wëther opened and closed in a heartbeat, and she was greeted by the scent of saltwater and the rush of fresh air.

Day 181
CHAPTER 50

"Why did you do this to me?"
I found myself in a disorienting space, suspended between the familiar life I knew and the elusive one I desired. Caught in the interstice of time and its fate, I struggled to comprehend my surroundings. I've never been here before, and I wondered if it was the power of the three world elements that had sent me to this place. Unlike Purgatory, this place was bright and filled with air that tasted sweet, it resembled Paradise, yet a mirrored version designed to deceive those daring enough to traverse the fate-binding line between worlds.

As my bare feet made contact with the ground, water rippled around my toes, casting its reflections across the endless expanse. The sky, or perhaps a ceiling, displayed hues of blues and pinks, adorned with splashes of white.

"You took my life." Kaed said, and while he never appeared in front of me, I knew he was saying those things directly to me. "I read your letter."

"I want to die." My voice raw and woven with pain.

"You are the villain, Azahara." I hated the way my name sounded coming from him, with all that hate and anger. "You deserve to suffer."

"You won't even let me explain..." There were no tears that came, even though I wanted to cry. The fear that if I didn't, I would explode and take whatever there was left of my life with me.

"There is no room for explanations from a murderous monster."

I stumbled, my knees colliding with the floor, a soft splash accompanying the impact. As I peered down into the water, expecting to catch a glimpse of my reflection, there was nothing but ripples dissipating from the disturbance.

"You once told me that you would choose me. Then, tomorrow, in this lifetime, and the next." There was silence, and so I continued, "Choose me over them, and I can explain everything. Allow me to fix this."

"You truly are a manipulator," his words cut deep, the pain unbearable. I couldn't fathom a worse feeling. "I knew what you were, yet I still fell for your lies."

"I never lied to you!" I screamed, and the once-beautiful place around me cracked and began to shatter. My sanctuary, my lifeline, was crumbling. "I love you! I fucking love you so much. Don't do this, please!"

"I will not stop until you are dead. For everything you have done to me, and the people I've sworn to protect."

"Because of your duty..." My breaths came heavy, and despite the ample air, my mind wrestled with the notion of suffocation. "You... You coward..."

I don't think he spoke again, and I wasn't sure if I had blocked him out or if he had vanished. In this place, I contemplated trapping myself—a realm of solitude, walking the line between this world and the ones beyond. Here, I could avoid hurting another soul. The pain would be minimal, and I could come to terms with the loneliness. It was warm, a comforting warmth without being overbearing.

"Please, Azahara, don't do this. Allow me to heal you!"

"Jayce." He was trying to save me.

Don't fall back into the darkness. I needed to allow him to help me. I couldn't run away, as desperately as I wanted to.

"Baby, heal, it's okay, wake up. Come back to me."

As if being torn through an unending portal of blinding lights, she plummeted, the sensation of seconds stretching into an eternity of minutes, hours, and days. The boundless vortex carried her through a kaleidoscope of potential lifetimes, none of them her own. Her mind struggled to grasp the unfolding chaos, and she instinctively closed her eyes, afraid of witnessing realities she didn't want to confront.

"Come back, we love you—I love you—don't leave us." His voice became the lifeline she desperately clung to, the singular thread that could rescue her from the chaos within herself.

"Ladybug please!" "Sunshine." "Aza!" "Ounr!"

Finally finding herself back in her body, she slowly peeled her eyes open, keeping them at half-mast. A loud, harmonious sigh reverberated around her, and several faces came into view, though she didn't fixate on any one in particular.

Jayce pulled her up against his chest, his hand gripping her arm. She could feel his Magic pouring into her, and she leaned her head against him.

"Sweetheart, allow yourself to heal, please," his voice carried pain.

"He..." her words emerged, shattered and almost in a whisper, filled with agony, "he tried to kill me..."

His hand tightened, "I know—"

"He hates me." Tears traced a path across her temples, her gaze shifting to Jayce's deep amethyst eyes, now glossed over. "He called me... a monster."

He lifted her, wrapping his arms around her as he rocked her gently. She sobbed against him, feeling strong arms enveloping her from behind, another set snaking around her head. More bodies pressed in, creating a nest of warmth around her.

"Help..." she whimpered, her voice desperate. "Help me..." Her grip on Jayce never faltered. "It hurts."

Her cry resonated so forcefully that even Ilkiz whimpered in response. In the aftermath, the Dragon herself seemed to join in the lament. The agony and torment enveloping her heart tugged at the threads of their bonded spirits. This pain surpassed any death she had endured before—drowning herself in the sea, cutting herself till she bled out, the rope around her neck, the blade through her heart—none of it compared to this.

The pain was suffocating, while bringing her back to life. A back and forth that would never end. It would continue to destroy her, only to repair itself, preparing to repeat the cycle once again.

Jayce... please...

"Tell me what you need."

Put me to sleep, I don't want to feel this. I can't. I want to die. It hurts too much...

Without a word, she sensed him guiding her backward, the surrounding figures fading away as his hand tenderly traced her cheek. The currents of Magic shifted, pulling her back into the comforting embrace of darkness. Like a soothing touch, it offered a semblance of peace, and the pain began to ebb. A layer of warmth surrounded her, and in that moment, all she yearned for was to linger in this tranquil embrace indefinitely.

"You are a fucking monster."

After two days of continuous sleep, she awoke to find Jayce by her side, his soft eyes reflecting nothing but pure love. She had feared that he would have sympathy or pain marring his face when she saw him, but thankfully, it was anything but. He deserved to feel neither of those things and remembering how hard he had tried to get Kaed to come with them, he didn't deserve to feel pain. He had done everything right, and she wanted nothing more than to shield him from any hurt.

Her arms opened, and he promptly enveloped her, pulling her into his lap and wrapping his arms around her waist. Although she felt markedly better than after the events in the Kingdom, the lingering pain in her heart stayed.

As she tightened her arms around him, she pressed her forehead into the crook of his neck. His wings unfurled, and without hesitation, encircled both of them, curling around her arms and cocooning them in their embrace. The ensuing darkness that enveloped them further pacified her. The wings quivered and shifted, settling against her skin.

"You aren't hurt, right?" she finally whispered against his skin.

"Physically, no, I'm not hurt," he replied, his arms tightening around her, drawing them as close as possible. "But my soul hurts for you. It's beyond words." Determined not to cry, she nuzzled against his shoulder before tilting her head back slightly, just enough to look up at him.

"I don't want you to hurt at all, please," she murmured, bringing her hand around his back, placing it on his neck, and then to his cheek. "How is everyone else?"

"Worried," he answered promptly, his hand coming up to rest over hers. "There is no rush, but they want to see you. Karver, Illyan, Zhal, and the rest of the crew. Though I think those first three should take precedence."

She nodded, subtly leaning away from him as if to rise, yet he held her firmly in place. "Wait," his hand gently lifted her chin. "You don't need to go right now." Her lip trembled, and she couldn't quite fathom why. The purity of his expression and the unconditional care he emanated made her feel all the right things in that moment. "Stay with me, just for a little, please." His hand traced along her jaw, behind her ear, and pulled her into a kiss. She didn't pull away or hesitate, only letting out a soft sob as she leaned into the embrace.

Tears streamed down her cheeks, and as he poured his passion into the kiss, she tasted the salt in her mouth. It wasn't just her who had gone through hell that day; he had too. Jayce would never say it, but witnessing what they did to her must have torn him to pieces. Failing to save the one person in this world who mattered as much to him as he did to her was his own version of torture.

They kissed for what felt like an eternity, and he only leaned away to pull her back into his arms when she was out of breath. His fingers laced through her hair, and as he took a deep breath, he rocked her ever so slightly. "There will be no more kindness from me to those that hurt you. No plan worth enacting that would have them harm you," he declared. He released the air in his lungs and nuzzled his head against her neck. "Tell me to go and destroy them all."

"*Me too—*" Ilkiz boomed in her head.

Ilkiz...

The air in her lungs got caught in her throat, "Jayce..."

"Send me to destroy our enemies; command me so that I may put their heads on spikes as reminders that anyone who even **thinks** about harming you—" He pulled her back, his eyes filled with rage and unfiltered power, "will suffer that same fate."

She closed her eyes, envisioning the lifeless gazes of those whose heads would stand as a stark warning. Their severed heads would serve as symbols of what awaited anyone who dared to threaten her. They were not only a threat to those who might challenge her but also a warning to the gods themselves—a reminder of what they would face if they ever dared to come for her. It was a potent message, resonating not only in the divine realms but also across both the Fae and mortal realms.

With unwavering confidence, she knew that Jayce and Ilkiz would be her protectors, standing by her side through it all. It wasn't just them; Xol, the twins, Zhal, Illyan—they would all be there, alongside Alyse and the crew.

While she yearned for that more than words could convey, she shook her head. His strength didn't waver; he watched her with the same determination in his eyes. "I need you here, with me," she sighed. "If we are to destroy our enemies, it will be together. I won't send you, or anyone—" *that includes you, Ilkiz,* "to fight my battles. We will do this together; there is no other way."

That handsome smile she loved crossed his lips, and with it, his expression relaxed.

"We will destroy them," she said with confidence. "We."

"We will," his hand rested on her cheek as he placed his forehead against hers. "My girl, protecting an ancient Dragon, a Yuul, a very old Fae—will you ever let us protect you?"

She nodded, "You all safeguard what is most important to me, you protect what keeps my heart beating: Each other." He kissed her again, and she was lost between him and the bed beneath her, his body engulfing her and claiming what was his.

While she could have stayed entangled in the sheets with Jayce indefinitely, she knew there were people she needed to see. She had asked him to call in Karver first, and then she would see Illyan and Zhal.

As the door opened, she stood from the bed and watched the dark, beautiful Fae saunter through. Jayce crossed the room before she did, wrapping his arms around his brother in a near-death grip of a hug. The sounds of their hands patting each other's backs echoed through the room, and she smiled so widely that her eyes began to sting with the tears brimming in them.

Karver then pushed Jayce aside, "Alright that's enough, let me see our girl."

She laughed and ran to him, his arms wrapping around her waist and spinning her several times. Tears ran down her cheeks as she clung to his neck with such a grip, fearing he'd portal away and be gone again.

"Mmm! Mm, mm!" He hummed and held her tight. "That was torture, just so you know." His voice felt like the Mother telling stories to her children. "I blame the overbearing one for keeping me away for so long." She could hear Jayce groan.

"Do you know, anytime I talked to him, he would never ask how I was doing, but go straight to you? Sheesh—chopped liver here," Jayce said playfully.

Karver put her down, moving her hair away from her face. "It's good to see you and finally be back at your side."

She released a laugh that intermingled with soft bouts of tears. "I'm so glad you're home, Karver." That made him smile wider, but it quickly turned to a scowl as her fist connected with his chest, and he winced. "That's for lying to me though."

"Ouch—" he rubbed the spot of impact, "Did you hit him? He made me keep the secret."

She glanced over at Jayce, who raised his hands. "Please, I'm fragile, remember?"

Rolling her eyes, she returned her gaze to Karver, maintaining a smile. He sighed and placed both of his hands on her shoulders. "I'm so, so sorry—" her expression shifted. "I had no idea what was going on. Jaakobai's Magic is far stronger than my own, and I couldn't even tell I was in his masking ward." He sighed, and she took a shaky breath. "I wasn't even aware they had your family. The King must've been suspicious of me, and with Goddrick knowing who Jayce was, that is likely where it stemmed from."

She shook her head, "Don't apologize, I know you would have done whatever you could if you knew. To be honest, I'm glad you stayed in the dark. It likely kept you safe."

Seeing Jayce shake his head and step beside her, his arm coming across her shoulders. "Always protecting everyone, my goodness."

Karver swatted him away, "Hey, it's my time, back it up lover boy." The three of them harmoniously laughed.

"Why don't you two catch up," she suggested, slipping away from the two of them. "I need Illyan and Zhal—Karver, we can chat afterward—oh, also." She looked between the two of them. "Be nice to Xol, I swear it, or I'll throw you both off this ship." The two of them laughed again, and as she was leaving, she saw them embrace once again. They wouldn't say it, but they missed one another more than they'd admit.

Closing the door behind her, several faces turned to her, none of which were Illyan and Zhal. Putting her hand up to Carmen and Alyse, she shook her head, mouthing "after." They both seemed to understand but gave her the biggest smiles and eyes that threatened tears. Alyse, bless her, pointed toward the helm.

She moved quickly, the soft pitter-patter of her feet against the wood echoing behind her. As she took the steps up, the all-too-familiar seven-foot-tall, ebony-skinned warrior stood with her hands crossed over her chest. The lanky, nearly the same height, pale Fae leaned over the ledge looking out to the vast sea. They both looked exhausted, but they were alive. That was what mattered more than anything.

With another step in their direction, Zhal turned her head with her normal stoic, uncaring expression. That was, until her eyes connected with hers. The pure shock that turned to actual tears in her eyes hit her like a rushing horse, causing her knees to weaken.

Her feet kept her in motion, closing the distance between them. As she got closer, Illyan stood and turned as well. The few feet between them were crossed with a charge, and she launched herself up and into Zhal's arms. She gripped around her neck as though it were her own lifeline, holding on as if her very existence depended on it. Zhal's arms were tight around her waist, and as though forgetting her strength, she slightly loosened, likely fearful that she would injure her.

Illyan was there, their arms finding her hips and holding her from behind. When Zhal felt him, she lowered her, and they cocooned her between them. Her feet dangled, and she was once again reminded of her shortness compared to these two; and she loved it.

"Aza..." Zhal whispered against her, "I—"

Azahara put her hand up to the back of her head, brushing down her braided hair and cupping the back of her neck. "I know... gods, I know—I'm so sorry for ever leaving."

"We missed you, so much. By the Mother, we missed you." Illyan said through their tears. Feeling them tremble, she slowly released Zhal, and she conceded. Allowing her to turn then and embrace Illyan, who placed one hand on her head and the other behind her back.

Zhal took Illyan's place behind her, arms wrapping around her waist and keeping herself close. They stood like that, for several beats, allowing the moment to sink in, that they were finally back together after so many days apart. They had so much to catch up on, and she wanted to know everything that happened, but for now, she only had one question that needed answering...

When she pulled away, they both took one of her hands, "When did Kaed..." She bit her lip, and swallowed back the lump that was forming, "When did he wake up?"

Illyan shook their head, "We have no idea. When they found us, Kaed was still in that frozen state. We were just as surprised when he walked out as you were."

Zhal squeezed her hand, "We would have never left him." Her words sent a chill down her back, and her eyebrows furrowed.

"I— I know, it's okay." Surprisingly, she didn't begin to break down. While that pain in her heart still lingered, having them here with her kept the bleeding at bay. She shook her head and leaned back towards them both. They each wrapped their arms around her.

Illyan asked, "What now?"

With a resounding sigh, Azahara rested her head against Illyan's chest, looking out at the deck where Jayce and Karver were stepping out of her quarters. His eyes immediately found her and gave her a smile. Around him, Xol, Alyse and the rest of the crew were gathering. She could see Kaen, who had a few bumps and bruises, but alive thankfully, and Akua.

Everyone was alive.

They were heading back to Ilkiz now, nothing but the sea around them, running from the threat that would plague her for centuries if allowed.

Leaning back from them, she looked between their gazes.

"Rest," she whispered, sensing the surge of power tingling between her fingertips and the raw energy coursing under her skin, "I fear our battle has only just begun."

Chapter 51
Kaed Blackfyre

Kaed had his fingers gripping through his hair, sweat pillowing at his forehead. He hadn't even realized he was down on his knees, the strength in them weak if not present at all. There were several hands on him, trying to assist in any way they could. Feeling nauseous, he put his hand over his mouth, trying to fight back the vomit that was threatening to show itself. *That witch*, whatever she had done to him several days ago, still affected him nearly four days later.

After too long, the effects began to disappear, and he began to feel some semblance of normal. He pushed to his feet and stood.

"Commander Blackfyre, are you all right?" When he looked over, it was an officer with the White Cloaks, his hand gripping his shoulder. "We can alert—"

"No, I'm fine." His voice stern and held no room for further questions. "Thank you."

The last week had been trying, but none more so than having to hear her through his mind. Who had given her that right? After everything that she had done, why would she even try to attempt to convince him? Had he not made it clear to her by nearly killing her that she was unwanted?

After waking from being **dead**, to find himself back in the Kingdom with his mother and, who he now knew as Goddrick, waiting for him, nothing made sense. It had all been too much to comprehend, but as they both began their tale of the previous year that seemed to be a complete fog, it all circled around one individual that had completely ripped away his life: Azahara.

Even just thinking about her name made him sick.

His fist knocked rapidly on the door at which was his destination.

"Come in," a male voice called, and Kaed entered quickly.

Within the spacious room in the Keep, stood Goddrick, and to his right, a female Elf. The room was lit by the wide-open window, the light bouncing off the gold accents in the room. When the god turned to him, he smiled, "Ah—Kaed, thank you for coming. Have you met Zephyra?" The female turned and smiled at him. While she was beautiful, long brunette hair that reached down to her hips, stunning slanted gray eyes and perfectly pointed ears, nothing sparked his interest.

"It's a pleasure, Zephyra." Kaed bowed his head politely, and she did the same. Her bright red lips stayed smiling as she took him in.

"The pleasure is all mine," she tucked her hair behind her ear sheepishly.

"If you will excuse us, Zephyra."

She nodded, and made her way around Kaed towards the door. He turned to watch her go, and something tore at his stomach for taking a second glance. A ripple thrummed through his chest, and he brought his gaze back to Goddrick.

"Beautiful, isn't she? She provided us with some good information and has become quite the asset."

"Yes, very much so," He moved further into the room, and didn't question the information. There was already too much for him to unpack, having every piece of detail broken down would only weigh on him more.

Goddrick took a seat, gesturing for him to take the one adjacent from him, and crossed his legs. While he had no interest in men in the slightest, Goddrick was quite the figure. He exuded ethereal prowess, and when looking at him, one would know he was not of this world.

"How are you?" Goddrick asked.

"Not well," He answered truthfully, "Whatever she did to me by way of reaching through my mind is still plaguing me today. The memories you helped me get back, they are still so shattered."

Goddrick clicked his tongue against his teeth and sighed, "I know, for that I am sorry." He was so genuine, and the thought that the witch would try to spin every evil thing she had done on a god, astounded him. They were there to protect the mortal realm, not seek its destruction. "When she gave her blood to you, she had the power of not only a god but that of

Death. It will be hard, if not impossible, for me to bring them back as they once were."

He shook his head, "You do not need to apologize, ever." Putting his head into his hand, he groaned, "I just want to understand what I am up against, and to make sure that she can't slither her way back into my mind. Turning me back into her...puppet."

The god held sympathy in his expression, "I, too, was once a slave to her seduction, Kaed, and I am a god. She holds more power than that which was given to her."

"How, though? I just don't understand." He was angry, not at Goddrick, but at Azahara. "Why me?"

A pained expression crossed Goddrick's face, "It was all to get her where she is now. You had connections that she didn't. She played everyone like a fiddle, and no one would stop her. I mean, did you see her?"

Kaed hated that the moment he saw her, his knees felt weak. She **was** the epitome of beauty and grace. When she saw him, it was as though she was throwing herself at him, and he was ready to do the same. His heart felt light, as though elevated beyond this realm. He felt like he loved her, but Goddrick had warned him of the lingering effects of her power on him. That she had seduced him into taking her to bed, *Kaed, fuck*—. His head shook violently, a memory seeping through.

He felt Goddrick lean towards him, "My blood will counteract hers, all you need to do is drink it. I know that is strange but, it will help." He was grabbing a glass from the table closest to them, his nail drawing a line across his thumb, drawing thick black liquid. Draining some into the cup, he handed it to him.

Kaed took it, but just looked at it, "Will it ever stop?"

"Probably not," he confessed. "Not until she's dead at least."

"I stabbed her through the heart," Kaed spat, anger lining his words, "Yet she lived. What kind of creature—"

Goddrick cleared his throat, interrupting him, "She's equivalent to a god now, no mortal weapon will kill her. Death will not separate her from this existence." He leaned back then, looking out the window beyond Kaed's shoulder. "You are going to play a pivotal role in her demise, Kaed, but it will not be easy."

He once again looked down at the glass with the blood of a god swirling in it, "How can I, a mere half-breed elf, kill a so-called god?"

"You can't," He watched as Goddrick laced his fingers together, "So, I will take her away from these realms, where she can't hurt anyone ever again. Imprison her, as I was for centuries."

Kaed felt a strange conflict build in him at her being imprisoned.

"Your role will be a bit different." There was a brief pause before he continued, "She *will* come for you."

He felt his nostrils flare, and his body trembled, "I don't understand…" his grip on the glass felt too strong, and he feared shattering it in his grasp. "Why?"

"She loves you, in her own twisted way. She'll try to convince you that what you had was real. Try to make me out to be the source of her turmoil." Goddrick was so matter of fact that he didn't need his elf trait of knowing the truth to know he was speaking it. "She likely has done that with everyone around her, played the victim—played innocent to her darkness. They don't understand that at the end of all of this, she plans to wipe them all out. Reshape this reality for a new one."

His eyes widened, "What? Like—what Rah did nearly seven thousand years ago?!" His voice was raised, and he had to take a step back, or he would begin to lose control of his emotions.

"Exactly like that," The confirmation was shattering.

"Why—this realm needs fixing, but it isn't broken. Why would she—"

"Because, Kaed, she feels this world has brought down upon her only heartbreak and pain—"

"Okay?" He quickly cut him off, "Everyone has heartbreak and pain. She just murdered my mother without remorse, and I don't want to completely wipe out millions."

Goddrick nodded, staying calm, and Kaed wished he had his resolve, "You are strong and a male with a clear mind. Capable of controlling your emotions. She feels everyone has wronged her enough that this reality shouldn't exist and should be rewritten with her in mind."

While Kaed disagreed with Goddricks remark, he understood its meaning.

Goddrick continued, "I don't believe why she is doing it matters, just that she is. All she needs now is Magic."

When he had asked what type of Magic she used on Goddrick to subdue him, his confession that it was the might of Ilkiz, he nearly lost it. This world, Magic, Power—it was all too much. None of it should exist, especially when someone like Azahara could wield it for evil.

"Jaakobai is still recovering, and while they are attempting to reattach one hand, the other was not recovered." Kaed had nearly passed out watching that huge Fae rip both of Jaakobai's hands off.

"She warned you not to touch her." Were the words he said just as they were torn from his person, as though nothing more than pulling a leaf from its branch. He, along with Azahara, terrified him.

"That Fae, the one that did that to Jaakobai, who is he?" He asked, not necessarily carrying, but when he came for Azahara after he'd stabbed her, the way he held her was—

"Another puppet in her play. Jayce, from what I could get from Jaakobai, is the oldest living Fae. Meaning he will be just as big of a problem as Azahara."

"I don't have much memory to speak of, but I don't recall him ever. I remember the lanky Fae, Illyan and the Væragi, but not him." He confessed, and even just thinking about the two of them, his head began to swim. The glass in his hand lifted to his lips and he drank from it, not giving it a second thought.

"No, he showed up after you died." Somehow, that did not make him feel better. "We were both easily replaced, Kaed."

"Kaed, come on, we need to go—"

But why did he reach for me too?

"Kaed, please. Come with us."

They both were reaching out for me... why?

"It seems so." Kaed finally responded, the memories fading and returning was his anger. "Doesn't matter. Beautiful or not, she's still a monster." Not realizing it until it was too late, the glass shattered in his hand and bounced on the floor.

Without reacting, he just looked at Goddrick, who met his gaze, "Tell me what needs to be done to destroy her."

A Special Thank You:

My Street Team
Angi Brock, Brittney Gribble, Brittany Wray, Conner West, Cynthia Underwood, Dee Harford, Devynn Fisher, Enola Henderson, Holly Antle, Jessica Morris, Rebecca Hughes, Shanda Hall. Expressing my gratitude for having each and every one of you in my life is a challenge beyond words. Your support means the world to me, and no amount of gratitude could ever suffice. However, I'll keep saying it, because you all deserve the world and to me, you are all my Sunshine's.

My Readers
Without you, there would be no reason to write this story. Thank you so much for reading the second installment in The Keeper Series. My hope is that it heals you in a way that it healed me writing it. Everyone deserves a Jayce in their life, because you truly deserve the world, and he would give it to you without question.

It is okay to be scared.
It isn't okay to give up.
Keep fighting, Sunshine.

About The Author

M. L. Burns (Mel) has been writing for nearly eighteen years and began her journey with short stories and text-based role-playing. She writes in the third-person point of view (POV) limited while dabbling into first-person POV, focusing on the Dark Romance Fantasy genre, with an emphasis on character development and low-fantasy world-building. Her debut novel, "The Hourglass Keeper," the first book in the Keeper Series, is set to release on November 30th, 2023.

She lives in Spain with her husband and daughter. When she isn't working her day job or writing/reading, she enjoys exploring Europe as her new backyard, playing video games, and engaging with her readers.

MLBurns_Author   MLBurns_Author

Printed in the USA
CPSIA information can be obtained
at www.ICGtesting.com
LVHW040023230424
778120LV00019B/58/J